## The attacker brought his arm up and then smashed the stone against the side of Malden's temple.

Bright lights flashed behind Malden's eyes and he felt his consciousness swim inside him, blackness surging up around his mind to carry him into nothingness.

"Oh no, not yet," the attacker laughed, and slapped Malden hard across the face with a bare palm. Instantly Malden snapped back into his own head—and back into the pain that surged through his skull. "I wish you to know my name. That way, when your soul is cast into the pit, you can tell the Bloodgod who sent you."

"Verr . . . wellll," Malden slurred. His tongue could barely move in his mouth.

"My name is Prestwicke. I like all my kills to know my name."

"Ki . . . k-kills," Malden said.

"Yes, I was hired to slaughter you, Malden. It's my trade."

ANY WAY YOU WANT IT—SPECIAL EDITIONS, EXCERPTS AND MORE
Another thrilling novel in the bestselling series . . .

# Books by David Chandler

*The Ancient Blades Trilogy*
DEN OF THIEVES: BOOK ONE
A THIEF IN THE NIGHT: BOOK TWO
HONOR AMONG THIEVES: BOOK THREE

# A THIEF IN THE NIGHT

## THE ANCIENT BLADES TRILOGY: BOOK TWO

# DAVID CHANDLER

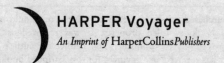

HARPER Voyager
*An Imprint of HarperCollinsPublishers*

This is a work of fiction. Names, characters, places, and incidents are products of the author's imagination or are used fictitiously and are not to be construed as real. Any resemblance to actual events, locales, organizations, or persons, living or dead, is entirely coincidental.

**HARPER Voyager**

*An Imprint of* HarperCollins*Publishers*
10 East 53rd Street
New York, New York 10022-5299

Copyright © 2011 by David Wellington
Excerpt from *Honor Among Thieves* copyright © 2011 by David Wellington
Cover art by Richard Jones
ISBN 978-0-06-202125-0
**www.harpervoyagerbooks.com**

First Harper Voyager mass market printing: October 2011

Harper Voyager and ⑂ is a trademark of HCP LLC.

Printed in the U.S.A.

10 9 8 7 6 5 4 3 2

*For G.G. and D.A., on the outer planes*

# ACKNOWLEDGMENTS

A criminal mastermind is only as good as his co-conspirators. The usual suspects are responsible for the contents of this book as much as me: Alex Lencicki (wheels), Russell Galen (the bagman), Diana Gill (demolitions expert), and Will Hinton (eagle-eyed lookout) aided and abetted its creation. Fred Van Lente was the perfect inside man. I could not have asked for a better crew of accomplices.

DAVID CHANDLER
New York City, 2011

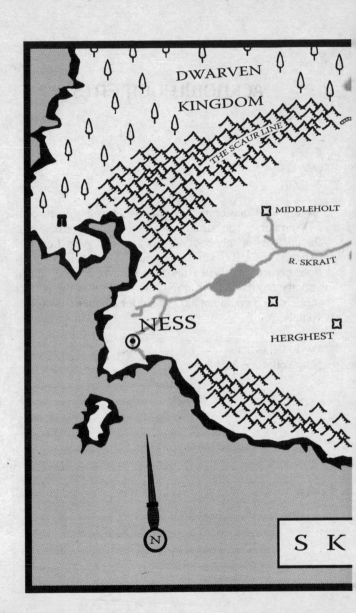

# A THIEF IN THE NIGHT

# PROLOGUE

In a place of stone walls, attended by his acolytes and warriors, the Hieromagus knelt in the dawn rays of the red subterranean sun. Both sorcerer and priest, he wore a simple garment decorated with jangling bells. The sound of them was meant to draw him back to the real world, to the present, but for now he silenced them. For now, he needed to remember.

The ancestors spoke to him. For those long lost, forgetting was a kind of death. They pulled desperately at him, trying to draw him into memories of ancient forests, of a time before the first humans came to this continent. Before his people were destroyed, driven away, forgotten. He saw their great battles, saw the works of magic they created. Saw the small, tender moments they shared and the guilt and shame they tried to put behind them. He saw kings, and queens, and simple folk in well-patched clothing. He saw Aethlinga, who had been a queen—the seventy-ninth of her dynasty—but who became something more. A seer. A diviner. Back then, in the depths of time, she had become the first Hieromagus. Just as he was to be the last.

His body twitched, his eyelids in constant motion as if he were dreaming. A serving girl mopped his forehead with a piece of sponge. He tried to wave her away, but lost in reverie, he could only raise a few fingers a fraction of an inch.

*"I came as soon as I saw the sails. I knew you would want to see this with your own eyes," the hunter said. Together the two of them climbed to the top of a forested ridge that overlooked the southern sea. One tree, an ancient*

*rowan, stood taller than the rest. Aethlinga was old and frail but still she climbed the branches for a better look.*

*Out at sea the ships stood motionless on the curling waves, their sails furled now, their railings thick with refugees. Less desperate than they might have been. They had reached their destination. Down on the shore, boats were landing, long, narrow wooden boats crammed with men. Hairy, unwashed, their lips cracked and cratered with scurvy. Their faces gaunt and grim after their long voyage.*

*Iron weapons in their hands.*

"What are they?" the hunter asked. "They look a bit like ogres, but . . . what are they? What do they want?"

The Hieromagus's lips moved, eight hundred years further on. "They want land. A place to make a new start. What are they? They are our death."

It was very difficult to tell, inside the memory, where the Hieromagus ended and Aethlinga began. He had seen this particular vision so many times. Remembered it, for simply to recall was a sacred rite. This was the history of his people. The thing that could never be forgotten.

*Later, when the first skirmish was over and the men from the boats lay bleeding and cold on the sand—but others on the ships still stood out on the waves, watching—Aethlinga went to a private grove deep in the forest. A place where the ancestors wove through the tree branches, whispering always. She had her own sacred memories to recall.*

*But now she turned her face to a pool of water, a simple looking glass. She looked into her own eyes. Formed her own memory. "I know you will see this," she said, and she spoke a name.*

She spoke the true and secret name of the last Hieromagus. This memory was for him.

*"I need you to remember. Not the past this time, but the future. Look forward and find what is to come. I have glimpsed it as well, and you know I would not ask this, were it not utterly necessary."*

The body of the Hieromagus, so far away now, convulsed and shook. The serving girl drew back in fear that he would lash out and destroy her. It had happened before.

Some memories were less pleasant than others, and this was the worst of all.

Except—this one was not a memory at all. Instead it was foresight. For one like the Hieromagus, who saw past and future all at once, the distinction had little meaning.

Looking forward he saw the knight. He saw the painted woman. He saw the thief. As he had so many times before. Always before he could put their images out of his head. Tell himself it would be many years before they arrived.

Now they crowded in on him as if they were shouting in his ears. He could no longer push them back, nor did he seek to. He only endeavored to separate them, to let them each speak in turn.

*"Some demons are smaller than others,"* the woman said, and it was her, though the images were gone from her skin she was the same one, and then a twisted hand crashed across her cheek, knocking her to the ground.

Her, the Hieromagus thought—her—it was the one he sought, but in the wrong time—she was cut loose from him still, but so close, so—

*A man with the features of a priest, but the eyes of a murderer. This one only smiled, and did not speak. This one showed only the teeth of a predatory animal.*

He dared not look on that one too long, even in memory.

*Two knights with the same name, one dissembling, not a knight at all. He was something else entirely, something hated, and yet he was the key to liberation. A draft of burdock root, certain oils most precious, blisswine. An elfin queen throwing herself across a bed in the attitude of a whore.*

Closer now—closer, but fragmented. The Hieromagus beat feebly at the floor with his fists, trying to force the memories—the forebodings—into proper shape. Into an order he could understand. He must see the path. He must choose for his people.

*Three swords, deadly swords. Something worse, something far worse, a weapon of incredible potential. Two men pushing a barrel up an incline of stone.*

Yes. Yes, he had it—

*A flash of light. A burst of energy, searing and brilliant. Molten stone flowing down a corridor.*

There, that was the future he sought. The one he'd glimpsed so many times, only to turn away in fear. The one he'd convinced himself was still a long way off.

This time he must watch the images all the way through. See it all.

*"Malden!" the painted woman called out to her lover, desperate, watching him walk toward utter and certain death. The sword in his hand would be of no help.*

So close now. After so long. So many years of dreading what was to come. Of trying desperately to find a way to forestall it. When it could never be prevented.

*The human knight leaned down over them, his face warped by hatred. Spittle flew from his lips as he barked at the bronze-clad warriors. "You're going to die. Every last one of you will die! It's less than what you deserve for what you did to Cythera!"*

The hatred—the death that was coming—the tumult—

*"He knew," the painted woman said. Her voice thick with loss, with dread at the sacrifices that had been made. "The Hieromagus had seen the future. He saw this, all of this. He knew that what he'd seen could not be changed. That this was the only way for his people to survive."*

The eyes of the Hieromagus opened like window shutters being thrown back.

"No!" he screamed.

No.

*He saw the dead laid out in heaps before him. He saw himself, the Hieromagus saw through his own eyes, crawling over a pile of bodies, his feet treading on the faces of the ones he loved.*

No . . . not like that. It couldn't come to that, to so drastic a turn. And yet . . .

It would. It must.

The painted woman was correct. What was foreseen could not be changed. And there was only one way forward now. No turning, no detour was possible, though the way was choked with death and destruction.

He opened his mouth to speak. It was hard, so very hard to get the words out. He felt so very far away.

"They're coming," he said, and the warriors and acolytes stirred, traded terrified glances. Grasped hands in hope. "Very soon now, they will return for us."

Much muttering, much grave discussion followed in that place where the underground sun burned red. Yet the Hieromagus heard none of it, for his memory was not yet done. There was more to see.

*Back in the sacred grove, Aethlinga watched the visions with him. Her face, so slender and beautiful, was deformed by fear and the sorrow for what was to come. For what was to come to him.*

*"Be strong," she said. "I know what we ask of you. There is no justice in it—but you were born to perform this task. This bitter cup is yours to sip alone. I am sorry."*

# PART I

# The Getaway

# CHAPTER ONE

A thin crescent of moon lit up the rooftops of the Free City of Ness, glinting on the bells up high in the Spires, whitewashing the thatched roofs of the Stink. The furnaces of the blacksmiths in the Smoke roared all night, but the rest of the city was asleep—or at least tucked away in candlelit rooms with closed shutters.

It was the time of night when even the gambling houses started to close down, when the brothels shut their doors. It was the time when honest men and women retreated to their beds, to get the sleep they needed for another long day of work on the morrow. Of all the city's vast workforce, only a handful remained at their labors. The city's watchmen, of course, patrolled the streets all night long.

And, of course, there were thieves about.

Malden moved quickly, running along the ridges of the rooftops, hurrying to make a clandestine appointment. He made as little noise as a squirrel dashing along, and he was careful not to let himself be seen from the street level. For all that, he made excellent time as he leapt from one rooftop to another, following routes he'd learned through years of practice, knowing without needing to look where he should put his feet and where a roof had grown too soft to take his weight. He danced among the Spires, swinging from stone carvings, launching himself across narrow alleys. His route led him around the broad open space of Market Square, then downhill across the tops of the mansions in the Golden Slope. He was very close to his destination when, through the sole of his leather shoe, he felt a shingle crack and start to fall away.

Malden froze instantly in place, careful to keep his weight on the broken shingle as the rest of his body swayed with momentum. He checked himself, then bent low, his fingers grabbing at the broken shingle before it could fall into the street below and make a noise. Very carefully, he laid the pieces of the shingle in a downspout, then dashed forward again. It was very nearly midnight.

He reached his destination and clung to a smoking chimney pot, his body low against the shingles to minimize his silhouette. He had arrived. His eyes, well adapted to the dark, scanned the sides of the houses around him, looking for any sign of movement. He spied a rat scuttering through an alley twenty feet below. He saw bats circling a church belfry two blocks away. And then he found what he was looking for.

Across the street three men dressed in black were climbing a drainpipe on the side of a half-timbered mansion. When the one on top reached a mullioned window on the second floor, he wrapped his hand in a rag and then punched in the glass.

It made enough noise to scare cats in the alley below. Malden winced in sympathy. Had he ever been that noisy? He knew, from long experience, what the three thieves must be feeling. The blood would be pounding in their veins. Their heartbeats would be the loudest sounds they could hear. The thing they were about to do could get them all hanged, following the barest formality of a trial.

The one on top—the leader, he must be—reached inside the window and slipped open its catch. He opened the casements wide, then disappeared into the dark house. The other two followed close on his heels.

Malden shifted his position carefully, to make sure his legs wouldn't cramp while he waited. He had to give them time to do the job right. He watched as a light appeared in the next window over, then as it moved, bobbing and darting, through the house. The thieves took their time about their work, perhaps because they wanted to make sure to get everything.

Grunting with impatience, Malden wished they would hurry up. Down in the street a man of the watch was coming this way. He wore a cloak woven with a pattern of eyes, and carried a lantern held high on the end of his polearm. The watchman barely glanced at the houses on either side of him, but if he should catch sight of that candle moving stealthily through an otherwise dark house, he might grow suspicious.

Malden would have been smart enough to bring a dark lantern with a shield over its light, and shone its beam only when absolutely necessary. Of course, Malden would have been in and out of the house already. And he wouldn't have required two accomplices to burgle a house that size.

The thieves were lucky—the watchman saw nothing. He walked on past without so much as a glance at the mansion. When he was sure the man was out of earshot, Malden carefully stood up, then took a few steps backward to get a running start. With one quick bound he leapt across the alley and onto the roof of the darkened mansion.

The thieves were on the ground floor. Most like, they heard nothing as he landed, as soft as a pigeon settling on the roof. He lowered himself over the edge and placed his feet carefully on the open windowsill, then slid inside, as easy as that.

He took a moment to glance around him and study his new surroundings. He was in a bedroom, perhaps the chamber of the master of the house. The bed had a brocade canopy hung above it to keep insects from pestering its occupants. The floor was strewn with rushes scented with a faint perfume. Against one wall stood a pair of wooden chairs and a washbasin. Underneath the bed he found a dry chamber pot.

Malden could hear the thieves moving about on the ground floor. How smart were they? he wondered. He needed to make a judgment. If they were at all clever they would leave the same way they came. Leave as little sign of forced entry as they could. If they were fools they would exit by the kitchen door on the ground floor. An easier method of escape, perhaps, but it would put them in full view of the windows of four other houses—and thus, potentially, any number of eyewitnesses.

No, Malden thought. This bunch wouldn't be that stupid. Cutbill—the master of the guild of thieves in Ness, and Malden's own master—kept his eye open always for real talent in the criminal professions. Cutbill had singled these men out, of all the freelance thieves in the city, as his next assignment. And Cutbill never sent him on such a mission if he didn't have good reason.

So they would leave through the upstairs window. Which meant he had to wait a little longer. Malden swept his cloak back to uncover the bodkin in its sheath at his hip. Then he reached into a long wooden case he kept strapped to his thigh and drew out three slender darts. He was very, very careful not to touch their tips.

"Make haste, make haste," one of the thieves hissed from the stairs. Another grumbled out some profanity. There was the old familiar clink of metal objects bouncing in a sack. And then the first of them stepped into the bedroom, eyes peeled, watching the shadows just in case.

He did not think to look down, and so he stepped right into the chamber pot, which Malden had placed before the doorway.

"Son of a whore," the thief howled as he tripped forward into the room and went sprawling past where Malden lay on the bed. The other two rushed into the room after their fellow. One held the candle high, while the other had a wicked long knife in his hand. All three of them held bulging sacks.

"What is it?" the one with the candle demanded. His face was yellow in the guttering light and his eyes were very shiny. The one with the knife was quicker, and spied Malden even as he sat up in the bed.

"We're tumbled!" he cried, and rushed forward with the knife.

Malden flicked his wrist and a dart went into the knife-man's chest, just above his heart. As the candle holder turned to look, Malden pitched his second dart and caught him in the neck.

The one who had stumbled on the chamber pot managed to get back to his feet just as Malden readied his third dart. The thief began to cry out in fear just as Malden made his cast. The dart hit him in the tongue and he went silent.

The three thieves turned to look at each other, knowing the jig was up. One by one their faces fell. And then they slumped to the floorboards with a treble thump.

When he was sure they were all down, Malden stepped out of the bed and went to look in their sacks, to see what shiny presents they'd brought him.

## CHAPTER TWO

It was not more than an hour later when Malden heard the master of the house come home. He had been out at a gaming hall until closing time, as he was prone to do every night. Malden had done his research on the man, following him for the last three nights all the way from the Royal Ditch back to his home. Typically the man lost more than he won, and he would be followed all the way home by his long-suffering wife, who begged him every night to give up his expensive hobby. The man never said a word, merely took his drubbing as his due. The two of them would be accompanied by a bodyguard and a linkboy who lit his way through the dark streets. Malden closed his eyes and listened as the householder paid off the linkboy and then set his bodyguard to stand watch in the main room of the ground floor. The wife moved straightaway to her chamber, as she did every night, perhaps exhausted by the long journey through the night streets, perhaps simply desiring to get away from her wastrel mate. Malden heard her splash her face with water from the basin, then call for her handmaid, who would not be coming.

The master of the house climbed the stairs ponderously, pausing now and again as if he were so drunk he could not walk a straight line. He came immediately to his strongroom, which served him both as office and sanctum. Before he opened the door, he called for his own servant, a valet, who was also conspicuously absent.

"By the Bloodgod's eight elbows," the merchant swore, stumbling inside his strongroom. "Someone strike a light, anyway. Who's here? I can hear you breathing in there. I promise you, Holger, if this is your idea of a jape at my expense—"

The light from the open door spilled across a glittering treasure, gathered and neatly sorted on the rich carpet of the strongroom. Silver plate and cutlery had been stacked beside bags of coin and fine porcelain. Good clothing, the lady of the house's jewelry, and even the more expensive sort of cooking spices had been laid out there. The master of the house inhaled deeply to see all his worldly goods of value arrayed so.

Malden struck flint and lighted a taper on the table before him, the table that normally served as the merchant's desk. "Close the door," he said.

The merchant's name was Doral Knackerson. He was not the wealthiest man in the Free City, but he was far from the poorest either. He owned three tanneries down in the Smoke. Malden had walked by those workshops often enough to know the particular gruesome stench of rendered animal carcasses. Strange, he did not detect even a whiff of that unforgettable smell on Doral's person. It was as if the merchant were unwilling to visit his own property.

The man was middle-aged, with silver wisps of hair around his temples and none up top. He dressed well, but in the specific shabby-looking finery that rich men wore when they went abroad into the less reputable parts of town. He had a stack of coins in his hands—it seemed for once he'd left the gaming table richer than he'd arrived. The silver spilled from his fingers and rolled across the floor as he stared at Malden.

"Thief," he whispered, then opened his mouth to shout it.

Malden forestalled him by stabbing his bodkin into the surface of the merchant's desk. The knife was no longer than Malden's hand, from the tips of his fingers to the heel of his thumb. It had no edge at all, but only a very sharp point that dug easily into the soft wood of the desk.

It was not a particularly effective or very deadly weapon. But it was good for sending a certain kind of message, one that Doral Knackerson must have received loud and clear. He closed his mouth again without so much as calling for his bodyguard.

"Close the door," Malden said again, very softly.

Doral did as he was told. Malden had made extensive inquiries regarding Knackerson before he came here, and of all the people he had asked, none described Doral as a fool. Good. That would make this much easier.

"You'll hang for this, thief. Cut my throat, take my belongings—what will you, but you'll hang for it. Or you may leave right now, empty-handed, and I'll say nothing of this intrusion to my close personal friend, the Burgrave."

Malden smiled. "I'm not here to rob you," he said. "Not tonight, anyway. In fact, my purpose here is quite the opposite. I happened to be strolling past this fine home tonight when I discovered these," he said. He glanced to one side.

The bodies of the three thieves he'd surprised lay sprawled on the floor there, facedown.

Doral's face went white.

"They were busy at amassing this collection of your goods," Malden said, and gestured at the valuables piled on the carpet. "I stopped them before they could make good their escape."

The merchant stared hard at Malden with shrewd, half-closed eyes. "You're no watchman. None of them would lie in wait for me like this."

Malden chuckled. "Oh, no. Just a citizen looking after his neighbor. By way of profession, I am the agent of one of your fellow burghers. A man of some influence in the city, though he rarely appears at the moothall. You'll know his name, if you think for it."

Doral pursed his lips. He did not require much prompting. "Cutbill. The guildmaster of thieves."

"You make his name sound like a curse. When the man in question is about to become your fondest friend." Malden shrugged. "These three were none of his. They were private operators, of a kind he despises. They were smart enough to make note of your movements, and even to bribe your servants to sleep elsewhere tonight. They were not clever enough to evade me."

The merchant shook his head. "Say what you want. What your master wants, rather. I like not this feigned civility from a man who threatens me with a knife."

Malden shrugged off the man's brusqueness. "My master wants nothing. He wishes to give you something you clearly need. Protection. Cutbill can make sure you are never bothered with this unpleasantness again. You see how easily unprincipled rascals made entry to your house. You see how close a thing it was, that you were robbed tonight. Why, if I hadn't been here, you'd only now be realizing how much you had lost. There must be . . .

let me see . . . fifty gold royals worth of plate and jewels here, and the clothing would fetch some good silver coins if sold to the right consigners. Why risk losing so much, when Cutbill can ensure the safety of your belongings for so little?"

"How much?"

Malden pulled his bodkin out of the desk's top. "One part in fifty of everything you earn. To be paid monthly, in silver. A trifle."

"That's just robbery by another name," Doral spat. "I won't pay it."

"Ah, no man would submit to such blandishment, be he a creature of honor. I told Cutbill you were too high-minded to accept his offer. Alas, he bid me make it anyway. Very good. I'll take my leave now, with compliments to you and your lovely wife." Malden stood up from behind the desk and sketched a graceful bow.

"If I see you again—"

"Oh, you shan't," Malden told the merchant as he strode toward the door. "When next I come, you won't see me at all."

He walked directly past the merchant and reached for the latch of the door.

He didn't make it that far.

"Wait," Doral said. "We can negotiate something, surely."

"I listen attentively," Malden said, and leaned up against the wall.

# CHAPTER THREE

It was a long ride from the Golden Slope to the Ashes. Malden had a small wagon and an old, spavined horse to drive down the steep hill that took him from the houses of the wealthy through the district of workshops and manufactories called the Smoke. There he entered a maze of narrow streets that led farther downhill into the Stink, where the poor had their homes. It was just as he entered that zone of wattle-and-daub houses, where the streets and the alleys between them were hard to tell apart, that he heard the first groan from behind him.

The wagon appeared to be full of hay. If he were stopped, Malden could claim to be making a delivery to the stables of an inn nearby—it was close enough to dawn to make sense for such traffic—but if a watchman heard the hay moaning in pain, he might ask questions that Malden would find uncomfortable to answer. So he pulled his team into a very dark, very deserted byway, and leaned back over his cargo. He thumped the side of the wagon very hard with the pommel of his bodkin and waited until he heard another grunt. "I know you can hear me," he said to the hay. The three men underneath it, the thieves from Doral's house, were just now waking from their drugged stupor. They would be unable to use their limbs for a while yet, but their ears would be fully recovered. The drug Malden had used on his darts was measured out quite carefully, and he knew its effects well—he'd even tested it on himself, to be sure of its efficacy. He knew how groggy and listless it would leave them, and how unable to defend themselves.

Still the hay rustled as they tried to rouse themselves

and escape. Malden sighed and said, "If I tell you to be quiet, I expect you will try to shout. It's what I would do in your situation. Allow me to point out one thing, however. If I wished to kill you, I could have done so quite easily, hours ago. Instead I did you a very great favor: I saved you from the hangman's noose. I'd like to do you another favor, but it depends on my getting to my destination without incident. You may therefore remain silent, and keep your groans to yourself. Or I can stop your breath right now, while you're still too weak to fend me off. Do we have a deal? Cry once for yes, or twice if you wish to die."

"Oooh," one of them moaned.

"Pluh-pluh-pluz," the second begged.

"Gah," the third one muttered. That must be the one he'd struck in the tongue.

"Very good. Lie still, then, and you'll live, for now." Malden got his horse under way again and headed for the Ashes.

That ancient district of the Free City of Ness was named for a calamity that happened well before Malden was born, the Seven Day Fire that claimed half the city. There was very little evidence of the conflagration left in Ness, save for a small zone of houses that had been so decrepit before the fire—and their owners so desperately poor—that they had never been rebuilt. The Ashes had become a section so desolate no one ever wanted to live there again. It was a grim place of streets that verged on nothing but charred ruin, all of it hid during the day by the shadow of the city's towering wall. It was a place decent folk—and thus the city watch—never ventured.

Malden had come to know it well. He could find his way through the labyrinth of vacant lots and piles of rubble, through the lanes where weeds grew up through the soot-stained cobbles and moonlight soaked everything a sodden gray. He knew just where to turn, and, more importantly, just where to stop.

He stood his horse in the middle of a street and leaned

forward on the reins. The horse snorted in the cold air, mist making twin plumes from its nostrils.

He did not wait long. Glancing over at a collapsed house to his left, he saw a flicker of motion, and then a boy no more than seven years old stepped out into the street. The boy lingered in a door frame that was warped out of true by fire and time. He wore a tunic made of patched-together rags, and his face was filthy with ash. In his hand he held a stick, no longer than his diminutive forearm, with a two-penny nail driven through its end. A poor urchin's eye-gouger, that weapon. Malden had no doubt he was well drilled in its use. The boy, one of a small army of orphaned children with nowhere else to go, worked for Malden's master. The children made sure no one entered the Ashes without being seen, and, if they were unwelcome, made sure they didn't leave again.

Malden nodded at the boy, then made a complicated gesture with his fingers. The boy nodded in return, then stepped back into the darkness and was gone.

The entire interchange took five heartbeats to complete, but it spoke in an elaborate and eloquent vocabulary. The message was plain: Malden had three new recruits with him. He had not been followed. He needed to speak with the boss. The boy had understood, and would see to everything.

Malden jumped down from the seat of his wagon and walked around to the back. He shoved the straw away and let the three men sit up. As they rubbed at their numb faces and shook out their deadened legs, he studied them carefully. They were scrawny, shortish men dressed in dirty clothing. They didn't look like much at all. He knew their type all too well. Men broken down by poverty until they were willing to take the risk of being hanged rather than go another day without coin. Men who labored at menial jobs when they could, or relied on their families for a few coppers to keep them from starving to death when no work was available. Men who had spent every day looking at the houses of rich merchants and wondering why fate had denied them such luxury and comfort. One of them, Malden knew, was a cousin of Doral Knackerson's valet. It had been his brilliant idea to buy off the servants and burgle the rich man's house. It must have seemed like such a foolproof plan.

"I've taken your weapons, and the few coins you had on you," he told them. "The drug I gave you has no lasting effect, but it will leave you weak for tonight. I really don't recommend making a fuss now. You've been given a second chance and I hope you will all take it. The job you did tonight was a clumsy affair, poorly planned out and executed with only a modicum of skill. It was enough, however, to gain the notice of my employer."

The three of them stared at him. One of them mouthed *Cutbill*, but was smart enough not to breathe the name aloud.

Malden nodded. "You may know that he runs all the crime in this town. You three thought you could go into business for yourselves. That shows initiative, but also stupidity. No one steals a copper farthing in the Free City of Ness without attracting his attention. You made a choice to try anyway, and now you are under his most exacting scrutiny. You have another choice to make, right now. You can get up, and walk into that building over there." Malden pointed at the ruin of a feed store across the street. It had no roof, but three of its walls still stood. Only darkness lay within. "A little girl will take you from there to a place where you can sign on with my crew. Your other option is to walk back up that hill," and here he pointed behind him, "and look for honest work, and forswear ever taking up thieving again."

"Do you know how hard it is to get a decent position just now?" one of the thieves demanded. "The trade guilds say who may work, and who must starve. And you have to pay them just to get on a list of men waiting for a chance."

Malden felt little pity for the men. He himself was the

son of a whore. He'd never known who his father was, had never had any family to fall back on. He'd been far more desperate once than these men would ever get. Yet he was going to offer them the same hope he'd clutched to himself.

"My guild," Malden said, "is willing to welcome you in, tonight."

The thieves fell to communing with each other, in the mode of desperate looks and shrugs and shaking of heads. The one with the hurt tongue—the valet's cousin—seemed to be their leader, since the others turned to him as if begging him to make a decision. He ended this silent conversation with a grudging nod.

"You'll not regret this, good sir," one of the others said. He jumped down from the back of the wagon and ran toward the ruined feed store.

Another laughed out loud. "When I saw you on that bed, I thought I was dead as an elf," he announced, and followed his accomplice.

That just left the leader, whose tongue was still swollen in his mouth. He stared at Malden for a very long time. He was making it clear he didn't think Malden had done him any favors. But eventually he, too, took what was offered.

# CHAPTER FOUR

Malden grabbed a sack of coins from the wagon—Doral's first payment, made in advance—and walked away from the horse and its burden, knowing they would be taken care of by the children. The urchins who lived in the Ashes, orphans all, were desperate, violent little sprites but they worked hard for the pittance Cutbill gave them. It was their only way of getting food other than catching the district's vast number of feral cats and roasting them over open fires.

Malden turned a corner and walked into the ruin of an old inn. Three old men waited for him there, ancient graybeards who nodded and smiled as he approached. They were sitting on a coffin in the middle of an abandoned building, just as they did every night. The old grand masters of the guild of thieves.

"Well met, Malden," Loophole said, raising a hand in welcome. Malden took it warmly and smiled. "More grist for the mill?"

"The wheel of the gods grinds slowly, but it grinds the barleycorn exceeding fine," Malden said, making sure to use the night's password. He bowed and started to walk past the old men, when 'Levenfingers stopped him with a discreet clearing of the throat.

"Someone's been asking for you."

Malden stopped where he was and turned to look at the oldsters. It was Lockjaw, he who rarely spoke at all, who gave him the news.

"It's nothin'. Just some fool poking around where he don't belong."

"What kind of fool?" Malden asked. "The heavily armed kind?"

'Levenfingers sighed. "The children spotted him, an hour hence, just on the edge of the Ashes. Little fellow in very plain clothes. Not a watchman, nor a bravo with a grudge. Looked more like a priest."

"Perhaps he came to save my soul," Malden suggested.

"He got naught from the bairns, save a nasty look," Loophole told him. "He was smart enough to clear off after that."

"It's nothin'," Lockjaw said again, and waved one hand in dismissal.

"I appreciate the warning, all the same," Malden said, feeling distinctly uneasy. Cutbill kept his headquarters in such a forlorn place specifically so that approaching strangers would be conspicuous solely by their presence. Anyone asking for him who knew where he worked should be considered potentially dangerous, no matter how holy their intentions.

Nor could Malden afford to be reckless. Collecting protection money for Cutbill might seem like an easy job, but it actually held far more danger than straight thievery. When you robbed someone, if you did it correctly, they never knew who had done it. Doral, though, knew his face now. If Doral cared enough to spend some money, it would not be difficult for the merchant to learn Malden's name. After all, he was making enemies these days, enemies who knew where to find him.

Brooding on this, Malden passed the old men and opened a trapdoor hidden in the debris of the fallen inn. He headed down a short flight of stairs and pushed aside a tapestry to step into a room full of warmth and light. The din of the place overwhelmed him as he walked inside, right into the middle of a dice game in full swing. The gamblers gathered up their money and moved backward to let him through, some of them touching their hoods in salute. Malden was greeted warmly by the guildmaster's new bodyguard, a swordsman in red leather named Tyburn, and the pair of working girls who were keeping him company. Having grown up in a brothel, Malden knew the girls well and bowed as deeply to them as he might to a pair of fine ladies. They giggled and batted their eyelashes at him.

Slag the dwarf was hard at work, as always, at his chaotic workshop in one corner of the room. It looked like he was making a grappling hook, bending rods of iron in a vise. His mop of ragged black hair was greasy with sweat and he swore liberally as he twisted the metal.

"I owe you a debt of gratitude," Malden said. "Those darts you made me worked a trick."

"They ought to. I sighted them in myself." The dwarf glared up at Malden with wild eyes. "And you owe me nothing, you bothersome bastard. You paid for them, didn't you?"

"I suppose I did," Malden admitted with a laugh.

"Then leave me be, so I can get back to my own business," the dwarf finished, and turned away without another word.

Malden shrugged and made his way over to the massive door in the far wall that led to Cutbill's office. He knocked the requisite number of times before opening it. Stepping inside, he felt an edge of cold iron kiss his throat.

He never had gotten used to that sensation, though it was hardly the first time he'd experienced it. He held still until the owner of the knife withdrew the weapon and stepped back behind a hanging tapestry before Malden could see his face.

Sighing, Malden stepped into the office. It was grandly appointed, with a massive wooden desk and a cheerily glowing brazier giving heat. The walls were covered with rich tapestries, woven with gold thread that caught the light.

Cutbill, however, sat on a stool in the coldest corner of the room, facing a lectern on which was propped a massive leather-bound ledger book. He was making notations in its pages with a quill pen. The guildmaster of thieves didn't look like much to see, not at first glance. He was a small man, thin, with little hair and a pair of dark, beady eyes behind his long nose. He did not look up as Malden entered.

Malden placed the sack of coins on the unused desk and then leaned his hip against its solidity. It had been a long night and he longed to be abed, but he had to make his report first. Cutbill was a stickler for detail, and liked everything done in a precise way. His exactitude had bothered Malden once, but in the time he'd worked for Cutbill he'd learned just how necessary the details were. Cutbill's -operation was vast, and one man alone could barely keep all the figures straight, even a man with Cutbill's great talent for order. One slip-up could see the entire organization hanged. So Malden had learned to accept, and even appreciate, Cutbill's niceties. Even when he was so tired he was seeing spots before his eyes.

"You were successful, I see," Cutbill said. He made another notation in his ledger, then turned back several pages and consulted a figure.

Malden didn't question how Cutbill could know that before he'd even given his report. Cutbill had a way of always being three steps ahead of anyone he spoke to. "A new customer, and three new recruits."

"Hmm." Cutbill sounded vaguely amused. It was hard to tell—the guildmaster never smiled, and certainly had never laughed in Malden's presence. But Malden was beginning to learn his moods all the same. "That makes ten new clients you've recruited in two weeks," Cutbill went on. "I wonder what will happen if you keep operating at this pace. By way of a hypothetical, what would Ness look like if the entire population of the Stink were on my payroll at the same time, while every citizen in the Golden Slope was receiving my protection? Would we completely eliminate thievery in one fell swoop?"

"Perish the thought," Malden said. He scowled into the middle distance. "I can't imagine a more boring possibility."

"Hmm." It was as good as a belly laugh, coming from Cutbill. It seemed the man was pleased with his work. Well, that was something.

Once upon a time Malden had hated Cutbill with a passion. The old man had blackmailed him into coming into the guild, just as Malden had browbeaten the three thieves that night. But rather than just welcoming him in with open arms, Cutbill had exacted a ridiculous payment for the right to work as a thief in Ness. A hundred and one gold royals—a vast fortune—to be paid before Malden could earn a single copper for himself. He'd made that payment, though nearly died in the process. Other people had died, though no one the world would miss. Once the price was paid, Malden had believed he would go on hating Cutbill for what he'd been put through. He'd been convinced he would spend the rest of his life looking for a way to put the man in his place.

And yet over the months that followed, something strange had happened. He actually came to respect the guildmaster of thieves. He would never go so far as to say he liked the man. Yet as he had watched Cutbill plot from his tiny office in the Ashes (as far as Malden knew, Cutbill never left the room), he began to see something of the man's brilliance. The way he played the various factions of the city off one another. The way he kept his people out of harm's way, and his thieves' necks out of the noose. Cutbill could be a vicious schemer, and he was not above having people killed if they got in his way. Malden imagined the man had not a single moral compulsion in his slender skull. Yet by operating in such a ruthless fashion, Cutbill managed to save lives, to put money in pockets that had been empty, and to ameliorate some small portion of the city's misery. It was almost enough to make Malden think the guildmaster had a heart after all.

Cutbill gestured at the night's takings. "You may take your cut from the bag. I don't need to count it."

Malden stood up straight. That was a level of trust he'd never anticipated from Cutbill. He reached into the sack of coins and took out twenty small gold gravines. One part in ten of all he'd earned—the going rate.

"Just write me a receipt, if you'd be so kind," Cutbill said. He put his pen down for a moment and actually looked up. "You know, Malden, I've been meaning to talk to you about something. I'm worried about you."

In the middle of scribbling his receipt on the desk, Malden managed to misspell his own name.

"You . . . are?" he asked, trying not to sound too surprised.

Cutbill frowned. "You've been taking on these protection and recruitment assignments more and more often. I might begin to suspect you were looking to move up in the organization, if I didn't know you better. This sort of work is hardly fit to your temperament. You're a housebreaker, not a kneebreaker. Blackmail and extortion are foreign to your character—if you take a coin from a man's pocket, it seems to actually pain you to smile at him afterward. It's one of the things I like about you. You're the most honest thief I know."

"I didn't know you took such a personal interest," Malden said. In truth, he found it rather disturbing.

"Do not give me too much credit," Cutbill said. "A happy worker is a good earner, that's all. I like to keep my people happy when I can. So I would like to know—why do you keep taking assignments you must hate?"

"For the money, of course. They pay so much better."

Cutbill picked up his pen and looked down at his ledger. The time for concern and caring, apparently, was over. But then he surprised Malden again. He nodded vigorously, though he didn't seem convinced. "I'm all for uncomplicated cupidity, of course. Greed is a wonderful motivator. But would you indulge me and answer one more question? What is it that you plan to buy with all that money?"

"A house," Malden admitted. "A fit place for a fine lady."

"Indeed? Malden the thief looks to marry? Fascinating," Cutbill said, and wrote a number down in his ledger, as if he'd taken the empirical measure of Malden's heart. "Does this most fortunate creature have a name?"

# CHAPTER FIVE

"Cythera should be here by now," Sir Croy said, and paced across the floorboards for the hundredth time. "And Coruth—where is Coruth?"

Sir Croy was a knight of the realm, a man of action. He'd spent his life fighting demons and sorcerers, defending the weak and protecting his king from danger. He had faced down deadly monsters and desperate enemies and never quailed in the face of certain death.

Today he felt like every nerve in his body was twanging with panic. He felt faint, and flushed, and like he might be sick.

He stared over at Malden, who stood at the side of the hearth, leaning on the mantel. Tapping his foot on the floor in impatience.

"I beg you," Croy said, as his stomach flopped about in his midsection, "stop that tapping! I swear, Malden, you seem more nervous than I feel right now."

The thief's eyes went wide, as if he'd been caught cheating at cards. He licked his lips and said, "Do I?"

"If someone walked in right now, they wouldn't know which of us was getting married today," Croy said. He laughed to cover up his distress. "Just—be calm, will you? It would help me."

Malden's face froze, his expression unreadable. Then he smiled, though it seemed he had to force himself. His foot stopped its infernal tapping and he laughed at Croy's joke. "You're right, of course. I have no reason to be nervous. I suppose I was simply agitated in sympathy with your plight. But please, Croy. Be at ease."

Might as well ask a goblin to be pious, Croy thought.

He went to the window for the hundredth time, then back to the hearth. "Is she late? Perhaps she's not coming at all," he said. There was something strangely appealing about the idea. If she didn't come—if she had been detained by some small accident, something harmless but which required her attention, then he wouldn't have to stand here feeling like a newly anointed page facing his first sparring match. But if she didn't come—if she didn't come—what would that mean? Would it mean she'd stopped loving him? Would it mean she had broken her pledge to him?

Why wasn't she there already? Didn't she know how important this was to him? He felt that if she didn't come he would die on the spot.

"You spent ten years wooing her," Malden said, favoring Croy with a knowing smile. "A few minutes more won't erase that."

"Of course. Of course you're right," Croy said. Good counsel—he knew it as soon as he heard it. Malden had a way of seeing things, of putting things in perspective. It was one of the things Croy valued in him.

It was more than a trace unusual that a knight of the king and a common thief would share this bond of friendship. Scant months earlier, Croy would never have associated with his sort. Yet the two of them had been through so much together, there was no one else Croy wanted standing beside him this day.

They were alone in a private room above a tavern. The room had been rented for the full afternoon and made cheery for the occasion. A fire had been lit in the hearth, though autumn was still young and there was only a hint of chill in the air. A table had been set out with wine and meats and bread and cheese. Strings of flowers hung from the walls, bright and colorful in the dusty light that streamed in through the open window.

Also on the table was a rolled up parchment, a pot of ink, and two quill pens already cut and ready for use. The parchment was a copy of the banns of marriage, and once

Cythera signed it, Croy's life would change forever. She had only to step up to the table, lift her pen, and—

Croy jumped when he heard someone shout in the room below. Just a man calling for ale, he told himself. The common room of the tavern, just down the stairs, was full of men drinking and gambling, two of the most common labors in the Free City of Ness. They made far more noise than Croy had expected. He'd wanted this room to be perfect, this room where all his dreams were set to come true. He'd wanted everything to be . . . perfect.

"Do you think she'll like the place?" he asked. "It was all I could arrange on short notice."

"I think she will be so busy looking into your eyes that she will forget what land she is in. Here," Malden said, and grabbed Croy's arm. He yanked downward on one sleeve of the knight's leather jerkin where it had bunched up. "And take this to mop your brow," he added, handing Croy a cloth.

Croy grimaced and wiped sweat away from his face.

"Ah," Malden said. "I hear the carriage."

At that moment Croy felt his heart stop in his chest. He raced over to the window and peered down into the street, just in time to see Cythera step down into the mud.

The footman of the hired carriage squawked and rushed to help her, but she had not waited for him. She could be headstrong, at times, and she would need some training before she could be presented at court, but—

—but she was beautiful. Especially today.

She wore a velvet gown, the finest he'd ever seen on her. Her dark hair was gathered in thick braids entwined with golden bells. Her skin was fair, with only a hint of red on her high cheekbones. A tattoo like a vine wrapped around her forearm. As Croy watched, it bloomed with pink wisteria flowers. It was not a tattoo at all, he knew, and it betokened something darker than ornament. It was her curse—or perhaps her gift—that she could absorb magic into her skin. Curses or baleful spells cast against

her would manifest themselves as painted vines and flowers on her body, blossoms that were never still. Once those
painted blooms had been like chains that bound her to her
dead father, the dread sorcerer Hazoth. Croy, with Malden's help—he could never forget the debt he owed the
thief—had laid the sorcerer low and freed Cythera from
that slavery. In gratitude Cythera had agreed to marry him
and make him happy. Now, wherever they'd come from,
the painted vines seemed to only enhance her delicate
beauty.

She entered the tavern below to much comment and ac-
claim from the men in the common room. She must have
made some small jest, for Croy heard the men laughing in
response. Then he heard her footfalls coming up the stairs.

The door opened and a boy showed her into the private
room, where Croy and Malden stood together waiting for her.

She smiled for them both, and let them kiss her hands.

Croy tried to speak, but then he grimaced with pain as
he heard a man in the common room announce he was
going to be sick.

"Boy," Malden said, snapping his fingers for service,
"close that door. We like not all this noise." The serving
boy rushed to do as he was told.

Croy opened his mouth again, intending to speak, and
found he could not. His tongue would not lift from the
floor of his mouth.

For a moment the two of them just looked at each
other. Croy tried to smile and felt his lips tremble, so he
pressed them together tightly enough to still them. This
served only to make a flat, grim line of his mouth, as if he
dreaded what was to come next.

Cythera's face fell.

"Give me a kind word, Croy," Cythera begged. She
reached forward to take his hands. "Tell me I look beautiful, please. I spent so long coming to this favor. I put on
this uncomfortable dress. All for you."

He drew back a pace and stared at her. How could he be

so nervous now? He could scarcely credit it. He felt as if his feet were not touching the floor, as if his legs dangled in empty air. He'd been working toward this day since the first time they'd met, years ago. He'd slain monsters for her hand, had brought her and her mother out of sorcerous slavery to reach this exact moment. He'd never lacked for courage before.

Now, it seemed, he had not the bravery to even open his mouth. "You," he managed to stammer out, "look—"

There were no more words in his head. He could not speak.

"When he saw you from the window," Malden told her, "he used up every word he knew, words like 'enchanting,' 'divine,' and—of course—'beautiful.' "

Croy stared at his friend, unsure of what was happening.

The thief raised his eyebrows and tilted his head in Cythera's direction. What was he trying to communicate? Croy was unsure.

After a pause for breath, Malden went on. "He even swore on the Lady's holy name that he had been struck through the heart, by that invisible arrow whose wound no physic can heal, save the kiss of the archer."

From below came the sound of an old drinking song, sung well off key.

Cythera didn't seem to notice the music. "*He* said all that, did he?" she asked.

"Indeed, milady," Malden said, and bowed.

"Well, then he has said enough. Would someone be kind enough to pour me a cup of wine? I think I need to sit down. This corset is tighter than what I'm used to."

Malden rushed to help her. Croy couldn't move. She sipped at the wine the thief offered her and gave him a smile of thanks.

"When my mother arrives, we can get this formality out of the way, and then—" Cythera stopped speaking because the serving boy had let out a stifled yelp. "Ah," she said, not turning in her chair to look. "That must be her now."

The witch Coruth stepped out of the hearth and brushed sparks from her cloak. She must have come down the chimney in the form of a bird, Croy thought. He supposed if you were a witch you didn't need to travel in the way of common people.

Coruth had a wild tangle of iron gray hair and a nose so sharp it cut through the air like a ship's prow through the sea. She stared around at each of them, with an especially long and pointed glance at Malden, and then said, "Why is the thief here?"

"The law requires a witness," Cythera said. "After all, this is a legal contract of marriage. Once I sign it, I will be bound to marry Croy, or suffer quite severe penalties." She gestured at the roll of parchment. "Malden was kind enough to offer his services."

Coruth's thin mouth curved upward in a smile like a sharpened sickle. She was staring still at Malden, who couldn't seem to meet her gaze. Croy wondered what the witch found so amusing. Then again, he told himself, maybe he didn't want to know. The things witches found entertaining were not always pleasant for common folk. "Handy fellow, your thief. What's that singing?"

"We are above the public room of a tavern," Cythera explained.

"Hmm. Well, then what are we waiting for? Sign this thing, and then we can eat." Coruth sat down heavily in one of the chairs.

"Yes, of course." Cythera picked up one of the pens and smoothed the parchment out with her other hand. Then she stared down at the banns and laughed. "It's odd, I can't seem to make out the words. I have tears in my eyes, yes, that must be it. Tears. Of joy. Sir Knight, would you come over here, please, and show me where to put my name?"

Croy's head snapped upward and he blinked rapidly. Suddenly he felt in possession of his own body once more. He rushed to stand behind her and put one hand on her shoulder—her very warm and very soft shoulder—as together they looked down at the paper.

"My love," he said, "you seem ill at ease. I think I know why."

"You . . . do?" Cythera said. Strangely enough she glanced over at Malden as she said it. Croy wondered why. Perhaps she was hoping the thief would give her his support as well.

"Yes, of course," Croy said. "After waiting so long, this day must seem like a dream. After all you've been through, all the suffering and hardship. But I assure you, once you sign this paper, I will take full responsibility for you."

"Responsibility," Cythera said, very softly, but she lowered her head so the bells in her hair jingled.

Words came easily to him now. Perhaps too easily—they spilled off his tongue before he'd even thought of them.

"In full. I will protect you," he promised. "I will never let you near any harm, ever again. I will whisk you away to my castle, where you will be served night and day, all your needs met, all your requirements seen to on the instant. Why, you'll never need to lift a finger again. You'll never need to leave the castle at all. And when our children come, you will be complete as a woman. Think of how fulfilling it will be, to raise our sons and daughters far away from this noisy throng, this vulgar city."

Malden gave a cheer. "And that's exactly what you want, isn't it, Cythera?" he asked. "What you've always dreamed of."

Cythera looked up at the thief and scowled. "Indeed. As I've told you many times, Malden."

"Then you should have no trouble signing this paper," the thief said. "Once you do, there's no going back. You'll spend the rest of your life with Croy. You'll be his property."

"In a legal sense, perhaps," Croy said, hoping Malden wasn't going to scare Cythera off. What was the thief thinking, saying that? "But in a spiritual sense, it'll be the other way around. I'll be your slave. Forever," he promised.

"Sounds like a bargain," Malden announced, and he laughed as if he'd made a hilarious joke. "Sign now, and let it be forever. Or—"

"I've never been happier to write my name, Malden!" Cythera said, her voice almost a shriek. Nerves! So many raw nerves in the room, Croy thought. If only she would get this over with and let everyone be at peace!

He could say no more, only watch as Cythera moved her quill to dip it in the ink pot—

—and flinched as a scream came up from the room below. Her hand jumped and she knocked the ink pot over, spilling ink across the table.

"What was that?" she asked, lifting the parchment away from the expanding pool of ink. "Did everyone hear that?"

"It was nothing but men carousing," Coruth insisted. "Sign, now. I'm hungry."

"I could have sworn it was—"

Cythera did not have a chance to finish her thought, because just then something hit one of the walls of the tavern hard enough to make the entire building shake. A candle fell from a sconce on one wall. Luckily, Malden was quick enough to grab it before it could land on the floor rushes and set the place ablaze.

The sound they heard next was even more startling— booming laughter from below, the sound, surely, of a demon exulting over deadly mischief. It was followed by the sound of a man crying out in dire pain. There was no more singing from below, no sound of clinking tankards or muttered jokes.

Suddenly everyone in the room was looking right at Croy. Croy, who had sworn an oath to protect the people of Skrae. They were looking to him, he knew, for an explanation of the noise. Well they should, he thought. As a knight of the king, it was his sworn duty to keep the king's peace—which, by the sound of it, was being violated most egregiously in the room below.

If he were truly honest Croy had never been so grateful

for a distraction in his life. "I should go investigate that," he announced. "Wait here. I'll be right back." He was already headed down the stairs.

# CHAPTER SIX

A flying tankard full of beer nearly struck Croy's face as he hurried down the stairs. He dodged and let it smash messily against the wall. Leaping down the last few steps, he pushed his way into a throng of people in the common room, all but a few of whom were trying desperately to get out. Some hurried up the stairs, some rushed for the door or ran toward the kitchens. For a moment even Croy had trouble swimming against the tide of panicked humanity—but then, suddenly, the room was cleared, and he was standing alone.

Alone save for a barbarian in a wolf fur cloak, and the six bravos who had stayed to fight him.

The bravos were of the ordinary sort who haunted every tavern in the city, men of Ness who were good with a blade or a club but lacked any other trade. When they found work it was as bodyguards or hired thugs, but they spent most of their time drinking, gambling, and whoring. They dressed to intimidate, in boiled leather or in black cloaks, and they went everywhere armed. The six facing the barbarian carried knives as long as their forearms. Illegal, of course, but easily concealed. One—obviously the smartest of the lot—had a buckler on his left wrist. They had formed a rough semicircle before the barbarian and were edging back and forth, trying to get behind him.

Their opponent stood head and shoulders taller than any of them. His head was shorn down to mere stubble and the lower half of his face was painted red, as if he'd been drinking blood. Under that paint huge white teeth showed, for he was smiling. Beaming. He was either very drunk or very confident.

Croy flicked his eyes to the side to learn how this had started. He saw a man slumped against a cracked wooden pillar behind the barbarian. That accounted for the great crash he had heard, which shook the tavern like an earthquake. He was certain the column had not been cracked when he came into this place earlier.

The barbarian reached up and unlaced the front of his cloak. Pushing it away from his shoulders he revealed rippling muscle beneath—as well as a small arsenal of weaponry. A sword hung from his belt, reaching near his ankle. A cruel-bladed bearded axe hung at his other side. Knives were tied to his upper arms and a mace dangled on a thong at the back of his hip. He reached for the axe first.

One of the bravos danced forward, knife slashing up from a low start. It was a good strike, timed perfectly. The barbarian brought up one massive forearm and took the cut on the back of his wrist. Blood ran down toward his elbow. Before the bravo could finish his swing, the axe came around in a powerful arc that carved right through the bravo's leather pauldron and sheared off half his bicep. The bravo howled and spun away from the melee.

One of his fellows tried to duck low under the axe and get a knife point into the barbarian's ribs, but the barbarian stepped aside at the perfect moment and the knife missed him entirely. The axe swung back and the end of its haft came down hard enough to crack the attacker's skull. As the bravo fell, the barbarian kicked his insensate body away, so as not to tangle his footing.

The man was fast, and exceeding strong, Croy saw. He

would make short work of his six assailants if he wasn't stopped. Rushing forward with his hands held high, Croy called, "Fellows, good men all, stop this now, let us converse and see if—"

His words were lost in the noise as the barbarian's mace—held in his presumably weaker left hand—caught a third bravo in the stomach and sent him sprawling across the room. The injured man screamed with a horrible wet sound that suggested half his innards had just been ruptured.

The remaining three all rushed the barbarian at once, their knives flashing high. The one with the buckler took a mace blow perfectly, catching it on the small shield and knocking it backward toward the barbarian's face. The barbarian took a step back, surprised at this resistance—the first real challenge he'd met—and another bravo took the opportunity to lunge forward with his knife and prick his chest. The barbarian howled and brought his axe around to slice off his foeman's cheek. The axe was red with blood when it came back, whirling in its master's hand. Continuing his swing, the barbarian brought it behind his back and embedded it deep in the buckler, splitting the wooden shield and the wrist that held it. Two more bodies struck the floor.

Croy felt no fear at watching this spectacle of gore. He had trained himself, over the course of many years, to ride the wave of giddiness that threatened to freeze him to the spot. He took another step forward and raised his hands again for attention. "Stop this. Now," he said.

"Just a moment," the barbarian said. Then he swung around on one foot, his mace whistling through the air. The final bravo had edged around behind him and was about to stab him in the back. Instead the mace shattered the bones of his forearm and he dropped the weapon. For a moment he stared at his hand dangling at the end of a crushed arm, and then began to scream.

There was no other sound in the room. The air seemed

to hang perfectly still, as if it had turned to glass and held every object secure in its place. Croy felt rooted to the spot, unable to move an inch.

It was no magic spell that made Croy feel that way, but the simple focus of battle joined. It was clear this barbarian would not surrender without a fight. Based on what little Croy knew of his people, that was no surprise. The barbarians of the eastern steppes were born warriors all—they spent their entire lives hunting and fighting, and they were renowned for their pure bloody courage. Only a thin range of mountains separated their land from the kingdom of Skrae, but that fluke of geography was a true blessing. If the barbarians ever came to Skrae in pursuit of conquest, even Croy doubted the kingdom could stand for long against them.

Now he was face-to-face with a perfect specimen of that warrior culture, and he didn't know if he could prevail.

"I believe you wished to say something," the barbarian said. His lips drew back in what might have been a friendly grin—if the posture of his body and the set of his muscles didn't suggest he was about to spring forward in a deadly attack.

Croy scowled and drew his sword. He had trained for fighting himself. He had made a study of taking down opponents like this. He considered his strategy in the moments he had left before the attack came. He could parry the axe, he knew, if he used a cross slash cut, but that mace was too heavy and the arm that wielded it too strong to be effectively blocked. He would need to duck under its swing, and lunge forward at the same time, bringing his sword down in a weak slash that might—

"Ghostcutter," the barbarian said, as if greeting an old friend. He nodded at the sword in Croy's hand. Then he flung his arms out to the sides and dropped both axe and mace.

Croy frowned. "You know my blade?" he asked. The sword he wielded—the only weapon he'd brought to the signing of the banns, and that only for ornament—was famous in certain circles, of course. It was an Ancient Blade, one of seven swords forged at the dawn of time to fight no lesser opponents than demons themselves. Ghost-cutter was made of cold-forged iron, with one edge coated in silver. Runnels of melted silver streamed across its fuller. It was made to fight against magical creatures, curses, and the abominations of foul sorcery. It was damned good at cutting more mundane flesh as well.

"I should recognize it anywhere," the barbarian said. He drew his own sword and launched himself forward, straight at Croy, in a fast cutting attack that would have overwhelmed a less disciplined warrior's defense.

The two swords clanged together with a sound like the ringing of a bell. When two well-made swords met like that it was called a conversation, for the repeated ringing noise as they came together and checked each other's strikes. Croy knew this conversation would be very short—if he didn't cut the barbarian down in the next few seconds, the other man's strength would end the fight before it had a chance to properly begin. The first clash nearly brought him down. He struggled to hold his parry against the strength behind the blow, his eyes fixed on the point where the barbarian's foible met his forte. The weakest part of the barbarian's blade, up against the most resistance Croy could offer, and he barely held his ground. Iron slid against iron with a horrible grinding that would blunt both edges.

Then the barbarian's blade burst into light.

It was no reflection of a candle flame, but the pure clean light of the sun, and it came from within the metal of the blade itself. Croy was blinded and shouted an oath as he jumped backward, falling on his haunches away from the light. He flung up Ghostcutter before him in hopeless defense. If he could not see the barbarian's next attack, he could not properly meet it. The man could kill him a hundred different ways without resistance.

Yet when Croy managed to blink away the bright spots

that swam before his eyes, he found not a sword pointed at his face, but a massive hand reaching down to help him back to his feet.

"Dawnbringer," Croy said, with proper reverence. "You wield Dawnbringer."

"Yes. Will you take my hand," the barbarian asked, "and call me brother?"

Croy grasped the barbarian's wrist gratefully, and allowed himself to be hauled to his feet. Dawnbringer was already back in the barbarian's scabbard. Croy sheathed Ghostcutter, and stepped forward into a warm embrace.

# CHAPTER SEVEN

"I think . . . they're hugging each other," Malden said. He was lying on the stairs above the common room, watching the fight and reporting on it to Cythera and Coruth, who were standing in the doorway of the private chamber. "They've put their swords away. They're . . . talking. They actually look quite friendly."

"Good. It's over," Coruth said. "Now we can eat." She stepped back through the door and disappeared. Cythera glanced down at Malden, threw up her hands in resignation and followed.

Malden found the two of them sitting at table, picking apart a cheese between them. "But," he said, "it was—it looked like it was to be a fight to the death. Clearly they were going to kill each other."

"Yet for some reason they've decided not to," Cythera pointed out.

"You saw the big man, though. He's a beast! The blood-lust had him. What kind of man can just go from wanting to kill an enemy to embracing him like that?" Cythera shot him a knowing look, and it was Malden's turn to shrug. "Other than Croy, I mean. I admit that's exactly the kind of thing Croy would do."

Cythera and Coruth nodded in unison.

Croy had a sense of honor that other people often found confusing. Malden thought of it as sheer stupidity, but sometimes he was glad enough for it. One of the knight's tenets was that he tried never to let anger overcome him when he was fighting, so that he never struck anyone down for ignoble reasons. More than once Malden had benefited personally from that compunction. "I still don't see it, though. The barbarian just left six men in a moaning heap. He maimed some of them for life. Now Croy's acting like this fellow's as blameless as an honest priest."

"Don't try to figure out Croy's reasons," Coruth said. "You'll tie your own brains in knots."

"I usually just wait for him to explain himself later," Cythera pointed out. "He's never shy about telling me how things ought to be. Or how he thinks they should be, at any rate."

Malden pursed his lips. "I noticed that earlier. When he was talking about how he would lock you away in his castle so you could have his babies. He made it sound quite . . . safe."

"There are worse things in this world than being secure."

Malden stopped himself from speaking. He wasn't sure how much he could say in Coruth's presence. Yet he longed to be alone with Cythera so he could discuss things with her. There had been a time when she seemed to care for him. More than that, perhaps. She had seemed to love him. After her father died, and she was free to renew her pledge to marry Croy, that all seemed to just melt away.

For her, anyway. Malden's feelings for Cythera were just as strong as ever.

When Croy invited him here today, to witness the banns, he had accepted in a state of pure denial. He couldn't believe Cythera would actually sign the document and go through with the marriage. She seemed so nervous—almost as nervous as Croy. Malden had been certain she would say no at the last moment. Reject Croy, refuse to marry the knight, because she still loved him.

But then the barbarian had shown up and thrown everything into disarray. And now Malden had no idea what to think.

"Cythera," he said. "You and I should have a talk at some point, about—"

"Malden," Cythera said, cutting him off before he could finish his thought, "the watch will be here at any moment. They'll have a lot of questions, and they may try to take this stranger away. In the meantime, we have a moment's peace. It's even quiet for—"

They all flinched then as the booming, demonic laughter came once more from below. Malden tensed and reached for the bodkin at his belt, but when there was no sound of ringing swords or screams of agony, he dropped into a chair and shook his head.

"—mostly quiet, for now," Cythera amended. "We'll all have to leave very shortly, so perhaps we should make use of this groaning board before we have to flee."

Malden could see the wisdom in that. He nodded, but said, "Later, then. But we will speak, won't we?"

"As you wish!" Cythera said, seeming more than a little annoyed.

Malden knew better than to push the point. He took an eating knife from the table and speared a slice of ham. He glanced over at Coruth. She was downing a goblet of wine so fast it was spilling down the front of her tunic. If the witch had read anything into the conversation between the thief and her daughter, she seemed oblivious now.

"He's a barbarian," Coruth said when she had emptied her cup. She reached for the flagon to refill it. "If you're wondering."

"You didn't even see him," Malden said.

Coruth grabbed a roasted leg of chicken from a plate. "Don't need to."

Malden frowned. "You sense his nature, on some subtle current in the ether? Is that it? Have you plumbed his heart with your witchery?"

"Don't need that either. Only a barbarian laughs like that. Like his death could come for him at any minute and he's looking forward to it." The witch put down the bone she'd been gnawing and sat back in her chair. "They're different, out there on the eastern steppes. Unsophisticated, some might say. They live in a more violent world, that's for sure. They have no gods but death, and they fight like animals." She stared into the middle distance and smiled. "Make love like animals, too."

"Mother," Cythera said, spreading butter on a piece of brown bread, "if you know that from personal experience, I'd prefer not to hear the story."

Heavy footsteps came clomping up the stairs, and the two swordsmen bustled into the room. The barbarian had a fresh bandage around his forearm, but the bleeding wound on his chest was left exposed. He had one massive arm around Croy's shoulders.

"Everyone," Croy said, "I'd like you to meet Mörget."

Malden rose from his chair and wiped his hands on his tunic. He glanced toward the window, wondering how fast he could get out of the room if he had to. It wasn't that he felt he was in any particular danger. Looking to the nearest escape route was simply his natural reaction when being introduced to a very large man covered in weapons.

Croy introduced his new friend to the ladies, and then to Malden, who stuck out one hand to grasp. The barbarian stared at the hand for a moment, then looked away.

"I beg your pardon, sir, if I have offended," Malden said.

"Little man, forgive me. In my land we touch only those we love, or those we plan on killing."

"Like . . . Croy," Malden said, nodding at the arm that held the knight. "Do the two of you know each other from some previous battle?"

"We never met before today," Croy assured the thief.

"Then—"

"Mörget is an Ancient Blade."

"Oh!" Cythera said, and Malden nodded, because that explained everything.

Croy bore the sword Ghostcutter, and it defined his life. Before it had been given to him his father had carried it, and before his father a whole succession of knights wielded the sword. Each of them had groomed his own replacement, so that the sword would always have a noble bearer. Croy had spent his entire youth training just to be worthy to hold it. To listen to him talk of his sword, the knight was far less important and less valuable than the piece of iron he wore at his belt, so when people asked him what kind of man he was, he claimed he was an Ancient Blade—speaking for the sword, which had no voice of its own.

The wielders of those swords were sworn to various oaths, one of which was that they would aid each other in noble quests. Another was that if they ever broke their vows, the other six were bound to hunt them down and slay them, so that the blade they had dishonored could be recovered and passed on to a more worthy owner.

Which meant that Croy and Mörget would either be fast friends from now on, or Croy would have to kill Mörget without warning.

"I believe I told you once that only five of the swords were accounted for here in the West. Two others were lost to us, among the—the barbarians."

Mörget pursed his lips and tsked. "The clans of the East," he corrected.

"Yes, of course," Croy said, "the clans of the East. Well,

it turns out they weren't lost at all. The clans have had them for centuries, and they've been honoring the blades just as we have, and keeping them for their holy purpose."

"We have sorcerers beyond the mountains," Mörget added, "just as you have them here. Someone must fight them. I, myself, have slain more than one dozen with Dawnbringer." He drew the sword from its sheath and jabbed it toward the ceiling. "May I live to slay a dozen more, or die with blade in hand!"

"Yes, may you do that," Malden said. He went to the table and picked up a pitcher of ale. "Should we drink to it?"

"I never drink spirits," Mörget insisted, putting his sword away. "They dull the senses, ruin the body, and make a man unfit for battle. Do you have any milk?"

"There's cream here," Cythera suggested, and pointed out a ewer.

The barbarian picked it up like a cup and quaffed a long draught. Then he grimaced and shook his head. Cream was smeared all around his mouth, obscuring the red paint there.

It did not, in Malden's eyes, make the man look comical. He could have been wearing a wig of straw and a fake pig snout over his nose, and still Malden would not have thought the man looked like a clown. Not when he knew how much iron Mörget was carrying under his fur cloak.

It was not that Malden was a coward, after all—he was not opposed to personal risk if there was any benefit to be had from it. It was merely that he understood that courage in the face of certain doom was folly. He would no sooner laugh at this barbarian than he would put his head inside a lion's mouth to prove his manhood.

While he was brooding on this subject, Malden heard the door of the tavern open with a crash. He glanced at the window again. "I believe the watch have arrived," he said, and was proven right when a voice below demanded to know what had happened. "As well met we may be, we would be just as well advised to be elsewhere now."

"Agreed," Coruth said. She stood up from the table and grabbed for Cythera's hand. "It's time to go home."

Cythera began to protest but the witch had already started to change shape. She and her daughter transformed into a pair of blackbirds that darted out the window, and before anyone could react or speak they were gone.

"Witchcraft," Mörget said, staring after them. There was a bloody look in his eye.

"Let us follow them, by more prosaic means," Malden suggested. He went to the window and saw its ledge was wide enough to stand on. "The roof of this tavern is connected to the roof of a stable next door. From there we'll have to cross Cripplegate High Street." He looked over at Mörget. "Do you know how to climb, milord barbarian?"

The barbarian opened his mouth and let out another booming, murderous laugh. "Like a goat, boy!" he claimed, and threw himself out the window with abandon.

The watchmen were already coming up the stairs. Malden followed Mörget, with a trace more care. Standing on the ledge outside, he looked back in at Croy and gestured for him to follow.

"But the banns—we never signed them," Croy protested, staring at the parchment on the table. Black ink had soaked into the contract and obliterated half of its calligraphy.

"The wedding will have to wait," Malden said. "Such a shame." Then he reached in to grab Croy's arm and pull him toward the windowsill.

# CHAPTER EIGHT

Malden scampered up onto the roof of the tavern and braced himself against a chimney, then reached down a hand to help Croy up. This was not the first time he had brought the knight up onto the rooftops of the city. Always it was a painful process. Croy could never seem to find proper handholds, and the boots he wore were wholly unsuited to running on uneven surfaces. Always Malden had to help him over every obstacle and show him where to hold on and where not to put his weight. Making matters even worse, the knight didn't seem capable of moving quietly even when walking down a crowded street. His baldric slapped against his chest with every step, his sword clattered in its scabbard.

Mörget, it seemed, was different. He was already halfway across the roof of the stables when Malden caught sight of him. The barbarian leapt from the roof ridge of the stables to a broad lead gutter as nimbly as a bird, and perched there on hands and feet in such a way that even his great bulk didn't strain the drainpipes. Malden scurried across a bank of shingles to join him, then beckoned for Croy to come as well.

The knight looked game enough, but halfway across his foot slipped and he began to tumble. Malden raced toward him to try to steady him but Mörget beat him to it, rushing over and picking up Croy in his two giant hands while Croy's legs still flailed in the air. The barbarian set Croy down carefully and they all three peered down into the high street. A market crowd had gathered there, perusing the wares of an endless line of ramshackle wooden stalls. Pigs and small children ran in and out of the throng and someone was walking a pair of cows uphill toward a slaughterhouse. Smoke from the stalls of food vendors wafted on the air.

"It's too far to jump," Malden said, pointing at the roofs of the shops and houses across the way. Nearly ten yards of open air separated the climbers from that goal. "But up there, we can make use of that canopy." He indicated a broad roof slope sticking out from the second floor of a blacksmith's shop. It covered the open part of the shop below, where horseshoes and andirons and skillets were on display. "From there we jump to the balcony across the way, and then up over the roof beyond."

Mörget nodded and raced toward the blacksmith's, even as a watchman poked his helmeted head over the roofline and called for them to stop.

Malden dashed for the canopy and made the jump easily, landing on the balcony across the street and gesturing for the swordsmen to follow. Croy nearly mistimed the jump but at the last second Mörget gave him a boost that sent him clattering and sprawling onto the balcony beside Malden. The watchmen came boiling out onto the roof of the tavern they'd just fled so precipitously, even as Mörget boomed out a laugh and flung himself over the street.

Half the shoppers in the market looked up in surprise and terror, perhaps thinking some storm cloud had passed over their heads booming with thunder. They could only stare upward in wonder as the thief and the knight followed suit, without quite so much noise.

"Now," Malden said, "up and over. And—please you—discreetly."

Mörget frowned in mock shame and hauled himself up onto the slate tiles of the roof above. Malden helped Croy do the same. They left the watchmen behind, staring across the street at them, unwilling to make the jump. Rather than waiting for the watchmen to shout for reinforcements, Malden led the two warriors up and over a roofline, then along the gutters of a row of houses and over a narrow alley until a quarter mile of rooftops lay between them and any possible pursuit.

"Enough, Malden, enough," Croy gasped, unable to stand upright after all that bounding and jumping. "We've lost them, I'm sure of it." He sat down hard on the slates, with his legs dangling in the air.

"We could have just stayed and fought them off," Mörget suggested. "You made it sound as if an army was after us, when it was just five little men with halberds."

"I'm sure you could have smashed them into paste," Malden said, scowling, "but then you *would* have had an army after you. Don't they have watchmen where you come from? If you fight one, you have to fight them all."

"Men whose only job is to watch their fellows and make sure they are not breaking laws? Why would we need such a thing? In the East, when a man wrongs you, you go to his tent and call him out to fight. You pummel him until he apologizes, or pays you what is owed. It's a very simple system, but it works."

"And what if you call out a man who has done you some injury, but he's bigger than you, and he wins?" Malden asked.

The barbarian squinted in confusion. "I wouldn't know."

Malden shook his head. "Well, here, when you attack six men in a tavern with an axe—"

"Come now, I didn't *kill* any of them."

"—the watch will send as many men as it takes to cart you away. Then they put you in gaol to wait for a trial."

"I would have died before they put me in a cage," Mörget said.

"Or afterward, when they hanged you. They would have probably arrested Croy for helping you, and detained me on pure suspicion because I happened to be nearby."

"Thanks to Malden it did not come to that," Croy said, and slapped the thief on the back.

"I suppose I owe you at that," Mörget admitted.

"Think nothing of it. But perhaps you'll tell me one thing. Why did that fight start in the first place, and how did it get so out of hand? Normally a tavern fight ends with bruised knuckles and maybe a chair being broken over someone's head, not axes and maces and faces getting chopped off."

Mörget shrugged. "A man insulted me. He besmirched my honor."

Croy nodded in understanding but Malden had to look away.

"You Ancient Blades and your honor will get me killed one of these days. All right, what did he say? What was such a dreadful blasphemy?"

"He saw me drinking milk and said I was the largest babe he'd ever clapped eyes on. I thought it a nice jest, and saw no harm in it."

"Men in taverns often joke and make sport," Malden said. "It means nothing."

"But among clansmen, one must always respond to a jape with another. So of course I had to tell him that in my country, even infants were bigger than the men that I'd seen in this city. He didn't like that much." Mörget shrugged. "He tried to grab my arm—as I have said, that is forbidden to strangers in my land. So I picked him up and threw him against a pillar. I thought that was the end of it, until I saw his friends drawing their knives."

Malden made a mental note never to try to shake the barbarian's hand again. "All right," he said, "that explains how we all came to meet. But now, tell me, pray thee, what you're doing in the Free City of Ness in the first place. We don't get . . . ah, that is to say, a man of your people is a rare sight this far west." Malden had grown up hearing horror stories of the barbarians, of how they ate their own babies and that their women were all seven feet tall. As an adult he'd often heard them spoken of in hushed tones, as it was commonly believed that the barbarians would sweep over the mountains any day and invade Skrae and enslave them all. It was all hearsay, of course. He had never met a barbarian before, nor ever expected to.

"Ah!" the barbarian said, and looked like he might start laughing again. "I am glad you asked. I am looking for Sir Croy."

Malden was confused. "Well, you found him—but did you expect to find him in that tavern? It's not the sort of place he normally frequents."

Croy himself was still trying to catch his breath. His eyes were locked on Mörget's face.

"I knew nothing of him, until now, except his name. Perhaps I spoke wrong," Mörget said with a frown. "I am looking for another Ancient Blade. I am looking for the help of an Ancient Blade. It did not matter which one. I have sought them for a very long time, looking anywhere men with swords gathered. Until today my search was fruitless. From town to town I wandered, asking everywhere. Few men would even speak to me, but in the town of Greencastle I was told there was not one, but two such men in Ness. Sir Croy, and Sir Bikker—champions of your king, each of them bearers of a puissant sword. Ghostcutter and Acidtongue, they are called. I was told that Sir Bikker would be found in a place where ale is sold, if he could be found anywhere."

Malden and Croy traded a glance. Until a few months ago that might have been true. Bikker had been in Ness— though that man had fallen a long way since he'd been one of the king's champions. He'd hired himself out as a sellsword to the sorcerer Hazoth and the traitor Anselm Vry. And then he'd put himself at odds with Malden and Croy. That had nearly ended in both their deaths. Instead—

"I'm afraid Bikker is dead," Croy said, still a little out of breath.

"Dead?" Mörget asked.

"He broke his oath," Croy said, nodding, as if that explained everything.

Apparently it did, as far as Mörget was concerned. "Ah.

So you had to strike him down. I understand. It is part of our duty, our sworn duty, we who bear the Blades."

Malden didn't want to talk about Bikker. The dead man had caused him a great deal of trouble once. "Well, you found the other one, anyway. The other Ancient Blade in Ness. Now, what do you want with Croy?"

"There is a task I must perform. The other part of our oath must be fulfilled." The barbarian's eyes had gone out of focus, as if he was looking at nothing but the inside of his own skull. As if his thoughts were very far away.

Malden scratched at an eyebrow. "If you specifically need the help of an Ancient Blade, that suggests just one task I can think of."

"Indeed. I am hunting a demon."

Croy jumped to his feet, all sign of weariness gone from him. "Where?" he demanded.

# CHAPTER NINE

There was no word Malden knew that could get Croy's attention better than "demon."

The world had its share of monsters. Up in the Northern Kingdoms there were still bands of goblins on the loose, and the occasional troll for a knight to test his steel on. Malden himself had met an ogre, and knew stories of everything from the dread Longlegs of the Rifnlatt to the dragons of the Old Empire. All such creatures could be felled by good swords or by magic, it was said. Demons were different.

They were not of the world. They did not belong there. Instead they were creatures of the Bloodgod, and they abided in his Pit of Souls, that place where all men were eventually judged and punished for their sins. Demons were normally trapped down there with eight-armed Sadu, but they could be summoned to the mundane realm by sorcerers who sought to tap their incredible power. Such a pact was illegal and utterly forbidden, and with good reason. Demons did not hail from the world of living men, and in that world were unnatural things, unbound by natural law. They were enormously powerful and almost impossible to kill. The sorcerer Hazoth had called up two of them before he died, and either one of them might have destroyed all of Ness if they had not been stopped.

Luckily for Malden and his fellow citizens, Croy had been there to slay them. Ghostcutter had prevailed against them, just as it had been made to do. The Ancient Blades had been forged for just that purpose.

And over the last eight hundred years they'd been quite successful at it. The men who wielded them often died in the process, but the swords had all but eliminated demonkind from the world. Now the existence of a single demon anywhere on the continent was a rare—but utterly fearful—occurrence. If the barbarian had encountered one, Croy had no choice but to go and slay it.

"You must tell me everything," Croy said.

The barbarian nodded. "And so I shall. Two years ago I was hunting in the mountains at the western end of our land," he said, squatting down on the tiles. "I was after a wild cat that had already tasted human blood, and found it to be good. I went into the hills with only a knife and three days' food in a sack. Just having a bit of fun, you know."

"Yes, of course," Malden said. "Fun."

Mörget squinted at the sky. "I followed the cat's trail until I ran out of food, and then for five days more. Its spoor took me ever higher, up to a place where the trees grew no taller than saplings, and then to where they thinned out until there was nothing but lichens to eat, and springwater to quench my thirst. From time to time I found the remains of some creature the cat had killed—or so I thought. The carrion was broken open, crushed and sucked dry.

"On the sixth day I found the cat itself, and all its bones ground to dust. There was not much left of it save the head and one paw. The rest had been . . . dissolved, yes, I think that is the word I mean. Eaten away as if by acid. It was then I knew I hunted bigger prey than I thought.

"I made a hunting blind in the cave of a raven, and sat me down to wait. It was another seven days before I caught my first good sight of the thing I tracked. It came to me at twilight, moving along the bare rock face of a cliff. It was about fifteen feet long, though it was hard to mea- sure. It did not climb, you understand, for it had no legs. It crawled—no, it flowed like water along the rock, living water." Mörget clenched his fists in frustration. "I describe it poorly. I have not the honeyed words of a westerner, for- give me."

"It's all right," Croy said. "Go on."

"Its skin glistened like autumn moonlight on a brackish pond. The skin had no regular form, but flowed and oozed as it moved. There were shapes under that skin, shapes like hearts and livers and even human faces, that pressed up against the skin from inside, mouths open in soundless screaming. I decided then this was no natural beast."

"A fairly safe conclusion, it sounds like," Malden agreed.

"I made myself still, and did not so much as breathe as it came ever closer. I did not wish to scare it away. It came up to the mouth of my cave, and still I held myself in readiness, my knife in my hand. It came inside, into the darkness, and I could barely see it. It flowed up over my bare feet and my flesh screamed at its alien touch, but still I made myself like a statue. It climbed up my body, faster now, as if it had become excited, as if it hungered for me. It was only then I struck.

"Yet how to slay a beast with no muscles, no bones? I stabbed at the shapes like hearts and livers and faces, but my knife could not puncture its slimy skin. It flowed over my chest and part of its substance oozed up to my face. It tried to fill my mouth and nose so that I could not breathe. I stabbed and pulled at it, to no avail. I wrestled with the beast, rolling on the floor of my cave, tearing at it with my fingers. I was so close to death I could feel her hands upon my shoulders."

"*Her* hands?" Malden asked.

"Death is my mother," Mörget said. It sounded like a litany, something the barbarian had said so many times it would spring to his lips without bidding. "When I die, she will be there to bring me home. But not that day! With all my strength I fought against this demon, aye, for demon it had to be—I fought for long hours as it wrapped around me like a cloak, smothering me. Would it absorb me, I thought, until mine was one of those screaming faces I'd seen under its skin?

"Strength did not matter to the beast. It yielded every time I grasped it, stretched like dough in my hands. Always it covered more of me, always it sucked hungrily at my more solid form. Then, of a sudden, I was *inside* the beast. It had swallowed me whole. My lungs cried for breath, my skin burned as if I'd been doused in acid. I could just see by the light that streamed in through its translucent hide. Before me were the livers and hearts and faces—faces attached to no skulls, faces with no eyes, like living masks. There was another shape inside there, one I had not seen before, just as a man will not see a piece of glass that is under dark water. This was the biggest of the shapes, a thing like a clear egg full of worms. With the last of my strength I grasped it with my hands and started pulling it apart. It was more solid than the rest of the beast, and when I broke it open, it bled. Could I breathe then, I would have laughed, for I knew death favored me still. The beast trembled and shook and spat me out all at once, dripping from my skin to the floor of the cave. It raced away from me, for it knew I was going to slay it. I tracked it all that night, though it moved far faster than a man on that rough terrain. I tracked it up the mountainside, until it came to another cave, which I thought must be its lair.

"This new cave was far deeper than I expected, however. It proved to be the mouth of a tunnel that led deep into the heart of the mountain. Nor was it any natural cavern. Had I not been so hot for the thing's destruction, I would have noticed how regular the floor was, how the walls had been carved out of the rock by metal tools. The tunnel went down and down until it came to what looked like a blank wall. There was no light down there, so at the time I could not see that a solid block of stone filled the tunnel, a block cut almost to the exact dimensions of the shaft. I was just in time to watch the thing flow around that block, to ooze through the hair-thin gap between the block and the wall. It nearly got away from me. I managed at the last only to stab at it one more time, and to pin one of its hearts to the floor. It tore itself in half to get away from me, so desperate was it to escape.

"I had not killed it, I am sure of that—the part that got away still lives. What remained behind shriveled rapidly, parts of it drying out and turning to dust, other parts melting and soaking into the floor of the tunnel. I put the heart in a sack and brought it down the mountain, to my father, who is called Mörg the Wise. He is a man of great learning, they say, and it was he who told me of demons, for I had never heard the word before. He told me how they are hauled up out of the pit, and how they take forms unseemly to man. He said that if such a thing was haunting the steppes, all of our clan were in great danger. I said I would take a band of men back up to the mountain and slay it, but he shook his head. He had something else in mind.

"In the eastern land of my birth, no boy becomes a man, not truly, until he hunts and kills an animal of his father's choosing. I had thought this cat, the poor creature I originally tracked, would be the prey that made me a man. Yet my father laughed at the prospect. After all, I had not killed the cat myself, but only seen what did it. He demanded that I track and kill the demon properly—with a tool that was made for such work. And that was when he gave to me Dawnbringer, and made me swear all the vows of an Ancient Blade. I will not be allowed to marry, or sire children, or lead men to battle, until this demon is destroyed.

"I do not think my father knew how hard that would prove. Or perhaps he did, and wanted me to show that I had not just manhood within me, but greatness."

# CHAPTER TEN

"I returned to the shaft many times, trying to plumb its secrets," Mörget went on. "It was very deep, running almost three hundred feet down into the mountain. Its walls were perfectly square, cut with precision. The block of stone at its end was cut to almost exactly the dimensions of the shaft. I brought men up there to break through the block, thinking to find my demon waiting just beyond where I could challenge it to single combat. It was not so easy as that. I soon discovered there was not one block, but four of them. They were plugs, you see. When the shaft was finished, its makers brought these four giant stones up the cliff face and slid them down the shaft to seal it forever.

"I could not rest, though, until my demon was destroyed. The blocks were broken one by one, shattered with iron picks, their pieces dragged back up the shaft with the strength of our backs. When we reached the fourth block, we were surprised to find a dwarven rune carved into its face. The thorn rune, which every man knows."

"The rune of death and destruction," Croy said. It was true that everyone learned that rune early on. When a dwarf decided something was too dangerous to meddle with, it was wise to take heed.

Mörget nodded. "When we broke through that block, we found it was all a trap. A great underground river was being held back by the stone. The water burst through, filling the shaft and nearly drowning me.

"The demon's lair could not be breached that way. I needed another route in.

"For months I searched, looking for another shaft. There was none. I traveled far and wide seeking out wizards who could see inside the mountain, to tell me how I could find my path. The effort I spent was wasted. Yes, they told me, there is a demon in there, which I already knew. Yes, they said, there were tunnels and even whole caverns inside that mountain where the demon could hide. Bah! Useless. At last one told me something I could use. He said to go to the library at Redweir. There I would find my answers."

"That must have been daunting," Croy said.

"Oh?" Malden asked.

"Redweir is a city of Skrae," Croy said.

"Even I know that," Malden replied.

"It lies on the far side of the Whitewall Mountains from Mörget's home."

"How was that a problem?" Malden asked.

Croy shook his head. "Forgive me, Mörget, if I say anything that offends. But the . . . clans of the eastern steppes have been enemies with the land of Skrae since . . . well, for hundreds of years. It's only an accident of geography that keeps us from total war." He looked at Malden the way a teacher will look at a recalcitrant pupil. "You don't know any of this?"

"I've spent my entire life in Ness," Malden explained. "I never needed to know anything about maps or mountains."

Croy nodded sagely. "This continent is split in half by a range of snowcapped mountains, called the White-wall. The mountains are impassible, save in two places, both narrow defiles that are open only in the summer. The passes are well guarded on both sides, on the Skrae side by our soldiers, on the other side by the clans, so that no army can pass. If Mörget wanted to travel from his own land to Redweir, the easiest way would be through those passes, but we would never allow even one clansman through—for fear an army would be right behind him."

Mörget laughed with excitement. "Give us one chance only, and we'll do it, too! You're right, the men at the passes would not let me through, even when I told them I was on a sacred quest. Just as we would not permit one of your warriors to travel east and live, no matter what flatteries and pretty turns of speech he offered," Mörget said. "Yet come to the western lands—and Redweir—I must. So I took the long way around. I traveled halfway around the continent, on ships that sank and by trade routes beset by bandits. Along the way I taught myself how to fight against magic."

"How?" Malden asked.

"By finding sorcerers and slaying them, of course. Many times death whispered in my ear, but never did she claim me." He shrugged. "It was a long journey, and I needed something to do to pass the time.

"At last I came to Redweir, and the library there, which contains more than one thousand books. The customs of the place were strange to me. I could not read your languages. I had to teach myself even the shapes of your letters, and then I had to do many labors for the librarians before they would allow me to even see their books. But eventually I learned what I sought. The shaft I had found, the mountain I wished to enter, was known well to the sages on this side of it. The entire mountain was hollow on the inside, carved out by ancient hands. I learned that no one knew of the shaft I had found, but that on the western side there was a grand entrance to the mountain. I took this as a sign. I could not return to my homeland, not yet. I must enter the mountain here, from this side, if I were to slay my demon."

"This mountain," Croy said, "I fear I know its name."

"I think you might," Mörget said. "It is called Cloudblade, for the way it splits the storm clouds with its sharp peak. I think perhaps you also know the name of what lies underneath it. Yes, my friend. I learned that the place I sought was the Vincularium."

Malden frowned. He had never heard the name before. It had to be very old, though, because it sounded like a word from the language of the Old Empire—a language no longer spoken in Skrae, and used now only by the Church and by scholars. He knew only a few words of that language, but perhaps enough to know what the name meant. "The . . . Chained Place, no—the House of Chains?" he asked.

"Yes," Croy and Mörget said together.

"What's a House of Chains?" Malden asked.

Mörget glanced at Croy. "He knows little of maps, aye, but nothing of his own history."

"Again, I've lived in Ness my entire life. What do I care about the rest of the world? But come, indulge me. What, I ask once more, is a House of Chains?"

"It's . . . a tomb," Croy said. From the look on his face it was a lot more than that. "A very . . . old tomb. It was built by the dwarves, a long time ago. They say it fills half of the interior of Cloudblade, and that it is a great labyrinth of traps and pitfalls. They also say it is haunted."

Malden touched his eyes with his thumb, an old gesture for warding off ghosts. He was not a superstitious man by nature, but no good ever came of disturbing the dead.

He shivered as he imagined the place. He'd heard far too many frightening stories about the underground lairs of the dwarves. In his day the dwarven kingdom was a small land just north of Skrae, a place of silent forests and cold, deep lakes. The dwarves themselves never went to the surface because they preferred to live underground. They had a handful of small cities up there built into old mine shafts where they worked tirelessly at their labors and only ever emerged to trade their wares for Skraeling gold. Once, though, their borders had extended much farther. Before mankind had come to this continent, the dwarves had been of much greater numbers and power. Most of their underground works were forsaken as their population dwindled. There were old abandoned dwarven cities left behind all over the continent—they were found as far away as the Northern Kingdoms and even on the Islands of Blue Mist, far to the east. No one ever went into those forgotten places, though, and for good reason. There was no telling what was down there—what hazards a grave robber might encounter, what terrible traps they might set off. The dwarves held many secrets, but everyone knew how clever they were with their hands, and how utterly deadly their safeguards were. Such places were not meant to be violated.

"Sounds terrifying," he said, without a trace of flippancy.

"It is my destiny," Mörget insisted.

"Well, that explains what you're doing in the West," Croy said. "But not why you came to the Free City. The mountains of the Whitewall are a hundred miles from here."

"I knew I could not storm the mountain on my own," Mörget said. "I learned many lessons on my travels. I learned when I could rely on the strength of my own back, which is almost always. And I learned that there are some few occasions when I must find help. This demon is stronger and more dangerous than any creature I've fought before. Even with Dawnbringer in my hand it will be a challenge. I came for others who might help me defeat it—others sworn to that cause, in fact. I came looking for you, Croy. To ask for your assistance."

Croy leapt to his feet—and nearly slipped and fell on the slate tiles of the roof. "Of course," he said. "Of course I will help! I am honor bound." He drew Ghostcutter and pointed it at the sun. "How could I refuse? Truth be told, I'm grateful for the chance. We had some trouble with demons here in Ness a while back, but since then I've heard nothing of them. I'd thought they were killed off, every last one, and all the sorcerers who might summon them."

"There is at least one more," Mörget said. "Perhaps we will have the honor of slaying the last one in the world."

"That would be a tale to tell," Croy agreed. "I am at your service, brother. Ghostcutter and Dawnbringer will drink demon ichor once more. I wonder—should we summon the others? Sir Orne, Sir Hew, and Sir Rory are all here in Skrae—the bearers of Crowsbill, Chillbrand, and Bloodquaffer. They would rally to our cause on the instant."

Mörget looked sheepish. "If it's all the same, brother . . . it is hard enough for me to admit I need the aid of one fellow Ancient Blade. Glory shared amongst two is glory halved. Split five ways . . ."

"I understand," Croy said. "But two of the swords are kept by your people. What of Fangbreaker? I'd have thought you would go to its wielder first."

"The one who bears Fangbreaker is not my brother," Mörget said, in a tone that suggested he would not explain further.

Croy looked almost relieved—maybe he didn't want to share the glory either. "Very well. The two of us will leave as soon as possible. Ah—and there will be traps."

"Aye. The Vincularium is full of 'em," Mörget said. "Or so say the books at Redweir."

"Well, then, your luck is with you today. When it comes to traps, and defeating them, there's none more skilled than Malden."

The barbarian turned a suddenly interested eye on the thief. His red mouth split open in a wide grin and he started to laugh.

"I beg your pardon?" Malden asked, looking up at Croy.

"It'll be good sport," Croy told him with a wink. "You'd be doing a work of great worth. And of course, the Vincularium is rumored to be stuffed full of treasure." He looked down at the thief as if that final word was the goad that would move him to acts of unrivaled heroism.

# CHAPTER ELEVEN

"So of course, I told him to jump in the river. Head-first," Malden said, when he'd finished recounting the barbarian's story.

Cutbill had wanted to hear everything, and Malden did not stint on any detail. The guildmaster of thieves listened attentively, all the while scribbling long strings of figures into his ledger, as if Mörget's tale was a matter for scrupulous bookkeeping. "You said that? To the barbarian?" he asked, finally looking up.

"Yes! I did. Or, rather, I told Croy to do that. I told Mörget I wasn't the man he was looking for, but thanked him very much for considering me. I'm not stupid."

"Hmm," Cutbill mused. He flipped to an earlier page of his ledger. "Well, that's settled, then. There are demons afoot once more. Of course, something will have to be done about that—we can't have such creatures at large."

"Yes, yes, it must be vanquished. But they hardly need my help with that. The two of them have their magical swords. They're perfectly adequate to the task."

Cutbill shrugged dismissively. "Still, I can see why they'd like to have someone along to take care of the traps. A sword—even a magical sword—is of little use to a man who has fallen into a bottomless pit. But you turned down their offer, quite reasonably. It does sound like a dangerous undertaking."

"Positively foolhardy," Malden agreed.

"Quite. Though I imagine that for Sir Croy the risk is half the reward. This will give him the chance to prove, once again, just how heroic he is. He'll reap a great bounty of honor and glory."

"I suppose such things are what you desire if you're a titled man's son, and there is no need to ever work a day in your life."

"I imagine that would be nice," Cutbill said.

"He's going to get himself killed. Him and the barbarian both. As for Mörget, well, good riddance. That man is a threat to decent society. It's just a matter of time before he kills someone just being here in the city."

"It's for the best, then, that he leaves soon." Cutbill put down his pen and rubbed his chin. "And yet I do not wish him ill."

"Well, of course not," Malden said, raising one eyebrow. He wasn't sure what Cutbill was on about but he could tell the man was already forming a scheme. "I mean, at the very least, I hope he survives long enough to save us all from the demon, but—"

Cutbill lifted his pen for silence. "Hmm. He wants someone to deal with the Vincularium's traps. I'll have to think of someone I could send his way. Just in the interest of getting him out of my town faster."

"Much joy it gives them both, I hope. I'll have nothing

to do with this tomb. As I told them, in no uncertain terms. Of course, then Croy had to go and suggest the place was full of treasure. As if that was all it would take to make my ears prick up. There's more to life than money."

"There is?" Cutbill asked, as if he'd never considered the possibility.

Malden had to think about that for a moment. "Yes, there is. There's living to spend it."

"Interesting," Cutbill said. He picked his pen back up. "Just the other day, you were telling me that you needed a large sum of money for a specific reason. Tell me, how is that project going?"

"I thought it was dashed to pieces," Malden admitted, thinking of Cythera. She had not signed the banns of marriage after all. "But there may be some new hope. All the same, there are easier ways to get the money to buy a house than crawling around in haunted tombs."

"Most assuredly. Though . . . I might suggest, Malden, that you go and ask someone about the Vincularium. Specifically, about who is buried there."

"Some moldy old king or other, I have no doubt," Malden said.

Cutbill frowned. "The treasure is likely to be . . . considerable."

"The entire interior of that mountain might be made of gold, for all I care. I'm no grave robber."

"Ah. So it's because of your deeply felt respect for the dead that you won't go."

Malden wrestled with himself. He didn't ordinarily lie to Cutbill. The man had a way of seeing through to the truth no matter how honeyed a tale one spun. This time, however, he found himself completely incapable of telling the truth.

"Yes," he said.

"Very good," Cutbill said. If he believed Malden or not didn't seem to matter. He wrote in silence for a while, then put down his pen and folded his hands in his lap. Malden had worked for Cutbill long enough to know what that meant. He was about to do something devious. "Malden. Would you do me a favor? Go out to the common room and ask Slag if he would be kind enough to come in here for a moment."

"Certainly," Malden said. He was mostly just glad not to be the object of the guildmaster's plotting. Outside, he found Slag constructing a boiled leather cuirass, laying long strips of hardened leather across a stiffened shirt and then affixing them in place with paste. When Malden approached him, he cursed volubly, but after a moment the dwarf came trooping along after him into Cutbill's chamber. He had a scowl on his face, as usual, but he had always been an obedient employee.

"This had better be good. My glue's getting tacky."

"It will only take a moment, I assure you," Cutbill said. "Malden here has turned up a very interesting piece of information. It seems there's a barbarian in town who is forming a crew to go and open the Vincularium. I thought that would be of some small interest to you."

The scowl went slack on Slag's face. "Huh," he said.

Malden rubbed at his chin. He'd never heard the dwarf stymied for a curse before. What was Cutbill up to?

Slag failed to give the game away. He stood there looking pensive but said nothing more. Eventually Cutbill looked up and gave the dwarf a pointed look. "That's all. You may return to your work."

Slag nodded and turned to go. He stopped before he reached the door, however, and turned to address Cutbill. "Sir," he said. Malden had never heard the dwarf use an honorific before. Interesting. "Sir, if it's all right with you. Well. You know I'm in here every fucking day, and most nights. I work hard, don't I? And I serve you well. I haven't even been sick a day for—how long?"

Cutbill tilted his head to one side as if trying to remember. Then he stuck his thumb in the ledger book and opened it to a page quite near its beginning. "Seventeen years," he said, after consulting a column of numbers.

The dwarf nodded. "Aye. Well. I think, suddenly, I might be coming down with somewhat. Somewhat lingering."

"That is unfortunate," Cutbill said. The look on his face was not what Malden would call sympathetic, but then he couldn't imagine Cutbill showing fellow feeling for anyone. "You'd better go home, then, until you feel well again. Take as much time as you need. I don't care if it takes weeks and weeks."

"Thank ye, sir," Slag said, and left the room.

When he was gone, Malden stared at the guildmaster of thieves. "What was that about? What's he after?"

"Like I said, Malden, you might do some asking around about the Vincularium. In this case, it might interest you to know who built it. Of course," Cutbill said, and flipped back to his current page, "it matters not. Since you have already made up your mind not to go."

# CHAPTER TWELVE

Croy and Mörget set about at once outfitting themselves for the journey. There were so many things to buy—a wagon to carry their gear, supplies to make camp in the wilderness, lanterns and climbing gear for inside the Vincularium. Croy had rarely been as happy or excited as when he looked over the growing pile of equipment.

Of course, Mörget had no money, so Croy had to pay for everything, but that did little to dampen his enthusiasm. He'd always considered money to be something you spent, not something you hoarded. He was glad to foot the bill for such an important endeavor.

While he arranged for the packhorses they would require, he was approached by a messenger with a letter from Cythera. He blushed, having almost forgotten the events of the previous day, when he'd come close to marrying her. Her message said she wished to meet with him and discuss a matter of importance—almost certainly about the banns, he decided. He sent the messenger back with instructions on where she should meet him.

Croy was just trying on a new brigantine when Cythera arrived at the armorer's shop. He glanced up at her with a smile and turned the doublet inside out, showing her the thin plates of bright case-hardened iron inside the canvas.

"Of course, this will be little use against a demon," he said as she came and took his hands in greeting. "Especially this one, which can simply flow through the cracks between the plates. Yet there may be bandits along the way, and other dangers yet unguessed once we get inside the Vincularium." He everted the doublet again and showed her the elaborate pattern of brazen rivets that held the plates fast. "Rather beautiful in its way, hmm? But of course, one doesn't choose armor for how it looks."

"Perhaps you'll marry me in it," she told him, then leaned close to whisper, "of course, you must remove it before the wedding night, or I shall be quite sore the next morning."

He flushed red and stepped away from her. Picking up a round shield, he held it high between them. "Now, this will stop any blow. Yet it's light as a buckler, made of basswood in overlapping strips, then faced with boiled leather. Truly exquisite craftsmanship. As you would expect from a dwarf of Snurrin's reputation."

The proprietor of the shop bowed low, his head dropping nearly to the level of Croy's ankles. "Your very presence in my shop only serves to enhance my meager fame, Sir Knight."

The armorer looked like any other dwarf from Croy's experience, with corpse-pale skin (dwarves shunned the sun's rays, being subterranean by natural inclination) and a tangled mass of dark hair sticking up from his scalp. Yet he had never heard a dwarf speak so prettily—or with such couth. Normally they swore oaths and laced their sentences with profanity as much as did sailors. It was the reason Croy patronized Snurrin. Though the dwarf was known to be the most expensive armorer in the Free City, Croy knew he wouldn't be embarrassed by strong language while picking out his panoply.

"I'll want to see this brigantine proofed, of course, but I think it will suit," Croy said. He smiled sheepishly and then let out a little laugh. "Ha, I have made a jest, I think. This suit of armor, you see, will—"

"Fie!" the barbarian shouted, coming out of a fitting room near the back of the shop. He was naked save for a pair of faulds that wouldn't quite buckle around his waist. For a man as large as Mörget that was a lot of nudity. "Have you nothing big enough for a real man? Or do you make armor only for tiny creatures like yourself, shopkeep?"

Croy saw Cythera staring at the barbarian and took her elbow to lead her toward the back of the shop. There was a yard behind the main building, where a number of Snurrin's human apprentices were cleaning hauberks and coats of plate. To get the blood and sweat and less identifiable substances out of the metal armor, they loaded each piece in a barrel full of sand wetted down with vinegar, then rolled the barrels endlessly back and forth across the yard.

"A rather tedious method of doing one's laundry," Cythera observed.

"Armor must be cleansed after every battle or it rusts. I expect you to have little knowledge of what it's like to wear a rusty hauberk, but I assure you, it's unpleasant," Croy told her. He could remember plenty of times in the field when he'd had no chance to keep his mail clean. The chain mail had chafed his skin until it was red and raw. "But this is what I brought you to see." He led her to a wooden post mounted near the back of the yard. A crosspiece stood at its top and padding wrapped around the two beams of wood, while a hank of straw had been nailed to the top like a wig. It looked to Croy like an emaciated scarecrow. He slipped the brigantine over the wooden form and then took Cythera back to a table near the door where wine and three cups had been provided. There was even an awning to keep the sun off the two of them while they waited. In short order, Mörget emerged from the shop, holding a barbute helmet big enough to make soup in. It looked like it might just fit his massive head. It had a sharply pointed nasal and an elaborate aventail of mail to protect the neck.

"This is all he had," Mörget said with a shrug. "I've never favored armor anyway. It's always too heavy and slows a man down."

Snurrin came out of the door next, a broad-brimmed hat on his head to protect his eyes from the sun. He held a crossbow in his arms that was almost as big as he was. The dwarf did not seem overly taxed, however, with the work of cranking the bow to its full extension, or with loading a heavy quarrel. He mounted the weapon on a forked stand, sighted on the brigantine, and bowed.

"Perhaps you'll do the honors?" he asked Mörget.

The barbarian waved one lazy hand. "You go ahead."

The dwarf frowned in shame and looked to Croy.

"He can't do it," the knight said. "I imagine you don't know about Skraeling history. We signed a treaty with the dwarven king many centuries ago, back when we finished off the elves. Until that time men and dwarves were only the loosest sort of allies, you see, and after the long and wearying battle we waged against the elves we had no desire to fight another. So the dwarves kept their kingdom, and their borders were guaranteed, but in exchange they had to agree never to harm a human being. Now all dwarves are forbidden by both law and honor to use weapons—even the weapons they build themselves. It's part of our alliance with them."

The barbarian looked confused. "But how do they defend themselves, then?"

Croy laughed. "Why would they need to do that? We protect them. In fact, we made it a law that any man who harms a dwarf is subject to being roasted alive. I assure you, the dwarves of this city are the safest of all its citizens. No one would ever rob them or harm a hair on their heads."

The barbarian squinted at the dwarf. "You agreed to that? Really?"

Snurrin smiled and bowed low again. "I assure you, sir, I was not personally consulted, seeing that I was not to be born for many centuries. But I find the arrangement quite suits my taste. It's a dangerous world and I am most grateful for the protection the laws offer me."

Cythera smiled knowingly at the barbarian. "They make it sound so very courtly and noble, don't they? Don't let them fool you. There's a reason the king of Skrae keeps his dwarves so close to his bosom. They're the only ones who know how to make good steel. If he wants proper weapons and armor, he has no choice but to appease them."

"That's interesting," Mörget said. "Quite interesting. Very well, then." The barbarian stepped up to the mounted crossbow and squeezed the trigger.

With a resonant *thwock,* the quarrel slammed into the brigantine just to the left of center, high up on the chest. For a moment it stuck out straight from the armored doublet, but then drooped and fell away.

"Oh, well made, well made," Croy said, jumping up and applauding vigorously. He rushed over to the brigantine and stuck a finger through the hole the quarrel made in the canvas. "The plate beneath is barely dented!" he called back.

"I'll hammer it out anyway," Snurrin insisted. "Now, for the shield and yon basta—yon warrior's helm," the dwarf said, nearly slipping into vulgarity, if not an outright obscenity.

The shield and the barbute were mounted on the wooden form, and Snurrin began to crank his bow back to tension.

"Croy," Cythera said, grasping the knight's hands.

He squeezed her hands in return but his eyes were fixed on the shield. He barely heard her, for he was working out in his head what device he would put on it. As a knight errant, he was not permitted a proper heraldic coat of arms but he could paint it with some element of his family crest. Some way for anyone who saw him holding it to know who he was.

"There's something I want to tell you," Cythera went on.

"Hmm?" he asked. "Oh, yes, of course. That's what your message said. I'm sure we have much to talk about concerning the wedding and such. What is it in particular you wished to discuss, my pet?"

Mörget stepped in to fire once more. The crossbow's string thrummed with pent-up energy waiting to be unleashed. "It's not about the banns." Cythera took a deep breath, then said, "I've decided I'm going with you."

The quarrel leapt from the bow and smacked into the shield, this time sticking in place with its deadly point fully penetrating.

"I—I beg your pardon?" Croy asked, turning in his seat.

She had his full attention now. "I'm going with you to the—" She glanced over at the dwarf to make sure he wasn't listening. "—to the Vincularium. I will accompany you and Mörget."

"I can't permit that."

Cythera frowned. She must have known he would say as much. He was sworn to protect helpless women, the aged, and the infirm. There was no way he could take her into a place of danger.

"As your husband—" he began, but she shook her head.

"You are not my master yet," Cythera said. "Once I sign the banns, you will own me like chattel. That is the law. But until that moment, I make my own decisions."

"That's . . . true," Croy admitted. He liked this not at all. "Yet I am also leading this expedition, and I will choose who accompanies me."

"I thought this was Mörget's quest," Cythera pointed out.

"Aye," the barbarian grumbled, making Croy jump. He must have forgotten Mörget was in earshot.

"Then tell her she cannot come," Croy insisted. "Questing's not for women. It just isn't done!"

Mörget shrugged. "In my land, our women accompany us whenever we travel."

"But you're nomads! And from what I've heard, your women are nearly as big and strong as you."

"Aye," the barbarian said, with a wistful look in his eye. "They're huge."

"This is completely different," Croy demanded. "Cythera, this won't be like a coach ride to the next village over. This is going to be a demanding trek through wild lands full of danger. And then there are the perils of the Vincularium itself."

"Aye, a place full of ancient curses." She held up her left arm and showed him the writhing painted vine that wrapped around her wrist. It was longer than when he'd seen it last.

He understood her meaning, of course. Coruth, her mother, had gifted Cythera with the perfect charm against both curse and enchantment. When magic was directed toward her, she absorbed it into her skin in the form of what appeared to be tattoos. Later on she could discharge it as well, once sufficient malefic energy had been stored.

"Cythera, I beg you, forget this folly," he said. "The place we go to is one of the most dangerous in all of Skrae—in all the world. If something happened to you there how could I go on living? How could I ever forgive myself? I love you more than my own life."

"I know you do," she said, "but—"

"Do you not love me?" he asked.

Her face went pale.

Croy was not a man given to manipulation, and preying this way on her feelings made him feel soiled. Yet how could he give in to her mad demand? He could understand why she was angry, but he could only hope she would get over it before he returned.

She took her time framing her reply, yet when it came, it was devastating. "Let me make this plain, Croy. I will not sign the banns until you have safely returned from this venture. I have no desire to be a widow even before my wedding ceremony. To ensure that you return safely, I will go with you, and protect you from threats that Snurrin's armor cannot. I'm afraid you cannot gainsay me now."

"I—but—you can't—" Croy sputtered.

"Mörget," Cythera said, "I am asking you directly. May I join your expedition?"

Mörget frowned. "I see one problem with it."

"Thank you," Croy gasped.

"We don't have enough horses," Mörget said. "I suppose we'll need to buy some more."

# CHAPTER THIRTEEN

Malden knew if he wasn't going on Croy's grand adventure, he needed to get back to work. He wasted little time finding his next assignment, though of course he had to tarry until nightfall before he could begin to work.

Cutbill had a lead that took him into the Royal Ditch, the valley just north of Castle Hill that was formed by the course of the river Skrait. The narrow streets atop the ditch were lined with gambling houses and brothels, with drug dens and pawnshops that asked few questions. Old, familiar territory for Malden, though little that went on there was truly lucrative enough to interest him anymore. What the Royal Ditch did possess to compel him was a scattering of old friends.

He found one shortly after dark, exactly where he expected her to be. Every part of Morricent's face was painted, with the white lead caked so thick around her eyes that it hid all the wrinkles. She'd been at work in Pokekirtle Lane long enough to know all the tricks of her trade: she doused herself in sweet perfumes, she pitched her voice unnaturally high, like an infant's, she wore her hair down with green ribbons woven amongst her curls, like a twelve-year-old girl celebrating her first chapel ceremony. Yet Morricent was old enough to remember Malden's mother.

His mother, who had spent some time in Pokekirtle Lane herself, though she died before she needed to start painting with white lead.

Malden had been born in a whorehouse, and spent his childhood inside its walls, working first at cleaning it and then later learning how to keep its books. When his mother died during his adolescence he'd been forced to leave and find his own way in the world—a hard thing for a penniless boy with no family. Yet he had not been cast out without pity. The whores of Ness were a close sisterhood, and they stuck together better than any guild of workmen. Malden was guaranteed a warm welcome now whenever he stopped in at any brothel in the city, and even the semi-independent streetwalkers knew his face and always had a smile for him. Morricent was no exception.

"Malden! You've come to keep a girl company on a wretched night," Morricent cooed as he leaned up against her particular stretch of wall. The bricks were wet with mist, and dark clouds covered the moon. It was indeed a bad night to be out of doors, especially while wearing as little clothing as Morricent did. One more trade secret. "Such a warmhearted fellow. Here, come help me chase away the cold." Morricent's hand was already under Malden's tunic, plucking at the belt that held up his breeches.

He grasped her wrist and pulled it gently free of his clothes. As he lifted her fingers to his lips, instead, and placed a gentle kiss on the back of her hand, her eyes grew wide.

"Milady," he said, "nothing would please me more, save—I have business tonight, pressing business."

He released her hand. She closed it fast enough to keep from dropping the coins he'd slipped into her downturned palm.

"Gareth sent me to you, saying you might have some information for me." Gareth was Morricent's pimp. Not a bad sort, as they went—mostly his role was to collect the money his stable of women earned. He never beat them and was actually just a middleman for a wealthy gambler named Horat, who paid the city watch to stay out of the Royal Ditch. Horat, in turn, answered to Cutbill, whose interests ranged far and wide.

"I'll tell you anything you want to know, Malden, of course. You don't have to pay for *words*."

"Ah, but I impose on your valuable time. I understand you had a customer last night, a hairy fellow with a mole on his cheek just here." Malden indicated the spot on his face. "Talkative cove. Wanted to brag all about something big he had planned."

Morricent nodded and leaned close to whisper. "He said he would take me someplace nice, next time. A room at an inn, even, with wine and sweetmeats, instead of a bare patch of wall and a sprig of mint to freshen my mouth after, like usual." She shrugged. "I hear promises from that sort all the time, so perhaps I did not look sufficiently convinced. He wanted me to believe he was about to come into money, so I would fuss over him like a real lover. So he told me about this job he had lined up, told me all the angles, and I had to admit it sounded like a nice bit of work. Simple as sifting flour, he kept saying, and no crew to split the swag with."

Malden got the particulars from her, then bowed and took her hand again. "He's one of your regulars?" he asked.

Morricent nodded.

More coins flowed into her palm. Silver this time. "After tonight," Malden said, "you may see a lot less of him. Even if he does come back I'm afraid there'll be no room at an inn."

Morricent's fingers rubbed at one of the coins he'd given her. Malden knew what she was doing—even without bringing it to the light she could tell by the feel what denomination he'd given her. "Methinks I can get my own room now, and all the sweetmeats I like, and a bed for just me. Now that's a rare enough thing to be treasured. Thank ye, Malden," she said, and kissed him on the cheek.

He was enough of a gentleman to wait until he was out of Pokekirtle Lane before wiping her white lead off his face.

The job was going to take place that very night, halfway across the city. He had to hurry if he wanted to catch Morricent's client in the act. This wasn't a typical housebreaking either, and he had to think on how he would get his wrench into the would-be thief's works.

Malden always thought best up in the clear air of the rooftops. He moved quickly, jumping across alleyways and making good time across the sloped roofs of the Smoke, the zone of workshops and tanners' yards that separated the wealthy uphill parts of the city and the poorer districts down by the wall.

Some of the manufactories and smithies of the Smoke were open all night. The big furnaces there that smelted iron were never allowed to die down, because it cost too much to get them back up to heat once they were cold.

Similarly, there were some industries so in demand that the shop masters kept their apprentices working at all hours, taking their places at the workbenches or sleeping in their communal beds in shifts. Therefore Malden had to be careful as he ran along the roofline of a fuller's shed and then up the brick side of a sifting tower beyond. If he was seen now he could get away easily enough, but any honest citizen who spotted him up on the rooftops would know he was at no legal business. They would call out "Thief! Thief!" and the hue and cry might alert his mark. That would ruin everything. The mark might run off, forgetting his scheme, thinking it too risky—or at the very least he would be overly cautious, expecting someone to come up behind him at any moment and put a hand on his shoulder. That would make Malden's work difficult. It could also make it dangerous. The mark would be armed, and desperate enough to attack at the first sign of trouble.

No, if he was to take this man, he needed to have the advantage of surprise. It was the best lesson he'd learned from Cutbill—if your mark knew you were coming, the game was already fouled. Better the mark never saw him coming. Never, in fact, guessed that anyone was on to him.

Morricent's regular was a wheelwright's apprentice named Pathis. He'd reached the grand old age of thirty without ever advancing in that career—either he was too lazy to apply himself, or his master had no faith in his abilities. Trapped in employment of the most menial kind, knowing he was too old now to ever make a change, he must have spent every day scheming, trying to think of some way to get enough money together to start a new life. Perhaps Pathis had never heard of Cutbill, nor that there was already an organized army of criminals in the Free City. Certainly he had no idea that freelance larceny was frowned on by the powers that be.

So when an opportunity came along, an easy way to make some quick coin, Pathis had jumped at the chance. It might have been the first enterprising thing he'd done in his entire life, and it might well be the last. The shop where he worked stood next to a hire paddock, an empty lot between two workshops that was rented out to farmers bringing their livestock to market. He must have seen the vast number of animals that went through the paddock every day, and thought of the price each one would fetch. Of course, it wasn't easy to steal sheep or cows or horses, since every animal was branded with its owner's mark, and no one would buy livestock from a thief without knowing its provenance.

No one, that is, who wished to butcher said animals for their meat, or sell them on to others. Yet two roads down from the wheelwright's shop there was a tannery. Pathis could hardly have avoided noticing *that*—the reek the place (and all the others like it) gave off, of death and acrid dissolution, was what gave the Stink its name and low rents. Tanners needed animals all the time, and weren't likely to ask too many questions. Animals were their stock in trade. Dead ones, anyway.

And so one simple, ugly, brilliant, nasty idea had flourished in the otherwise barren garden of Pathis's mind.

Malden climbed to the top of the sifting tower and had an excellent view of all the surrounding streets. He did not know if Pathis would come from his shop, or from his home down in the Stink, or from some tavern after building up enough liquid courage to carry out his foul employment. But from atop the tower Malden could be sure he'd see the would-be thief coming.

He did not have long to wait. Pathis appeared in Greenmantle Stair, coming up the hill from the Stink, not even bothering to keep to the copious shadows of that dark night. He looked exactly as he'd been described to Malden, and he already had his knife in his hand.

Keeping out of sight, Malden started to climb back down the side of the tower, toward a dark alley near the hired paddock. It was time to get to work.

# CHAPTER FOURTEEN

The hired paddock filled most of the space between two multistory buildings, a patch of trammeled mud surrounded by a sturdy wooden fence. Inside, a few dozen head of swine were sleeping in the mud, huddled together for warmth. From time to time one would grunt, or a hoofed leg would twitch, but the animals suspected nothing of the grizzly fate Pathis intended for them.

Of course the paddock was guarded by night. No place in the Free City of Ness was left unwatched, given the constant threat of thievery. The guard here was just a boy, perhaps the son of the owner, perhaps just some local youth looking to gain an extra coin or two. He carried a stout quarterstaff and he stood his watch near the gate, leaning up against the fence. If he was not asleep standing up, he was certainly dozing—Malden could see that his head slumped forward on his chest and his shoulders were slack at his sides.

Malden slipped around the corner of the wheelwright's shop and into an alley that ran behind it, intending to take up a position where neither Pathis nor the guard could see him. He silently cursed the mud that sucked at his leather shoes, but he was an old hand now at lying in wait and had camped in even dirtier spots for longer than this would take. He kept his cloak wrapped around himself, covering his bodkin and anything else that might gleam even in the near perfect darkness. The cloak was a deep green, dark enough to look black, and he knew he was almost invisible where he perched behind the fence. He settled down to wait.

And wait. And wait. Where was Pathis? Malden had seen him no more than half a block away, coming hither with clear intent. He should have arrived already. Other than the dreaming pigs, nothing moved in Malden's vision. Nothing at all. He had expected the would-be thief to come in from the street, to accost the guard directly and then slip through the gate to get at the pigs. Would Pathis come from the rooftops, instead, thinking he could slaughter the animals and haul them out of the paddock without waking the guard?

Malden glanced upward at the roof of the wheelwright's shop. Nothing there. He turned slightly to get a view of the lastmaker's on the other side of the paddock. The roofline was clear. What was taking Pathis so long to—

With a muffled thump, a heavy weight fell from the roof of the wheelwright's and splashed in the mud of the paddock. Malden didn't so much as flinch, but his heart pounded in his chest. He shot a glance up at the roof of the wheelwright's again and saw nothing there. Without rising above a crouch, he circled around the edge of the paddock to get closer and see what had fallen.

Through the slats of the fence, Pathis stared up at him with glassy eyes. The fool's throat was cut from ear to ear.

The sudden intrusion had woken the pigs. They stirred noisily, grunting and squealing in their fear. Some were struggling to their feet, slipping in the wet mud. Malden was certain the noise would wake the guard, but the boy didn't stir.

Oh, no, he thought. No, it cannot be.

Legs bent double beneath him, Malden circled around the paddock a bit farther until he had a better look. The guard was dead as well, his throat cut just as savagely as Pathis's. The boy had been tied to the fence, his arms fastened around his quarterstaff to keep his body propped upright. In the darkness, anyone would have thought the boy was only sleeping.

Malden certainly had.

The pigs were all standing now and whimpering in their fear. They knew the smell of death and no one was left to calm them. The noise they made was like thunder crashes in Malden's ears. Surely anyone in the neighboring buildings would hear it, and wonder what had agitated the animals. Surely someone would come to investigate in short order.

When one is bent on criminal enterprise, and one discovers that even the slightest thing has gone wrong with the plan, the wise thief has but one recourse—to forget the night's business, and run as fast as possible to a place of safety. The city watch was never far away, especially in the Smoke. If he were discovered near the paddock, he would be blamed for two murders and clapped in irons, thrown in gaol, and hanged with very little to say about it.

He stood up straight and dashed for the lastmaker's shop. Up the wall and away over the roofs, that was the best course. He dared not go up the wall of the wheelwright's, for fear of whatever had killed Pathis. The lastmaker's shop was a two-story, half-timbered building with plenty of windows. An easy climb for one as nimble as he. This would be all right. He merely needed to escape. As for the mystery of what had gone wrong, he would gladly leave the pleasure of solving it to the watch. He grasped a timber and started hauling himself upward, and was ten feet off the ground before something hit him hard in the back and he slipped.

You didn't learn how to climb as well as Malden if you didn't first learn how to fall. He twisted in midair and got his hands and feet under him, ready to take the impact with the muddy ground below. Before he could land, however, a heavy, blunt object struck him in the stomach and he collapsed in a heap, winded and in pain.

He could hear someone coming toward him. Moving fast. Malden got his knees down in the mud and started to spring up to his feet. A forearm like something carved of stone smashed across his throat, and he fell down to sit in the alley, his back against the wall of the lastmaker's shop.

He had learned his lesson, and did not attempt to get up again. Instead he looked up at his attacker.

The man was short, almost as short as Malden, and even more slender. He wore an undyed woolen habit like a monk's, with a matching cowl covering much of his head. His face was round and merry, though his eyes were very small and very dark.

He looks like a priest, Malden thought. Just like the man who had come to the Ashes, asking for him by name, and been turned away by the urchins. The attacker had a stone in his hand, and Malden understood that the missiles that brought him down from the wall were simply that—cobbles pried up out of the street.

That gave him little comfort. He'd seen the urchins in the Ashes arm themselves with just such stones. If you had no other weapons, you could kill a man with one of those cobbles.

The attacker brought his arm up and then smashed the stone against the side of Malden's temple so fast he couldn't move to block the blow. Bright lights flashed behind Malden's eyes and he felt his consciousness swim inside him, blackness surging up around his mind to carry him into nothingness.

"Oh no, not yet," the attacker laughed, and slapped Malden hard across the face with a bare palm. Instantly Malden snapped back into his own head—and back into the pain that surged through his skull. "I wish you to know my name. That way, when your soul is cast into the pit, you can tell the Bloodgod who sent you."

"Verr . . . wellll," Malden slurred. His tongue could barely move in his mouth.

"My name is Prestwicke. I like all my kills to know my name."

"Ki . . . k-kills," Malden said.

"Yes. I was hired to slaughter you, Malden. It's my trade."

"Wh-Wh-Who?" Malden asked, wanting to know who had commissioned this murder. He did not expect the assassin to answer, nor did he.

Malden had many enemies, but he didn't think a killer like this would come cheap. Most of the people who wanted him dead would have simply hired a bravo, some thug with an axe. Such a killer would simply have waited for him to walk into a dark alley and then make short work of him before he could cry out.

This man was something far more sinister. Something strange. You paid extra for that in Ness.

But who could have sent him? Malden wracked his brains trying to think, because knowing who it was could make all the difference. It would at least let him know why he had been singled out. It had to be a rich man. The list of truly wealthy men who would want his life was a short one, but it started with the Burgrave, the ultimate ruler and lord of the Free City of Ness. Malden knew a secret the Burgrave would prefer to be kept.

In a fairer world, of course, the Burgrave would have owed Malden a favor. He had recovered the lord's crown when it was in the possession of Hazoth, and returned it to its proper head. In the process he'd saved the city from a usurper and ensured the continuation of the Burgrave's reign. In the process, though, Malden had learned things better kept secret, and that was always the best way to get oneself killed. In the end it had been Cutbill who saved Malden from a quick death. The Burgrave did, in fact, owe Cutbill a favor—quite a large one—and Cutbill had used it up for Malden's benefit. The Burgrave had promised Cutbill that he wouldn't slaughter Malden. Of course, that only meant the Burgrave's own guards and watchmen would not do the deed. If it could be done discreetly— and Prestwicke looked the discreet type—then perhaps the Burgrave was willing to break his promise.

It would not surprise Malden in the least.

Prestwicke reached up into one of his voluminous

sleeves and pulled out a bundle wrapped in waxed cloth. He unrolled it on the ground and Malden saw half a dozen knives of various sizes and shapes inside. "I was paid a certain fee to take your life. It is customary that the client pays a small additional sum to ensure that it is done quickly, with a minimum of pain."

"Thass . . . nice," Malden said.

"I regret to say, in this case my client declined to pay the surcharge." Prestwicke smiled broadly.

Malden's head was packed too tight with wool to allow much fear to stir his brains, but he felt his breath come faster and his heart start to race. He could barely move, certainly could not stand up just then. He still had the bodkin at his belt, but his arm felt dead as a piece of wood. Even if he could manage to draw the weapon, he had little doubt Prestwicke could kill him before he could strike.

*Think*, he told himself. But he could not—his head hurt too much.

*Talk your way out of this.* But he could barely speak.

Was this how he was going to die?

Malden lived with constant danger. The penalty of thievery in Ness was hanging, whether one stole gems and jewels or a crust of bread. Every day he risked his neck. Yet he had never been more afraid than at that moment, never more certain that his jig was up.

There seemed nothing he could do, no way to save himself. But then a miracle happened and gave him a distraction.

Behind Prestwicke the pigs screamed. The assassin looked up and away from Malden, just for a moment. It gave Malden a chance to glance down at the knives, laid out in careful order on their cloth. They were so close to his right foot, dim slivers of light in the dark.

He jerked out with his leg and kicked them away from him, sending them clattering down the alleyway.

Prestwicke growled in anger and punched Malden hard in the gut. Malden nearly vomited—the killer was far stronger than he looked.

"You dunce! Now I'll have to go collect them. And they'll be *dirty!*"

"Sssorry," Malden managed to say, when he stopped wheezing.

"And these beasts, why won't they be quiet? Don't they understand a man is working here?" Prestwicke demanded. "The watch will be on us at any moment, and they'll spoil everything. I'm of a mind to just strangle you now." The assassin stared out at the street, and Malden saw beads of sweat had broken out on his chin. "But no. We'll do this *right*. Next time I'll do it *right*."

The assassin stooped to grab Malden under the armpits. He hauled the thief upright onto his shoulders and carried him down the alley.

"Where?" Malden asked, deeply confused. *Where are you taking me?* he wanted to ask.

"I can't let the watch find you, not now," Prestwicke told him. "They would lock you away, and probably hang you. And I don't share."

Malden was too weak to resist as the assassin carried him far across the Smoke, well clear of the searching watchmen. Prestwicke seemed to have a real gift for evading pursuit—he ran mostly through dark alleys, but occasionally he had to cross a broad avenue, where even at this hour there were people abroad. Yet Malden would swear not a single eye fell on him and his captor as they hurried through the night. Whatever kind of man this Prestwicke was, he was even more gifted at clandestine work than he himself.

Eventually they came to an alley on the edge of the Stink, a dark way between two massive blocks of wattle-and-daub houses. Prestwicke dropped Malden on a pile of old rubbish—broken furniture and sticks of unidentifiable wood kept there to feed the hearth fires of the houses all around.

"I'll be back for you tomorrow night, when the proper hour comes again," Prestwicke said, staring down at him.

In Malden's dazed state the assassin seemed to be looming over him from a great height.

"Where . . . should we meet? I'd hate to miss such a— Oof." Malden's head felt as if it were full of rocks grinding together. "Such an important engagement."

Prestwicke sneered at him. "Run where you like. I'll find you wherever you go to ground. There's nowhere in Ness you can hide from me."

"That's awfully . . . convenient," Malden said. He was having trouble keeping his eyes open. "Since I—"

But Prestwicke had already gone. Malden didn't see his would-be killer leave, but one moment Prestwicke was there and the next Malden was alone in the alley, save for the rats that nested in the woodpile.

# CHAPTER FIFTEEN

A drizzling rain rolled down Croy's best loden cloak the next morning as he finished loading the wagon. He tied down a leather cover over the various supplies inside: barrels of smoked fish, rolled-up tents and camp gear, jugs of beer and a pail of milk for Mörget. Big coils of rope and mining gear—blocks and tackles, hooks and spikes, hammers and other tools—rounded out the load. The horses snorted in their traces, unhappy about being out in the wet, but they were good well-bred hackneys and would settle down once they were under way. The riding horses, a palfrey and a rounsey, were still under shelter in the stable behind him.

It felt good to Croy to get moving. It felt good to begin.

For far too long he had been a true knight errant—a warrior without a master, or any well-defined purpose. He'd been sworn to fight demons, but there were so few of them left now. He'd been sworn to defend the king, and then the Burgrave of Ness, but both of them had severed him from their service. A man like himself needed a reason to keep going, to stay strong.

Well, the Lady had provided that.

He knew nothing of this demon, not its capabilities or how great a danger it was to the world. Yet he was certain that it had to be destroyed, and that he was the man for the job. He, and Mörget, of course.

The barbarian came down from the door of the inn stretching and stamping, looking well-rested and ready to get under way. "Starting in the rain's a good omen," he said, looking up into the clouds. He opened his mouth wide to catch the raindrops, then swished them about his teeth and spat into the mud. "Means it'll be dry when we arrive."

Croy laughed. All deep thoughts about duty and purpose fled his mind with the excitement of the journey's commencement. "I hope you're right. It does mean we'll have to make a short day of it, and find some shelter before dark. It's getting cold early this year."

The barbarian went back inside to get a bundle that he dumped on the tailgate of the wagon. It clanked loudly as he shoved it in with the rest of the gear.

"Sounds like you've got half an arsenal in there," Croy said.

"All that I need," Mörget told him, with a shrug. "A man with a proper axe can survive in the wild longer than a man with a hundredweight of food and no axe."

Croy laughed. He was glad to have the barbarian along. Mörget was right, too—the food in the wagon would only last just so long, and he imagined they would have to hunt before they reached their destination, if they didn't want to starve.

Once everything was loaded they were ready to depart, and waited only on the two other members of their expedition. Slag the dwarf arrived first. Croy had been quite surprised when Slag had found him the night before and demanded to be included. Croy knew Slag only a little, through his connection to Malden, but from what he'd heard, the dwarf was an unlikely traveling companion. For one thing, all dwarves were known for their hatred of travel, even those who worked as ambassadors for their king and had to move from place to place all the time. And Slag was a city dwarf, accustomed to the refinements of Ness. By Malden's account he'd been a fixture in the city for many years.

Slag had given little explanation for why he wanted to leave just now, or why he would want to go to the Vincularium, but Croy supposed little was needed. Dwarves had built the place, after all, though so long ago none alive could remember it, surely. Mörget had been enthusiastic about allowing Slag to come along, saying that the dwarf would be useful in overcoming the Vincularium's many traps and blind passages. An important addition to their crew since the thief had refused to accompany them. Croy had offered no real objection. After all, Slag was a friend of Malden. That was enough to vouch for the diminutive man right there.

"Well met, friend," he said, and bowed to clap hands with the dwarf. "We ride today toward true adventure!"

"Picked a lousy fucking day for it," the dwarf replied. Without another word he climbed up under the leather cover on the wagon and curled around a barrel. In a few moments he was snoring.

Mörget and Croy exchanged a smile and went to get the horses. By the time they had them out of the stable, Cythera had arrived as well. Croy gave her a knowing look as she placed her own gear on the wagon. She was dressed in an old cloak with the hood up over her hair. It hid her eyes as well.

"Shall we get started?" she asked when Croy opened his mouth.

He had been about to give her a chance to change her mind, and remain in the city until he returned. Clearly she still intended to go.

"Very well," he said. "You take the palfrey. He's gelded, and a good ambler. Mörget can have the rounsey for now. That's a man's horse."

Cythera turned to face him, and he saw she was glaring at him under her hood.

"I meant simply that the rounsey will better bear his weight, that's all," Croy said, desperate to mollify her. "I'll drive the wagon for this first day."

Cythera said nothing more, but climbed onto the palfrey and kicked its flanks to get it moving. Croy had to hurry to jump up on the wagon and get the hackneys moving, just to keep up with her. She led them downhill, through the Stink toward King's Gate, which opened on the road toward Helstrow. They passed by a fish market on their way there, where poor women braved the rain to get the freshest catch, and then past a small churchyard. Croy frowned—that was a bad omen, riding past graves on the way to danger—but he did not call for a change of course.

Soon he saw the wall rise up before them, sheer and white and looming over the buildings that crowded around its feet. The rain had flooded some of the side streets, but the main way stayed clear. Croy leaned forward with his elbows on his knees and started lulling himself into the old familiar trance of the road. The rhythmic clop of the horses' hooves and the grinding of the wagon's wheels on the cobbles made a song of journeying. In a few minutes they would pass the gate and be on their way. The way would be long, and there would be obstacles to overcome, but he was on a quest again, a mission. How he had longed for—

Something heavy dropped onto the leather cover of the wagon behind him. Slag shouted out a curse as if he'd been struck. Croy pulled on the reins, and the hackneys whinnied as he slowed them. Turning around, one hand already on Ghostcutter's hilt, he stared with wide eyes.

"Room for one more?" Malden asked. He lay sprawled across the wagon's cover, as if he'd fallen there out of the thin air. For some reason his face was badly bruised and one of his eyelids was nearly swollen shut. "I have a sudden urge to get some country air," the thief offered, by way of explanation.

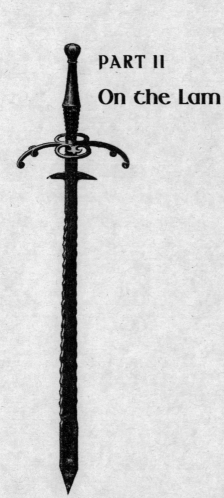

# PART II

# On the Lam

# INTERLUDE

Snurrin the dwarf armorer closed up his shop an hour early that day, sending his human employees home with a halfhearted excuse—he'd had too much sun, he told them, and needed to rest somewhere cool and dark or he'd be worthless for the next morning's appointments. The humans didn't seem to care why they were released early from their labors. As was typical of the gangly bastards, they were just glad for a chance to spend the evening in a tavern drinking away their wages.

"Fucking layabouts," Snurrin muttered once they were gone. It felt good to be able to swear like a proper dwarf, something he never did when humans were around. Humans, he thought, were so very tall and brutish, and so very good at killing one another, but they acted like strong language was more dangerous than any weapon in his shop. Utter one good profanity and half of them just fainted dead away.

He locked up the day's take in his strongbox, then cleaned up the workshop where he'd spent most of the day fletching crossbow bolts. When he was done he headed up to the top floor of his shop where he kept his living quarters. Heavy velvet drapes covered all the windows there, blocking out the fierce sunlight. They were tacked in place, but still a few errant beams of light broke into his room. More than enough to see by. Snurrin went to his desk and took out a long thin strip of paper. Using a heavy stylus of white lead, he wrote out a message in dwarven runes. When he was done the paper still looked blank, but if it were held over the proper sort of oil lamp for a few moments the runes would be revealed, as the particles of smoke adhered to the paper but not to the lead. What he had written was not for every eye to see.

Snurrin was no stranger to spycraft. Every dwarf living in Skrae—or at least every one loyal to the dwarven king—was expected to keep an eye on what the humans did, and report as necessary. The treaty between the crown of Skrae and the kingdom of dwarves was ironclad and made their two nations fast allies. That didn't mean they trusted each other for a moment.

When the message was ready, Snurrin headed up to the roof where he kept a wooden box sealed with a good stout padlock. Inside were a dozen bats each as big as his forearm, still asleep with their wings folded over them like cloaks. He picked one with three black dots painted on its back and rolled his message around its leg. The bat kicked and squealed in its sleep but was unable to shake the slip of paper loose. When Snurrin was sure it was done properly, he locked the box again and went back downstairs to take his supper. His work was done.

The city of Redweir lay over a hundred miles away, far to the southeast on the Bay of Serpents. It would take a human rider three days to cover that distance, even if he rode through the night and assuming he had fresh horses waiting for him at every stop on the way. A fast ship sailing with a fair wind might make it there in half the time. But even if the entire Free City of Ness had been swallowed up by a crack in the earth and dragged down to the pit of souls, no human in Redweir would hear of it and quicker than that.

The dwarves had a far more convenient method of getting messages back and forth between the two cities. That night when darkness fell, the bat would clamber out of a thin slot in the side of the box and wing toward Redweir. It knew the only way to get the objectionable piece of paper off its leg was to present itself to a certain dwarf who lived there. It would fly at full speed and arrive by dawn, when a minor clerk in the dwarven embassy at Redweir would find it just as he was headed for bed. The clerk would take the message—unread—directly to the Envoy of that city, who would know exactly how to make it legible. The Envoy would also know exactly what to do with the information Snurrin had provided:

> *BARBARIAN LEAVING TODAY FOR VINC*
> *MUST NOT FIND WHAT IS HIDDEN THERE*
> *THE KING GIVES THIS UTMOST PRIORITY*
> *HUMAN CASUALTIES ARE ACCEPTABLE*
> *SEND BALINT*

# CHAPTER SIXTEEN

The band of adventurers passed through King's Gate without any trouble—none of the guards were interested in stopping such a dangerous-looking crew from *leaving* the city—and before Malden knew it he was out in the world.

His reaction was immediate, and visceral.

Never, in his entire life, had he set so much as a foot outside the walls of the Free City of Ness. He was for the first time seeing that there even *was* a world beyond.

And it terrified him.

The land rolled like the waves of a vast ocean, a sea of tawny grain that never stopped moving under the lowering gray sky. In the distance the clouds broke and sunlight streamed down in impossibly long, straight rays to flicker on golden fields. A small army of peasants worked out there, bent over with sickles to harvest the glowing treasure. To the northeast a church stood white and straight, its spire pointing upward like an accusing finger. It looked terribly alone in that open space, its right angles and distinct shape like some piece of his life cut loose and cast down carelessly like a plaything by some cyclopean child.

Every hour of Malden's life to that point had been spent in narrow lanes, or climbing over rooftops, or in well-mannered parkland hampered by walls. Now there was nothing on any side of him that he could reach out and touch. If I were plucked up into the sky by some violent wind, he thought, and tossed out into the middle of the ocean with no land in sight, this is how it would feel. He felt exposed, naked, vulnerable in a way he distinctly disliked.

Over time this unease ebbed, though it never left him.

For hours they ambled through the fields under the blustery rain, never seeing more than the occasional distant group of laborers. The only way to measure the distance they covered was to count the mile markers that stood by the side of the road, simple piles of stones marked with the sigil of the local nobility: a crudely drawn stork or a pair of chevrons or just a simple crown. To Malden the symbols meant only one thing, really: all this land belonged to someone else. He was trespassing on someone else's property, and if they wanted to, they could run him off.

It seemed there was no place outside the city where a man could be free after all.

Despite his unease he soon found himself drowsing in his seat. He worried that if he fell unconscious he would slump and fall from the swaying wagon, and so was almost grateful when Croy began to sing a traveling song. It was a rather sentimental tune about a knight who went out riding to do battle for his lady's honor. Malden knew a far different version, a much lustier tale of a farmer's lovely daughters and dragons that disguised themselves as naked women (and only gave themselves away by a certain scaliness of their skin), but he knew there would be plenty of time to sing his version later. This journey was likely to take more than a week—no need to use up all his songs on the first day.

After about an hour's travel Cythera dropped back to ride beside the wagon. "I'm surprised to see you here," she told him, "though I'll admit I'm rather glad." She reached across to touch Malden's face. "Oh. You're hurt," she said.

Malden shrugged, even though it pained him to do so. "'Tis a trifle only," he told her.

"What happened?" she asked.

He puffed himself up and said, "A host of villainous assassins came upon me in the dark. Now, normally I would have been ready for them, but I was busy at that moment stealing the silver out of the moon, so they got first licks in before I knew what they were about. After that, of course, it was a done deal, and I left them in far worse shape than I found them."

She laughed, which made him smile for the first time in a day.

"Boasting's not your strength, thief," she said. "Regardless, I'm glad you weren't killed. Or arrested, for that matter. Was there much silver in the moon? It looks no bigger than a single coin held out at arm's reach."

"When matched with the gold I took from the sun, that's still a sum worth stealing." He glanced sideways at Croy but the knight made a good show of paying no attention to their talk. He was busy singing anyway, and was deep into a verse about the virtue of courtly love, so Malden felt he had a little liberty to spend. "I must say, if you're surprised to see me, I'm doubly so to see you. I didn't think you were prone to Croy's nature of folly."

"I've spent my whole life working for my father or my mother, almost every day of it inside Ness's walls. I wished to see the world one time before I was married. Once I am pregnant with Croy's get, there will be no more opportunities of this sort." She looked away from him and added, "Besides, there were certain temptations I wished to leave behind me."

"Like me," he said.

"Don't flatter yourself," she told him, looking straight ahead.

Malden shook his head. "I saw the way you hesitated when you tried to sign the banns. You aren't sure of your own heart, are you?"

"Malden . . . we've spoken of this before. You know my mind's made up. When we return to Ness I'll marry Croy. My life's course is sure and steady before me, straighter even than this road."

"I'll believe it when I see you wed," he told her.

Her eyes flashed when she turned to look at him. Her mouth set in an angry line. If she'd possessed her mother's gift for magic, he imagined she might have cursed him until his skin turned inside out, then and there. Instead she could only glare.

He met her gaze, measure for measure. When she refused to take the bait, however, he eventually looked away. After a bit of riding in silence alongside him, she spurred her horse and went back to riding in front of the wagon, by Mörget's side. It seemed their conversation was done.

The day passed, as days spent traveling in the rain will, with little talk and much brooding. When no one joined his song, Croy eventually fell quiet, though still he smiled as the road passed beneath them. Malden had never seen the knight happier. Even Mörget seemed listless and irritable when faced with the prospect of endless miles of plodding through mud and cultivated fields. Of them all, only Croy kept his spirits high, despite the rain.

Eventually the sun sank toward the horizon as they rode away from it, into the east. The sky turned yellow, then pink, and it was getting hard to see when Croy called ahead to Mörget to say they should stop for the night.

Thank the Bloodgod, Malden thought. His legs were

near as bruised as his face after eight hours on the wagon, and every stone and rut in the road brought new pain. He had never imagined he could get so tired from sitting all day.

Up ahead a milehouse stood in a patch of weeds by the side of the road. Before long Malden made out its sign, a crudely painted swaybacked cow. The king's law, Croy told him, required that houses of lodging like this be placed every ten miles on the road from Ness to Helstrow, for the comfort of travelers like themselves. Once Malden saw the place, he wondered what the legal definition of comfort might be. It was a ramshackle affair of only a single story, with a row of stalls to one side where horses could be stabled for the night. Its walls had been whitewashed with lime at some point in the past, but time and dust had robbed it of any cleanliness or cheer. Its thatched roof crawled with rats, but at least a little yellow light beamed out from its windows.

There was no stable boy to take the horses, so Mörget agreed to see to them—and sleep with them for the night. "I'm used to sleeping out of doors," he explained, "and would feel ill at ease in such a place."

Malden was more than glad to jump down from the wagon and head inside with the others. The common room of the milehouse proved as shabby as its exterior: a long room with a low, sagging ceiling, lit only by the guttering fire in its hearth. A cowhide had been nailed to one wall, its fur rubbed off in places by years of customers brushing against it. The room was empty save for themselves and the alekeep, who looked more tired than Malden felt. The man ushered them to a table by the fire and brought them what he had to eat. This proved to be coarse bread and pottage—a thin stew of vegetables, tasteless and fit only for the peasants who patronized what was known locally as the Cow. There was ale, though, which was more than welcome.

None of them spoke much while they ate, and by common agreement they retired immediately after their meal to the small rooms provided for them at the back of the house. Cythera and Croy each got their own room, while Malden and Slag had to share.

"What is this?" the dwarf asked when he saw their accommodations. The room was barely big enough for a pair of mattresses, which proved to be sacks of straw with musty blankets piled on top. When Slag pulled the blankets off of one mattress, dark things with many legs scuttled away from the light. "This is unacceptable."

"Call down to the master of the house, and bid him bring you a proper bed, then," Malden said. "I, for one, could sleep on a pile of leaves just now, with a rock for my pillow."

"Ha! Laugh now, jester. That's exactly what's in your future," Slag told him. "Once we cross the river Strow, this will seem like luxury. I fucking hate traveling. Nothing for it, I suppose. That damned wagon bounced and rattled so bad I couldn't get a wink of sleep today." The dwarf threw himself down on the bed with a deep sigh, and in a few minutes began to snore. That was the sign Malden had been waiting for. Tired as he was, he had to answer a question or he knew it would plague his dreams. Making no noise at all, he slipped out of the door of the room and down the hallway.

Cythera had taken the room nearest the front of the house because it was likely to be the warmest. Malden tapped lightly at her door—if she were already asleep, he had no desire to wake her. He waited a long while, thinking himself a fool, before the door cracked open and he saw one of her blue eyes peer out at him. The eye went wide when she saw him.

"Malden, what are you thinking, coming to me like this?" she whispered.

"I was thinking I might be welcome," he said.

"If Croy came in here right now—"

"He would slaughter me where I stand," Malden said. "I deem the risk worth the prize."

"I was going to say it would destroy him. His best friend, taking liberties with his betrothed! I ask again, whatever gave you the idea to come here like this?"

"The words you said today on the road put a notion in my mind. I could not rest until I found out exactly how you felt. You said I was a temptation."

"One I wished to leave behind." She reached for his hands. "Malden, I will not deny I bear a certain . . . affection for you. And I do owe you a debt. Without your help, both my mother and myself would still be enslaved."

"I didn't come here seeking payment for services rendered."

He could barely make out her face in the darkness, but he was certain the look in her eye then was one of utter relief. Had he insisted on a reward, would she have given herself? But of course, then she could never truly love him after. Malden knew enough about women to understand that.

"No," she said. "I know you don't see it that way. You're a kindly man, Malden, under all that arrogance. So—be kind. Let me repay my debt by never speaking of this to Croy. And in turn, do me another service, and forget this fancy."

A wiser man would not have tried to kiss her then. She did not try to stop him, but merely turned her cheek so he ended up kissing the line of her jaw instead of her lips. He sighed and lifted his lips to her ear.

"I see," he told her. "You've truly made up your mind."

"I've never suggested otherwise," she sighed. Was there regret in her voice, a certain heaviness, a longing? Or did he simply wish there was?

Malden nearly choked on the lump in his throat. He had hoped . . . well, he had hoped. And hope was worth exactly what it cost. "Very well," he said. "I will trouble you no more."

He slipped away from the door without a backward glance, leaned up against the wall outside his own room and waited for his heart to stop racing.

# CHAPTER SEVENTEEN

In the morning, Malden woke late, and came out to the common room to find that he could not break his fast—the kitchen was already closed. Remembering there was food stored in the wagon, he headed out toward the stables and found his companions there waiting for him. Cythera and Croy were already on horseback, looking impatiently toward the east, while Mörget and Slag had the wagon up on blocks. The dwarf was underneath its wheels, grunting and swearing as he worked on the wagon's undercarriage with a hammer and a wrench. The barbarian stood placidly by, ready to lift the vehicle by one end as Slag requested.

Eventually Slag emerged from beneath the wagon and told Mörget to remove the blocks. The barbarian kicked them out of the way and the wagon dropped heavily onto its wheels—and bounced up and down for a while before coming to a stop. As Mörget strapped the two hackneys into their harness, the dwarf explained.

"I spent all yesterday trying to sleep in this thing and failed miserably. Every time we drove over a pebble in the road I got thrown against this berk's pile of iron weapons," he said, nodding his head in Mörget's direction. "So I fixed it."

Malden looked underneath the wagon and saw a cunning arrangement of leaf springs mounted to the axles. "So now it will bounce and rattle even more?" he asked.

"I fixed it," Slag repeated, one eye squinting nearly shut. "I'm a dwarf. Trust me. You'll be happier this way, too."

They got under way quickly enough then. Mörget proved to have an easy hand for the reins, and while the wagon did sway more than it had before, Malden soon realized the dwarf had done something right. When the wagon wheels passed over deep ruts in the road, the wheels went up but the body of the wagon did not, and when the wheels dropped into ruts, the springs kept Malden from flying off his seat. It was almost like the wagon was suspended above the road, held up by invisible hands.

The only disadvantage of the rebuilt wagon was that it made it even harder to stay awake. After a mostly sleepless night, and unable to stretch his legs, Malden found himself dozing constantly, only to be awakened with a fright as he realized he was about to slump over to the side and fall from the wagon—or worse, to lean over and rest his head on Mörget's shoulder. He was uncertain what the barbarian would do if he inadvertently touched him, but he was sure it would be painful.

Watching the fields of wheat go by on either side only made things worse. The mile markers were too far between to hold his attention. Cythera rode far ahead of the wagon, so he could not talk to her, and Croy was singing again. There was nothing for it but to talk to the barbarian.

Fortunately Mörget seemed to love the sound of his own voice. He told Malden many tales of his native land, few of which Malden could understand. Apparently there was no feudal system at all on the eastern steppes. No villeinage, no manorial obligations. No kings or knights or lords either. That sounded fine—wonderful, in fact, to someone with Malden's political sympathies—until you learned what the barbarians had in place of those institutions. "The strongest man rules, as chieftain," Mörget said. "This is the basis of all our laws. If you disagree with his policies, you challenge him to a fight. If you win, you get to be chieftain and make your own rules."

Malden frowned. "But surely some young fool with muscles but no brains could become king of you all, then."

"Aye," Mörget said. "And often does. But such rarely last long. No matter how strong a man's arm may be, there's always someone stronger out there, waiting."

Malden frowned. "But what of justice? What recourse do the meek have, if the strong decide what is right?"

Mörget laughed, loud enough to make Slag shout for peace. The barbarian shrugged and told Malden, "In Skrae, I've met many such as you. Philosophers and priests, two things we have none of on the steppes. They've tried to explain this justice to me, and other abstract concepts, and yet all I hear is the voices of children saying, 'It's not fair, it's not fair.' Where they got this idea that life was meant to be fair remains a mystery to me."

Malden tried to imagine how he would survive under barbarian law, and the prospect made him queasy. "If every chieftain makes his own laws, what is to stop him from saying that murder is no crime, or that a man may lie with his sister if he chooses?"

Mörget shrugged. "In principle, I suppose, it is possible. Yet I've never heard of a chieftain that would ignore such basic laws. If a man kills in cold blood, we run him through with a sword, that's always been the way. If a man rapes another man's daughter or wife or mother, we strangle him."

"What if . . . just hypothetically, here—a man were to steal another man's property? Say, his horse blanket. Or something trivial like that."

"What's the penalty for such in your Free City?"

Malden shrugged. "Hanging."

"Ah! You see, there's where your civilization breaks down. You put a man to death for stealing? Regardless of why he did it? What if he only takes a loaf of bread, to feed his hungry family? That is senseless cruelty!"

"I always did think the penalty too harsh," Malden agreed.

"Yes, in the East we are far more humane. We do not kill our thieves. We simply cut off their feet and leave them crawling in the dirt like the dogs they are."

"Oh," Malden said. "But then—how would such a thief feed his family after that? He would be reduced to begging."

"We have no beggars in my country," Mörget said.

"No?"

The barbarian laughed again. "If a man cannot feed himself, we make him a slave. We would never let someone starve!"

"Ah," Malden said.

"You know—sometimes I think if my people overran this country," Mörget said, gesturing at the fields of wheat, "it would be a good thing for your people. You're so soft! You need a good war to toughen you up. Make you remember what is important in life."

"You'll forgive me," Malden said, "if I hope it never comes to that."

The barbarian laughed. "Don't worry, little man. You've got a whole mountain range protecting you. A wall to keep us out." He chortled so exuberantly he nearly dropped the reins.

"And knights like Croy to defend us," Malden pointed out.

The barbarian stopped laughing on the instant. He turned a shrewd eye toward Croy, who was singing some old ballad, a duet with Cythera. "It'll be interesting to see what he's made of, when we face our demon. Whether he can fight or not."

He wasn't laughing when he said it. A fact that made Malden uneasy for reasons he couldn't quite explain.

# CHAPTER EIGHTEEN

They covered twenty miles that day, pushing the horses near their limits. "I always thought men rode horses to go farther and faster than they might afoot," Malden told

Mörget, when they came to a stop outside another mile-house. "But I think if we walked we'd make better time."

"Bah! Horses are meant for running short distances, not this ambling gait we force them to. A man walking can cover more ground than a horse in a day," the barbarian said. "Yet not while carrying so much on his back." Mörget reined in the horses by the stables—this milehouse looked almost identical in design to the Cow—and thumped the side of the wagon to wake Slag. The dwarf came stumbling out into the dusk and squinted at the place's sign.

"This place is called the Sheaf of Wheat?" Slag asked. "First the Cow. Now the Wheat. I wonder what will be hanging on the wall inside? What fucking wonderful imaginations these farmers have."

Croy leapt down from his horse and slapped the dwarf on the back. Slag nearly sprawled forward in the dust. The knight explained, "There are seven milehouses between Ness and Helstrow. They are named after the Seven Munificent Blessings of the Lady. Come, you'll forget the name once you have a quart of ale down your throat."

Croy headed inside, with Cythera following so close behind Malden didn't even have a chance to catch her eye. Clearly she'd meant what she said last night.

"Lad," Slag told him softly, "if your rival was any less trusting than Sir Croy, you'd have a long piece of steel sticking out your back already. Let her be."

Malden felt his cheeks burn. He shot a look toward Mörget, but the barbarian was already leading the horses away. "I don't know what you're talking about," he said to Slag.

"Fine. But if you go slipping out of the room again tonight, try not to be so damned noisy about it, all right?"

Inside the common room of the Sheaf of Wheat, Malden found familiar surrounds—right down to the dozy alekeep behind the bar. This time at least the place wasn't completely deserted. A man in a dusty cloak sat near the fire, drinking brandy from a wooden cup. He glanced up as they entered and studied each of their faces, then glanced toward their belts to see what weapons they carried.

Either a thief or a watchman, Malden thought, judging by the professional efficiency of the man's scrutiny. Malden glanced at the man's own belt and saw a stout cudgel there, painted white and kept where it was visible. The symbol of a reeve, an overseer of peasants—but this was no mere farm supervisor. He must be a shire reeve, then. The local enforcer of the king's laws.

Eating in the same room as a lawman made Malden uneasy, but he hadn't broken any laws since leaving Ness, so he tried to ignore the feeling. It didn't help that the shire reeve kept glancing his way, as if he recognized Malden from somewhere.

When he had finished his pottage and ale, Malden announced he was exhausted and would go to bed right away. Slag came with him. "You've been sleeping all day," Malden pointed out, when they were alone together in their room.

"Aye, as is only natural for a dwarf. I don't intend to sleep tonight, but read. Do you mind a bit of light while you take your rest?"

Malden shrugged. "I think I'll be asleep soon as I lie down. A candle won't bother me." In the brothel where he grew up he had learned how to sleep through noise and other distractions. Yet despite what he'd said, he did not go to sleep right away. He watched the dwarf take a hand-sized book out of his pack. It looked very old, the leather cover worn bright orange at the edges and cracked along the spine. Like any book, it must have been quite valuable, and Malden had an eye for expensive things. "What book is that?" he asked.

Slag shook his head. "Naught for you, so keep your thieving hands off it. If you must know, it's a classic of dwarven literature. *Harnin's Stone Surfaces and Bond Griding Manual*. A masterpiece of strength of materials ratios and specific density tables. Every placer miner and stone carver in my country owns a copy. It's also the only written work to mention the Vincularium."

Malden was bone-tired but this interested him. Despite Cutbill's suggestion, he'd never managed to ask anyone about their destination. There had been two main reasons for that: for one, he'd been afraid to demonstrate his ignorance in front of Cythera, and for the other, he didn't actually plan on going as far as the Vincularium. He intended to part ways at Helstrow, where he'd be safe from Prestwicke and also from the demon Croy and Mörget were chasing.

Yet he had to admit a certain free-floating curiosity about the place the rest of them were headed. "It's a tomb, yes?" he asked, because he figured the dwarf had to know.

"Aye," Slag said, and turned a page. "You certain this light isn't keeping you awake?"

"Certain. A tomb for a dwarf, I think—which would explain why you're so intent on going there. You don't want to see your ancestral crypts defiled."

"There you're wrong. Dwarves built the place, but we weren't the last to live in it. You called it a tomb, and aye, it is. But before that it was a prison."

Malden's eyes widened. He had no desire to rob graves, but breaking into prisons was perhaps worse. The thing about prisons—and this was common knowledge for a thief—was they were hard to get out of once you were inside.

"Was it a prison for dwarves?" Malden asked.

"No. For elves."

Malden sat up on his mattress and stared.

"Aye, the fucking elves," Slag said, putting his thumb in the book to save his place. "What do you know about the elves, Malden?"

The thief searched his memory. It was a common enough expression to say that someone or something was "dead as an elf." Everyone knew Skrae had been infested with elves once, and that now they were gone. But that was almost all they knew. "Pointy ears, right? And evil, they were supposed to be evil. Sometimes people say 'sharp as an elf's ear,' and I've heard a man called 'wicked as an elf' for beating a whore."

"The ears, yes, those were pointed. As for evil, well, let me tell you something you can learn from. When a man speaks ill of the dead, and calls the corpse evil, you can bet your fundament he killed the poor fucker, and needs an excuse. I don't suppose the elves were any more evil than you or me. Well, me anyway. But they fought a war with the humans, and they lost, so now they're remembered as wicked."

Slag looked up at the ceiling as if reading a page of history there. "In truth, I know little more than you do about them. They lived long lives, it's said. If they didn't die in battle, they could expect to see their eightieth birthday."

Malden gasped. That was twice as long as a human's average span in Skrae. Eighty years seemed to him an eternity. "But they're dead now. What happened to them?"

"Men did. Humans forced them out of their lands. They tried to make a final stand in the Vincularium. The last of their kind went into that place eight hundred years ago, and never came out. They starved to death, most like, or turned on each other. A prison and a tomb, as I said."

"A place like that must be haunted."

"It's fucking likely, yes."

"Death would wait for anyone who ventured inside."

"Almost assuredly. Now, unless the sound of my voice is lulling you to sleep, perhaps you'd do me a favor and let me read, hmm?" Slag asked. "I want to plumb this volume for any clue as to what awaits me."

"You want to know how you're going to die?"

Slag gasped in frustration and slammed the book down on the floor. "At least that way I won't look so surprised when it happens, now will I? Shut your gob, lad, and let me read!"

# CHAPTER NINETEEN

The following day the sun was warm and rippled along the surface of the road, while a soft breeze bowed the heads of wheat. Croy rode on the wagon while Malden drove. Between the demands of watching the horses and the knight's singing, Malden had no trouble staying awake this time. They made good time in the morning but had to slow their pace in the afternoon as foam slicked the backs of the hackneys and it was clear they were pushing the horses too hard. Still, by the time pink clouds began to gather in the sky, they could already see Helstrow on the horizon—the halfway mark of their journey.

The royal fortress stood in a wide bowl of land cleared of trees and rocks, to allow better fields of fire for the archers on its walls. In shape it looked like a great ship, with a sharp prow and a high stern castle—that must be the king's palace, Malden thought, a stand of spires and high towers. The fortress stood astride the river Strow, from which it took its name. A hundred flags flew from its high places, and knights in bright armor rode in and out of its three massive gates on endless patrols.

East of the fortress, across the river, an ancient forest grew. Croy told Malden it was the last of its kind in Skrae, a thicket of ancient trees that cloaked the foothills of the Whitewall Mountains. To find a forest that old anywhere else, Croy said, you'd have to go as far north as the dwarven kingdom, for the dwarves cared little for the surface world and had never cleared their land in the endless demand for firewood.

"This forest," Croy told him, "has survived only because no one is willing to get so close to the Vincularium just to chop down trees."

Malden had a choice to make, whether to part company here and lose himself in the streets of Helstrow—where surely there were things to steal, and a living to be made—or to press on with the party and become a grave robber (and, likely, a meal for a demon). While he was pondering that, however, he was asked for his opinion on another matter.

"The only bridge over the Strow is inside the fortress," Croy said. "We'd have to enter the gates to cross."

"That shouldn't be a problem—you're still a knight of the realm," Malden pointed out. "Even a knight errant should be able to talk his way in."

"The difficulty is on Mörget's side. A barbarian in Redweir or in Ness is a curiosity, even a wonder. Inside Helstrow, he's an act of war. One reason the king stays here is to keep his army close to the Whitewall, where he can respond quickly in case the barbarians flood through the mountain passes."

"Is an invasion really that likely?" Malden asked.

Croy glanced over at Mörget, but the barbarian was out of earshot. "The people of the East live by conquest. They do not farm, so simply to feed their people they must constantly raid the freeholds and villages of their neighbors. Mostly they harass the hill people north of here, on the border between Skrae and Skilfing, but they've long had their eye set on richer bounty. If they were allowed through the passes, though . . . yes. I am certain they would try to conquer us. The threat they pose is real—and kept in abeyance only by constant vigilance on our part." Croy shook his head. "If Mörget is discovered in Helstrow, we'll be taken as spies or traitors or worse. And you've seen him. He's hardly inconspicuous."

"Is there another option?"

Croy frowned, a rare expression on his face. "The Strow is too deep and runs too fast to ford anywhere on its length. We can head downstream a few miles, build a raft, and pole the horses across—but that's not without its dangers. The current is so swift we could be capsized and drown."

"When choosing between two evils," Malden said, "my mother always said, make sure you get paid in advance. It seems to me we cannot predict what will happen if we enter Helstrow. Any number of things could go wrong. The river may be treacherous, but at least we know what we face."

"I think you're right. But it will add a day to our journey. Thank you, Malden."

"For my counsel? I'm surprised you even asked for it."

Croy smiled at him. "You count yourself so worthless sometimes. You're one of the most canny men I've ever met," he said. He reached over and slapped Malden on the back. "I know you weren't born a nobleman, Malden, but you have true honor in your soul. I've seen it. There are great deeds in your future."

Guilt washed through Malden's veins, a feeling he'd hardly expected. If Croy knew what kind of dishonorable things he dreamed of, concerning Cythera . . . "I think you do me too much credit."

Croy shrugged. "I suppose no man can take the measure of his own mettle. Once we're across the river we'll discuss this again."

Malden wasn't sure what to make of that. Did Croy suspect something? Was he trying to put him off his guard? There was no way to know.

Croy stuck two fingers in his mouth and whistled loud enough to hurt Malden's ears. "Ho, friends!" he shouted. "Up ahead the road forks. Turn south!"

"South?" Mörget asked. "Away from our destination?"

"Put faith in me," Croy said, and the barbarian just nodded.

The two warriors trusted each other implicitly, Malden realized. Mörget didn't question Croy's instructions unduly, because he knew they shared a common interest. And now Croy was trying to bring Malden into that same confidence. It gave him chills.

And a very strange sort of pride. Not that he intended to

live up to this newfound trust. But it was . . . nice, perhaps,
to have a man like Croy think highly of you.

Malden laughed to himself. He'd been spending too
much time with the knight errant. He was starting to believe in Croy's folly himself. Best to nip that in the bud.

The road duly forked, and Croy wheeled the wagon to
the south, so that the setting sun was on their right shoulders. The horses were dragging their feet by the time, a
mile later, they pulled into the stable yard of a milehouse.
They were on the road to Redweir now, and Croy told
Malden that the milehouses on this road were named for
the Nine Learned Arts. The sign out front depicted the
constellation known as the Troll, and the house was called
the Astrologer.

Inside, the walls and ceiling were decorated with tin
stars, and instead of the usual dreary room they found
music and warmth and a boy carrying two flagons of ale.
He nodded them toward one of the available tables. This
place was not crowded by any measure, but at least it saw
some decent custom. The men gathered at the tables were
mostly merchants and tradesmen, travelers on the road between Redweir and Helstrow. Men who might have a coin
to spend. They were laughing and their faces were bright
with drink.

"Now this is more to my liking," Malden said, and
called for food. What came to the table was pottage again,
but a bit of bacon had been stirred into the bowls to give
the stew a measure of flavor. He downed his bowl in a
hurry and ordered another, as well as more ale.

It might, after all, be the last meal he shared with the
dwarf and the knight. It might be the last time he ever saw
Cythera. He intended to get drunk.

Croy went to bed early. Cythera stayed long enough to
watch a band of musicians strike up their first song. The
music was as rustic as the instruments—a shawm, an old
plucked dulcimer, and a fiddle—but boisterous and full of
life, and the songs retained their traditional, and therefore

mildly obscene, lyrics. Malden found himself slapping the table in time, and even Slag nodded his head to the rhythm.

When the first song ended, to much cheering, Cythera rose from the table and took her leave. "If I stay, I'll be dancing before long, and shan't sleep at all," she told them.

Malden nearly fell over his chair as he jumped to his feet. "Pleasant dreams, dear lady," he said.

She looked quizzically into his eyes for a moment, but when he added nothing more she nodded to Slag and headed back to her private room.

"You haven't an arsehole's chance with that one," Slag said when Malden sat back down. "What woman would trade a knight for a thief? Unless human women are so different from the dwarven kind."

Malden shook his head. "Some of them, perhaps. Slag, tell me, does Cutbill have an agent inside Helstrow?"

"If he does, he never told me," the dwarf replied. "You think I'm privy to his secrets? And why do you even ask?"

"A wise man would never set foot inside the Vincularium. A wise man would run now, while he still had the chance. Oh, I know you have your reasons for going onward with this crew," Malden said. "Even if you won't share them. Probably a hoard of dwarf gold hidden in there somewhere, left behind an age ago."

Slag's face refused to show any emotion. Which told Malden he'd come close to the mark, at least.

"Yet," the thief went on, "I'm more likely to die than get rich if I go. I had considered the possibility of making my own way from here."

"You mean to run off without a word of explanation, is what you're saying," Slag said.

"I'll head for Helstrow and find my fortune there," Malden whispered. "Better a live thief than a dead hero, no?"

"Well, if you do go," the dwarf said, and pursed his lips as if he'd bitten into a lime, "good luck go with you, son."

"There. It's not so hard to wish a man fortune, is it? I know curses are easier for you, so I'll ask no further benediction." Malden rose unsteadily from the table. He should have taken his time with that fourth pint of ale, he thought.

"You're going right now?" Slag asked.

"No, no, no, no," Malden said. "Just outside. For a piss."

The dwarf looked like he didn't believe this, but it was true. Malden was in no shape to walk a dozen miles that night, not without some sleep. If he did run off, he would do it just before the dawn.

He stepped out into the cold night air, leaving the music and the fire behind him, and wandered down the dooryard of the milehouse toward the privy. Overhead an army of stars marched across a perfect dark blue sky.

Malden had built a kind of life for himself in Ness. He could do it again in Helstrow, he was sure of it. The decision would be easy, if not for—

But he did not finish that thought. Just as he was about to take down his hose, he heard a sudden sharp crack behind him. He jumped in the air and spun around.

Standing behind him was a man dressed in a heavy cloak with a hood that masked his features. He had a white stick in his hand, which he slapped against the wall of the milehouse. "Going somewhere?" he asked.

# CHAPTER TWENTY

"You," Malden said. "I've seen you before. Back up the road a ways. You're—"

"I'm the man no mischievous little peasant ever wants to meet," the man said. Malden was sure he knew the man now, even if his face couldn't be seen. This was the shire reeve he'd seen back at the last milehouse. The one who'd sized him up like a horse he wanted to buy. "I work this road looking for runaways. Most don't give me such exercise as you." He swept back his cloak and Malden saw a long-handled hammer dangling from his belt. "You're looking at a beating, no matter what. But you can save yourself from being hobbled if you play nice."

Hobbling. The very word made Malden's blood freeze. It was too gentle-sounding a word considering what it meant—leg-breaking was perhaps more precise. It was the traditional punishment for villeins who ran away too many times from their farms.

Malden licked his lips in fear. "I have no idea what you think I've done, but—"

"Your master sent me to bring you home, boy."

"Master? I don't know what you're talking about," Malden said. "I'm a citizen of Ness, a free man. I'm traveling with a knight of the realm, Sir Croy. He'll vouch for me if we just go inside and rouse him."

The shire reeve chuckled. "You've got a silver tongue in your mouth, I'll give you that. Most folk I catch can barely mumble the king's speech. That must have helped you trick yon bunch into letting you ride on their wagon. Did you tell them all that guff about being a citizen? Do you think they really believed you? Look at you, son. You're as thin as a switch, and near short as a dwarf. You've got the look all over you of one born poor. You can put on fancy city clothes if you like, too, yet it don't make you a gentleman."

Malden glanced to the left and the right, looking for a good escape route. Unfortunately none presented itself. The privy stood well off from the main building, and he doubted he could outrun the shire reeve. Yet if he could just get inside the milehouse, he knew he could wake the others and they would explain everything. If he could—

"Hold," he said, thinking of something. "You say my master sent you? Pray tell, what was his name?"

"I should think you'd know that yourself," the shire reeve said. "Prestwicke. His name is Prestwicke. He sent me word of your description, and coin to pay for your capture in advance. When I spied you last night I sent a message back. He'll be here tomorrow to collect you—whether or not you can walk then."

At the sound of the name Malden's heart raced. He'd come all this way to get away from Prestwicke, but it seemed the assassin wasn't going to give up that easily. He had no choice now but to escape. If Prestwicke came for him, he knew the bastard would never let him get away again. "Very well," he forced himself to say. "I'll go quietly. Just let me do one thing first."

"Come now, what could you possibly hope to achieve by—"

"This," Malden said. He drew his bodkin from his belt in one quick motion and flicked it toward the shire reeve's face. It was no throwing knife—it had no edge, just a poorly sharpened point—and he knew better than to think it would actually hurt the man. The shire reeve didn't know that, however, and as Malden had expected he flinched and took a step backward as the tiny knife flew past his ear.

It was just enough to ruin his balance. Malden rushed toward him with one shoulder down and caught him in the midriff, knocking him off his feet. He didn't stop to admire his handiwork but kept running, across the road and into the field of wheat on the far side. Behind him he heard yelling but he didn't bother listening too closely—he could guess what the shire reeve was shouting about.

The stalks of wheat, pale in the moonlight, bowed and bent aside as Malden hurtled through them. He would run a dozen yards and no more into the field then double back, he figured, and race for the door of the milehouse. Hopefully the shire reeve would get lost in the wheat while trying to stop him. Hopefully—

A sharp pain exploded across Malden's buttocks. He was lucky he'd been doubled over, trying to keep his head down below the level of the wheat. If the hammer had taken him in the back it might have broken his spine. It was one of the worst blows he'd ever taken, and it sent him sprawling in the mud. His breath burst out of him and his hands grabbed at the yielding wheat as he tried to scrabble back up to his feet.

A boot pushed down on his back and ground him into the dirt.

"That," the shire reeve said, "was a fool's gambit. You think I never chased down some farmhand in a field before?"

Malden could think of several witty quips to come back with, but he lacked the breath to form them.

"I can see you're a lively one," the shire reeve said. "Well, I got a cure for that. Tell me, boy. Which knee you want to keep? Left or right?"

Malden fought and struggled and just managed to roll over onto his back. He looked up at the stars and the great shadow of the shire reeve above him, and the silhouette of the hammer in the man's hand. His heart beat so fast in his chest he thought it might burst. "Please," he begged. He'd spent much of his life as a thief waiting to be measured for a hangman's noose. He'd thought often of what he would say to his executioner, what final words he would impart on the world. All that came out of his mouth now was, "Please."

Even vain hopes are answered, sometimes.

There was a sound very much like the noise a scythe makes when it cuts through a sheaf of grain. A few drops of dark rain pattered on Malden's cheek. And then the shire reeve's head fell from his neck to land right in Malden's lap. The man's body stayed standing a moment longer, then slid to one side and crushed the wheat down flat.

Another shape was revealed behind it. A much larger shape, that of a man holding a massive bearded axe.

"The fool woke me up," Mörget said, "when he rapped on the wall with that little stick of his. I was enjoying my rest."

The blood started flowing once more in Malden's veins. It still ran cold, though.

No. Oh, no. It couldn't be.

Not a shire reeve.

Among the criminal fraternity of Ness there was a certain understanding. Thieves occasionally fought one another. Sometimes footpads had to hurt someone to make their nightly wages. Every thief owned at least a knife, and often far more serious weapons, and they knew how to use them. But not even the most hardened thug in the Free City would think of attacking a watchman.

The agents of the law had their own fraternity, and they punished those who killed their own without mercy or question. If you slew a watchman, you were signing your own death warrant. They would never stop until they caught the killer.

And that was just for average everyday watchmen. The shire reeve was—had been—one of the most important officials of law in the entire kingdom.

If you killed a man like that, you might as well slit your own throat next. And Malden knew to a certainty that after the law dealt with Mörget, they would come after him as an accomplice. The facts didn't matter. The law would have its due.

"That might have been a foolish blow," he said. "Though I do thank you for it."

Mörget squatted down a little and picked the head up from Malden's lap. "No, it was a clean cut. Look."

Malden shook his head. "Mörget, that man was an official of the crown, and when he turns up missing they'll hunt high and low for his killer. Nor will they think that disturbing your rest justified your crime."

"Ha! Let them come. I'm afraid of no watchman."

Malden shook his head. "Please, listen to me, friend. You know how to chop off men's heads—I know about the law. We have to hide the body. Just to make sure it isn't found until we're long gone from here. Once we're across the Strow, away from civilization, maybe we can breathe easy again."

"Justice! Law!" Mörget mocked. "Just words, little man."

Oh, this was bad. Very, very bad. Malden could hear his heart pounding in his ears. He could feel sweat pooling in the small of his back. What if someone in the milehouse heard the shire reeve shouting? What if they were coming even now with torches and swords, looking to see what was the matter?

What if the shire reeve had told someone, anyone, about the peasant named Malden he was hunting? What if Prestwicke came in the morning and—

No. He couldn't think about that. He couldn't think at all, there was no time for it. He needed to act.

Malden got to his feet, then reached down to grab the shire reeve's ankles. The shire reeve was bigger than he was, and Malden didn't think he could drag the man very far on his own, but if Mörget would just help—

"Catch," the barbarian said.

It was all Malden could do to drop the dead man's ankles and bring his hands up. He neatly caught the shire reeve's severed head, then almost dropped it again when he realized what Mörget had thrown to him.

The barbarian bent down and lifted the body easily, slinging it over his shoulder. "Where do you want it?" he asked.

"Deeper in the field is our best bet," Malden said. "He won't be discovered until this place is harvested."

Together they covered up all evidence of what had happened. The hardest part was washing the blood from his tunic. Malden was convinced the keeper of the milehouse would come out and demand to know what they were doing in his horse trough, but somehow they avoided detection.

When it was done, Mörget returned to the stables, while Malden slipped inside and headed for the room he was supposed to share with Slag. He stopped outside the door and waited until he'd stopped shaking.

Inside, Slag was propped up on the mattress, reading by the light of a single candle. "Didn't have the liver for it, eh?" the dwarf asked.

It took Malden a moment to realize what Slag meant. "Ah. No. I won't be going to . . . to Helstrow, not now." Not until he was sure the shire reeve's death went unnoticed. Not while Prestwicke was out there somewhere, riding hard to catch up with him. All the horrors of an elfin crypt couldn't match what his misbegotten fate came up with on its own. "I'm coming with you."

"I thought as much," Slag said.

"You did?"

"You'll never leave Cythera behind. Not if it means losing her to Croy," the dwarf told him, and tapped the side of his nose.

Malden knew he couldn't tell anyone—not even Slag—what had happened, so he just said, "You've got me there, old man. You've got me dead to rights."

# CHAPTER TWENTY-ONE

The horses screamed as water jumped over the side of the raft and licked at their feet, but Croy didn't have time to soothe them. He was too busy pushing against a rock as big as a house that stuck up from the middle of the river Strow. Malden dipped his own pole in the water and added his strength, and between the two of them they managed to get the raft moving away from the boulder.

"Slag, are you sure this thing will hold together?" Cythera asked, fear pitching her voice high.

"Yes, I am fucking sure," the dwarf shouted back. Slag grabbed at one of the taut ropes attached to the mast as they were all swung about by the current.

Croy had planned on building a traditional raft, a square platform of logs lashed together, but the dwarf insisted he knew a better way. The thing he'd constructed looked more like a spider's web, with logs radiating out from a central upright mast. Ropes hanging down from the mast braced each log, allowing them to move back and forth and even up and down as the water surged beneath them.

"Another rock!" Cythera cried.

Croy shoved his pole down into the stony bed of the river and heaved once more. On the far side of the raft Mörget howled some barbarian war cry and leaned across the water, pushing them clear with his arms. The raft spun around on the axis of its mast like a wagon wheel, and the sky and the land flashed around Croy until his head felt light, but suddenly Cythera was laughing and the dwarf was jumping up and down, pointing at the far bank. It was only a few yards away. Croy jumped down into the water with a rope and tied off to a boulder there, his blood singing in his veins. He heaved against his line, and the raft beached on a bank of pebbles and sparse grass. Cythera untied the horses and they bolted gratefully for dry land.

Once everyone was safely ashore, Croy dragged their supplies off the raft and then fell back into a patch of grass and just stared up at the sky for a while, glad to be alive. "I didn't think we'd make it," he said when he had the strength to sit up again.

The knight rubbed at his wet face and looked around. He found himself on a grassy verge shaded by tall trees. The sun had just come up—for some reason, Malden and Mörget both wanted to get an early start, and they crossed the river in the first blue light of dawn. Under the canopy of leaves it might still have been night.

"I'm soaked to the skin," Cythera said, reaching for a horse blanket. "We should get a fire going and dry our clothes. Croy. If you please."

"Hmm?"

"I'm going to disrobe," she said, shaking out the blanket.

"Oh, yes?" He tried to look innocent.

"You could at least turn your back," she said.

"I thought, perhaps, as we are betrothed, you might allow me to . . ." He couldn't bring himself to say the rest. Especially with the way she stared at him.

"Stop thinking of me as your wife," she said. "At least until we return to Ness. I won't give you any excuse to send me home, not now. If you start thinking you're my master, you'll think you can order me around. Now. Turn your back."

Croy did as he was told. What choice did he have? It was clear Cythera intended to see this adventure through, regardless of how it made him feel. His back burned as if he felt her eyes on him. When she was finished and told him he could turn around again, he saw she was wrapped completely in the blanket, with only her feet exposed.

They were lovely feet.

He went to see to the horses. The animals looked grateful to be back on dry land, but still they whickered and bucked when Croy approached them. Malden came up behind him, standing well back, as if afraid of being kicked.

"Did we truly need to sell the wagon? With Slag's improvements, that was probably the most valuable piece of cartage in Skrae," Malden pointed out. "Are you sure we got good value for it?"

Croy laughed and nodded. Where they were going next there were no proper roads, and they would have spent more time pulling the wagon out of mud or levering it over tree roots than they did traveling. "For Slag, I found this pony," he said, pointing out the piebald colt. "A good courser for Cythera. And for you, a jennet."

Malden approached the indicated horse with a look of distinct fear. The roan looked back at him with pure apathy. The thief reached out tentatively to touch the animal's forelock but the jennet snorted and he yanked his hand away. "You got me a horse," he said. "Croy, I'm afraid to tell you this, but I never learned how to ride."

"I assumed as much, and so chose the gentlest, most kindly dispositioned animal I could find. Don't worry. She'll do all the work. You just need to hang on."

"Well," Malden said, taking a step back, "I'll do my best."

"I have something else for you as well," Croy said with a sly grin. He'd been waiting a long time for this.

He went over to where their supplies were piled in a heap and took out a long bundle wrapped in oilcloth. "You didn't need this back when we were in civilized country, but now we're properly in the wilderness I want you to have it." He unwrapped the bundle to reveal a sword in a thick scabbard. He held it out toward Malden in both hands.

"Ah," Malden said. "A sword. I don't think I want to wear a—"

"Not just any sword," Croy said. "I believe you know this one." He drew the sword carefully from its special glass-lined sheath. In the firelight it looked ragged and notched, and when it caught the light the blade was revealed as nothing more than a corroded and pitted bar of iron with a weathered point. As soon as it was exposed to the air, however, glistening drops of fuming liquid began to break out upon its length, like steaming sweat.

"Acidtongue," Malden whispered.

The name was said loud enough to get Mörget's attention. The barbarian had been chopping firewood. Now he stormed over to where Croy and Malden stood. He stared with open and unaffected lust at the eroded sword.

"One of the seven," Mörget thundered. "Another Ancient Blade! You had this the whole time, Croy, and never mentioned it to me?"

"It is not mine to speak for," Croy explained. "Its previous wielder, Bikker, was my teacher. I was forced to slay him in a duel of honor. Now I seek a proper replacement, someone I can train in its use. I've had Malden in mind for a long while."

"Me?" Malden asked. "But—why? I'm no knight. I'm barely a free man, as far as the law is concerned. And I've never waved a sword around in my life."

Croy nodded solemnly. He had known that Malden would doubt himself. Humility was a great virtue, one of the hardest for a knight to keep. Malden, with his low birth, would have an advantage there. "Traditionally it is knights who wield the swords. That makes sense—knights are trained in the use of such weapons, often trained from birth, as I was. My first toy was a wooden sword, did you know that? You, Malden, were born to a different estate. You were never trained for this. Yet this is not, as you say, the first time you've ever waved a sword around. You did it once before—with this particular blade."

The thief blanched, but he nodded. "I suppose I did."

"This runt?" Mörget asked. "Could he even lift a sword, if he had one to hand? I think it unlikely."

"You weren't there," Croy said. "Together, Malden and I faced the most powerful sorcerer in Skrae. A magician who thought nothing of summoning demons to do his bidding. One such creature was sent to hunt down Malden and destroy him. I wounded the beast with Ghostcutter, but I was too fatigued and injured to finish the job. Malden had to take up Acidtongue then and slay the beast. He did it without thinking, without hesitation. I've never seen such courage."

"It was that or let the thing eat me," Malden said. "I was so scared I thought I might soil my—"

Mörget chuckled. "You think there's some difference, little man, between terror and bravery? They're like the moon in its phases. Sometimes it waxes, and sometimes it wanes, but it's always there, all of it. We just don't see it all."

"Since that day," Croy went on, "you've shown true courage often enough—not least of all when you agreed to come with us on this quest. If we're going to fight a demon—if you're going to become one of us and pledge your life to fighting them—this is the perfect opportunity to start learning how."

"You want me to become an Ancient Blade," Malden said. "Like you." The thief didn't seem to believe it was even possible.

The knight and the barbarian looked at Malden expectantly.

"I'm not meant for your squire, friend," Malden insisted. "I'm not really the sword-slinging type. Please, I thank you, truly, but—"

"Just hold it a moment. See how it feels," Croy insisted.

Malden stared at him. Then he glanced toward where Cythera and Slag sat by the riverbank. Croy wondered what he looked for from the two of them. He must have found it, though, for Malden took the sword by its hilt. He nearly dropped it—Croy supposed the thief was unused to a sword's weight—but then he managed to swing it through the air. Drops of potent acid flicked through the dark and sizzled in the undergrowth.

Malden took a step toward a nearby tree and brought the blade round in a wildly swinging arc. Croy winced at the poor swordsmanship, but he cheered as the sword smashed into the tree trunk with a noise like a hundred angry snakes. Malden jumped back as the tree toppled and fell with a great crash, its leaves thrashing and its branches snapping when it dropped to the forest floor.

The stump it left looked burnt around the edges, but in the middle the cut was clean. After a moment sap started to ooze from the sundered tree.

"In Sadu's name," Malden breathed.

Croy coughed politely. The swords were consecrated to the Lady, after all, and not to the Bloodgod.

"Croy," Malden said, "I can see you mean this as an

act of great friendship. I have to admit I'm . . . touched."
The thief stared at the ground. "I worry I don't deserve
it, though. There have been times I've not been as—
faithful—a friend as I might. There have been times I've
proven I don't deserve this gift." Malden's arm shook as
he spoke, as if great emotion were flowing through him.
The tremor made flecks of acid rain on the carpet of pine
needles below their feet. "There's something I must tell
you. Something you don't want to hear—"

Croy held up one hand for silence. "Let the past be forgotten now," he said. This was a sacred moment. The passing on of an Ancient Blade was a holy rite. "Prove to me,
from now on, that you deserve to call me brother."

"If you do not want the blade, little man," Mörget said,
"I will be glad to take it from you. By force, if necessary."

Malden laughed, but Croy nodded sagely. "It's one of
our vows," he said. "If a wielder of the sword proves un-
worthy, he must be challenged and killed on the spot."

"I suppose," Malden said, "in that case I'd better hold
on to it. For now."

# CHAPTER TWENTY-TWO

There was still plenty of daylight left, so the companions
loaded up their gear and got on their horses. Mörget
and Croy were old hands at riding, of course, and Cythera
knew how it was done. Slag needed some help getting on
his pony but once on its back he seemed stable enough.
They all had to wait while Malden tried to mount his

jennet. He was nimble enough to jump up into the saddle, but once seated he found himself too far off the ground and started to grow dizzy and had to climb back down. It was ridiculous. How many times had he hung from finger grips off the spire of the Ladychapel in Ness, a hundred feet above the cobblestones? Yet the way the horse refused to stand still gave him vertigo. Mörget offered to strap him in with leather lashings, as was sometimes done for invalids and the very ill who nonetheless had to ride. Malden refused. He would do this. He had to. He could not turn around now. Half the country was after his blood—not to mention Prestwicke.

Eventually he managed to keep his seat and hold the reins as he was shown. The jennet had already proved herself a patient beast, and now she started walking with no compulsion, following the other horses. It was just like Croy had said, she did all the work. Malden clutched to the cantle of his saddle and tried to not fall off.

There were no roads, nor even any trails through the forest. No one lived there—the place was as deserted by human industry as the farmlands had been full of it. The riders had to pick their way around thick copses of gnarled trees and boulders overgrown with bright green moss. Croy led the way. He had an uncanny knack for knowing where the best route could be found. The others followed in single file. Slag rode his colt just in front of Malden, but the dwarf seemed as poor a horseman as the thief, because the colt kept stepping off the chosen path, its short legs finding better purchase elsewhere as they climbed over a fallen log or down into a defile. Then Malden's horse would follow the colt, and everyone would have to stop while all the horses were brought back in line.

It made for slow going. Malden had plenty of time to listen to the sounds of the forest, which constantly startled him in a way that the shouts of soldiers or the crash of thunder never could. Each bird sang with a song he'd never heard, every frog's croak was the roar of some massive beast. At least the endless maze of trees felt enough like the walls of a city's houses that he did not feel so exposed, as he had out in the fields of wheat.

Yet so preoccupied with the sounds of the forest was he that he did not notice in time when his jennet decided it had found a better path and led him deep into a stand of trees. He suddenly looked up and realized he could not see Slag ahead of him.

He was lost.

Well, the others couldn't be too far away, he decided. He shouted "Halloo!" and called Croy by name, and pulled up on the reins as he'd been shown to make the jennet stop. The horse, which clearly had decided she knew better than her rider, kept plodding onward, picking her way through a rank of ferns tall enough to brush Malden's knees.

"No, no, I said stop," Malden told the horse. There was a proper word to use, wasn't there? He'd heard drovers in the city use it, to command their teams. "Whoa," he said, and the jennet stopped instantly.

Malden didn't. He wasn't braced for the halt, and though he managed not to be thrown, he was pitched forward across the jennet's neck and one foot came loose from its stirrup. Clutching hard to the horse's mane, he cursed himself and tried to get back into the saddle.

That was when Malden heard the buzzing.

He froze, every sense tuned to that strange noise.

It had not sounded friendly.

Morning light streamed down through the trees, dancing around the shimmering leaves to dapple patches of undergrowth with sudden, blazing color. The wind that shook the branches never let up, and carried no sound but its own rising and falling susurration. Malden turned around as far as he could in the saddle to see what was behind him. Nothing but rocks and trees and briars.

"Did you hear that?" Malden asked the horse.

She had. Her ears stood straight up and she pawed nervously at the ground. From her demeanor he could guess her feelings: she very much wanted to run away, but her rider had given the command to halt.

"That's the problem with having a foolish master," Malden sympathized. "Perhaps I should take your counsel." He wore no spurs, but when he touched his heels to the jennet's flanks, she walked forward readily. Malden craned his neck to peer around him, looking for the source of the buzzing noise, and—

It came again, even louder, very close now. He nearly jumped off the horse's back so he could go running and screaming through the woods. But no. Surely he was safer on horseback. He reached down to touch the hilt of his bodkin. Then cursed himself as he remembered he had Acidtongue tied up behind the saddle. Surely the magic sword was the match for anything short of a fire-breathing dragon.

To his left, something crashed through the foliage. Malden wheeled around to that side and the jennet did likewise, snorting in panic.

The thing that came out of the woods was as big as a cow, and it gleamed with iridescent colors when the sunlight struck its back. Two stunted, cloudy eyes stood on either side of a curved black beak, below which spiky mandibles clicked together. The beast's massive oblong body stood supported on six slender legs that bent in all the wrong directions. Coarse black fur covered those legs, though the rest of the animal was smooth and covered in plates of armor.

The thing reared up and snapped at the jennet with its compound jaw.

Malden reached back to grab the hilt of Acidtongue and slapped the jennet's rump instead, because he could not see what he was doing. He couldn't take his eyes off the monster that bore down on him.

The horse, perhaps thinking her master had finally come to his senses, did a very horselike thing and bolted. Unfortunately Malden was leaning backward at that precise moment to reach the sword. He had to slip his feet out of the stirrups to get it.

The horse went forward. The thief went backward, head over ankles. He crashed to the leaf-strewn forest floor with a thump that took his wind.

The jennet disappeared between two thickets of trees. The monster ran forward, barreling right for Malden's prostrate form. Malden grabbed for the bodkin at his belt and brought it around in a wild arc, slashing at the thing's face.

The creature took a nimble step back, avoiding Malden's swing. Its jaws clacked together and Malden pulled his hand back. Carefully, he got to his feet. The monster tried to circle around behind him, so he turned with it. It lunged forward—he jabbed, and struck, but the point of his bodkin only scored the leathery hide on its beak.

Malden recovered and started another swing, intending to cut at its eyes. Surely they must be a weak point in its armor, he thought. He must strike true to catch such tiny targets. Yet as he leaned forward into the stab, the monster's carapace split open, two pieces of its shell peeling back as long glassy wings burst free and buzzed savagely.

Malden danced backward as it jumped up into the air and smashed into him. He was knocked back, his heel caught on a rotten log and he fell, his bodkin flashing wildly before him as the monster bore down on him from above. He threw up his free arm to fend it off, and the mandibles grabbed at the sleeve of his jerkin.

"No!" he shouted, certain it would snap the bones of his arm like so many twigs. The weight of the creature fell on him and he was enveloped in its strange reek, an acrid stench like nothing he'd ever smelled before. The mandibles closed on his arm and he yelped in anticipation.

Yet the pain did not come. The thing gummed at his sleeve, and Malden realized it did not have any teeth. It could grasp him, and drool on him, but it lacked the equipment to actually bite him.

It buzzed angrily and its skinny legs batted at his face, the hairs there feathery soft. It tried to crush him under its massive bulk, but it proved surprisingly light for something so large.

If it wanted to kill him, it was going to have to sit on him until he starved to death. Malden almost laughed as he understood. This was no monster bent on devouring travelers who strayed into its forest. It was some leaf-eating insect, grown overlarge, yes, but as harmless as a pill bug. It must have attacked him only in desperation. Had he stumbled across its nest? Was it protecting its young?

Then he heard shouts and the crashing clamor of horses running through the forest. Suddenly his companions were all around him, and he called to them that he was all right, that it was nothing.

Apparently Croy didn't hear him. Ghostcutter came up high and flashed down, slicing the insect's head from where it seamlessly joined its thorax.

Stinking yellow blood poured down over Malden's face in great gouts. He choked and spluttered as some of the foul stuff got in his mouth. That was the worst injury he'd taken from the animal.

"You didn't need to do that," he said as Croy helped him up to his feet.

"I just saved your life," the knight insisted. He looked perplexed.

"No, no, it was harmless—look—it doesn't even have any teeth."

Croy picked up the severed head of the beast and poked inside its mouth with a finger. "I thought you were in peril," he said. "You were down on the ground and that thing was on top of you."

Malden wiped at his face and chest. The yellow slime had positively ruined his clothing. It stank of the animal's alien odor and clung to his fingers like thick mucus. "Gah," he said. "I need to find a stream so I can wash this off."

"There's one just up ahead," Cythera told him. "We

were trying to ford it when we realized you were missing. Then when your horse rejoined us, missing her rider, we knew to come look for you." She frowned and looked away. "Mörget—what are you doing?"

The barbarian had his axe out and was cheerily butchering the giant insect. "Slag says we can roast this for dinner. It'll be good to have fresh meat."

"I think I might be sick," Malden said.

The dwarf, still sitting his pony, just shrugged. "More for the rest of us, then. Though I'll tell you, you're missing out on a fucking delicacy. I haven't had a good giant cave beetle steak since I left my country. You can get it in Ness, dried and salted like jerky, but it's just not the same."

Croy looked incredulous. "You've seen such a beast before?"

"Oh, aye," Slag told him. "There's some mines in the dwarven kingdom just crawling with the things. Normally they live underground. What this one's doing up here in this blasted daylight, I can't say. Must have climbed up out of a crack in the rocks and got lost. They're sodding stupid like that."

Malden studied the eyes of the dead beast. "Out of its element," he said, thinking perhaps that explained its aggression. A humble creature, a harmless feeder on fungus and subterranean plant matter, suddenly lost in a world of painfully bright light full of strangely soft but dangerous monsters. He could not help but feel sorry for it.

"Wait," Croy said. "If it's a denizen of caves, by nature—does that mean what I think it must?"

"Aye," Slag told him. "It could only have come from one place. This means the Vincularium must be right around the next fucking bend."

# CHAPTER TWENTY-THREE

Croy and Mörget studied a map for a while, then they all mounted their horses and headed to the northeast. The way led up a slope, at first gradual but ever steepening. At times they crested a ridge of land and could see out beyond the trees and across great vistas of green valleys to hills in the distance. Then the trees began to grow thinner on the ground, and shorter of stature, and soon the sunlight that burst through the gaps between their branches was strong enough that Slag could not bear it. He put on a wide-brimmed hat and rubbed burnt cork under his eyes to cut the glare, but eventually he was forced to throw a cloak over himself and allowed Croy to lead his pony on a line. To keep the horse from panicking, the dwarf rigged up an ingenious device—a set of square iron plates mounted on the colt's bridle, which kept it from looking to either side or behind. It could only see Croy's horse ahead of it, and instinctively stayed in line.

Malden kept an eye on his own horse, not wishing to be separated from the others again. The jennet seemed badly spooked after her encounter with the giant beetle. It didn't seem to help that Malden still stank of the thing's thick blood. He had to whisper soothing words to her constantly lest she panic and run off. He was barely aware, then, when they crossed some invisible border and suddenly were out of the forest. It was not until Croy called for them all to look up that he raised his eyes from the ground.

He saw at once they had climbed a great hill that stood at the foot of a great towering mass of rock—the Whitewall, the chain of mountains that separated the land into eastern steppes and western plains.

Beyond that wall lay the land of Mörget's people. It

was better than any fortress wall could be at keeping the two countries apart. The mountains were too tall to be climbed—Malden had heard that men who tried climbed up above the air itself and smothered, drowning for lack of breath. The mountains were so high that their peaks were swathed always in snow, for which fact the range was given its name. Only in a few places was the terrain low enough to be passable—places that were heavily guarded for that reason.

Tallest of those mountains was the one called Cloudblade, which formed the keystone of that endless range. Its jagged top, like the roots of an extracted and upturned tooth, did indeed cut through the clouds overhead, and pennons of mist streamed from its rocks. Above a certain height nothing grew on its slopes, and only the pale rock that formed it was to be seen.

About a third of the way up the slope, the vestiges of an ancient road ended at a pair of massive stones carved into the shape of upright menhirs. It was hard to judge their height from such a distance but Malden thought they had to be taller than the spires of the Ladychapel. Strung between them like the laces of a corset were countless chains, brown and red with ancient rust.

"The House of Chains," Malden said aloud.

"What do you see, lad? Tell me what you fucking see," Slag demanded from underneath his cloak.

"A doorway tall enough for the Bloodgod to walk through without bowing. Chains as thick as Mörget's waist, unbroken for centuries."

"Aye, that's the place." Slag wrestled with the cloak until one of his eyes peered out of the shadows. "Oh, aye."

They climbed as high as the horses could take them, intending to reach the entrance before sunset. The hills refused to make it easy. They had to force their mounts over long stretches of broken rock and up through a defile where some house-sized stone had cracked in half, leaving a passage as narrow as a man's outstretched arms. They emerged into a barren waste of stones that shifted danger-ously underfoot, where only a few sparse clumps of grass grew up through the scree.

It was as desolate a waste as Malden could imagine. A thin cold wind touched the rocks with icy fingers, while thin rivulets of water trickled past below the fallen stones. Had he been told no human being had entered that land in a thousand years, Malden would not have been surprised.

He was quite startled, then—as was Croy's horse—when an emaciated man wearing nothing but a loincloth stood up from behind a rock and hailed them all.

Croy wheeled his horse around to keep it from bolting. One of his hands reached down to touch the pommel of Ghostcutter. The other he raised in a gesture of greeting.

"Well met, Sir Croy," the stranger said. His voice was scratchy and thin, as if he had not used it in many months. "I am Herward, a humble servant of the Lady."

"You know me?" Croy asked.

Malden didn't like this at all.

The hermit bowed low and touched the stones. "We have never before met," he said, as if this were a small, unimportant detail. "Yet I know you! For one night, as I lay in my stony bower, a vision came to me in my sleep. A dream, you may well call it! Yet 'twas as clear as day, and as vivid. I was told of your coming."

Malden tried to catch Mörget's eye, but the barbarian had backed his horse a few steps and was focused entirely on the hermit.

"A knight of honor, bent on holy quest. With him a mighty warrior of the East, and a lady who must be pro-tected at all cost."

"Don't forget a pissed-off dwarf," Slag insisted, "and a thi—" He glanced at Malden, who realized he'd been about to say "thief." "An, erm, a whatever the hell this idiot is."

"Well met, Herward," Croy said. He took his hand off the pommel of his sword and reached out with both hands, as if he would embrace the hermit. "If you serve the Lady, you are my friend, and I thank you for this welcome. What else did She say, in this vision? It may be crucially important to our task."

Herward scratched viciously at his armpit. Malden could see that the skin there was already badly irritated. Now that he'd had a chance to look at the holy man, he saw just how unhealthy the poor fool was. His wild hair and beard had fallen out in patches where ringworm and probably mange had afflicted him. His sun-baked skin was so dry it cracked around his nails and in other places looked as scaly as snakeskin. His eyes were as yellow as his teeth.

How long had this man been living in these rocks, with no human company at all? Malden couldn't guess. Yet he had heard tales before of madmen, seized by holy zeal, who sought out the truly desolate places, there to worship in silence and utter privacy. He'd heard there were holy men who went to live at the bottom of abandoned dwarven mines, so they could be closer to the Bloodgod and his pit. Then there was supposed to be a hermit in the hills above Redweir who only came out to scream obscenities and throw his own waste at passing caravans. The drovers who passed that way considered it good luck to be so assaulted.

From what he could see, Herward was just as crazy. Malden tried to get the jennet to take a step back, out of range of flying excrement.

The hermit stared at Croy for a long while, saying nothing. Then he pulled at his beard and said, "She showed me your face, and his, and hers. She said I must aid you in any way I could, and allow you to pass as high as the gates of the House of Chains. She said I would be rewarded."

"In what aspect did She appear to you?" Croy asked.

Malden's eyes widened. Was the knight really taking this seriously?

Herward bent low and placed his forehead against the rocks. He was certainly limber for someone who probably lived on lichens and whatever grubs he could dig out of the stones. "She appeared to me in the form of the Crone. As an aged women, bent with the blessings of motherhood and the bounty of long years. She had hair the color of old iron, and a fearsome cast to her eyes."

Cythera slumped in her saddle and covered her mouth with one hand. "Oh, Mother, tell me you didn't . . ." she moaned, though not so loud that Herward might hear.

# CHAPTER TWENTY-FOUR

"Please," Herward said, "let me show you what meager hospitality remains in my power." The hermit started walking away without another word. Malden got his jennet moving to follow, but when he looked back he realized he was the only one to do so. He looked at the others, wondering what was going on.

Cythera moved her horse near to Croy's courser and whispered something in his ear. He nodded, and the two of them cut away from the group, heading up the hill rather than following the holy man. Mörget had taken up a position near the head of the trail, where he could watch their rear, as if he expected the shire reeve and an army of knights to come after them. Slag stared up at the entrance to the Vincularium, perhaps impatient to get inside after so long on the road.

"Come along," Malden said to the dwarf, and with a curse or two the dwarf followed where the hermit led. He left Mörget to his own business.

The thief and the dwarf headed back down the hillside

a way, then up another slope where the horses had trouble finding solid footing. The hermit climbed over the rocks like a mountain goat, never looking back. As they neared the top of the hill, Malden expected to see a crumbling shack or perhaps a simple monastic cell, just big enough for one hermit to crouch inside.

He was not expecting to find a fortress up there.

Not that it was such a grand thing, really. The structure could have been dropped into the Market Square of Ness and fit easily. It was not so large as a castle, nor so well made. Its walls were of unmortared stone piled together in thick sloping walls. It showed signs of immense age, one whole wall having been smothered by clinging vines, its stones bleached white by centuries of sun. Yet it looked strong enough to withstand a cavalry charge, or even a siege if it came to that. It had towers at two of its corners, though one had collapsed into a pile of rubble. A massive iron gate stood rusting at its front.

A hundred men could have barracked inside its walls. From that position they could hold off a small army. They also had a perfect view of the entrance to the Vincularium, and with longbows they could hold off anyone who attempted to enter the tomb, or leave it.

"Was this place built before the Vincularium was sealed?" Malden asked.

"Oh, no. After," Herward assured him. "A hundred men waited here, for a hundred years, to make sure the door stayed sealed."

"They must have feared the elves greatly," Malden said, as the hermit shoved on the creaking iron gate and gestured for them to ride inside.

"Oh, the Elders were deadly warriors," Herward agreed. "Every man of that race was skilled with a blade. Their archers could outshoot any man now living. Worse still, they didn't fight like honest men. They would come out of the trees just long enough to slaughter a few of us, then slip back into the forest again where we could never find them."

"The Elders?" Malden asked.

Slag explained. "That's what the elves called themselves. They believed that dwarves, humans, goblins, and the rest were all descended from them. That we were all degenerate sports of their master race."

"They had some terrible magic as well," Herward went on. "They could butcher a man in his sleep from a hundred miles away, if they only had a hair from his head or a piece of cloth he'd once worn. Why, just giving an elf your name was enough. They could use it, gain power over you. You understand why we had to kill them all."

Malden climbed down from the jennet and tied her to a post in the yard of the fortress. The place was a husk, he saw, nothing but a few walls still standing after so much time. A ruin.

"The war lasted for twenty years. Half a man's life, but the blink of an eye to them. Here. Let me show you something I've found," Herward said, his face lighting up with joy. He rushed through what had been a doorway—now it was just a hole in one wall—and busied himself in the shadowy room beyond. "Come in, come in!" he called. "Come see the prizes of my collection."

Malden approached, and then stopped when he smelled the place. It must be where Herward lived, he thought, though it was also possible he used it as his privy. Maybe both. "So you collect things?"

"Yes! Come see!"

"You don't collect your own droppings, though?" Malden asked, just to be sure.

The hermit poked his head out through the empty doorway again. "What are you talking about?"

"Your, ah—your . . . Slag?"

The dwarf dropped from the back of his colt with a thud. "He's asking if you save your own shit. To throw at folks, or some other barmy purpose."

"Shit," Herward said, as if he'd only heard the word once, many years before. "Shit. Oh, no. I don't defecate."

That got Mörget's attention. The barbarian had stopped just inside the gate, perhaps expecting a trap. "Every man shits," he said.

Herward shrugs. "I don't eat, you see. The Lady sustains me on black mead. No, I haven't tasted food in nearly a year. So I don't defecate. I do urinate quite often." He gestured again. "Now, please, come here!"

Malden and Slag approached the doorway but didn't step inside. The room beyond was hard to see, but it must have been an arsenal at some point. Bundles of swords and spears filled all the available space. Suits of armor hung from the ceiling, as if knights of old were sleeping up there in net hammocks. The armor looked subtly wrong to Malden, until he realized that the breastplates were far too slender for a human rib cage, and the helmets too long.

Moreover, all of the weapons and armor gleamed like gold.

"There was a battle here, long ago. The Elders fought a running retreat all the way to the entrance of the House of Chains, with the combined army of our king and all his bannermen hounding their heels. Many died on both sides. Now, so long hence, I still find their things here out among the rocks. When I find a good piece, I bring it back here to polish it and bang out the dents with a hammer." Herward squinted at them. "Not sure why I do it. Maybe to help pass the time. Look at this."

He handed Malden a shortsword with a square tip. The blade was notched and quite dull, but had not rusted to pieces like an iron sword would. It didn't feel quite as heavy as he'd expected, though.

"Bronze," Slag said.

"Are you sure?" Malden asked. It had occurred to him that Herward had so many golden swords he might not notice if one went missing. "It's not gold?"

"I'm a fucking dwarf. I know my metals. That's bronze."

Herward nodded happily. "The Elders wouldn't touch

iron. Supposedly it interfered with their magic. Everything they made was of copper or bronze or brass."

Malden made a pass through the air with the sword. "Well, that explains how we were able to beat them, eh? We had iron weapons. Clearly superior."

"Bronze is as strong as iron, and carries just as sharp an edge," Slag told him. "Also—it never rusts. It gets a nice patina, but it never corrodes. You come back here in a thousand years, these swords will be just as strong."

"There has to be something wrong with bronze," Malden pointed out, "since we won with our iron."

"It's more expensive, is your main downside."

"Then we . . . we won because we were . . . our hearts were pure, or some such," Malden said, trying to remember old stories he'd heard as a child. "Because our cause was just?"

"You beat them by outbreeding them," Slag said. "An elf lived near on a century, and never had more than one child. You lot bred like rats when you came over here."

Malden frowned. He wasn't sure what that meant. "What do you mean, when we came over here? We've always lived on this land."

Herward clucked his tongue.

"Wrong again," Slag explained. "A thousand years ago this whole country was covered in a thick forest, right? All those fields of wheat were so many trees. Nobody ever cut them down, so they grew thick. My people, the dwarves, lived under the ground, and we had no use for that much wood. The elves lived in the forest, aboveground. Then the humans came, from the south. First they were just explorers. Looking for new lands to name after themselves. The elves laughed at the idea, but they didn't drive you off, because they didn't know what was coming. We barely even knew you were here, because you didn't dig deep enough to disturb us. Should have paid more attention. It was missionaries, what came next. Then traders, and trappers, and then followed the fucking settlers. They had families that had to be fed. Every generation of humans chopped down more trees, to make more room for their fields. Finally the elves started noticing what you were doing to their homeland."

"What happened then?" Malden asked.

Slag flicked the sword with his fingers to make it ring, a high piercing note like two blades coming together. "You weren't the kind to leave peaceful like, not once you had your sodding big paws on a piece of earth. So it came down to you or the elves. This is where you finally wiped them out."

Malden looked out through the gates of the fort, at the entrance to the Vincularium on the opposite slope. Though he could read and write and do figures, he'd never had any formal education. Certainly no one had ever told him this dark secret of his own history.

# CHAPTER TWENTY-FIVE

Croy followed Cythera as she turned her horse up the ancient road that led up the mountain. "He seems a pleasant enough fellow," he told her, because she'd said she wanted to get away and talk about Herward.

"I'm sure he's harmless," she said. "You should know, however, that he is not communing with your goddess."

Croy frowned. "You doubt his sincerity?"

"I doubt his sanity. I know for a fact he didn't see us in a holy vision. You heard the way he described the Lady in his dream. It didn't sound familiar?"

"He described the Crone, which is one of the Lady's primary aspects. She might also have appeared as the Mother, or the Maiden. Why She chose one over the other is a mystery to me, but She rarely reveals her plans to us."

"He was describing my mother," Cythera told him.

Croy shook his head. "Now that's just silly—"

"My mother is a witch," Cythera said. "As you know. Placing visions in the minds of lunatics is hardly stretching her powers. She must have sent him this vision the same day that we left Ness."

"It's blasphemy to impersonate the Lady," Croy said. He thought of the witch, safe and comfortable in her lair in Ness, reaching across the world to cloud the minds of men, and he wanted to—well, he wasn't sure what he wanted to do. Certainly rushing back to the city to slay his prospective mother-in-law didn't feel like the kind of thing a noble knight would go in for. But surely there must be some retribution.

"She was only trying to protect us. She wanted someone to watch over us. And Herward can definitely be of help. For instance, we can't very well take our horses inside the Vincularium. Someone needs to watch over them."

"I had considered that," Croy said. "I was hoping we could give you the task."

Cythera sighed. She stopped her horse in the middle of the road. "I thought you might say that. I'm sure you've spent this entire journey trying to think of ways to keep me from entering the tomb with you."

"It won't be safe for a woman. There's a demon in there."

"Croy, I can take care of myself. I'm not some helpless damsel to be locked away in a tower." She dismounted and rubbed her horse's nose for a while, before dropping her reins to the ground. The palfrey was well trained, and knew that was the signal to stay put. She proceeded on foot, then, toward the massive gates of the Vincularium.

They were far more imposing from close up. The massive square pillars rose to dizzying heights above Croy's head, and the chains between them proved so thick and solid that he could not begin to imagine how they had been forged. While rust pocked the surface of the iron, there was no doubt in his mind those chains would last another thousand years before they corroded away.

Behind the chains, recessed from the menhirs, stood a solid wall of enormous granite bricks, sealed with black mortar. The dwarven thorn rune—sign of death and destruction—had been carved deeply into each of the bricks, a warning to anyone who might try to unseal this massive portal.

Croy took a step closer and something crunched under his boot. He looked down and saw a scorched human skull staring up at him with empty eye sockets.

"Cythera, don't look," he said. The bones could only distress her. He glanced around his feet and saw more bones there, some shattered, some black with soot. He saw bits of cloth and metal amidst the bones, but no swords or armor. Were these the remains of past grave robbers? "And don't come closer. In fact, get back on your horse and ride back to the others. This isn't a good place."

She was already walking past him, however. "These chains—what purpose do they serve?" she asked.

"What?" Croy replied. He was trying to kick broken shards of bone off his foot. "They held in the elves, of course."

"No, they didn't." She was dangerously close to the entrance. "They attach to nothing but the columns. They do not brace the seal, or even touch it. They're just strung across the gate, so that anyone trying to enter must duck underneath them. Yet that could hardly slow down an elfin warrior."

"Wait," Croy shouted as she ducked to look under the chains. "Don't—"

He rushed toward her, but as he came close to the lowest chain he felt a sudden, searing pain in his head. Sweat burst across his back and he felt dizzy. The whole world started to spin. He reached out to steady himself, hand up to grab the chain above him, when he felt Cythera's hands push against his chest and he went sprawling backward.

The heat and disorientation left him instantly, though he was already overbalanced and fell to clatter among the bones.

"They're cursed," Cythera said. "The chains are charged with magical power—Croy, get away, quickly. There are currents in the ether here, wild eddies, and I can feel the puissance growing—it's going to discharge!"

Croy desperately wanted to get up and run. Yet he could never leave Cythera there, alone and defenseless. He struggled to his feet and lurched forward, intending to grab her. He saw terror streak across her face and was certain they were both about to die.

Then she reached up, with both hands, and grabbed a link of the chains.

Croy lacked the special senses that allowed witches and sorcerers to view the winds of magical energy that swept through the world. He could not feel the lethal power that flowed into Cythera then, nor the shockwave that burst outward from her body and swept across the land.

Yet he could see the painted flowers and vines that erupted across her face and hands, as if an invisible tattooist were working with demonic speed to cover every portion of her flesh. Vivid roses and tulips bloomed and withered on her cheeks and forehead. Creepers wrapped around her wrists and fingers, growing a thousand times faster than the plants they resembled. Her fair skin turned dark with the painted vegetation, until he could no longer make out her facial features at all.

"Cythera!" he shouted, because she was gasping in pain.

"I can't contain it," she moaned. "So much—so much power!"

This was the gift Coruth had given to her daughter.

Cythera was immune to magic in all its forms, for rather than pervading her, arcane energies could only crawl upon her skin in the form of images. As Croy watched, the brambles on her neck thickened and sprouted long, vicious thorns. The flowers on her palms dripped with poison. Malevolent eyes peered out from behind the leaves that curled and dried up on her chest.

"I have to release it. Croy—get back!" she screamed.

The more magical energy she stored in her skin, the more likely Cythera was to release it inadvertently. She could only hold so much. If she touched Croy now, all that power would flow into his body, and he had no protection from its evil. He scuttled backward, all thoughts of saving her flown from his mind.

Moving with terrible slowness, careful not to release her burden before she was ready, Cythera climbed through the chains and made her way to the brick seal beyond. Then she thrust her palms against the stone blocks, and the painted flowers on her skin writhed and twisted as if they were being consumed in an inferno.

Under her hands the bricks shimmered and glowed. Light seeped out from between her fingers as the stone seethed and bubbled and flowed. A stream of red-hot molten rock oozed down the face of the seal, then rolled across the ground to lick at the scorched bones. Croy rushed back and got the horses clear before the burning stone could reach them.

In the cold air the molten rock cooled quickly, like candle wax on a table. Though still hot to the touch, it stopped glowing and lay still. When Croy was certain he would not be incinerated, he hurried forward to search for Cythera. He was very careful not to touch the chains, though this time he did not feel dizzy when he approached them. Cythera must have absorbed the magic that had previously coursed through them.

He found her by the seal. A broad fissure had been

melted right through the bricks. At its base the fissure was wide enough for a man to crawl through. Beyond, past the seal, was only darkness.

Cythera sat on the ground near the opening, hugging her knees to her chest. She was weeping, but her skin was clear. There was not a single tattoo anywhere on her that he could see.

"It's open," she said. "We can go in now."

# PART III

# Some Light Grave Robbing Required

# INTERLUDE

The keeper of the milehouse known as the Astrologer always thought he had been blessed with the perfect life. There was a steady trade on the road between Redweir and Helstrow, so he was not reliant for his income on the local farmers. He was close enough to the king's fortress that bandits never raided his house. Having once been the son of a farmer, expected to follow in his father's footsteps and work a tiny strip of land until he was bent double and decrepit at twenty-five, he counted himself especially lucky that now his main occupation was giving orders to serving boys and pouring the occasional tankard of ale.

The night the priest came, however, the keeper would gladly have traded places with the lowest serf in Skrae.

"I have simply come for my property. Once it is in my possession, I will leave peacefully," the priest said. He didn't look like so much, this little man from Ness who dressed in an undyed habit. The knife in his hand was tiny, the blade no longer than a child's finger.

When he'd come in demanding information, the keeper had been busy counting the coins in his till. Figures were not the keeper's strong suit and he'd lost track. He supposed he might have been a little abrupt when he told the priest to have a seat and shut his mouth.

He'd had no idea how fast things would happen then, how the knife would blur through the air, while the priest's face transformed into the countenance of something from the Bloodgod's pit.

The keeper stared down at the cut on his arm. It was only perhaps an inch long but it was bleeding furiously.

He pressed down hard on the wound with a bar towel but in seconds the cloth was red right through. "I'm telling ye, friend—I don't know anything of what you're asking! I never heard naught of this shire reeve. Please, just let me bandage this—"

The priest never raised his voice. He never got angry. But the knife in his hand flicked back and forth, cutting at the air. "You're lying to me. The shire reeve wrote me just days ago. The message was posted from this house. He claimed he had my property and that I could come collect it at my leisure. Well, here I am. Where is the shire reeve? Where is what is owed to me? Should you lie to me again, I'll cut your other arm."

The keeper of the house looked up at his patrons, a dozen or so assorted merchants, tradesmen of various occupations, and three dwarves up from Redweir. They had all jumped back from their tables, abandoning both food and drink to press up against the smoke-stained walls. He'd get no help from that quarter.

"There was a man—a day or two back, sure," the keeper said. He was beginning to feel faint, probably just from the fear. He took a step back, away from the priest, and nearly slipped on the pool of his own blood that was ruining his floor. "Might have been a reeve of one sort or another. I didn't see if he carried no white stick, but mayhap that was just under his cloak. He had the look of a lawman."

"Good," the priest said. "That's a good start."

"Figured he was just playin' at it, though, for he skipped out before he paid his bill. Figured he was some tricky thief."

"He was an official of the crown. Now. As to my property."

"I know nothing 'bout that," the keeper said. "Please!" he begged as the knife came toward him again. "Please—whatever it was, whatever it was worth, take it out of my till, and be welcome to it! Just—just put the knife away. I beg you!"

"All your coin won't pay what I'm owed," the priest said. "I've come for a man, a bondservant who ran away from me. His name is Malden. What of him?"

"Malton, you say?" the keeper asked. "I'm not so good with names—"

"A slender fellow, of no great height. Wears a green cloak. He would be traveling with a number of companions—accomplices in his flight."

"Aye, aye!" the keeper almost laughed with relief. "Aye, they were here, too, the same night as your reeve. He was with a fancy looking gentleman, a lady, and a dwarf. And—And a great big dog-hearted bastard with half his face painted red. That one they made sleep in the stables like the wild man he was. Now, *they* paid their bill, and left before dawn the next day. Please—no more!"

The knife was inches from the keeper's face. It seemed to float in the air, as if unconnected to the priest's hand. The keeper could see his own reflection in its red-smeared blade.

"One more question, only, and then I'll give you my thanks and take my leave."

"Anything! I'll tell ye anything!" Whether it was true or not, the keeper decided. This was not a man who accepted "I don't know" as a correct answer.

"When they left, which way were they headed?"

The keeper belched mightily as a wave of nausea swept through him. He had no idea how to answer that. He hadn't watched the travelers depart—he'd been inside, fast asleep, and only knew they'd gone because the stable boy told him so. He had to guess now what the priest wanted to hear. And if he guessed wrong—

"They headed east," someone said.

The knife was gone. The keeper sagged backward against the bar, unable to stand a moment longer. The priest was across the room now, standing over a man wearing the mask of an itinerant barber-surgeon.

"They headed east," the man repeated. "I'm coming

from that direction, and I passed them just as they left the road. It looked like they were headed down to the river, though for what purpose I can't imagine."

"You've been very helpful," the priest said. The knife disappeared and he smiled at everyone in the room, taking his time to beam at each patron in turn. "I do apologize for the excitement. Please, go back to your meals. I will not keep you any longer."

And with that he left, headed back out into the night. As easy as that.

The barber-surgeon rushed over to where the keeper lay, facedown on his own bar, his legs tangled in the stools. With deft hands the healer pulled the bar rag away from the wounded man's arm and studied the cut. "By the Lady's elbows," he swore.

"It's just . . . a little scratch," the keeper insisted.

"He pierced the major vein of your arm without so much as palpating for it," the barber-surgeon insisted. He reached for a pouch at his belt and brought forth a long strip of dirty bandage. "It normally takes me three tries to find that vein, even when my patient is restrained so I can take my time. Who was that man? Where did he train? At the University at Vijn, perhaps? They bring up fine doctors there, it's said." The barber-surgeon worked quickly at stanching the flow of blood.

"Will I live?" the keeper asked.

"Oh, surely," the barber-surgeon told him. "Eat plenty of fish taken from a cold stream, and purge three times a day with an emetic I give you, and you'll be back on your feet in no time. Of course, the wound might fester and then you'll lose the arm. But you'll definitely survive."

"Excuse me," someone said, but the keeper couldn't see who it was. "Excuse me. Hey! Down fucking here!"

Despite how faint he felt, the keeper leaned over the side of the bar and looked down to see one of the dwarves staring up at him. The keeper was used to getting dwarves in, since there were so many of them at Redweir and they often traveled to Helstrow on business. He'd barely been aware of the three of them before this, except for the fact that one of them was female. You almost never saw female dwarves this far south.

The one addressing him was male, a skinny, tiny fellow with a bushy beard and hair like a mop that should have been thrown out years ago. His eyes were beady and dark but they shone with purpose.

"You said somewhat about a wild man, with a face painted red?"

The keeper frowned. Not again, he thought—no more questions! "Aye," he replied. "Now, if you don't mind, I'm—"

"He was traveling with the other bunch? You're sure of it? Think hard on it, man. This is important!"

"Aye, aye, you daft little thing," the keeper growled. There were spots dancing before his eyes. That couldn't be good, could it?

"And they went east? Toward the forest there, and the mountains beyond? You weren't lying just to throw that other fucker off the track? Excuse me! I need to know this!"

The barber-surgeon answered for the keeper, who was having trouble breathing properly. "Yes, yes, just as I told that butcher. East!"

The dwarf nodded and ran back to his fellows. They whispered amongst themselves for a moment, then raced out of the common room in the direction of the stables. The keeper never saw them again.

At least they'd paid in advance.

# CHAPTER TWENTY-SIX

The five of them made a simple camp just outside the seal. There they ate a final meal in the sunlight before heading in. Mörget roasted the cave beetle steaks and served out large portions to each of them. "We'll need our strength," he explained. "We may be in there for several hours before we find the demon."

Malden stared at the meat he was given. It was white and stringy and still attached to a piece of shriveled shell. "I've always found it best to exercise on an empty stomach," he protested.

"Don't be such a ninny," Cythera said, laughing at him.

Malden felt his cheeks grow red. He took a small bite of the meat, and was surprised, to say the least. "Ha! This is actually pretty good. A little like crabmeat. And a bit like venison." He ate it all, and then had another serving. There was none left by the time Herward came up to their camp, his nose twitching in the air.

"I smelled your repast," the hermit said. "Not that I would ever consume flesh. Oh, no. Never. But I'll admit the odor was tempting."

Croy shrugged. "Then I am glad to say we have nothing to offer you, for I would hate to lead any man to sin."

"Yes . . . that is good." Malden could hear Herward's stomach rumbling. "It is what She would want—"

The holy man stopped speaking then. He seemed transfixed as if by a vision.

Malden followed his gaze and saw him looking at the entrance to the Vincularium.

"The Lady be praised," Herward said, staring in mortal dread at the opening in the seal. "She has ordained that what was closed, now may be opened."

Malden rolled his eyes but said nothing. In his experience it was a bad idea to try to disillusion the religiously insane. Herward's cosmology depended on everything that happened making perfect sense in the context of his faith. Upsetting that turnip cart would do no one any good.

"The chains?" Herward asked. "They were enchanted . . ."

Cythera put a hand on the hermit's shoulder. "The crone of your vision allowed the enchantment to be removed," she said. Malden silently applauded her tact. What she said was entirely true. It was Coruth who had appeared in that vision, and it was also Coruth who had given Cythera the power to drain the curses from the chains. "Clearly she approves of our enterprise."

Herward nodded. His eyes weren't focusing, Malden saw—they were looking at something invisible. The hermit dropped to his knees, his hands clutched together before him. "The Lady be praised! How long have I waited for this! I've spent years of my life studying the Elders, winkling out their secrets. How many times have I dreamt of this, of walking up here and finding the way open. How much can I learn from this place? I cannot begin to tell you what this means!"

Mörget laughed. Cythera shot the barbarian a nasty look, but Mörget simply shrugged. "Why then, little man, it should be your honor to go inside before us!"

Herward turned toward the barbarian and for a moment his eyes cleared and Malden could tell he was gripped by a sudden fit of lucidity. "Inside?" he asked. "Actually . . . go inside?"

He turned to face the opening. That dark, forbidding hole in the seal where the breath of ancient times stirred restlessly. Anything could be in there, anything at all, but most likely nothing friendly.

Every eye was on Herward as he took a step forward, then another. Even from a distance Malden could see how badly the hermit's hands shook. Herward reached up carefully toward one of the chains, but his hand didn't make contact. Instead, he cleared his throat, and stood up straighter, and said, "No. No . . . the vision was clear. I am to aid you, not join you. Someone must stay here and see to your things, yes?"

Croy walked over to the hermit and nodded sagely. "It's what She would wish, I think."

"Indeed. Her name be praised," Herward said, and rushed back to stand behind Mörget and Slag, who were the farthest from the opening.

Croy stayed where he was. The knight bent down and looked into the hole, and Malden saw that he wasn't shaking at all. If anything, Croy looked like he was about to run forward and squeeze himself inside, to get at the demon in there as fast as possible.

Malden had to admit that Croy had courage. He supposed that was what made him a knight in the first place—that willingness to throw himself into danger for a noble cause. For the first time in a while, he realized he actually admired the man.

"Malden," Croy said, "would you be so kind as to take a look, and say if we must proceed?"

"Me?" Malden asked.

But then he remembered why he'd been brought along on this journey. He was the one who was supposed to clear the Vincularium of its deadly traps.

Maybe he should have run off for Helstrow after all, and taken his chances with the law. Nothing for it now, though. He came up next to Croy and then crouched down to look at the hole. "It looks big enough for us to crawl through," he said, rubbing his chin. He reached up to touch the stone where it had warped and flowed. It was cool to the touch now. "And I suppose there are worse ways to enter a place than through the front door."

"Not your usual method of ingress, eh?" Slag asked. The dwarf peered into the darkness beyond the opening and pulled at his beard.

"In my line, the back door is often preferred, yes. Let's

take a look." Malden lit a lantern and shone its light inside. He saw dull-colored rock, mostly. A wraith of mist swirled inside the opening, droplets of water catching some subterranean breeze and then flinging themselves outward, through his light. Nothing moved in there. Most like, nothing had moved in there for centuries.

He started to crawl inside, but Croy grabbed his shoulder and pulled him back. "Herward is saying a prayer for us," the knight told him.

"Oh, good. I'd hate to go in there without divine sanction."

The prayer was a long one, but Malden consoled himself with the knowledge that the holy man would be taking care of his horse while he was inside. For free. When it was done, Malden looked at Mörget, who was sharpening his axe with a whetstone. At Slag, who was trying to peer around Malden's arm for a better look inside. At Cythera, who failed to meet his gaze. And then at Croy, who set his jaw in a determined angle.

"Shall we go inside now?" Malden asked, and gestured toward the opening.

"You first," Slag suggested.

# CHAPTER TWENTY-SEVEN

Malden crawled forward on his hands and knees a few feet and then slowly stood up. The light coming in through the fissure behind him illuminated no more than a patch of marble floor. On either side, and as far above him as he could imagine, lay nothing but darkness and stale air.

His eyes burned with the dark almost at once. His skin tingled and the hair on the back of his neck stood up. Because his vision was next to useless, his other senses leapt to fill the gap in what he could perceive. He heard water dripping, somewhere far off. The echoes it made seemed to roll across vast smooth expanses of stone. He smelled the must of centuries, old dust and a hint of decay. His fingertips felt extremely sensitive, as if he could reach for the great darkness before him and stroke it like fur.

Not that he would probably want to.

No one had been in that room for centuries, he thought. And the last people to come through this way—the elves—had good reason to regret it. They must have believed they'd found a safe haven, a place they could fortify in their war against humanity. Instead they'd found their deaths.

Would the darkness in such a place, abandoned for so long, begin to congeal? Would it take on some semblance of life—or at least, harbor some emotion? Malden told himself he was just being silly. That the still air inside the Vincularium could not become angry on its own. There were probably ghosts inside, remnants of the elves who'd perished here. There was certainly a demon in there. But the Vincularium itself was just a pile of old stone. It could not resent his presence. It couldn't hate him, or want him to leave.

No matter how much it felt that way.

"Is it safe?" Croy said from behind him.

Malden couldn't help but jump. He didn't turn around—he imagined the daylight outside would be blinding after his eyes had adjusted to the darkness. Instead he fought to control his breathing and said, "Nothing has jumped out to devour me yet."

He was aware of the others coming in behind him. He could hear them grunting and scraping their way through the narrow opening, each of them in their turn struck dumb once they were inside by the profundity of the darkness. Mörget took a step forward to put down one of their crates of supplies, and the rustling of the barbarian's clothes was like summer thunder reverberating off rain-lashed hills.

Croy lit a lantern, a great flaring light that made Malden blink as his eyes watered. The candle inside the lantern flickered wildly in some unfelt breeze and then steadied, and light streamed out across the open space of stone.

The marble floor stretched ahead as far as the light showed. A pair of stout, twisted columns held up a roof that was high enough that the light couldn't show it, leaving it shrouded in pitch-darkness. Something moved on one of the columns, inching through the lantern's glow, and Malden nearly turned and dashed back out of the Vincularium, but then he saw it was only a millipede, no longer than his finger. Its glossy shell was translucent and he could see its clear blood surging through its body. Lifting feathery antennae into the dusty air, the insect turned and started crawling away from the light.

Mörget started forward, one fist raised as if he would smash the thing.

"Be careful," Croy whispered. "We don't know what we're walking into."

Mörget grumbled with impatience, but he stepped back again.

Cythera lit another lantern and pressed it into Malden's hand. It had a looping handle on one side and he gripped it hard, like a man dying of thirst will grab onto a tankard of ale.

"So far so good," Cythera said. She smiled at him. Obviously she meant to reassure him, but the light streaming upward across her face made dark pools of her eyes and made her look much more like a witch than Coruth ever had. He expected her to start cackling at any moment.

"There should be an exit from this room straight ahead," Slag said, gesturing into the dark.

"All right," Malden said. "I'll make sure it's safe."

He was known in certain discreet circles as a master
at evading traps. He'd bested the houses of sorcerers and
the palaces of nobles because he could keep his wits about
him and he knew when to step lightly. In all the Free City
of Ness there was no one more qualified for it. And only
a fool would think the way into the Vincularium would be
free of pitfalls or snares. Dwarves were famous for their
mistrust of interlopers and trespassers. The places they
built underground were never meant for human intrusion,
and over the centuries they'd become geniuses at constructing deadly surprises as a way of safeguarding their
premises.

They also tended to have a lot of treasure, which attracted thieves. Over time those of Malden's profession
had learned ways to overcome or simply avoid dwarven
traps. Of course, the traditional way to do that was to send
one person forward ahead of the group, and if they didn't
die screaming in some horrible contraption, then you knew
the way was safe. It looked to Malden like had been chosen
for that honorable role.

He stepped out between the columns, careful to test
the marble under his feet with each step. More columns
loomed out of the darkness, perhaps a whole row of them.
That was the obvious path, the way anyone coming inside
would be expected to take. Safer to take the long way
around. He turned to his left and raised his lantern high.
There was a wall in that direction, so he moved slowly
toward it and then reached out to touch it with one finger.
The wall shone under his light, and he saw it was made
of the same polished marble as the floor. A frieze ran along
the wall just a little above Malden's eye level, carved with
dwarven runes he couldn't read.

"Slag," he called, and his voice boomed in the stone
hall so much that he ducked his head and pressed his back
against the stones. "Slag," he said, in a much softer voice,
"can you read this inscription?"

The dwarf came out of the dark toward him and peered

upward at the frieze. His mouth moved silently for a while as he read. "Names, that's all. It's a standard formula," Slag said, when he'd read enough. "It lists the dwarves who built this place, as well as the names of their fathers."

"I was worried it might be warning us that only death awaited those who passed through this hall," Malden said. That was the kind of thing he expected to find in a forbidden crypt.

"This was a city, before it was a tomb," Slag told him. "When we lived here, there would have been fires burning all day and night in this room, and cups so full of mead you would never see their bottoms. This room would have been used for receiving visitors from the surface—elves or humans, anyone willing to trade with us." He shook his head. "No, this was not a place of death, lad. Not till later."

Malden nodded and headed forward, along the wall. He was trying to get a sense of its dimensions, but that proved difficult when his light couldn't reach all the corners at once. The columns ran beside him, one every fifteen feet or so. Then he came to the far wall, and turned to his right, and moved forward again. Eventually he came to a wide stone door, no more than six feet high, mounted in a stone arch. The latch of the door was simply designed and had no lock. Cool air streamed through the crack between the bottom of the door and its jamb. He checked its hinges and all along its top, and found nothing to worry him.

"All right," he said, "come the way I did, all of you. I think it's safe."

Croy, Cythera, and Mörget came quickly to join him. Slag seemed to be taking his time. Before he entered the circle of light shed by Malden's lantern, they heard him snuffling, and when the light touched him it gleamed on the tears in the corners of his eyes.

Malden panicked a little, but fought his fear back down. "Slag—what is it?" he asked. "What's wrong?"

"Nothing, lad, nothing. I just feel like I've come home, is all."

# CHAPTER TWENTY-EIGHT

The door opened easily on its hinges. It didn't even creak. After eight hundred years, that was a small miracle—but Malden knew that dwarves built things to last.

Beyond lay a passage with smooth walls that curved down. A bronze handrail ran along the wall at waist height for a dwarf. Its shine was gone with age, but it ran unbroken as far as Malden could see. He stepped into the passage, and when nothing tried to kill him, exhaled deeply. Then he started downward. The others followed more slowly.

"Take care," Cythera said.

"My eyes are open. Yet most likely," Malden said, "we won't run into a trap for a while." He was expecting to find traps near the entrance, because they would have been needed back when this place was closed up. Something was required to keep the elves inside long enough for the exit to be sealed behind them. He was trying to think like a human general who died centuries before he was born. How would you layer your defenses? You expected the elves to try to break out en masse. "The barrier Cythera brought down would have been more effective if you weren't expecting it—if the elves thought the way to freedom was clear. So there should be a good open run between the chains and the next trap. Also, we're going the wrong direction, as far as the trap-makers were concerned. They *wanted* the elves to come down here unhindered. They just also wanted to make sure they didn't get out again. So the traps will be laid to stop elves coming from inside, heading out. So it's possible we'll walk right past a trap without setting it off, because it only works one way. Of course, we need to find that trap anyway, since we'll be coming back this way on our way out."

Croy looked skeptical. "What makes you think there will be any more traps at all? There was enough power in those chains to decimate an army."

Malden laughed. "I suppose there was. But you're a soldier, Croy. Tell me, do you put all your troops in one formation and just assume the enemy will attack head on? If you did that and they simply flanked you, you would lose every time. No, you need to have multiple ways of stopping your enemy. Herward said the elves were famous for fighting dirty, and we know the people who sealed them in here were terrified of them ever getting out. Fear can be good sometimes. Paranoia makes you think of everything. There will definitely be another trap. And it won't be magical."

"No?" Mörget asked. He looked a little foolish, ducking down to keep from striking his head on the ceiling. "Why not? Magic works."

It was Cythera who answered that. "Magic was a good choice for the trap outside—it doesn't wear off or rust or fall apart over time. But it isn't perfect. Anyone with arcane training and enough power can defeat a magical trap. And we know the elves were gifted in that regard."

Malden nodded. He lifted his lantern high and looked back. The corridor had curved enough that he could no longer see the door behind him, nor anything in front of him. Judging by the echoes of his footfalls, the downward passage went on quite a ways. "It'll be a mechanical trap. That was one advantage the humans had over the elves, superior tools and metals." He thought of something then, something nasty. "And of course, they had the dwarves helping them, didn't they?"

Slag looked away from his gaze. "Aye," he said.

"I thought so. Humans didn't put those dwarven runes on the entrance and on the block in Mörget's shaft. So the humans who drove the elves in here had dwarven allies. Which begs the question of why the elves thought they would be safe in a dwarf city."

Slag fidgeted with a piece of wire in his hands, but eventually he answered. "For a couple reasons," he said. "For one, we'd already abandoned this place. The whole dwarven race had moved north by then. We knew the bloody humans were going to take this whole land, so we just got out of their way rather than fighting them for it."

"You said there were a couple of reasons," Malden pointed out."

"Well," Slag said, "I suppose the elves didn't know whose side we were on."

"They thought you would be opposed to human intrusion as well," Croy said, running one hand along the smooth wall of the passage.

"It probably helped that we told them as much." Slag sighed deeply.

"What?" Malden asked, surprised.

"Eight hundred years ago, my people signed a treaty with yours. You didn't kill us, and we wouldn't fight you. There was more to it, of course, things we had to offer to keep you off our necks. We agreed to make steel for you, for instance. Truth be told it was a pretty lousy deal for us. We gave up a lot. But we knew it was the only fucking way we could survive." He sighed again. Malden could tell he didn't want to say any of this aloud, but felt he owed them all an explanation for some reason. "Before that, before we signed the treaty, we were actually allied with the elves."

"You were?" Croy asked.

"You have to understand," Slag went on, "when you first showed up, looking like bloody apes, waving your iron spears around and claiming this land was yours, it didn't look like you had a chance. The elves had held this land for ten thousand years, or so the story went. We figured they'd make fucking mincemeat out of you and that would be that. So of course we allied with them. We're a practical people, in case you missed that fact. But once you started winning—when the elves started losing battles and such—maybe we switched teams. And maybe we did it in secret, all right?"

"So when the elves came here, looking for shelter," Malden said, "they thought you were still their allies."

"I'm not proud of what my ancestors did, except in how if they hadn't, I wouldn't fucking be here right now. The elves came to us for assistance when they knew they were going to lose. When there were so few of them left that they couldn't keep fighting. They asked us for counsel. We told them to come down here. It was a good defensible position to make a stand. It also had a back door."

"The shaft that I found on the eastern side of the mountain," Mörget said.

"Aye. Every dwarven city has its secret exits. Usually dozens of 'em. We told the elves they could pretend to hide here, then slip out to the east. There weren't so many humans on that side, back then. The only thing they didn't realize was that when we abandoned this city it started flooding almost immediately. The exit shaft was already under the water table. If they wanted to get out that way, they were going to need to hold their breath for a long fucking time."

Mörget scowled. "I lost good men in that shaft. But it wasn't enough to flood the exit," he said.

"No. The humans didn't think so. They didn't want even one elf to get out. So they told us to block the shafts. We slid stone blocks down from above, just to make bloody sure no elf got out. Now, an elf might be able to swim enough to get to the shaft, but nobody could hold their breath long enough to knock their way through fifty tons of granite."

Malden cast his mind back through the ages and shivered. They came down this way full of hope, he thought. They marched down this very corridor thinking they were on their way to a new life. And all they found was darkness and death.

He was on the threshold of the scene of a great crime, he thought. How had his ancestors slept at night, afterward?

Probably just fine. As far as they were concerned, they had finally won a long and bitter war. One act of monumental treachery meant peace and safety for all their children. Yet surely, when they thought about what they'd done . . .

"The poor elves," Cythera said, her voice thick with emotion. Clearly her thoughts had tended the same way Malden's had.

"Don't pity them overmuch," Croy insisted. "They were evil, after all. A decadent and cruel race. They slaughtered our missionaries in ways I won't describe while a lady is listening. They worshipped nothing but their own ancestors. They even sacrificed their own people for magical power."

Malden thought of what Slag had said, how he defined evil. It was what you called your vanquished enemies when you wrote the scrolls of history later. How much of what Croy said was true, and how much was made up after the fact, as an excuse for what had been done?

"What needed to be done, was done," Mörget insisted. "That's all. You win a war any way you can, and worry about the casualties later."

# CHAPTER TWENTY-NINE

When Malden found the trap, he had to smile. It was the most elegant kind of trap, and often the hardest to find—a hazard hidden in plain sight.

The spiral passage led downward for hundreds of feet

and then opened into a wide arch looking out on a natural cavern far larger than their paltry light could limn. The walls on either side of the arch were of uncut rock, rough to the touch and streaked with mineral deposits that glittered when he moved his lantern over them. The floor of the cavern was made of blocks of rough-cut basalt. He could feel how uneven they were through his soft leather shoes. It looked like the dwarves hadn't cared enough about this chamber to ever bother finishing its construction. Malden knew how thorough dwarves were, though, and he was sure that was an intentional semblance.

Running through the middle of the cavern was an enormous crevasse in the rock, a canyon carved by some turbulent subterranean river aeons ago. He could hear water rushing by at the bottom of this defile, perhaps fifty feet below. It looked like a perfectly natural feature, a crack in the earth that even the dwarves could not heal. Malden wondered if it was more than met the eye. He tied his lantern to a rope and lowered it carefully down into the crack to get a look at its walls.

Just as he'd thought, the sides of the crevasse were smoothed out by dwarven tools. Every ledge had been rounded off, every crevice filled in with mortar. If you fell down into the crack, it would be impossible to climb back up. Yet to an uninquisitive eye, it looked perfectly natural.

The dwarves had placed a bridge across it, a wide, inviting path with high rails on either side to keep passersby from falling off the edge. A dozen men could walk abreast on the bridge—or rather, a dozen soldiers could march side by side. It looked like it could easily hold their weight. Nor was it a particularly long bridge, as the crevasse was only ten feet across.

To someone like Malden, who had spent years learning to look for subtle and carefully hidden traps, it positively screamed of danger.

He stopped Mörget before the barbarian could set foot on the bridge.

"Hold," he said. "Let me take a look, first."

Mörget scowled and studied the bridge. "It looks more sound than many a bridge I've crossed over in my time."

"I have no doubt it will hold your weight—for a time," Malden said. He tied off the rope holding his lantern so both his hands would be free, then picked another rope from the supplies. "Slag, drive a spike into that stone there," he said, pointing at one of the basalt blocks, "and tie this rope to it. I trust your knots."

"Oh, any knot I tie will hold the fucking moon down," Slag insisted, perhaps thinking his workmanship was under question. He did as Malden asked, then handed the free end of the line to the thief.

"Look," Malden said, "how this end of the bridge is so well supported." He lay down on the basalt and peered underneath the bridge. A buttress of ornate stone scroll-work held it up. "Yet on the far side—it's not as strong." The buttress there was cunningly carved to look much the same as its brother, but a close inspection showed it was made of thinner beams and the scrollwork looked lighter and finer. "Mörget," he said, "take hold of this line and pay it out as I instruct."

The barbarian did as he was told. Malden crawled forward and lowered himself carefully over the edge of the crevasse. Just as he'd thought, he was unable to find handholds in the smooth rock, and could only hang from the rope like a sinker on a fishing line. As he dangled, one foot against the wall to keep himself from spinning, he looked up at the near buttress from underneath.

In his lantern light there were clear seams in the scrollwork.

Also just as he'd thought.

"Give me six more feet of line," he called, and his body jerked as the barbarian let the rope slacken and he dropped another six feet into the fissure. He had a moment of panic as he heard the hemp rope creak, but it held his weight. "All right, that should be enough."

He put both of his feet against the stone wall of the crevasse and bent his knees up to his chest. Then with one quick spring he pushed against the wall and swung out on the rope, toward the far side of the gap. His fingers splayed outward to try to grab the far buttress, but he missed entirely and swung back, barely catching himself against the near wall before he smashed his teeth out on the rock.

"Malden!" Cythera cried, her face popping over the edge so she could look down at him.

He smiled with all the bravado he could muster and gave her a cheery wave.

"All's well," he said. "I just misjudged the distance. Mörget, give me another three feet."

The rope creaked again as Malden dropped deeper into the fissure. He braced his feet once more and pushed hard for another swing. This time he managed to grab onto the far side of the crevasse and haul himself up onto its rim before the rope swung back. "More rope," he called, "and Slag, toss me a spike and your mallet." Mörget paid out the line and Malden tied it off on the far side, yanking it tight so it stretched across the fissure like a bowstring. "Now," he said, "everyone stand back."

On the far side the others did as he said. Malden approached the bridge and tapped it with his toes. It held—he expected it to—but he made a point of not putting his full weight on it. He found his balance and struck it with his foot again, this time bringing his foot down as hard as he dared.

The bridge dropped under his blow, the whole span of it falling away as it swung down into the crevasse. The side of the bridge closest to Malden had been held up by only a weak latch, while the scrollwork buttress on the other side was in fact a massive hinge.

Malden looked down into the crevasse and saw swirling darkness below. Twenty, maybe thirty soldiers could have gotten onto the bridge before it fell, and all of them would have fallen to their deaths. They would have been the best knights the elves could muster, the vanguard of their army. The message would have been very clear.

Malden walked back across the crevasse on the tight rope he'd strung between the two spikes. Foot over foot, his arms held out at his sides for balance. He'd done it before a million times. He made a point of bowing toward Cythera before he leapt back to the safety of the basalt.

"The rest of you will have to go hand over hand, I'm afraid. A less dignified method to get across, but far safer," he said.

They divided up the supplies into five knapsacks. Mörget took the largest share without complaint. Anything they couldn't carry they left behind as a cache for later. That significantly increased their mobility, but still it took the better part of an hour to get everyone across, each of them crawling along the rope, hand over hand, helping each other as much as they could. Cythera, surprisingly, had the hardest time of it. She was nimble enough, and so light the rope barely sagged under her weight, but she had to cross with her eyes clenched tightly shut. Malden knew the signs of someone with a fear of heights, and he spoke gentle words to urge her across before she opened her eyes and looked down. If she did that, he knew she would freeze up and be unable to cross at all.

He had a bad moment when Mörget started swinging across like a monkey, hand over hand with his legs dangling over the drop. The rope creaked and sagged as he stretched out its fibers and Malden worried it might just snap. Which he found he truly didn't want it to do. True, if Mörget fell here and perished in the water below, then his own life would become a jot less dangerous. But it would also mean he would have one less warrior on his side when they eventually met the demon.

No, let Mörget kill his beast—and then all bets were off, and the barbarian could get himself killed however he pleased. Until then, Malden thought, he would do his best to keep him alive.

The rope held, despite Mörget's antics. It was stout, strong stuff from the best of Ness's ropewalks, and it had never gotten wet or been coiled improperly. Malden had taken care of it himself during their journey—every thief knows that his life will some day depend on a strong rope, just as he knows he may one day swing from one. All of Cutbill's employees treated ropes with respect.

However, when they were all across, Croy looked back with skeptical eyes.

"It'll be hard getting back across the same way on our way out," he said. "Especially if we're in a hurry."

"You expect ghosts to chase us off?" Malden asked.

"Just considering all possibilities. That's something I learned from you."

Malden sketched a bow in his direction. "You are too kind. All right, from here I think we'll be safe. That should be the last of the traps." He strode across the basalt flagstones to a door in the far wall. This one stood barely five feet high. As Malden flung it open, he stepped back to bow and gesture through the door with one hand. "Mörget," he said, "do watch your head."

Had he not been so cavalier, he would have walked right through the doorway—and impaled himself on the iron spikes that came slamming through to meet him.

# CHAPTER THIRTY

Croy called out in shock, but Malden was already in motion, dropping to a crouch and rolling out of the way as the spikes slammed through the doorway and bit hungrily at the air where he had been.

Malden scuttled away from the spikes on his hands and heels. When it was clear they weren't going to shoot outward from the door or knock back into the crevasse, he shook his head in relief.

The spikes were six inches long, protruding point first from a wooden board. A complicated arrangement of springs sent the board flying into the room when the door was opened. The tip of each spike glistened with droplets of liquid.

"Poison, almost certainly," Malden said as he rose to his feet. "Interesting. I wonder why it was set to trigger from this side? Surely—"

A loud, rhythmic clanging noise interrupted him. The noise ratcheted up in volume, and then the five of them jumped in surprise as the board began to retreat back to its previous position, drawing back through the doorway. A spring mounted to the back of the door slammed it shut again once the spiked board had returned to its starting state.

There was a very loud click, like a dead bolt being shot into place, and then silence reigned once more. It was as if Malden had never opened the door.

"Ah," he said.

"Fucking brilliant!" Slag cried.

"Ingenious, definitely," Malden agreed. "But it raises a question. If we want to proceed, how do we get through that door?"

The dwarf pondered for a moment. "Trigger it again. Then we wedge something in between the board and the doorjamb. Something strong, like one of Mörget's weapons. He's got a whole fucking wardrobe of the things under his cloak, surely he can spare one, right? Then we all heave on it until something breaks."

"Something inside the mechanism that propels the board?"

"Or the weapon. In which case we try again."

Malden nodded, seeing the wisdom of this plan. "Very well. In that case—"

He stopped because Mörget was already standing to one side of the door and pulling on its latch. Malden jumped back as the board of spikes came bursting into the room again, exactly as before. Mörget roared and jumped between the board and the jamb. Instead of sacrificing one of his weapons, however, he got his own shoulder into the narrow space.

The clanging, ratcheting noise came again as the trap tried to reset itself. Mörget's face twisted into a grimace of pain as the back of the board tried to crush his body. Yet he was braced well and he pushed back with the arm he had thrust into the mechanism. The ratcheting noise made a pathetic series of clicks as the barbarian heaved and shoved, sweat breaking out across his forehead and running down across the red stain around his mouth.

And then something broke.

Malden couldn't be sure at first if it was the mechanism or one of Mörget's bones. But a moment later the barbarian screamed in rage and gave one last heave, and the board tore away from its springs. It went flying across the room, inches from impaling Cythera, and then slid over the edge of the crevasse to disappear from sight. A moment later Malden heard it splash into the river below.

"Grab the door," Mörget howled. Croy rushed in to grab it before it could slam shut on Mörget's body. Slag ducked under the knight's arm and attacked the spring on the door with a wide-bladed screwdriver. In a moment he had that spring disabled as well.

Mörget stepped away from the mechanism and rolled his shoulder as if it was slightly sore.

"My way works, too," he said.

"So much for the element of surprise, though," Cythera pointed out. "That made enough noise that I'm sure even the demon heard it. We'd be wise to press on now and get away from here as quickly as possible, before it—or anything else—comes to investigate."

"You mean the ghosts of elves?" Croy asked. "Do you sense them?"

Cythera shook her head, but she didn't look particularly sure. "No . . . but . . . there's something here. Something that doesn't want us to go any further." She gave them all a weak smile. "Perhaps I'm just jumping at shadows."

"Some shadows are more dangerous than others," Mörget pointed out. "The woman is right. We need to keep moving."

Malden approached the open door and held his lantern inside. He could see the clockwork that had operated the trap, much of it now broken and bent out of shape. Beyond, there seemed to be a large open space. He crawled over the gears and into the room there, and then called back for everyone else to follow.

The room beyond the door had a low ceiling, though Mörget was able to stand upright once he was inside. It was broader than it was deep, and the walls were of finely dressed stone. A pair of broad doorways led out of the room, farther into the city, but they could not be reached immediately because someone had constructed a barricade before them. It was a clumsy affair of broken furniture and low walls made of sacks filled with sand, studded all over with wooden spikes. The spikes pointed toward the door Malden had just come through. He approached one and gave it a push, and the wood collapsed under his finger, rotten through and as soft as paper. In fact the entire barricade looked like it might collapse into dust if he gave it a good kick. The furniture was falling apart and the sacks of sand had been nibbled at by insects until they leaked in a hundred places. "Ah. Well, this explains one thing," he said.

"What's that?" Croy asked.

"I wasn't expecting that last trap to be triggered from that side because I expected all the traps were meant to keep anyone from getting out of the Vincularium. Clearly, though, the elves wanted just as much to keep anyone from getting in. Tell me, Croy, would this make a good defensive point to ward off invaders?"

"Yes, certainly," the knight said. "Presumably the trap on the door would stop the first one who tried to come through. The noise it makes would alert you that someone was trying to come in. The invaders would be unlikely to fall for the trap twice, but by the time they disabled the mechanism, you could have a dozen archers here, protected by this defensive works, and they could hold off all but the most determined attackers."

"The elves thought they were going to be attacked," Malden said, climbing over the barricade. From the far side he could see how easily a man could duck down behind the gathered junk and be shielded from incoming attacks. "They must have believed that the humans would come in here after them and finish the job. The last thing they expected was that they would be sealed inside and left to rot."

"Sounds good, lad," Slag said. "Too bad your theory is horseshit." The dwarf was busy examining the clockwork that had propelled the spiked board.

"Oh?" Malden asked.

"Two reasons. No elf ever built something this complicated. They lacked the skill. Secondly, the buggers all died off centuries ago." He ran one finger across the teeth of a heavy gear. "But the oil on this thing is fresh."

# CHAPTER THIRTY-ONE

"Then—someone else has been here. And recently," Cythera said.

"Most like they're still here," Slag insisted. "And they didn't want us coming in."

Croy frowned. "It doesn't seem like Mörget's demon would be capable of building that trap."

"It had no hands," the barbarian agreed. "The woman had a sense something was here. Now we know it's more than just intuition. There's someone else in here with us."

"But who?" Croy demanded. "This place has been sealed tight for centuries. The demon seems able to come and go, but only because it can flatten itself so that it fits through narrow cracks in the earth. We know no human has ever despoiled this place—the chains out front were still intact, and their enchantment had never been discharged. Moreover, if any man of Skrae had ever come here before we would have heard the tale."

"Grave robbers, perhaps," Malden said, though that failed to counter most of Croy's points. It was all he could think of.

For a while they all just stared at each other, fear passing from one to another as their eyes met. This was not something they'd prepared for.

"Whoever they are," Slag said finally, "even if they didn't hear all that noise—they'll probably come check their trap from time to time. And when they do, they'll see that someone broke their fucking toy. They'll know we're here, too."

Croy drew Ghostcutter from its sheath. "We need to be on our guard from this point forward." He saw Mörget's axe jump into his hand. "Everyone," the knight said, "get back behind this barricade, while we scout the way forward."

Mörget moved without instruction to one of the two doors leading deeper into the Vincularium. The barbarian shoved his helmet down over his shaved head and nodded to indicate his readiness. Croy moved to the other door and stood to one side of it. Whoever constructed the door trap might even now be aware that it had been triggered. He had no conception of what might come to check on it, but he was ready. Carefully, in case there were more traps, he pushed down on the latch of his door. It swung open easily, revealing only darkness beyond.

If anyone was out there, they needed no light to see by. Croy considered extinguishing his group's own lanterns, but he had fought in darkness too many times to think that wise. A man fighting without a light was as likely to strike down a friend as a foe. He looked across at Mörget, who opened his own door. No spikes jumped out, nor did the ceiling of the barricade room fall in, nor did the room fill up with boiling oil. All to the good.

Lantern in one hand, sword in the other, Croy stepped through his door. Beyond lay a room so large his light failed to illuminate anything but the wall behind him. The floor was made of cobblestones like a city street, smoothed down by time and commerce until they were nearly as flat as flagstones. He took a few steps forward into the darkness but failed to find another wall. Soon he was standing in a rippling puddle of his own light, with darkness beyond him in every direction.

He turned to look behind him and could just see the door he'd come through. Standing next to it was its twin. Mörget stood framed by the light coming in through that door—it seemed both doors opened on the same chamber. Croy wanted to call Mörget out to join him but dared not make noise. He could hear nothing but the omnipresent sound of dripping water and the roaring of the air as it rushed past his ears. There could be a host of demons all around him, with slavering jaws and squirming tentacles, but if so they were not pressing their attack.

After considering his options for a moment, he headed back to the barricade room. "All right," he whispered, "everyone, come with me. But we must remain absolutely silent!"

He had no idea what was out there in the enormous room. Yet it would be foolish to simply wait in the barricade room for the enemy to arrive. He would look for another defensible spot, one the unseen opponents wouldn't be watching.

The five of them moved in absolute silence—or as close as they could manage. Mörget's arsenal rattled and clanged under his cloak, and Slag's tools jangled in his purse. They headed left, along the one wall Croy had found, the outer wall of the barricade room. The wall was made of white brick, roughened here and there by centuries of dripping water. Croy had expected to follow it to another wall soon enough, but after a hundred feet or so he found nothing. The wall seemed to go on forever, featureless and unchanging save that every twenty feet it was braced with a massive column, ten feet square, that ran straight up into the darkness over their heads.

He kept going. After passing another five columns, he saw Malden waving to get his attention. Croy nodded, but placed a finger across his lips to indicate the thief should remain silent.

Malden grimaced in annoyance, then set his lantern down and pantomimed what he'd wanted to say. He held up one hand flat, the fingers pointing straight ahead, then pushed his other hand past it, curving away from it.

Croy frowned and tried to puzzle out the meaning. Then he had it. Malden was saying that the wall they followed was curved.

The knight ran his hands along the smooth bricks, trying to feel the distortion. It was very slight, and very subtle, but once he saw it, it was obvious. The wall was definitely concave. They must be inside some enormous circular room, and he had been hunting for a corner. Had he kept going, he would eventually have returned to the two doors leading into the barricade room.

Slag, watching the interplay of gestures, nodded eagerly. He took a piece of charcoal from his purse and drew a large circle on the wall. Croy nodded in approval. Yes, he thought, we are in a round room, very good.

Slag next took out a ball of string dyed with spots along its length. Croy had seen similar strings used to measure out parcels of land—the spots would be a precise distance apart, and if you knew the distance you could tell how long a given piece of property was, or how wide. The dwarf handed one end of the string to Malden, then reached up to close his fingers around Malden's hand, indicating that the thief should hold the string tight. Then, lantern held high, Slag walked back the way they had come until Croy could barely see the dwarf's light swinging in the distance. Slag stopped at some arbitrary-seeming point, then hurried back and drew some dwarven runes on the wall with his charcoal. Croy couldn't read most of them but recognized some numbers.

The dwarf pulled at his beard for a while, then wrote a number along the outside of his circle. Some strange notation was involved, but Croy saw the figure 1570, and near it the fraction 22/7. Slag next drew a line across the circle, neatly bisecting it. Along this line he wrote 500. Cythera, excited by the numbers on the wall, tapped the 500 with her finger several times, and Slag nodded happily.

Then Croy understood a little of what they were doing. Slag had somehow worked out that the circular room must be five hundred feet—or yards—across. He didn't understand enough mathematics to know how they'd reached that conclusion, but he didn't doubt it was correct.

Cythera ran her finger along the bisecting line, stopped right in the middle and shrugged. She was asking what was in the middle of the room.

Slag frowned, then drew the dwarven spiral rune where

she'd pointed. The rune of uncertainty and doubt. Cythera stood up and pointed out into the darkness, directly away from the wall.

Slag shrugged, and started walking where she'd indicated.

Croy almost called out to stop him, but caught himself in time. Instead, he set off after the dwarf. What else could he do?

# CHAPTER THIRTY-TWO

The five of them moved cautiously toward the center of the room. Mörget moved restlessly around the rest of them, his axe always pointed toward the darkness. Slag moved forward as if there was nothing at all to worry about.

Croy wished he could feel as confident.

The Vincularium was supposed to be empty. That had been a fact of life for as long as he could remember. Every knight of Skrae knew the story of the place, and that it was shunned. The king—and the king's father, and all his antecedents, as far as Croy knew—had always treated the place as something to be forgotten about, a legacy of a dark past no one wanted to dredge up. Everyone agreed there was no need to guard it, because no one would be foolish enough to go inside. Whether or not it was haunted was a question of theology rather than anything practical.

Yet Mörget had tracked his demon here, and now they had proof they were not alone. It was not a question of whether they were in danger inside the abandoned dwarven city.

It was only a question of what form that danger would take.

The weathered cobblestones under their feet were the only thing Croy could see in that dark place. His lantern illuminated nothing else for a long while as they moved, so that he almost felt they were wandering through a limitless space with a floor and no other features whatsoever—some other realm, like the pit of the Bloodgod but with less tortured souls and more of the emptiness of pointless existence. He could imagine such a place as the afterlife for those who had been neither good nor evil while alive, those who had accomplished nothing at all. The thought sent a shiver down his back. For a man like Croy, who endeavored always to make the world a better place, such inactivity and pointlessness was the ultimate sin.

Such thoughts did little to ease his anticipations.

When he first spotted a faint pale outline in the distance, he thought his eyes were playing tricks on him. Yet as they approached, it became more distinct. Something square and light in color, maybe five feet high. When they came close enough to see it in detail, Croy thought it looked like a very small house. It had a peaked roof and plain walls. Dwarven runes were inscribed on one wall, but they were in a formal, overwrought script he could not decipher at all.

Slag saw Croy's interest and waved to get his attention. Then the dwarf pressed his hands together as if in prayer and closed his eyes.

Thinking he understood, Croy drew a small medallion from inside his tunic. The golden cornucopia was the symbol of the Lady, and he wore it always on a chain around his neck. He had received it when he made a pilgrimage to Her shrine at Strayburn. Now, he was asking if the little house was a dwarven shrine or altar.

Slag looked confused. Then he rolled his eyes. With a sigh that sounded like a windstorm in that silent place, he lay down on the cobbles and repeated his earlier gesture, hands pressed together and eyes closed.

Croy understood then, and took an immediate step backward. The little house was a dwarven sarcophagus. Definitely something he wanted to avoid.

Unfortunately he had little choice. As they proceeded farther toward the center of the enormous chamber, more of the mausoleums appeared in their light. First a rare scattering, then more and more until they had to wind their way between the closely spaced tombs, climbing over some in places. They came in a variety of shapes and sizes—some were just slabs set into the cobbles, others stout obelisks, and one was even spherical, standing on four stout legs. Yet they were alike in their plainness and height. None were so high Croy could not see over them.

A city of dwarven dead, a field of ancient bones hidden away in the darkness under the world.

Such a place could not help but be haunted. The hair on Croy's neck stood on end, and he wanted to be away as quickly as possible. Yet the demon must lie somewhere beyond. Only duty could get him through that terrible place.

In time the tombs grew farther apart, and eventually the last of them fell behind, just a pale shadow in the dimness. They kept walking, moving toward the center of the chamber. It seemed impossible that such a large space could exist under the ground, yet the cobbles showed no sign of giving out.

At least—not until they did, with a suddenness that nearly spelled Croy's doom. Without warning the floor simply ended, opening up into empty space. He managed to stop well clear of the edge, but Malden had no warning and blundered into him from behind. Croy spread his arms and legs to try to balance on the edge, but one of his feet went over and he felt his balance shifting. It seemed he was falling into the gloom, into nothingness—and his panicked brain thought that pit must go down forever.

Then Mörget's massive hands caught his arms and roughly hauled him back, away from the edge. Croy let out a desperate breath and calmed himself. He brushed down the front of his brigantine and tried to control his vertigo.

Malden mimed an apology, spreading his hands outward in supplication. Croy nodded brusquely, then reached up to quietly slap Mörget's arm in thanks. The barbarian just shrugged.

The five of them spread out along the edge, their lights showing only where the floor ended and the abyss began. The edge was curved, like the wall they'd left behind, but it was more obvious here. It seemed the center of the round room was only empty space.

It was not perfectly featureless, however. The little light that strayed down into the abysm showed it was lined by a sheer wall of closely fit bricks. Knobs of some colorless fungus stood out from the bricks like ears and noses.

Slag held up one hand, two fingers pointing down. He bent and then straightened each in turn to suggest a pair of legs walking down a flight of stairs. Croy nodded and together they headed around the edge of the pit, careful to watch their footing.

They found no stairs leading down. However, off to the left the featureless floor was interrupted by a pillar of smooth rock that stretched upward into the dark. The pillar stood athwart the edge, descending into the depths just as it lifted upward. Bolted to this pillar was a massive iron chain, as thick as Croy's bicep, that stretched across the pit, much like the line Slag had used to bisect his charcoal circle. Malden was already examining this chain as if he intended to walk on it.

Mörget stripped off his pack and rummaged inside it. He took out a carefully folded tent and started ripping it to pieces. It quickly became apparent what he had in mind. He broke a piece from one of the tent poles, then tore a strip of canvas and wrapped it tightly around the end of the pole. The canvas was waxed to make it waterproof, but that also made it highly flammable. Lighting it from the candle in his lantern, Mörget soon had a wildly burning torch in his hand.

Before Croy could stop him, the barbarian whirled around and tossed his torch far out over the face of the abyss. It fell rapidly away from them, letting them see a little more as it fluttered past.

The pit was illuminated only for a moment, but in that time Croy made out several interesting details. The opening in the floor was at least two hundred feet across. It was perfectly circular, and it was crossed only by three massive chains like the one Malden was investigating. The chains met in the center of the pit, where they anchored an enormous round globe of crystal, thirty feet across.

Croy could not begin to guess what purpose that globe served. He was far too busy, anyway, following the brand with his eyes as it fell into the depths. He could see the pit went down for hundreds of feet, maybe even a thousand. It was perfectly cylindrical in shape, and its walls were everywhere streaked and encrusted with the fungal growths. It was not, however, totally uniform. Around its circumference countless openings showed—some small and square, like windows, others very broad like galleries. The pit must be like a vast tower turned inside out, so that its various floors were on the outside of its wall. Floors was the correct word, he thought—from where he stood, he could look down on dozens of levels of the dwarven city. Every one of those galleries might open on whole suites of rooms, broad halls, winding tunnels—even other shafts like this one.

For the first time Croy had an inkling of the vast size of the Vincularium. He had seen what the dwarves called cities in the North, and was disappointed by how cramped and narrow they were. He had always imagined the Vincularium would be the same: a small village's worth of homes and workshops built into a series of enlarged mine shafts.

This city, though, might be as big as the Free City of Ness, if all of its houses and churches and palaces and shops and manufactories were stacked neatly on top of each other, then buried under a mountain. The entirety of

Helstrow could have been dropped into that central shaft and not filled its volume.

"By Sadu's burning arsehole," Malden swore aloud. After the prolonged silence, Croy felt the words like rocks raining down on his shoulders. He tried to shush the thief, but the others ignored him.

"Indeed," Cythera said. "Slag, did you have any idea it could be so big?"

Even the dwarf looked awestruck. "Fuck no."

# CHAPTER THIRTY-THREE

It seemed to take hours for the torch to fall through the shaft, though it must only have been a few dozen seconds. It landed on something wet, but it went out so quickly and so far away that it was impossible to tell what it had struck.

Then the shaft was dark again, and its secrets were hid once more.

"There used to be more of us," Slag said, when the shock of the Vincularium's size had worn off a bit. "More dwarves. There had to be."

"How many more?" Croy asked. It seemed the rule of silence was utterly broken. "I would imagine the entire population of the dwarven kingdom could live here, and not feel crowded."

Slag nodded. "Surely. There are maybe ten thousand of us left." His lips moved quickly, as if he were doing some calculation in his mind. "This place could have held millions. And just look at the design! Hmm. Interesting. Central shaft for ventilation and access. Stratified construction, probably with reinforcing spars on each level—of course, you'd need more at the bottom, to hold the weight of the upper levels, but then what keeps the mountain up? This is some very complex engineering." He shook his head. "We've lost so much. My people couldn't build one of these now if life depended on it."

"Slag," Cythera said, "that giant crystal ball hanging in the middle of the shaft—what is its purpose? Mother has one but it's only the size of a cabbage. She uses it to scry with. Is this something similar?"

"No fucking clue," Slag said. "But no. I can vouch for the fact no dwarf ever peered into a crystal ball." He strode away from the edge and took his piece of charcoal out of his purse again. For a while he just wandered around, looking for somewhere to draw more figures.

Poor dwarf, Croy thought. He's looked on the glory of his ancestors and now he needs to draw more magic charms to protect himself against sheer awe.

"All right," Mörget said. "Enough gawking. Let's make camp."

Croy stared at the barbarian in pure surprise. "Here? Now? When we know there's someone out there, willing to do us harm?"

"I'm tired. I'm sure the rest of you are exhausted. So yes, here. Unless you wish to trek back to the barricade," Mörget told him. "This is the most defensible spot we have. The—The upside-down graves over there," he said, gesturing behind him.

"Mausoleums," Croy said.

"The dead dwarves will screen one flank. Anyone trying to get through there will be slowed down, at the very least. On the other flank we have the pit."

"Something might come climbing out of it," Malden suggested.

"The mountain could fall on our heads at any time," Mörget pointed out in return. "I'll stand watch while you rest, little thief. Anything that comes out of the pit," he said, and brandished his axe, "will find me waiting."

They placed their lanterns together in poor imitation of a campfire and sat around them in a circle. Croy was not surprised to see that Malden fell asleep almost at once, or that Cythera lay down with her head against the thief's shoulder. He was glad they could take some comfort from each other's presence, his betrothed and his best friend. Slag sat unquiet, however, passing his piece of charcoal from one hand to the other. As for himself, Croy was unable to rest—he was too aware, always, of the vast quantity of darkness surrounding him. He must have been born on a sunny day, he thought. This impenetrable gloom frayed his nerves and made him jumpy. He would be all too glad when the demon was slain and they could leave again.

*Admit it*, he told himself. *You're frightened.*

Like most boys of Skrae, Croy had grown up believing knights were supposed to be fearless, that they charged into danger without a second thought. That illusion lasted until he fought in his first real battle. He'd vomited while he waited for the enemy to arrive, and tried to cover up his shame by burying his sick. Sir Orne, a fellow Ancient Blade, had laughed at him but then told him the secret of being fearless.

"It's an act. A mask you wear, to help frighten your enemies. Just as they pretend to be unafraid to frighten you. But honestly we're all ready to run away, every time, run until we find our mothers and can weep into their skirts."

"But how do you conquer the fear?" Croy had asked.

"That's one fight you can't win. All you can ever hope for is to keep your mask from slipping at the wrong time," Sir Orne had told him.

He'd never forgotten that lesson.

To pass the time, he spoke in low tones with Mörget and the dwarf.

"What can you tell us of this place?" he asked Slag. "You seemed as surprised as any of us to see how big it is."

"Aye, lad. There's little enough to tell, as even the most

learned dwarves think of the Vincularium as a piece of the past, perhaps better forgotten. It was a grand city in the days before men came to this land, but ye knew that already. I know it had a different name back then, which was Thur-Karas."

"What does that name mean?" Mörget inquired.

Slag shrugged. " 'Place of the Long Shadows' is the best translation I can make. Which means as fucking little to me as it must to you."

"It sounds baleful," Mörget said, looking grim.

"Names are often meaningless, or chosen for reasons we cannot fathom," Croy said. "My own, for instance, means nothing of value."

"Truly?" Mörget asked, sounding surprised. "I would think a man of rank like yourself would have a name of importance."

"You do me too much credit. My mother chose the name. Before me, it belonged to an uncle, her favorite brother. That's all."

"It must have come from somewhere," Mörget said.

Croy shrugged. "I imagine my uncle was named after another Croy, perhaps an ancestor. How far back that chain goes I cannot say. Malden and Cythera could probably tell you similar stories. Such is the custom in Skrae."

Mörget shook his head. "Names should have power. In my land, in the East, we say a man's name is his destiny."

Croy raised an eyebrow. "An interesting notion. So when you meet a man, you know something his character right away. Very practical."

"If you have to fight a man, you want to know if his name means 'killer' or 'coward.' It's useful information."

Croy opened his pack and took out a jug of ale. He sipped at it, then handed it to Slag, who took a deep pull on it. Mörget, of course, drank no spirits, so the dwarf handed it back to the knight. "So," Croy said, "what does Mörget mean? Something violent and forceful, no doubt." He pumped one fist in the air and laughed.

"Hardly. It means simply that I am the son of Mörg. Mörg's get."

"And who's Mörg when he's not at home?" Slag asked.

Mörget looked as if he'd almost rather not say. It was the first time Croy had ever seen the barbarian look less than enthusiastic about something. And yet he knew from Mörget's own lips that his father was a great chieftain of the barbarians, a commander of men.

"Sometimes they call him Mörg the Wise. He's the closest thing we have to a king," Mörget said, his eyes dark.

Croy spread his arms wide. "There you go. A proud name indeed."

The barbarian ran one thumb along the blade of his axe. "It is not meant that way. It is meant as a mark of shame. Among my people, no man is worth anything but what he seizes for himself. My name is meant to always remind me that I am not special, nor am I to be favored, just because I am the whelp of a great man. I must achieve something great in my life, or my people will always remember me as someone's *child*."

"Once you kill this demon—"

"Then I will change my name. I will have earned a better one."

"I can see why you would travel so far to carry out your quest," Croy said.

"Yes. And now you know about my name, for what good it does you. You. Dwarf."

Slag looked up. He'd started dozing halfway through Mörget's explanation. "Huh, yes?"

"Your name seems strange to me. What is a 'slag'?"

"Slag is a waste product of the smelting process. It's just what humans call me. A sodding insult, to be true, though mostly they mean it affectionately."

"I knew it was unusual," Croy said, slapping his knee. "I was under the impression all dwarf names end with the suffix 'in.' Like Murdlin and Snurrin and Therin."

"Many do. It means 'descendant of.' Murdlin, for instance, is the seventh direct grandson of Murdli, the dwarf who invented the blister process of making steel. One of our great heroes. In our land, that *is* a mark of honor."

"We come from very different worlds," Mörget told the dwarf.

"You're not fucking kidding."

Croy laughed. "But what's your actual name, then, Slag? I hate to think this whole time I've been calling you after some noxious substance, when you had a real, proud name I could use."

"It's not important," Slag told him.

"Of course it is," Croy said. "I have nothing but respect for you, and wouldn't want to insult you, even in affectionate jest. Why, I—"

"Be still," Mörget said, jumping to his feet. The axe in his hand pointed out into the dark.

"I told you, it's not fucking important," Slag said, squinting at Croy.

The knight was too busy staring at Mörget to hear him.

"What is it?" Croy asked.

"I hear footsteps. And they're close."

# CHAPTER THIRTY-FOUR

"Lad, lass, get up," Slag said, shaking Malden and Cythera to get them moving. Croy paid no attention as the dwarf explained what was happening to them. He had Ghostcutter out of its sheath and was busy preparing himself for a fight.

His first inclination was to douse the lanterns and hide. But there was no good place to cower, and he had a feeling that whatever was out there could probably see better in the dark than he could. It showed no lights of its own. He couldn't see it at all in the murk but he could definitely hear it now.

Its footsteps were dragging and slow but it was making no attempt to muffle them. And it made another sound, too, a rhythmic scraping sound Croy couldn't place.

"It's this way," Mörget said, and pointed into the dark with his axe. "And there's more than one."

Croy strained his ears to the limit of their ability to pick up sounds, but he lacked Mörget's wild-born sensitivity. The knight squinted his eyes against the musty darkness and tried to see something. Anything.

And then he had it. A figure, human-shaped, moving toward them very slowly. It wasn't walking so much as shuffling its feet forward. One arm held something that it dragged along the cobblestones. That was the source of the rhythmic scraping sound they had heard. By the sound of it, the figure was dragging a piece of metal along the cobbles.

"It's armed," Croy said, presuming the piece of metal had to be a weapon.

"They all are. And armored."

"All?" Croy asked, near panic. He fought his fear down. He had to keep the mask of fearlessness in place, if only for the sake of Cythera and the others. In a moment he saw two more figures, just behind the first. It was impossible for him to make out any real detail in the darkness, but they were definitely clad in metal that reflected more light than their pale faces. As they drew steadily closer, he could see a little more. The one in front was dragging a sword. It gleamed yellow along one edge. Like gold—or bronze.

He could see now they were not human. They were far too slender, even when covered in plates of armor. Their heads were longer than a human's, as were their hands. They wore helmets that hid their ears, but Croy was certain the ears would be pointed if he could see them.

"Elves," Croy said. "But how? There can't be any living elves down here, not after so long."

Apparently there weren't. As they came even closer, no more than twenty yards away now, he could tell they were dead. The one in front had no eyes in its sockets. Its long, thin nose was partially eaten away, and the skin of one cheek was furry with mold.

Malden came up beside Croy and stared at them. "Ghosts," he breathed, his voice thick with supernatural dread.

"No," Croy said. He had fought ghosts before. Those had been thin, ethereal things, almost invisible and utterly silent. The sound the lead elf's sword made as it dragged along the ground told him these were material creatures. Dead bodies, animated by some foul sorcery and made to walk again. "Revenants," he corrected. "Malden, keep Cythera safe. Use Acidtongue if you must—I don't care if you haven't been trained with a sword. Just don't let them—"

He stopped because he saw the other two revenants clearly. One had a grinning skull for a face, with tatters of skin hanging from its forehead to obscure one blank eye socket. The other had no head at all.

"Mörget, be ready," Croy said. He'd never faced a revenant in battle before, but had heard tales, and he knew a little of what to expect. "They will attack without attempting to parley. And they will not stop to beg for quarter. They want only our deaths."

"Death is my mother," Mörget said. "Let them come a little closer, so I can give her a kiss."

Croy had no doubt the barbarian thought he could take all three revenants on himself. If they had just been elves, or even just animated bones, Croy was certain the barbarian would defeat them handily. But if, as he feared, these were true revenants—spirits of vengeance, animated by a desperate hunger for justice—they would be far harder to overcome than any living opponent.

"Just be careful. Whatever you do, don't let them grapple you. They'll cling to your neck with preternatural strength and never let go."

"Consider me warned," Mörget said, and then he howled like a wolf.

The nearest revenant opened skinless lips and screamed at them, a dreadful sound of loss and rage that chilled Croy's blood. Then the three of them brought their weapons to bear and charged, no longer shuffling painfully but running with great speed.

The leader came straight at Croy, bringing its sword up and whirling it over its head, just as a living commander might to rally his troops. Its bony feet slapped on the cobblestones, slipping and sliding, but it never fell or faltered. In the space between two breaths it was on him, and its intent was clear: it meant to slaughter him as quickly and as violently as possible.

Fear surged through Croy's body, like rivers of ice coursing through his veins. He remembered another of Sir Orne's lessons. Fear could make a man run away—or it could make him fight like a wildcat, if he thought he had nowhere to run. Fear could be used, channeled. It could make a man fast and strong.

He brought Ghostcutter high and caught the bronze sword on his forte. He pushed the blow away from him and the revenant reeled. He spared a heartbeat-long glance at Mörget, and was glad to see the barbarian was not just attacking like a berserker—he was moving around to the side, to flank the three while he himself took the brunt of their attack.

Sound strategy—but it meant he was exposed to a torrent of blows. The skull-faced revenant had a double-bladed battle-axe that it brought around in a clumsy swing Croy had to jump backward to avoid. The headless one's sword came around in a wild arc, as if the revenant were merely waving it in front of itself, hoping that he hit something. The leader's sword came down in a powerful overhead driving cut, and Croy could only bring Ghostcutter up to catch the bronze sword on his quillions. He swung around to kick the revenant backward, then jerked his foot away as the dead elf's free hand reached for his ankle.

Mörget's axe took the headless one in the back, a clanging blow that might have cut a human opponent in half. The headless revenant staggered forward under the pressure, then straightened itself up and swung its blade again.

Croy ducked sideways, away from the flailing blow. The skull-faced one's axe was carving through the air toward him, but he knocked it away easily.

"Everyone, move back, away from the edge of the pit," he shouted. He didn't want to be driven into the dark abyss by force of arms.

He brought Ghostcutter down hard on the skull-faced revenant's shoulder, and the silvered edge of his Ancient Blade bit deep through the thing's armor. The skull-face split open in a scream that left its jawbone dangling from one joint. Croy pulled his sword clear of the wound and swung around for a strong cut to the thing's axe arm. The blow surely would have cut through the revenant's elbow if the leader of the dead elves had not chosen that moment to thrust its sword hard into Croy's side.

Pain burst through Croy's entire rib cage. It blinded him, and made him drop to one knee. He heard Cythera calling his name, but the blood pounding through his head made her voice distant and small.

He managed to force his eyes open and looked up just as the skull-face's axe came whistling down toward his scalp.

"No," he had time to say, thinking this was his death.

Instead Mörget grabbed the skull-face around the waist and heaved him off the ground. He rushed toward the pit, clearly intending to throw the revenant into the depths.

"No!" Croy howled again as the skull-face dropped its

axe—and wrapped both its bony hands around Mörget's thick neck.

## CHAPTER THIRTY-FIVE

The barbarian did not panic as the bony fingers dug deep in to the tendons of his neck. He brought his axe up and bit deep into the revenant's back, though the unwieldy position kept him from striking a true killing blow.

"Malden, help him," Croy called. He was too hard pressed to rescue Mörget himself. The headless revenant brought its sword around in a wild two-handed swing that would have taken Croy's own head off if he hadn't ducked out of the way. The leader of the revenants brought his sword up then and aimed a long-armed cutting stroke downward at his chest.

The knight was still recovering from the blow he'd taken to his side. The metal plates riveted inside his brigantine had held, and he knew he wasn't bleeding, but the shock of the blow still left his whole left side numb and stiff. Every breath hurt, even as his body surged and gasped for more air. He managed to bring Ghostcutter up to deflect the oncoming blow, but he took the leader's bronze sword on the foible, the weakest part of Ghostcutter, nearest its tip. Any living fencer would have sneered at that defense—it opened Croy up to a deadly remise, a continuation of the original blow that could pierce his throat or face without any difficulty.

The revenant wasn't as fast as a living man, however

strong it might be. It tried for the remise but Croy leaned back and the bronze sword point slid harmlessly past his cheek.

Rolling to one side, he thrust Ghostcutter hard up into the lead revenant's vitals. It was a blow that would have disemboweled a living opponent. The Ancient Blade met little resistance, even from the bronze cuirass the revenant wore. Once past the armor it felt to Croy like he was stabbing empty air.

Such an attack would do little to harm a revenant. They felt no pain and had no vital organs to pierce. They could not be killed by sundering their hearts or by loss of blood. The magic that animated them cared little for the state of their bodies, as it only wanted one thing—revenge. The revenant opened wide its mouth as if to mock Croy for such a pointless attack.

Croy knew what he was doing, though. He twisted Ghostcutter to the side, hard, and the revenant was jerked off his feet. He dropped in a heap of bronze armor and emaciated flesh. Croy jumped with both feet on its throat and felt the sickening crunch as the revenant's head parted from its body.

Its bony arms reached up to grab his legs, even still. Croy was ready and leapt away, Ghostcutter already swinging to strike the headless revenant in its chest. The other had been approaching steadily, waiting for an opening in Croy's defense. Maybe it thought it had found its moment, but this time at least it was wrong.

Mörget's earlier axe blow had already chopped the headless revenant near in half. Croy's blow finished the job. With a great clatter of bronze on the cobblestones, the headless revenant fell in two pieces, both twitching with rage.

Neither of Croy's opponents was finished—it took a long time to completely destroy a revenant, and a strong stomach—but he had bought himself enough time to look around and see what else was happening.

Mörget was on his knees, his hands clutching desperately at his throat. Malden had managed to use Acidtongue to cut the skull-face's arms off at the wrists, and the thief was chopping the handless body to pieces with the magic sword. The disembodied hands were still wrapped tight around the barbarian's windpipe, however. They were already dead—being severed from their body wouldn't stop them.

Mörget's face was turning purple. His eyes stood out of his head and his red-stained lips were pulled back in a grimace of agony. In an incredible display of fortitude, he managed to grasp one finger of the bony hands and tear it from its joint. He cast it away from him, into the darkness.

Croy jumped in and helped as best he could, pulling the fingers away from Mörget's flesh as the barbarian thrashed and heaved. Mörget was getting no air, though, and soon would suffocate if they couldn't get him free.

"Stand back," Cythera insisted, coming up behind Croy. "Damn you, get back! I can help him." Croy did as he was told and let her lay her hands over the bony digits that were choking the life out of Mörget. She closed her eyes and spoke some magic words—or perhaps just a prayer. Then she let out a deep gasp and staggered backward. The bony hands fell away from Mörget's throat, completely lifeless now.

Cythera's own hands writhed with dark tattoos. No flowers this time—only thorn vines and briars.

"They burn," she said. "So cold . . ."

The barbarian gasped for breath, but he was already moving. He grabbed the now headless lead revenant by the ankle and swung it around in a great arc. The revenant tried to snatch at Mörget, but before he could find purchase the barbarian had cast it over the edge of the pit. It disappeared instantly, and a few seconds later Croy heard a great splash from below. Mörget repeated this performance with the two halves of the headless revenant and the severed head of the leader.

And suddenly the five of them were alone again in the dark, all of them wheezing with exhaustion and fear.

"Is that the last of them?" Slag asked. The dwarf had a lantern in either hand, and he waved them around, trying to illuminate the vast open space. The candles inside the lanterns fluttered and sighed, and one of them went out. Slag shrieked and set it down, then rummaged desperately in his pack for flint and steel to get it going again.

Croy wanted to comfort and reassure the dwarf, but he was exhausted and pained by his wound. He could only listen to his heart pound in his chest and try to breathe. Then he saw Cythera staring at her hands and started dragging himself over toward her, to help in any way he could.

Mörget staggered over to where Malden stood, still gripping Acidtongue in both hands. Drops of vitriol spattered the cobblestones and made them smoke at Malden's feet.

Malden looked up at Mörget as if he expected the barbarian to strike him down where he stood, for not having saved him.

The barbarian stared back into the thief's eyes, his huge body pulsing with life. Then he slapped Malden hard on the back.

The blow sent Malden sprawling forward, to almost crash on his face. He caught his footing and whirled around with Acidtongue up and ready.

Mörget let out one of his booming laughs, this one hoarse and painful-sounding but no less enormous. "We have fought together," he told Malden, "and I call you brother! You may now touch me, without causing offense."

"Maybe later," Malden said.

# CHAPTER THIRTY-SIX

"Do you hear any more of them?" Mörget asked, when they'd all had a chance to catch their breath.

Croy shook his head and went back to tending Cythera's hands. She clenched and opened them stiffly as if they pained her greatly, letting out a little gasp with each motion. The skin under the tattoos was red and irritated. He blew on them and then rubbed them briskly, surprised to find them still ice cold.

She favored him with a smile. "They're already warming up again."

"I hate to see you suffer, even for a moment," Croy said, and delighted in the way her face lit up. "Tell me—how did you do that? I thought you knew only a few simple magics, but you worked a little miracle there."

She shrugged her slim shoulders. "It occurred to me that a revenant is, in essence, a walking curse. There is no curse I cannot absorb with my gift." She laughed, a little. "It was worth the attempt, anyway. I did not expect it would hurt so much, though. I could feel the thing's hatred when I touched it. It despises all life—wants nothing but to destroy us and all our kind. They would never have stopped if we hadn't fought them off. That kind of retributive magic is dangerous stuff."

"Will you be all right?"

She closed her eyes and leaned her head against his chest. "I think so. But Croy, this worries me. The kind of magic I felt there—it's not natural."

"There can be nothing natural about the dead coming back to life," Mörget said. "Death is my mother, and I know her ways. I've looked into the eyes of many men as they perished, and—"

"Please," Cythera said, interrupting him. "Let me finish. The magic I touched wasn't human magic. Not witchcraft, or sorcery."

Croy frowned. "But isn't that to be expected? They're revenants. We all know the old stories about such. It takes no spell to call forth a revenant. When a man—or an elf, presumably—dies as the cause of gross injustice, sometimes his soul refuses to depart this world. It reinvests its mortal form, and though it cannot stop the inevitable decay of the flesh, it can grant some semblance of life, for just long enough to claim vengeance."

Cythera nodded. "Aye, we know the story. Yet I always thought it was just that. A story. It occurred to me the first time I heard it that if every man who ever died by foul play came back as a revenant, the world would be choked with them by now. No, I don't think those were simple spirits of justice we faced. Or rather, it was not the circumstances of their death that brought them back. I'm certain that magic had some part in it. But that only raises another question. Who cast the spell?"

"Questions that perhaps will be answered in the fullness of time," Croy said.

"But perhaps we've gained one answer," Malden pointed out. "We know someone tended the trap we found at the first doorway. Now we know who it was."

"Are you sure?" Slag asked. "They didn't seem like the mechanical types, if you ask me."

"I'm certain," Malden said. "We knew there was something active down here. Something that wished us ill. Now we've found it, and overcome it. We should find no more resistance after this, I think."

Croy wished he shared the thief's optimism. "I'm just glad we all survived, and that we're safe. We can rest now, I think, and—"

He stopped speaking then, because he could have sworn he heard something.

Something moving, out in the dark.

Again.

"There. And there," Slag said. The dwarf pointed outward, into the darkness. He turned about on one heel and pointed in another direction. "And over there. More of them."

Croy froze in place and tried not to breathe. He listened, hard. In a moment there was no denying it. More revenants were approaching.

A vast horde of them.

Croy could hear their clumsy feet slapping against the cobblestones, their weapons dragging behind them. The occasional scream of a tortured soul split the dark. Long before he could see them, he could hear them.

And then the first of them came into the light. Some were mutilated beyond recognition, with limbs hanging by shreds of muscle, or missing entire body parts. Some wore armor that had already been hacked to bits centuries ago. Others wore no armor at all, but only robes and cloaks and tunics that had rotted away to bare threads.

Their faces were twisted, grotesque, withered to parody. A clot of greasy hair spilled down over an empty eye socket. A pointed ear gnawed on by rats stuck up from an otherwise bare skull. Noses were missing or had decayed to pustulant blobs of flesh. Teeth stuck out of battered jaws in random directions. Time and death had not been kind to the army that now approached.

That army did not care about its appearance. Croy felt like he knew their inner thoughts: they had only one goal, one desire, which was long-frustrated revenge. Their ancient enemy, the humans (and one hated dwarf, betrayer of their people) had come into their resting place and disturbed the silence. The intruders must be destroyed.

How long had they been down here, lying motionless on the cold cobbles, waiting for the chance to enact their terrible rage? How many years had passed since they died here—abandoned, starving, with no light even to show them each other's faces?

The dark air around Croy seemed to pulsate with their

hatred. As if it were a demon itself, ready to swallow them all as soon as their light flickered out. Of course, the revenants would get them first.

There were hundreds of revenants. Perhaps thousands. In the dim light there was no way to count them all.

And no chance, whatsoever, of standing against them.

Croy looked down at Ghostcutter in his hand. It was a good weapon, and had served him well more times than he could count. Yet he knew it was no match for an undead army.

"We need to get out of here," Malden said. The thief held Acidtongue like a talisman, like it would protect him somehow. It dripped its caustic bounty to fall, hissing and useless, on the cobbles.

Mörget studied the serried ranks before them, then turned to face Cythera. "You," he said. "Witch! Do something."

She shook her head. "I'm no witch. I'm just a witch's daughter. I know a few simple tricks, but—"

"Then try them now!" Mörget commanded.

Cythera scowled at him. Then she vanished into thin air.

"Ah," the barbarian said. "Not what I had in mind."

Croy sighed. They had come so far. There was no denying they were outmatched now, though.

"Mörget," he said, "I think it's time to retreat."

"There's no such word in my language," the barbarian told him. Then he shrugged. "Luckily we are speaking yours. But where shall we go?"

"We'll hack a path through them, get back to the barricade room. Find any way we can to slow them down, then leave. Reseal the Vincularium. Find some other way to slay your demon, at some later date."

"A meritorious plan. I see no error in it, save one."

Croy frowned. "You don't think we can carve our way through them?"

"Not all of them."

Croy nodded. He'd thought of that himself. But he could hardly surrender. The revenants would not take them prisoner. They would offer no quarter, no matter how hard the fight went for them. They would slay him and his companions without remorse and then return to their graves and sleep a righteous sleep. "We have to at least try. Better to die trying to save one's life than lay down weapons and commit suicide."

"Oh, I heartily agree," Mörget said. He dropped his axe to clatter on the floor. Croy stared at the weapon, then back at the barbarian. "Fear not, little knight. I'm merely freeing up my hands." He drew Dawnbringer then, the length of iron singing as it pulled free of its scabbard. "I need my best tool for this task."

# CHAPTER THIRTY-SEVEN

In the darkness, the revenants began to scream for blood. Croy could see more of them—a vast throng now, swarming around them, converging on their presence. Outside a narrow circle of light, they were everywhere. He could just glimpse them moving, stirring restlessly. They made him think of ants toiling ceaselessly in their warrens, climbing all over each other, heedless of jostling their neighbors. Never pausing, never resting.

Utterly silent.

He brought Ghostcutter up into a guard position. A position from which he could attack or defend instantly. Thus when something appeared just to his left, he very nearly slashed out at it, just by instinct.

Croy managed to stay his hand just in time. Cythera reappeared as mysteriously as she had vanished.

She grabbed his arm. "This is your plan? To go down fighting?"

"I don't see any option," he said. "I'm sorry, Cythera. I failed you. When I first agreed to let you come along, I failed—"

"Oh, be quiet!" she said. "There's still one way out."

"Point to it," Croy begged. "They come from every direction—"

"Of course! Every direction save down," Malden said. He sheathed Acidtongue, pulled off his knapsack and searched inside until he found a coil of rope. "There's a gallery about three levels below us in the shaft. If we climb down there, perhaps they won't follow."

Croy shook his head. The revenants were getting very close. "But our exit will be completely cut off—the revenants may not follow, but they'll remain here, waiting for us to return. If we go down there we'll be trapped."

"Better trapped than fucking dead," Slag pointed out. With Malden, he threw a rope over the massive chain that stretched away over the mouth of the pit. "Let me show you a proper knot, lad," he said as Malden kicked one end of the rope over the edge.

The closest of the revenants began to charge. Croy rushed forward to meet them, to slow their advance as best he could. It was too late—there was no way they could all get down the rope before the dead elves overwhelmed them. Croy hacked all around him with Ghostcutter, dodging blows. A bronze mace took him in the thigh and he nearly went down. A sword came at his face and he felt hot blood slick down his cheek.

Mörget waded into the melee, kicking randomly at the attackers, and sliced through a pair of skeletal hands reaching for Croy's throat. When Dawnbringer touched the undead flesh it burst with light, nearly blinding Croy.

The effect on the revenants was far more dramatic. They howled, not with rage this time but with pure mindless pain. They had no eyes, but that light, the light so similar to that of the pure sun of the upper world, seared their flesh wherever it touched them.

For the barest of moments the charge was broken and the revenants stopped attacking. They drew back, knocking down those behind them, as if a great wind had driven them there. Mörget boomed with laughter as he brandished the glowing blade high over his head. The revenants writhed and clutched at each other in terrible fear. One by one, though, they began to rally.

"The light!" Croy shouted. "It hurts them, somehow. They are creatures of darkness . . . perhaps, Malden . . . Get everyone down that rope. I'll hold them off as long as I can. If I don't make it, get Cythera out of here. At any price, keep her safe!"

"That goes for the fucking dwarf, too," Slag insisted. Then he grabbed hold of the rope and jumped over the edge of the pit. Malden and Cythera followed as quick as they could. Croy saw the rope twitch under their weight.

"You bought us a moment's grace," Croy said to Mörget. "Now, while they're dazed—get to the rope."

"And leave you here to die a glorious death—without me?" the barbarian laughed.

A revenant, faster to recover than his fellows, came running at Croy with his hands outstretched. A long dagger remained in its sheath at his belt—clearly he meant only to strangle the knight. Croy jumped to the side and cut the elf in two. Even before it hit the ground, the torso of the revenant started clawing its way toward him again, its hands going now for his ankle.

Croy stamped on it until it stopped struggling.

Instantly, though, there were a dozen more to take its place.

Mörget growled like a bear and brought Dawnbringer around in a fresh attack, the blade lighting up like a torch. The revenants drew back from the hated blade, but this time the light was not so effective. As the revenants directly before Mörget clawed at their skin and dropped their weapons, a new wave of them came shoving through, axes and cleavers and morningstars raised high in the dark air.

"The rope!" Croy called, because he saw something to waken new dread in his heart. A revenant had broken off from the main ranks and was clambering down the line, hand over hand.

"I see it," Mörget said, and scooped his axe up off the cobbles. With a good, hard fling, he severed the rope and sent the climbing revenant falling down into the darkness with a screech.

Croy could only pray that Cythera was already on the gallery, and not hanging from the rope when it was cut. *Lady*, he prayed, *give me strength to die as befits your servant*. He laid into the revenants, left and right and before him, with one last surge of courage. "This is it," he shouted. "This is how we die."

Yet even before his third blow fell, he felt a thick arm wrap around his waist and suddenly he was off his feet. "They want justice," Mörget shouted. "I deny them!"

And with that the barbarian jumped over the edge of the pit, pulling Croy with him. They fell through utter darkness for what seemed like hours but must only have been seconds. Without warning they struck black, icy water that filled Croy's nose and mouth and tore away his consciousness.

# CHAPTER THIRTY-EIGHT

Malden was halfway down the rope when he looked up and saw the revenant crawling after him. It had no eyes, but he could feel it looking back down at him—looking into him, with a hatred that could never be quenched.

The thief yelped in panic and scurried faster down the rope, toward the gallery where Cythera and Slag already waited. It was a narrow ledge of stone that jutted out from a wide opening in the side of the shaft. Clumps of fungus stuck to it in knobby shapes. Only darkness lay beyond that ledge, but to Malden it looked like safety, like life, and he had never been more desirous to crawl into a dark place and hide. The ledge was twenty feet below him, and if he jumped to it now he would probably break his legs.

Above him the revenant scuttled on the rope like a spider. It howled in malevolent fury and redoubled its speed. One of its bony hands reached to snatch at his hair.

And then the rope broke.

For a moment Malden felt as if he weighed nothing. As if the rope and the revenant would fall away but he would remain, pinned to the air, not falling but with nothing to climb down either. That he would hang there forever caught between death and life. Then gravity caught up with him and he began to plummet. Panicking, he threw out his arms and his legs, trying to clutch to anything that would hold him. The ledge came shooting up toward him and he thrust his hands forward, not caring if his fingers shattered on the impact. It would be better than falling into the abyss—he had no idea what was down there, and didn't want to find out. He spread his fingers wide to catch any part of the ledge that offered itself—and missed it entirely. His fingertips just grazed the rock and went on past.

"No!" he screamed, thinking he might fall forever. Before the word was out of his throat, though, something grabbed at the pack on his back and he was jerked upward, his whole body pinwheeling madly. Thinking the revenant had him he struggled like a cat in a sack.

"Stop fighting me," Cythera demanded. Malden looked up and saw her face, a pale oval in the darkness. She was sprawled across the gallery, holding him up with her own bare hands. Her face was a mask of strain as she tried to pull him upward, and her arms were stretched to their limit.

He grabbed not at her but at the stone ledge and hauled himself up. He saw that Slag had helped her by holding her feet—without the dwarf's extra weight, he might have pulled Cythera right over the edge with him.

"You saved me," he said once they both rolled to safety on the gallery floor. He leaned in close and kissed her passionately, and he didn't care who saw it.

Her eyes went wide and she pulled back, shocked. "Malden!"

"I can only beg your pardon," he said, "not your forgiveness, for I feel no remorse—"

"Malden! The revenant!"

A searing agony went through the thief's ankle as he felt bony fingers constrict around the muscle there. Malden's blood flowed out of his face as he sat up and saw the dead elf clutching to him, pulling itself up over the ledge using his body for handholds.

He kicked it in the face with his free foot, and its head came off its neck with a crackling sound. It didn't slow down at all. He kicked again and again as he tried to get Acidtongue out of its glass-lined scabbard.

The now-headless revenant grabbed his knees and pulled. Malden started sliding toward the edge, dragged by the undead weight. Cythera and Slag grabbed at his shoulders to pull him back once more but they couldn't help him fight. With desperate fingers Malden yanked the sword out of its sheath. The revenant grabbed his left thigh, its fingers sinking painfully into the muscle there.

"Get off me!" he cried, and jabbed forward with the sword. Droplets of acid flecked his clothes and he smelled burning hair, but the blade ran the revenant through. Malden jerked upward with the sword and the thing came in two, half of it sliding away into darkness instantly. The other half—a torso, an arm, and a leg—kept coming, the dead fingers snatching at the leg of his breeches. Malden hacked away at it until Acidtongue sizzled in the air and there was nothing left but a few bones twitching on the ledge.

He jumped to his feet and kicked the bones away. Behind him Slag and Cythera only stared at him in shock, as if they couldn't believe what he'd just done.

At that moment Croy and Mörget fell screaming past the gallery, dropping into the abyss like a pair of flung stones. Malden just had time to see Croy's face, his mouth stretched wide open as he shouted in panic. The two of them were gone in a flash.

He flinched.

"No," Cythera said. Her face was blank of emotion. Malden knew that wouldn't last. "Croy—was that Croy?"

Malden bit his lip. He couldn't answer.

"No!" She rushed forward to the very edge of the gallery and stared downward. "No! Croy! Croy, are you down there? Croy! Answer me!" She pulled off her knapsack and dumped out its contents. A candle rolled free and went over the edge.

Malden didn't know what to do. He reached out a hand to grab her but then he thought better of it.

"Lass," Slag said. "What are you fucking doing?"

"Looking for a rope. Do you have one? If we lower a rope, he can climb back up. Both of them can. Croy and Mörget. Croy! Can you hear me?"

The dwarf shook his head. "He's gone, girl."

"I heard a splash, I definitely heard a splash," Cythera said. She scattered food and climbing gear all over the floor. There was no rope in her pack, but still she kept looking for it. "They fell into water. They could have survived that fall."

"It's a long way down—"

She turned on the dwarf and grabbed his shoulders. On

her knees, she was face-to-face with Slag. She shook him violently. "They could have survived. If they fell into deep water, that could have broken their fall."

"I suppose it's possible," the dwarf said.

"Then we need to get a rope down there, so they can climb back up. Croy!" she shouted. "Croy! Do you hear me?"

The dwarf looked up at Malden as if he'd run out of ideas. The thief could only shrug.

"Croy! Croy! Mörget, can you hear me? Is Croy all right? Mörget! Are you down there?"

Malden had rope still in his pack. Knowing it would do no good, but unable to resist her horror and her grief, he threw one end over the edge.

"It's not nearly long enough," Slag pointed out, "even if they—"

"Be quiet, Slag," Malden hissed.

Cythera turned to face the dwarf with wild eyes. "They might have caught a ledge lower down. They might be down there right now, struggling to hold on, trying to climb up. Hold this rope! Hold it, damn you!" She grabbed the end with both hands and nodded at Malden, who did the same.

"Lass, we need to figure out where we are," Slag tried.

"Hold this damned rope," she screamed at him. Then she leaned over the edge. "Croy? Are you down there? Croy, answer me! I know you're down there! Croy!"

Malden held the rope, though his heart wasn't in it.

"Croy, just grab the rope," Cythera shouted. "Croy, you bastard! Don't leave me like this! Don't leave me alone here!"

She kept calling. Malden held the rope, and so great was her panic and her hope that he kept expecting a tug from below, some sign that Croy or Mörget had grasped the rope and was climbing up.

No such signal came. Eventually Cythera grew hoarse and stopped shouting. And that was when Malden was forced to accept the fact that the three of them were alone, trapped inside the Vincularium. A thief, a dwarf, and a witch's daughter. If there were more revenants to face, or if they came across the demon . . .

"Croy," Cythera wheezed. "Croy!"

# CHAPTER THIRTY-NINE

They had not had the presence of mind to gather up any of the lanterns during their descent to the gallery. What little light Malden had to see by came from above, and after a short while the revenants must have smashed the lanterns and suddenly the three of them were in total darkness.

"Blast," Slag swore. Malden heard him go through his pack. "I have candles, but no way to make a fucking light. Malden, do you have a tinderbox or—"

Green light burst from Cythera's palms. It was a sickly flame, a color no decent fire should ever be. "Quickly," she said. "I'm using the magic I stole from the revenant. It won't last long."

Slag rushed to get a candle's wick into the flame. Once it was burning—with a wholesome yellow light—Cythera let the green flame sputter out again.

"My thanks, lass," the dwarf said. He held the candle up to show her face. It was streaked with tears but she seemed to have recovered a measure of composure.

"I'm fine," she told him. She looked up at Malden next. "I'm sure he's still alive. But you're right, we can't get to him now. We don't have enough rope. So we need to find another way down."

Malden inhaled deeply. "I think, perhaps, the best way to do that would be to follow his own advice. That we should find a way out of the Vincularium altogether. Slag, you said there would be more than one escape shaft. I'm sure they're all sealed tight, but with a little work, maybe we can—"

"I can't just leave Croy here," Cythera said.

"Just so we can go and get some help," Malden assured her. "Even if we just go and fetch Herward to help us look."

"Croy sacrificed his own—" Cythera closed her eyes and breathed deeply for a minute. "He took a great risk for you. He might have died making sure you got down here safely. Will you run away now, when he needs the same consideration in return?"

"What good is his sacrifice, if we all get killed now?" Malden demanded.

"What good is a man, who will not risk a little to save his friend?"

"Are you calling me a coward?" Malden demanded. "Are you?"

"Everyone knows what you are," Cythera seethed back.

Malden's eyes went wide with rage. "At least I'm sensible enough to know when a cause is lost, and to—"

"How dare you." Her eyes flared with anger. She kept her lips pressed tightly together, as if afraid the next thing out of her mouth would be some devastating curse. She said nothing, though. She must have understood he was right. Saying nothing more, she turned away from him and strode off into the darkness. Only a few paces, though— not so far that he couldn't see her back.

"You're acting like a fool," he told her, because he couldn't help himself.

She whirled around to face him, and he was certain he'd made a terrible mistake. Cythera was no witch but it didn't take much magic to curse someone. She could turn his guts to jelly, or his skin to glass, with just an oath.

It was Slag who saved him, since he was incapable of backing down himself. "Hold! Hold," the dwarf said, coming between them. "Be at peace, both of you. Fucking humans. So swift to take offense. You should know that both of you want the same damn thing."

Malden turned to face the dwarf. "We do?"

Cythera presented her back to them both.

Slag shook his head and looked out into the darkness. "She wants to go·down below, to find her betrothed. You want to find an escape shaft. I can guarantee you there's none on this level. This place," he said, waving behind him with his free hand, "is all shops. We need to descend, to where the dwarves had their homes. That's where the shafts will be." He lifted the candle high.

For the first time, Malden actually looked at where he'd ended up.

The gallery was just a wide opening in the shaft, but beyond it lay a long, broad tunnel lined with low buildings. Each structure had only three walls and no roof— they were more stalls than true buildings. Inside most there stood a counter at waist height for a dwarf, about two feet off the ground. Each stall was festooned with multiple signs, engraved in dwarven runes that Malden couldn't read.

"So this is a dwarven marketplace?" he asked.

"It was, once," Slag corrected. His face brightened a little, to see the traces of his ancestors. "Imagine the kinds of merchandise you could get in a place like this. Rare ores, clever tools, exotic fabrics . . . and the trade goods, things we would bargain for with the elves and then you humans. There would have been hundreds of dwarves here, any time of the day or night, driving hard bargains, making alliances for trade, speculating on prices—"

"Robbing each other blind," Malden said. He lit a

candle of his own and went to the nearest stall. "There's
no security here at all. I can see three different ways to rob
one of these shops while the proprietor was standing at his
own counter."

"We don't fucking steal from each other, lad," Slag said.

Malden turned to face him and raised an eyebrow. "Oh?"

"Never. It's unthinkable for a dwarf to turn to crime.
Why would he? There's always work to be done in the
mines, for any that needs money. Good, honest work. I've
never understood why you humans would breed so fast you
had excess people just lying around, not a thing to do, and
not enough food to feed 'em." He shook his head. "Why,
crime's unknown in *our* cities. I suppose we murder each
other, now and again, when some bastard deserves it. But
thievery's not in our nature."

Malden gave him a sly smile. "It's in yours, though. You
work for Cutbill."

"Not as a thief," the dwarf insisted.

"No, you just make the tools that human thieves use."

Slag grunted in displeasure. "We make swords and
spears, too, but we don't kill folk."

"That just makes you an accomplice." Malden wouldn't
let it go. He was still burning with anger from when Cythera had called him a coward. "You're leaving something
out, Slag. There's something you're not telling me."

"Oh, be still, lad," Slag said, looking distinctly uncomfortable.

"Every liar has a tell. Some small twitch of the mouth
as if the lie stings them on the way out. A tendency to tap
their foot in fear of being discovered. Or perhaps they
close their eyes when they deviate from the truth. I'm not
sure exactly what yours is, but I know you're giving me
half-truths."

"Enough of this," Cythera said. She shrugged her pack
onto her shoulders and headed down the double row of
stalls. "You think the way down is through here?" she
asked.

"Aye," Slag confirmed.

"Then let's get moving. Malden, you can insult and bully us when it's time to rest. Right now I expect you to walk."

Malden winced. He didn't care for this change of disposition in Cythera, not at all. "As milady wishes, of course," he said, and sketched a courtly bow.

"Save the flattery for later as well."

## CHAPTER FORTY

The marketplace corridor led hundreds of feet back from the shaft. In its center it widened into a broad plaza where the stalls gave way to larger, more elaborate shops—shops with four walls, and even some tall enough to reach the ceiling. Their doorways stood open, showing only darkness inside.

"There would have been curtains in the door frames," Slag said, gesturing at one gaping portal. "They rotted away centuries ago, of course. Fucking time steals everything of value."

"Time's the greatest thief of all," Malden agreed. "What's that?"

He pointed at a massive pillar that stood in the exact center of the plaza, wider around than any of the shops. It did not run straight from the floor to the ceiling, but arced in a subtle curve. Thousands of brass tacks had been driven into the stone, at eye level for a dwarf.

"The tacks? The dwarves who lived here would post

messages to one another by tacking them to yon pillar. The bits of parchment are long gone."

"No," Malden said, "the—the thing the tacks are driven into."

"Hmm? Oh. That, son, is one of three main support columns of the entire city." Slag went over to pat it with one hand. "Now this is something. I did a little mathematics in my head before and the numbers are just beautiful. This place is a masterpiece. A fucking jewel. The whole weight of the mountain rests on those three pillars. They run all the way up and down—we saw their top ends on the cemetery level, where we came in."

"Only three columns to hold up so much?" Malden asked, feeling like the ceiling might come crashing down at any moment.

"They must be reinforced, somehow."

"By magic?" Cythera asked.

"Nah, lass, we never relied on anything so damnably fickle. They're reinforced with . . . I don't know, on the inside—maybe there's solid metal inside the stone. How they got it in, how they could forge beams so long, or how they could move them once they cooled . . . I'll admit I don't know the specifics. This is far beyond anything my people could build today."

"If it holds up so much," Malden asked, "shouldn't it be straight? Even I know a bent pillar won't carry much weight."

"Ah, but that's part of the genius! That's to take the strain when they're shifted."

Malden frowned. "Shifted? What could possibly move something so big? And if they're rooted in the rock of the mountain, surely they're as stable as the ground itself."

"But that's the thing of it, lad. The ground moves all the time. In winter ice builds up and cracks open rocks. In summer the sun heats the outside of Cloudblade and the rocks expand."

"Rocks . . . expand?"

Slag threw his head back and looked up at the ceiling. "Just take my word for it. The whole mountain moves, all the time. It's moving right now, just so slowly you can't see it. I know I'm not making this clear, but—you know how a drumhead needs to be tightened, ever so often?"

"I've never been very musical," Malden confessed.

Slag grunted in frustration. "Again, take my word for it. Most things expand when they get hot, and contract when they get cold."

"What kind of things?"

"Every fucking thing!" Slag threw up his hands in disgust. "Well, water doesn't. Water expands when it gets colder. But—everything else, more or less. All right?" The candle he held guttered and nearly went out. "There's no use explaining. Just know the mountain moves. If it rested on straight columns, it would just collapse whenever it moved up and down. The curved columns have a little give in 'em. They compress, just a little, to take the strain, then release that pressure when the forces equalize. Like the springs I mounted under our wagon, a couple days ago."

Malden was utterly lost. "Does it work?"

"This place ain't collapsed in a thousand fucking years. So yes."

"Ah. Good, then."

Cythera lifted her candle high and pointed farther down the marketplace corridor. Ahead of them it narrowed again. "Now that's settled, can we get on with this? Slag, you said there was a stairway leading down to the next floor, through here."

"Should be. Only it's not a stairway."

"I'll slide down a pole if I have to." Cythera led them down the corridor until they reached its end. The corridor emptied into a circular room with a vaulted ceiling. In the center of the room a round hole had been cut in the floor, and an identical hole opened above it in the ceiling. A thick chain ran through one and out the other.

"The House of Chains indeed," Malden said.

"This is a lift. It operates by the principle of—"

Malden's eyes went wide as he expected the dwarf to give him another lecture on whatever kind of magic the dwarves had invented here, which he was sure wasn't magic because everyone knew that dwarves didn't use magic. Except it would sound like magic, and work like magic. Rocks expanding in the sun. Ice cracking open the entire world. He could study a hundred years, he imagined, and not understand a word.

"Oh, never fucking mind. Take this." Slag handed Malden his candle. Then the dwarf grabbed the chain and heaved downward on it. It took his weight but didn't move. "It's stuck. Not too surprising, but damned inconvenient. You two wait here—I'll be right back." He climbed up the chain, hand over hand, and disappeared into the hole in the ceiling.

Leaving Malden and Cythera alone.

Malden knew he should say nothing. Cythera was sick with worry for Croy, and he should have let her be. The silence between them was unbearable, though. He was almost able to convince himself he was helping when he said, "I know you don't want to hear this, but there's a chance Croy is dead."

She stabbed one finger in his face. "If you say that again—"

He held up his hand for peace. "Cythera, believe me, I don't want him to be dead. I'm merely suggesting it might be worth considering what that means, just in case." He grimaced. "On the off chance."

"Liar," she said.

"I didn't say he *was*, just that he *might* be d—"

"You lied when you said you didn't want him to be dead." She stepped close to him and he expected her to slap him across the face. She didn't, though. She looked too angry to lift her hand. "Croy," she said, quite slowly, quite deliberately, "was in your way. You persist in this delusion that I'm secretly in love with you, and that I'm only betrothed to Croy for his money. You must imagine that if he was dead, then you could just scoop me up. Steal me away from him with no consequences."

"That's not fair," he insisted.

"It's true. The truth doesn't have to be fair."

"Damn you, woman. I—"

Malden stopped talking when the chain in the middle of the room started to rattle. He stepped back and his free hand went to the hilt of Acidtongue. Then a very strange thing happened, wholly outside the realm of Malden's experience.

A little room came down out of the ceiling and stopped exactly flush with the floor. Perhaps "room" was the wrong word. It was a cage of bronze bars, about five feet high and eight feet across. It had a door in the front that swung open, so they could see Slag standing inside. His hands were covered in grease that he wiped on a piece of rag. "Come in, then," he said, "if you're in such a bloody rush to go down. This is faster than any stairway."

# CHAPTER FORTY-ONE

Coarse sand crusted Croy's cheek, digging into his flesh. He could hear the gentle slap of waves nearby. He opened his eyes but saw nothing but darkness so profound it made his head ache.

Come to think of it, his whole body ached. He felt like

he'd been picked up by a giant and thrown hard against a stone wall. He felt bruised and battered, though no bones seemed broken. He was also soaked to the skin.

He knew immediately that he was alive. This didn't seem anything like the glorious afterlife the Lady promised her followers. It was possible that he had sinned in some way and was dragged down into the pit by the Blood-god, but he had always assumed he would go to the other place.

Anyway, it was too cold where he lay to be the fiery pit.

He sat up and ran his hands across his face, clearing off the grit. Then he reached down to his belt to reassure himself that Ghostcutter was still there. Reaching for its hilt was an old reflex, and the feeling of its grip in his hand never failed to calm him, no matter how frightful a situation he found himself in. Yet this time his hand closed on nothing. The sword was gone. He struggled around to reach for his pack—there was at least an eating knife in there—but the pack was gone too.

Croy almost never blasphemed, but he muttered a curse concerning the Lady's left elbow then. It wasn't particularly vulgar but it made him feel better.

He called for Mörget but there was no answer.

He got to his feet, his boots crunching on the pebbly sand. He had no idea where he was, though considering the darkness he decided he must still be in the Vincularium. Stretching out his hands, he walked away from the sound of the water, moving forward one tentative step at a time until his hands encountered a brick wall. He pressed his back up against it and tried to think of what to do next.

Feeling his way along the wall, he headed away from the sound of water. The floor was even and he only tripped a few times as he made his way up a modest incline. The bricks under his fingers were uniform in size and shape, and he counted them as he went along, keeping track of how far he'd gone.

Fifty feet along the wall ended. He reached around its

edge and found another wall at right angles to the first, headed away from him. He took a few halting steps forward but couldn't find a far wall, and decided he had come into a larger room.

How long could he keep doing this, he wondered, moving blindly forward with no weapons and no light? How long would it be before he stepped over the edge of some pitfall—or blundered into the resting place of more revenants?

As long as it took him, he decided. If he stopped now, if he did what he really wanted to do—which was to sit down, hug his knees, and wait for death to come—then he would be a failure. A disgrace. All his vows, all his beliefs, would be for nothing. He would die alone in a dark place and the best he could hope for would be that nobody ever found his bones. That nobody ever realized what a dishonorable end he'd found.

The one thing Croy still possessed was honor.

He could not stop now. Cythera was out there—somewhere—in the darkness. He had made a bad mistake by bringing her to the Vincularium, he knew. He had put her in mortal danger. He had no choice now but to find her and rescue her from this place. No matter what that took. No matter if he was killed in the process, because at least then he would die striving to accomplish something.

He put one foot in front of the other and walked forward, into the darkness.

One step. Another. He felt the floor before him with his outstretched boot. The stone below him seemed solid enough. Another step.

That was when he heard the chittering.

It was a soft sound, like leather being rubbed against leather. It was all around him. He could not imagine what nature of monster made that noise, but it came from every side at once. It rose and fell in pitch, like the song the crickets sang in the trees around Helstrow. A sound he'd known well as a boy. He associated it with long summer days playing with wooden swords and mock-jousting against the quintain. A sound that made him think of his mother's hands, and his father's beard.

Only now it was a hundred times louder, and it might come from the throat of the beast that finally slew him.

He reached up and touched the cornucopia charm that hung around his neck. *Lady, make me fit for Your purpose*, he prayed. Silently, of course. If he had to fight with his bare hands, he would. But if he could walk through this room without alerting the creatures in it, all the better.

Honor allowed a man to be a little bit stealthy, after all. If it made the difference between life and death.

He took another step forward—and walked right into something big and hard that scuttled away from him on many legs. The chittering sound increased in volume and intensity until he thought it would deafen him.

Then he heard another sound—the sound of metal striking stone. And a light erupted into life before him.

Croy threw a hand over his eyes to protect them, but the light was dying away again already. Metal struck stone once more, and Croy finally saw what he faced.

Mörget, holding Dawnbringer. The light came from the blade.

All around him stood giant cave beetles, as docile as cattle. A whole herd of them—enough to make the chittering sound. The same as the creature they'd seen up on the surface, what felt like a lifetime ago. The giant beetle that "attacked" Malden, and done no worse than cover him in goo. Malden realized that the monsters he'd thought surrounded him were, in point of fact, just livestock.

He imagined himself standing in a field full of cows with a hoodwink over his eyes. Would he have been as frightened? Would he have thought so hard about what honor demanded of him? He felt an utter fool.

"We won't starve, at least," Mörget said.

And Croy laughed until tears shot from his eyes.

# CHAPTER FORTY-TWO

Mörget had both their packs open and the contents spread out on the floor of the room. Everything had been soaked through when they hit the water, and he was drying out what could be salvaged. "The candles won't light," he explained. "The wicks are soaked through." He struck Dawnbringer against the floor, and Croy saw their equipment arrayed before him. No rope, nor any lanterns, but they had two of the tents and the bulk of the climbing gear.

"You shouldn't bash your sword about like that," Croy chided the barbarian. "You'll blunt its edge."

"Better that than going about blind," Mörget told him. "But all right, let us sit down in the darkness, and I'll tell you something of what happened."

It was good to hear Mörget's voice. It filled Croy with hope and cheer. He drank some ale from one of their bottles—the cork had held—and listened without hearing all of the words. He caught the gist, anyway.

Mörget had carried him over the edge of the shaft and together they hit the water very hard. They had sunk like stones in their armor, and should by all rights have drowned. Croy was knocked unconscious by the impact, but Mörget kept enough of his wits to swim for the surface. He had hauled Croy upward, hoping only that he was swimming in the right direction.

"In the dark, with my head ringing like a bell, it was not so easy to tell. Luck was with me, it seems. I broke free into air and gasped for breath, and knew I was alive. I wanted to stay that way. So I picked a direction at random and swam for the side of the shaft, pulling you along behind me. I think you swallowed much water and I was certain you would drown, but I did not wish to leave your body behind, even though it slowed me greatly."

"I thank you," Croy said. The barbarian had certainly saved his life. "You could have faltered under my weight, and then we would both have died."

"Bah, death is my mother! I don't fear her embraces. Anyway, I figured if you were dead, and I found myself trapped down here, I could always eat you if I couldn't find any other food."

"Oh," Croy said.

Mörget continued with his tale as if there was nothing grisly or disheartening about the prospect of eating a friend. "I found the wall of the shaft and then swam along it until I found an opening. I quickly discovered one fact about this place—the lowest level is completely flooded. We are now actually upon the second floor."

"Hmm," Croy said, and drank some more ale. The pain of his bruises started to fade.

"I dragged you up onto a gallery and tried to revive you, but to no avail. I pounded on your back and chest until you stopped vomiting water, but still you did not wake. For a long while I sat by your side, waiting for you to stir. Then I decided I would use my time better by learning where we ended up. You see what I found. There are more rooms beyond this one, which we will explore together."

"Ah," Croy said. He leaned his head back against the brick wall. "You deserve some reward for saving me, but I fear you will have nothing but my eternal gratitude, brother."

"Recompense enough, surely."

"Yet I have one question," Croy told him. "My blade, Ghostcutter. Was it lost when we struck the water? It is not on my belt. Nor is its scabbard."

"Hmm? Oh, no. I took it from you while you slept. I have it here on my belt now, next to Dawnbringer's sheath."

"That's very good news. I'd be breaking a powerful oath if I lost it."

"As I well know."

Croy hefted the ale jug. It was half empty. He must have been very thirsty. "Mörget," he said, when the barbarian didn't say anything more. "May I have it back?"

The barbarian boomed out a laugh. "Of course, brother! I was only keeping it safe for you!"

They laughed together, though Croy wondered what would have happened if he hadn't asked for Ghostcutter. The barbarians, he knew, would love to get their hands on more of the Ancient Blades. They were a people who subsisted on conquest, and they longed to take Skrae for their own—and possessing the magical swords would certainly help with that goal.

But no, surely Mörget wouldn't have kept the blade. Mörget had honor of his own, even if it didn't come from promises made to the Lady. Croy was certain the barbarian had meant no harm at all.

He drank more ale and put suspicion out of his mind.

They sat together, drinking and eating from their waterlogged food supply, while Croy regained some strength. Eventually it came time to begin exploring. Once the candles had dried out enough to burn, they each took one and waded through the herd of beetles. Croy counted at least sixty of the beasts, and while natural philosophy was not his strong suit, he'd spent enough time around farms in his youth to wonder what they were doing there. "The elves kept them here, mayhap as a food source. That much I comprehend. Yet that was centuries ago. They still act like a herd of livestock," he said. "Huddling together for safety and warmth. Wild animals don't flock so close. They roam farther, the better to graze on open land."

Mörget shrugged. "A mystery. Perhaps not the most pressing."

"Of course," Croy said, but he couldn't defeat his own curiosity. "I suppose it's possible they simply huddle together because of predators. Perhaps the demon comes down here and feasts on them from time to time."

"I hope it is so!" Mörget crowed. "Then we will see it soon, for it had a terrible hunger, if I remember correctly."

The presence of the demon might well make the beetles cower together, Croy decided. Though why, then, didn't they just leave? One of them had escaped the Vincularium, so why hadn't they all tried to get away?

Perhaps they were just too stupid. Croy shrugged. It was all the answer he would get, so he considered it answer enough.

The two warriors made their way out of the room, heading still farther from the shaft. The floor sloped very gently upward as they proceeded. Croy wanted to get up to the third level from the top—the level where Cythera and the others had gone—so he was glad for the rise in elevation, though he kept his eyes open for any stairwells or ramps that might lead up more quickly.

The rooms they explored, however, were mostly featureless and plain. Whatever purpose they had served when the dwarves carved them out of the rock was unclear now. There were signs that this level, too, had flooded at some point in the past. The walls were mottled with fungus and draped with a strange white plant like albino seaweed. Perhaps it was this strange vegetation that had drawn the cave beetles. Beneath the plant life, pale stains ran along the walls like a high water mark. In some places bits of ironwork must once have been stapled to the walls, but all that remained were dull red streaks where rust had claimed them. When Croy held his candle high, he could see long stalactites hanging down from the ceiling, like dripping candle wax cast in stone.

Mörget took the lead while Croy covered their rear. The beetles were no threat, of course, but the two of them had agreed it was best not to be surprised by any more revenants if they could help it—and there was always the demon to worry about. For the most part they moved in silence, but it seemed that Mörget couldn't bear the stillness, and after a while he broke it with a statement that puzzled Croy greatly.

"These rooms call to me," he said.

"In what sense?"

"When I think of the lair of a demon, this is much what I see," Mörget explained. "Dark, abandoned places, with a ready supply of game. Such are rare enough, but that is exactly what we have here. I think perhaps our fall was fortuitous. Perhaps it was fate that drove me down here."

Croy frowned. "Mörget—I want to vanquish this creature as much as you do."

"Of course! It is our very nature."

"But—we have to rescue the others first. And it would be wise to secure a way out of the Vincularium. Only then should we track down the beast."

The barbarian turned to face him full on. His features were quite calm—his mouth a straight line under its coat of paint, his eyes half shrouded by their lids. "I have a destiny to complete," he said. "It can brook few delays."

"Just one small delay. Maybe two," Croy said. "I believe you possess a code of honor just as I do. No honorable man would leave a woman or a defenseless dwarf to the horrors of this place. Have I misjudged you?"

The barbarian raised one hand in dismissal. "Of course not. Very well, we shall rescue the weaklings first. Unless, of course, along the way we catch sight of our quarry. We must not lose the opportunity if it befalls us." He turned and started walking up the slope again. "What about the thief, though?"

"Hmm?" Croy asked. Thoughts so occupied his brain he barely heard.

"Malden. Your friend. You did not mention him when you listed those you must preserve."

Croy tilted his head to one side, considering why he had omitted Malden from his list of objectives. "Ah. Well, he has Acidtongue. He can defend himself."

Of course, he thought, it would help if Malden knew how to use a sword.

The possibility that his slip had been meaningful, that

he left Malden out of his goals for a reason, troubled Croy, but he already had enough to worry about.

# CHAPTER FORTY-THREE

Malden climbed into the brazen cage and braced himself by holding on to one of the bars. He had to stoop or bash his head against the top of the cage. Cythera, standing beside him, looked as uneasy as he felt. "This—device—travels upward and down along its chain?" he asked. "Like a bucket on a rope, lowered into a well, and then brought back up by winding a windlass. Only—instead of water, this carries people."

"Brilliant deductive powers, oh gormless human," Slag said, rolling his eyes.

"But—what if the chain breaks under our weight?" Cythera asked.

"Then my ancestors built it wrong," Slag told her. "You're going to insult my ancestors now?" The dwarf closed the door of the cage, its hinges making a hideous squeal. "Malden, help me with this." A loop of chain dangled between them—not the same chain that held the cage in its shaft, but a much finer one that looped around a complicated arrangement of gears in the ceiling. "Just pull down, and keep pulling. Normally there would be a team of huge cave beetles at the bottom of the main chain, walking a wheel to make it move. This is just for emergencies, but it'll serve our purpose. No, no, no," the dwarf grumbled, "you're doing it wrong. Just take hold of one length of chain and pull down."

The chain Malden held was actually joined to itself in a loop. He pulled down on it and the gears in the ceiling creaked. The whole cage dropped a fraction of an inch—far too fast for Malden's liking. Slag grabbed the chain as well and together they pulled until the cage moved smoothly down through the hole in the floor.

It was not magic that moved the cage. Malden understood that. The chain he pulled somehow did the work, and it was his own muscles that moved the chain. Yet the chain moved so freely in its gears, and there was some strange proportion to it—he had to pull it a very long way, very fast, before the cage moved even a bit—that he knew he would never grasp the principles involved. The cage might as well be enchanted, for all he understood.

Yet it worked, he could not deny that. They descended through the floor below without stopping. Slag claimed it was a level of workshops and smithies. Malden could see very little of that floor by the stray beams of candlelight thrown from within their cage.

What he could see didn't please him much. Beyond the bars lay a vast expanse of dust and stone. He could make out walls of ancient brick, and a doorway, the door hanging loose by one hinge. The candlelight reflected dully from every surface, casting long shadows that danced around the stillness. There was nothing there to alarm him, nothing that looked like it would come racing out to snatch at his face. Yet the very quiet of the place, the sense of vast time and stone left undisturbed for centuries, was somehow worse than the sudden fear and desperate action of the fight with the revenants. Anything could hide back there. Great treasures piled in heaps, maybe—but far more likely dead things, laying sprawled on the floor like inert piles of bones, just waiting for a reason to rise again. A reason to climb stiffly to their bony feet and come forward.

He'd known he was a fool to come here. It was far too dangerous, and the constant fear was preying on him, making him act like a dullard. Making him angry and snappish, so that he'd fought with Cythera when he should have been comforting her. Reassuring her (despite the obvious fact they were far from safety), telling her everything would be all right.

Cythera pressed her face against the bars and peered out into the darkness. Perhaps she was thinking exactly the same thoughts. But he didn't dare ask. As angry as she was with him right now, he thought that saying anything might be a bad idea.

Yet he was glad when she spoke, if only because it broke the silence. "I am very glad to have you with us, Slag," she said. "I fear we would be utterly lost without you. You seem to know this place, though you say you've never been here before. Do you have some map of the Vincularium you haven't shared with us?"

"I don't need one," the dwarf said, grunting from the effort of constantly pulling the chain. "It's all fucking standardized."

"I don't know that word," Malden said.

"Big fucking surprise." Slag considered it for a moment, puffing his breath through his black beard. "Well—you know Kingsgate High Street, in Ness?"

"Yes, of course," the thief replied. A silly question. It was one of the main streets in the city where he'd spent his entire life.

"Well, would you be surprised to know there's a Kingsgate High Street in Redweir as well? And one in Strowbury?"

"Not very."

"Let me ask you another question—would you be surprised to learn that, in any of those cities, if you were to follow Kingsgate High Street all the way to the city wall, you would find it led to a road that took you to Helstrow, where your king lives?"

"That's what 'Kingsgate' means."

Slag nodded. "Now, imagine if every road in Ness had a counterpart in Redweir and Strowbury, and once you knew where, say, Pokekirtle Lane led in one of those cities, you could find a whorehouse anywhere you went. And every one of those brothels had the same name, and the same password to get in, and charged the same fee for a quick fuck."

"Slag—there's a lady present," Malden insisted.

"A lady who has walked past the bawdy house on Pokekirtle Lane many times," Cythera said, giving Malden an icy look. "Though of course I've never been inside."

Malden wondered if that was meant as an insult about his parentage—his mother had worked in a bawdy house, after all. He shook off the offense and looked back at Slag. "I think I grasp your point," he said. "So every dwarven city is built to the same plan. If you know where the marketplace is in the dwarven capital, you can find a similar marketplace in a dwarven city halfway across the world—or in a dwarven city that has been abandoned for centuries."

"Huzzah. You've finally fucking got it, lad."

Malden shook his head. "It seems that would take half the charm out of life. And Cutbill would lose half his custom if no one ever got lost in the Stink, back home, and needed an apparently friendly local guide to direct them back to the high street."

"Maybe so. Our way's a damn sight more efficient, though. For instance—I can tell, without even looking, that this is where we get off."

Malden looked outside the cage and saw another floor rising up to meet them. It was as dark as any other and he could see nothing to distinguish it. Slag showed him how to bring the cage to a gentle stop just even with the floor, and then he pushed open the cage door. "Let's go," he said. "Bring that candle over here."

Malden and Cythera followed him out into the darkness. This level seemed in far less pristine condition than those above. Piles of loose stone and rusting iron lay all about, and here and there a forgotten tool lay in the middle of the floor, as if it had been dropped in a hurry and never put away properly. Giant gears with stripped teeth leaned up against the walls, and everywhere chains hung down from the ceiling like rusting stalactites.

"I'll admit to a certain ignorance regarding dwarven living arrangements," Cythera said, her voice thick with suspicion. "Yet I have to remark—this does not look like a residential level, where we might find an escape shaft. And I know for a fact we haven't descended far enough to reach Croy."

"Er—yeah," Slag said, rummaging about in one of the piles of old iron. He found a piece of tin only lightly mottled with corrosion, and began bending it into a new shape. "This is still one of the workshop levels. But it's where we want to be right now, I promise. I know a shortcut."

"Do you?" Cythera asked. "A shortcut that leads to the residential levels, or one that will take us to the bottom of the shaft?"

The dwarf frowned and cursed as the sharp-edged tin bit into his hands. Then he let go and reached into the pile of scrap for a short iron spike. "Both," he told her. "Here, give me that candle."

She handed him the candle stub she held. He wedged it onto the iron spike and then stood up straight. He had improvised a simple lantern, using the tin as a reflector. The candle's light was almost doubled, and he even had a sort of handle to hold it by. "Come on. It's not far now."

He set off at a good pace, wending a course through the piles of refuse, farther into the darkness.

Malden glanced at Cythera, who looked intensely skeptical. Then he shrugged and followed the dwarf.

# CHAPTER FORTY-FOUR

Slag's path led them through the largest forge Malden had ever seen—a cyclopean vault the dimensions of which could only be vaguely hinted at by their paltry candlelight. Molds for casting iron stood in great tidy pyramids, some of lead and some of moldering wax that collapsed into greasy dust when he touched them. Farther along, a wide channel had been cut through the floor, then lined with bricks that glimmered eerily as Malden climbed over them. One whole wall had been constructed of iron plates thirty feet high. The plates were designed to be retractable with the use of long, stout poles. One plate hung crooked on a rusted hinge, and beyond them he could see a round space as big as a house, lined everywhere with the same shiny bricks. It must have been a furnace capable of generating unearthly amounts of heat, he decided. Strangely, there were no ashes on its floor, nor remnants of charcoal or other spent fuel. Instead a complicated array of pipes emerged from the floor, with holes bored in a regular pattern along their top sides. Above the network of pipes, stout chains held up a mammoth iron cauldron. Bright metal slag stained its sides.

"Is this where steel was made?" Malden asked. Steel—good steel—was the most valuable thing the dwarves made, and it remained a great mystery to Malden's people. Human blacksmiths could work wonders with iron, twisting it into fantastic shapes and objects of great utility. Yet iron could not bend like steel, nor was it half as strong. Iron blades lost their edge too quickly and could never cut through steel armor. If humans could make steel they would turn their hands to little else, he imagined, yet every time they tried, they produced only a brittle facsimile that shattered as soon as it was struck with a hammer. No human had ever seen the foundries where the dwarves made their strongest metal—the very process by which steel was forged remained a closely guarded secret. Any human who learned how it was done could become a very rich man in very short order.

Sadly, he was not to be that man. Slag snorted in derision. "Don't be a simpleton. Steel wasn't invented until long after this place was abandoned. Anyway, you don't need a forge that size for casting a few fucking swords. This was for the more exotic alloys. Come along away from there, please. And don't touch a fucking thing!"

It was too late. Malden had already bent to examine a pile of metal scrap, thinking he'd seen a glint of silver at its base. He reached for it, then jumped back in fear as the whole pile creaked forward and spilled out over the floor in a cloud of dust and flakes of rust. The noise was deafening as the metal clattered and bounced against the flagstones.

When the heap had settled down into a new shape, Malden straightened up and tried to regain some composure while Slag stared daggers at him. "Lesson learned," he claimed.

Slag spat in disgust. He led them past enormous presses and hammer mills, water-driven machines that he explained could take a piece of raw iron and flatten it into plates by row after row of trip-hammers. Malden had seen similar devices in human workshops in the Smoke back in Ness, but nothing on such a scale or so cleverly designed. Other machines, he didn't recognize at all, which hardly surprised him. "The guild of smiths would pay a fortune for this equipment," he pointed out.

Slag shrugged. "None of this would work anymore, even if you could get it out of here somehow." Malden saw he was correct. The iron parts had rusted clean through in places, and anywhere the wood remained it was crumbling to dust and riddled with wormcast.

Still, the technical expertise on display put anything he had seen before to shame. Ness was a working city, a place where goods were manufactured in huge yards and works, but compared to the dilapidated machinery they passed, even the finest and most up-to-date mills in the Free City might as well have been devoted to bashing rocks together to make stone axes.

"You could outfit an army with these works," Malden said, keeping his candle high so he could see everything. "Several armies."

"They did," Cythera told him. "The war between our people and the elves went on for decades. For us it was a time of unparalleled bloodshed and suffering. For the dwarves it was an era of great prosperity."

The dwarf shrugged. "Soldiers need iron they can trust. Bronze, too."

"Sadu's knucklebones. Slag—don't tell me your people sold to both sides." Malden was somewhat offended by the idea.

"It wasn't our war," Slag said. It was not an apology.

"But you were our allies!" Malden exclaimed. He knew that much of history.

"Aye, lad—once we knew you were going to win. This way."

The dwarf took them past a slightly more tidy version of the junkyard they'd originally come through. Here, piles of metal scrap were heaped against the walls, piled to the ceiling, sorted by type of metal. Malden recognized lead and copper and iron—all of them succumbing to inevitable corrosion. He saw piles of tin and pewter and brass. Some were comprised of far more exotic metals—they were perhaps alloys he'd only heard mentioned, like hepatizon or corinthiacum. There were many piles as well that he could not identify at all. There were metals that looked blue in the candlelight, and—most interestingly to a thief—others very nearly the color of gold.

"Did your ancestors ever work in precious metals

here?" Malden asked. "Silver, say, or orichalcum? Maybe electrum?"

Slag sighed and turned to give him a nasty look. "Yes, they did. But not in this foundry. Gold's rarer than ghost shit. You work it in small quantities, under special conditions, to make sure you don't waste so much as a speck of dust. If you're looking for treasure here you're wasting your time, I'm afraid. Anyway, when they left here, the dwarves would have been sure to take every damned ingot of— Malden! Away from there!"

Malden had been about to pick up a piece of straw-colored metal from one of the piles. He stopped with his hand a hairbreadth from it and looked up in surprise. "Why?" he asked. "Is this some secretly valuable metal you don't want me pilfering?"

"No," the dwarf said. "It's yellow arsenic."

The thief yanked his hand back at once. "Like the poison?"

"The deadliest kind, refined and purified. That piece right there is enough to kill half a fucking village."

"And it's just been left here, out in the open?"

Slag's eyes were wide with fear. "Out in the open? When this place was in use, only trained smiths were allowed in this room. Did you expect this place to be safe and friendly to any thief who broke in and made himself at home?"

"Hardly," Malden said. "Yet I didn't expect it to be as poisonous as a nest of vipers either. What were your ancestors doing with arsenic? Making tainted weapons for the elves to turn against *my* ancestors?"

Slag grunted in frustration. "When alloyed properly with copper, arsenic makes an incredibly hard bronze. Really now, lad, don't touch anything in here. This place wasn't meant for a playroom."

Malden moved as quickly as he could away from the piles of scrap metal. It seemed he couldn't do anything right. At least Cythera didn't comment on his foolhardiness.

The foundry complex didn't go on much farther. Slag led them past a workshop used for polishing metals, where the brick walls had been etched by noxious fumes. The place still smelled of rotting eggs, even eight hundred years after it had ceased to be used. Beyond that, the foundry ended in a massive stone door inscribed with dwarven runes.

"We need to get this open, and it'll take some work," Slag said. "Here, Cythera, hold the light so. Malden, find a bar of iron we can use to pry this. Something not too rusted, please."

"I'm not touching a thing," Malden insisted.

"Fine," Slag said, and sought out the iron bar himself. When he returned with a stout rod about seven feet long, Cythera was waiting for him with a look of suspicion. Malden was glad he wasn't the dwarf.

"Your shortcut goes through this door, does it?" she asked.

"Yes, lass," the dwarf said.

Malden was impressed. He'd seen card cheats bluff their way to riches with less innocent expressions.

"Is that why the door is labeled, 'Hall of Treasures'?"

"Ah," Slag said. "I, uh, I didn't—"

"You didn't know I could read dwarven runes."

"Not as such, no."

"I'm the daughter of a witch and a sorcerer. I was taught to read so I could decipher ancient manuscripts and grimoires. Dwarven runes are easy compared to some of the weird alphabets I've mastered." Cythera sighed and set her candle down on the floor. "I'm sure you have an excellent reason to waste our time. Well, get on with it—but I want to know everything when this is done. I want to know exactly why you're willing to let Croy die for what's in that room. Is the treasure truly worth that?"

Slag frowned. "I doubt you'll approve, honestly. But to me, well, I'd sacrifice about a hundred dimwit knights for this."

She turned her face away from him. "Just be quick."

Malden, however, reached eagerly for the iron bar. "Let's get to it, shall we?" he asked, with newfound enthusiasm. He shoved one end of the bar into the massive doorjamb and started to heave. Slag grabbed the bar as well, and together they started to make headway. The door ground noisily against the floor, as if it had swollen in its jamb, but it moved, inch by inch.

The door was almost open when Malden heard what sounded like an insect fly past his ear. Slag suddenly let go of the bar. Its weight doubled in Malden's hands without warning and it was all he could do to jump back as it fell clattering to the floor.

"Got too heavy for you?" Malden asked, wheeling around to face the dwarf.

Slag didn't answer. He was too busy trying to pull a dart out of his neck.

# CHAPTER FORTY-FIVE

Malden dropped the bar instantly. He grabbed up a candle and peered at the wall next to the door. It didn't take long to find what he was looking for—a hole bored into the stone, as wide across as his little finger, drilled at exactly neck height for a dwarf. It was hard to tell by candlelight but he thought there might be a spring inside.

A classic trap, and one he would have seen instantly if it had been set for a victim of human height. The hole would be drilled all the way through the wall, and the spring latched in place. On the far side of the wall there would be a bit of wire running from the door to the spring. When they opened the door, the wire snapped, releasing the spring. Anyone standing near the door would be shot with the dart.

As to who had set the dart, Malden had no clue—though he supposed it must be the same unknown person who had placed the spike trap back in the barricade room.

"Damn," he said. "So obvious, when you know it's there!"

"Aye, lad," Slag said. He pulled the dart free and threw it to the floor. "Smarts a bit." He looked up at Malden. When their eyes met, Malden knew instantly that something was wrong. He had a pretty clear idea what it was, too.

"I got so fucking close," Slag whispered.

"Oh, no," Malden said. "It can't be. I—I'm sorry, old man."

The dwarf nodded and looked away. Then he took two steps away from the door and let out a scream of pain that echoed around the abandoned foundry. The agony must have been excruciating, for he doubled over and his whole body shook.

Cythera looked over at Malden with wide eyes, then rushed forward with her light. "Slag—are you all right?"

"What a fucking daft question," the dwarf told her. "No, I'm not."

"Poison," Cythera cried as she bent down by Slag's side. The dwarf put an arm around her waist and let her help him off his feet. Gently, she laid him down on the floor, then emptied her pack and wadded it up to make a pillow for his head. He tried to sit up but she pushed him back down. "No, Slag," she said, "don't move, just—just rest."

"No," Malden said, clenching his eyes shut. "No, damn you. Not like this."

There was little he could do. He wrapped the end of his cloak around his hand and picked up the dart. It was made of very light wood and fletched with pigeon feathers. The point looked very sharp. There was no doubt in his mind that it had not been sitting there, waiting to kill some-one, for eight hundred years. The mechanism would have rusted away or the dart itself would have rotted. Someone had laid that trap recently, within the last couple of days. And it didn't seem at all like the work of revenants. They longed to kill the living, true enough, but they had far less subtle methods at their disposal.

A droplet of straw-colored liquid ran down the shaft of the dart, and he sniffed at it before dropping it again. "It doesn't smell like hemlock," he said.

"Lad," the dwarf said, staring up at Malden. "Lad, I'm fucking cold."

Malden nodded and took off his cloak. Laying it across the dwarf's body, he knelt down beside him.

Slag gave him a wry smile. He tried to say something more but then his body seized up and he could only tilt his head to the side before he started retching.

Cythera dropped to her knees by the dwarf's side. "Hold him," she told Malden. "He might hurt himself."

Malden clutched the dwarf's arms as Slag began to shake violently. Convulsions wracked his slight frame and his back arched unnaturally.

"There must be something we can do for him," Malden insisted.

"Just—Just hold him!" Cythera said, grabbing Slag's ankles. "This won't last very long. Not this time, I think."

Slag's body gave one last buck and then he fell back and lay still.

"Oooh," the dwarf said. "My back hurts."

Cythera brought her hand up to her mouth and gnawed anxiously on one fingernail. "You said it didn't smell like hemlock. The poison on the dart. What did it smell like? Did it smell of almonds? Or perhaps garlic?"

Malden shook his head. "No smell at all, really. It was the color of straw."

"Was it liquid, or was it pasty?"

The thief stared at her. "Liquid," he said. "What are you getting at? You knew he would have that fit. What do you know of poisons?"

She waved one hand in the air. "I mentioned that my mother's a witch, Malden."

"I have met her, you know," he protested. Then he shook his head and said, "She taught you something of poisons?"

"There are more reagents, tinctures, and orpiments in her larder than you'd find in an apothecary's shop. She uses them to brew potions, to make healing salves, special ointments—she taught me a little of the plants and compounds that heal, and, yes, a little of those that kill."

She jumped up and ran to where the dart lay. She studied it carefully, then took a droplet of the poison between two fingertips and rubbed them together briskly. "It's not hemlock, you're right. Nor hebon of yew, though the symptoms are close . . . maybe henbane? He's too lucid for it to be deadly nightshade."

Malden looked down at the dwarf. Sweat slicked across Slag's face, and his skin was a rosy pink—which looked decidedly unhealthy, since normally a dwarf's skin was whiter than snow. Slag writhed and pushed Malden's cloak off him, as if he had grown too hot. Consciousness had nearly fled him.

Malden ran over to where Cythera stood and whispered, "Will he perish?"

"Yes," she said, looking him right in the eye. "Whether it happens in the next few minutes, though, or as much as a day from now, I can't say. Not without knowing what kind of poison was on this dart, how much of a dose he received—and a hundred other things I can't begin to guess at."

"You must know an antidote, though. Surely there is one!"

"If I could get him out of here—if I could bring him to Coruth, perhaps. But she's hundreds of miles away."

"We have to try. If he has any chance at all." He reached over and took her hand. "Cythera, I know you won't want

to hear it. But this means we have to escape from the Vincularium as fast as we can. We can't go looking for Croy."

Her mouth formed a hard line but she didn't look away
from his eyes.

"You're right," she said. The words came as if they'd
been dragged out of her.

Malden nodded and turned around, intending to build
some kind of litter out of the tents they carried in their
packs. He stopped, though, when he saw that Slag was
crawling across the floor.

"Stop that this instant," Cythera said.

Slag halted his forward progress. Yet he looked up at
them and said, "Fuck off. I know I'm dying. You don't
have to fucking whisper about it. Before I go, though, I
have to see what's behind that door. I have to know if it's
still there."

# CHAPTER FORTY-SIX

"What was that sound, just now?" Croy asked.
      Mörget turned and shook his head to indicate
he'd heard nothing.

"It sounded like someone screaming, very far away."

The barbarian stopped where he was and tilted his head
to one side. "Nothing," he said. "Perhaps a gust of wind,
howling through these ruins. Did it sound to you like your
woman?"

". . . No," Croy admitted. "You must be right. Let's
hurry onward, all the same."

They had found a spiral ramp that led upward to a higher level. A thin stream of water rolled down the ramp and made their footing precarious, but Croy was able to climb with one hand along the rough stone wall.

At the top of the ramp they found a long, low tunnel, perhaps twenty feet wide, its ceiling not much higher than their heads. It ran away from them into darkness. Croy hardly trusted his sense of direction at that point, but he believed the tunnel headed back in the direction of the main shaft.

The floor was slick with water, and a thin vapor coiled around his ankles. The tunnel was filled with broad stone racks, standing in uniform rows. Each rack had four shelves, and each shelf was packed tight with a type of object he didn't recognize. They were cylindrical in shape, though some were squatter than others, and some taller. Each was wrapped tightly in coarse fabric with a broad weave. They gave off a peculiar smell of dampness and must, and Croy thought they must be rotting away after so long underground in the wet.

Farther along the corridor, narrow side passages opened to either side. Mörget took the one on the left, Croy on the right, and when they came back together in the center they each could report they'd seen the same thing—more long, wet corridors, more racks, myriad more cylinders wrapped in fabric. There were at least a dozen such tunnels, and every one was filled in exactly the same manner.

Croy's curiosity got the better of him. He mounted his candle on top of one rack to free his hands. Then he lifted one of the cylinders from the rack and carefully unwrapped it. It was heavier than he'd expected it to be, but once open, it crumbled and fell apart easily. Inside the fabric he found three pounds of stinking black dirt. Clods of it broke off and pattered down along his cloak and struck his boots. A trickle of fine dirt rolled down the sleeve of his jerkin. Peering close in the darkness, he made out pale shapes inside the dark dirt, so he broke open the larger clods for a closer inspection. Growing inside the dirt were yellow-white fans of pulpy fungus.

"This is a farm," he said, surprised. "Of course, the dwarves couldn't grow proper crops down here—but mushrooms prosper under the earth. They don't need the sun. All they need is a little damp. And some . . . night soil."

He stared down at his filthy hands.

Mörget stared at him. "What is that on your skin? It smells like shit."

Croy dropped the unwrapped cylinder. Hurriedly, he bent down and washed his hands in the thin stream of water covering the floor.

Mörget leaned over to sniff at one of the cylinders. Then he looked at Croy where he squatted. The barbarian let out a booming laugh that echoed wildly in the low-ceilinged tunnel.

"Ha ha ha," he crowed. "Ha ha! The fancy knight has gotten himself all dirty! This is funny!"

Croy fought down a homicidal impulse and breathed deeply to clear his head. It was, after all, a little funny. He forced himself to smile. Then he rose to his full height and bowed deeply.

Mörget was weeping from laughing so hard. He bent from the waist—it was not a bow—and then slowly straightened up.

Just in time for Croy to hurl one of the cylinders at his chest.

The cloth tore open on impact and three pounds of manure splattered across Mörget's laced-up cloak. Some of it got on his face.

"You—" Mörget howled, and his hands came up to claw at the air. His eyes went wide with pure, unadulterated rage.

Maybe, Croy thought, I just made a mistake.

As Mörget's hands started to come down, Croy dashed sideways into the racks. He ducked low to hide himself from view. He could hear Mörget rushing toward him, perhaps intent on slaughtering him for the insult.

The barbarian was twice Croy's size. He held an Ancient Blade equal to Croy's own, and plenty of other weapons he could use in his weak hand. If the two of them came to blows, Croy knew it would go hard on him.

He reached down to put a hand on Ghostcutter's hilt. The barbarian was only steps away. Croy put one foot forward in a strong defensive crouch.

Mörget came around the side of the rack, both hands filled with weaponry. Croy raised one arm to protect his face—

But it was no use. Both cylinders full of manure struck him square on, covering him instantly in filth.

"Oh, for fie," Croy said, spluttering as wet manure slid down his cheeks and matted his hair. He jumped forward but Mörget had already run away. As Croy came out into the main aisle between the racks, a steady rain of manure cylinders smashed all around him, knocking over racks, exploding on the wet floor until it was a slippery morass. Croy tried to return fire, snatching cylinder after cylinder off the rack, but he could barely sense where Mörget hid.

A cylinder struck Croy's shoulder and spun him around—but for a split second he'd seen Mörget's shaved head sticking up over a rack to his left. Croy ducked low, gathering a pair of cylinders up in his arms as he hurried forward. It was hard to keep his balance on the muck-covered floor, but just as Mörget rose to throw again, Croy leapt forward, twisting in midair, and cast first one then the other cylinder, at very close range and with all the power of his arms.

The first cylinder missed Mörget and burst against the wall behind him. The second, however, hit Mörget squarely in the face. The red stain on his mouth and chin made an excellent target, even in the low light.

Manure splattered over Mörget's features, masking him in excrement. The barbarian tried to howl but only gurgled. He reached up with filthy hands to claw at his eyes, then dropped to his knees and coughed desperately to clear his mouth. For a while he could do nothing but grimace and spit.

Croy slapped him on the back and a thick ball of manure shot out of the barbarian's windpipe. Mörget gasped for breath and nodded his thanks. When he could breathe again, Croy reached down with one hand and grasped Mörget's wrist tightly, helping him to his feet.

The barbarian laughed and shook his head. "It is like the olden days, when my brother and I would wrestle and play tricks on one another," he said.

"It's good to have a laugh now and again," Croy agreed. He sighed. "Ah, Mörget, here we are—surrounded by death and danger, our comrades in certain peril, lost in the dark in the lair of a demon."

The barbarian agreed with a hearty sigh. "What other treasures could life offer to a man?"

Croy's eyes went wide. This was a . . . treasure? And yet . . . he knew exactly what Mörget meant. Croy never felt so alive as when he was dodging certain annihilation, or cutting his way through a throng of enemies. As much as he wanted to rescue Cythera and Slag and get away from the Vincularium, there was a part of him that longed for adventures like this, and mourned how few of them fate presented to him.

"I'll miss this life," he said.

"You are expecting to die soon?" Mörget asked.

"Only part of me." Croy shook his head. "I fear the age of adventuring is coming to an end. My land is pacified, and from here to the mountains in every direction, it is turned to agriculture, and the good of mankind. All of Skrae is under the rule of the king's law. No more trolls scheming in dark forests. No more bandits preying on travelers in the hills." He laughed a little. "And every year, fewer sorcerers remain—the arcane arts are thankfully being lost. Now that Hazoth is dead, there are only two or three real sorcerers left in the world. And where there are no sorcerers, there can be no demons that need slaying."

"It is true. Too true," Mörget agreed.

"Well, no point in crying over future boredom when today is full of excitement," Croy said, brushing off his cloak as best he could. He would need to bathe before he saw Cythera again, or she would most likely faint from the smell of him. "We must press on." He sniffed at the air. The stench of the manure didn't bother him so much anymore—nor did it obscure other smells quite as much. He led Mörget back to the central aisle, then started once more up the tunnel, looking for another way up.

He sniffed at the air again. Something—maybe—reached his nose that was not the smell of excrement, nor of mushrooms, nor of general damp. Something sharp and slightly acrid. Something that tickled the roof of his mouth.

Looking back at Mörget, he placed a finger across his lips for silence. Then he drew Ghostcutter.

He had definitely smelled the smoke of a campfire.

# CHAPTER FORTY-SEVEN

Croy and Mörget moved forward silently, taking light steps to avoid splashing in the water that covered the floor. They both had their swords drawn but held low so they wouldn't glimmer in the light.

There was definitely light ahead of them, far down the tunnel. They had extinguished their candles. Croy could see very little. But his eyes weren't playing tricks on him—a flickering radiance came down the aisle, glinting on the wet floor.

He was unable to dispel a nagging thought. Nothing they'd seen so far required fire. Nothing they'd seen suggested there was a desire for warmth or light in this forgotten place. The fire might have been natural. The fungus they'd seen lining the walls of the central shaft might be flammable, and some strange alchemy of forgotten places might have started a blaze on its own. But he thought not—the fire was glowing too steadily, as if it had been tended with care. And a natural fire down here would have spread quickly, given enough fuel, while this fire seemed to be carefully contained.

Which left only one possible conclusion: they were not alone in the Vincularium.

He already knew that the demon haunted the place. He'd also seen the countless revenants up on the top level. He understood that the ancient city was not completely abandoned. Yet this fire suggested that things were far more complicated than he'd previously believed. The demon didn't seem intelligent enough to use fire. The revenants were creatures of the cold and the dark—they had shunned Dawnbringer's light, so why would they make a fire of their own? No, there must be living creatures here. Living people, who needed to stay warm.

He should have known earlier, he thought. The flock of beetles and then the farm of mushrooms should have spelled it out clearly. Farms did not prosper on their own. Someone had to be cultivating the fungus. If someone didn't come by periodically to harvest the yield, the crop of mushrooms would have died and rotted long since.

He looked back at Mörget and thought of how to proceed. There was no telling how many enemies might be waiting by that fire. Yet Croy knew he had to get through them. They'd found no other path toward the upper levels. If he wanted to go up, he had to go through whoever tended that fire. If he wanted to rescue Cythera and Slag, he needed to keep advancing.

The racks on either side provided excellent cover, but there was no way to move forward without heading up the center aisle. It was also their only path of retreat, should there be more resistance ahead than the two of them could handle.

"Do you see any other path but to charge forward?" he whispered to the barbarian.

"I've rarely needed any other," the barbarian replied.

Croy nodded. He frowned and looked forward again. Shadows flowed along the ceiling, as if someone had moved around the fire. "Together we run up there, as fast as we can, and surprise them."

Mörget nodded. "As it should be."

Croy shifted his grip on Ghostcutter's hilt. Then he held up three fingers. Mörget looked at them in incomprehension, then shrugged and ran forward, bellowing a war cry and brandishing Dawnbringer over his head.

For a second Croy watched the barbarian recede before him, aghast at how much noise Mörget made. He supposed it was honorable to let your enemies know you were coming, but still—

Oh, enough, Croy thought. Then he screamed, "For Skrae and her king!" and followed the barbarian in his headlong rush up the tunnel.

Croy could see nothing but Mörget's back. His feet kept slipping on the wet floor and his breath plumed out before him in the damp. His brains felt like they were rattling in his skull as his boots came crashing down, again and again, on the hard flagstones.

He thought he must be running to certain death—at least, certain death for someone. The long tunnel sped past him, rack after rack of mushrooms in their ordure, and then suddenly the tunnel opened up, widening out into a broad antechamber.

Mörget staggered to a stop. Croy saw the barbarian

standing over a very small campfire, turning his head back and forth as he sought something. Croy drew up beside him and looked down to see buckets of water sitting by the fire. Nothing else.

"He disappeared before I could cut him down," Mörget said. He sounded like a gambler who had just discovered a card cheat.

"He? Who did you see? I saw nothing," Croy told the barbarian.

Mörget frowned. "There was one person here. Small, perhaps a youth."

"A warrior of some kind? Was he wearing armor?"

"No."

"Was he armed?" Croy asked.

"I do not think so. I do not know if it was even a male. It might have been a girl. It was very small. Yes. Probably a girl, judging by the noise she made. She screeched a bit, then ran that way." Mörget pointed with Dawnbringer toward the wall of the tunnel. Croy saw no door there, not even a wide crack between the mortared bricks. "She simply vanished."

"Cythera can do that," Croy said, rubbing his chin. "She can make herself invisible, but only for a few moments at a time. You . . . you don't think it was Cythera?"

Mörget shook his head violently. "Definitely not. Cythera is bigger. You know, taller. And dresses in finer clothes. This girl wore only a much-patched shift."

Croy stepped over to the wall. He pounded on the bricks with the pommel of his sword. The hollow thud he made suggested there was an open space behind the wall—but what of it? What kind of girl could just walk through a solid wall?

"Whoever she was, she's gone now." Croy shook his head. He glanced down at the buckets by the fire. "I don't think she was a warrior at all."

Mörget turned to stare at him. "No. No. She was . . . very small."

Croy stared back. Was Mörget suffering a pang of conscience? If the girl had not fled, Croy was certain Mörget would have cut her down just on principle. Maybe he was doubting his whole philosophy, maybe he was wondering why he had devoted his life to mindless violence, and—

"I have not killed anything in days," Mörget said. "Now, I am cheated!" He bellowed in rage at the unfairness of it all. "Magic! She must have used magic, to vanish in thin air like that. She must have been a sorceress. And I could not reach her in time."

Croy frowned. He looked down at the buckets. They were simple, and crudely made from hammered sheets of tin. They leaked. "A witch, perhaps," he admitted.

"Who knows what dark magic she was about?" Mörget thundered. "At least, I can say I kept her from practicing her foul art."

Croy shook his head. The buckets didn't look like witch's cauldrons. They looked like the kind of simple implements one might find on a farm. He was pretty sure the girl had been tending the mushrooms, not some arcane ritual. "She must have been sent to wet down the floor of the farm tunnels. Mushrooms like the damp."

"She was just here! And then she was gone. Magic, I swear!" Mörget looked farther up the tunnel where it ran ahead into darkness. There were more racks that way, identical to the ones behind them. "She did not go that way. She did not hide behind one of the racks. She was just—gone."

"Hardly a wonder, in the dark like this," Croy protested. He leaned against the brick wall. "We had no light ourselves, and—"

Behind him the wall shifted. He thought at first it was collapsing under his weight, and he jumped away. When he looked back, however, he saw that a whole section of the wall was mounted on hinges. It was a hidden door. It must not have been closed properly, and now it had popped open on its hinges.

He reached forward and got his fingernails around the edge of the door. With a simple tug it swung open before him, revealing a side tunnel—just wide and tall enough for one person to walk through at a time. A secret passage.

A fresh breeze ruffled Croy's hair.

"It smells better in there, at least."

# CHAPTER FORTY-EIGHT

Malden heaved at the iron bar again, and the stone door grated against the floor. He put his back into it and grunted in frustration. Sweat made his hands slip and he jumped backward as the bar flew, spinning, to clatter on the floor once again.

He stripped off his cloak and pushed back the sleeves of his tunic.

"Do you want me to have a try?" Cythera asked.

Malden glanced over at Slag. The dwarf was lying on the floor, curled in a ball by the pain that wracked his muscles. His eyes were clamped shut and he was moaning softly. Better that than the screaming that came before, Malden supposed.

"I'm to blame for this," Malden said, running his hands across his breeches to dry them. "If I'd been thinking clearly I would have seen that dart before it struck him." He looked at Cythera's face, hoping to find compassion there. *No, there is no fault*, he expected her to say. *No, you are not to blame*.

"Yes," she said instead. "His death is on your hands."

Anger and guilt surged through Malden's chest. He grabbed up the bar and shoved it into the door frame once more. He braced his feet and pulled, and pulled, and—

—fell over backward as the door stopped resisting him and flew open on its hinges. The bar struck Malden's foot as it dropped to the flagstones, and he cried out as sudden pain raced up his leg.

"Damn! I think I might have broken a toe," he said, hugging the foot toward him.

Cythera ignored him and walked over the threshold into the Hall of Treasures.

"Wait!" the thief called. "What if there are more traps?"

But she was already inside, carrying Slag's makeshift lantern with her. Malden rose to his feet—the toe hurt, but he doubted that it was really broken. He bent over Slag and helped the dwarf stand on shaky legs.

"Can you walk?" he asked.

"For this I can." Slag stumbled forward, barely keeping his feet. Malden pulled the dwarf's arm around his waist and helped as best he could.

The room beyond the door was not large, at least by the standards of the rest of the Vincularium. It went back perhaps sixty feet and was a third as wide. Its ceiling was barely ten feet over Malden's head, and was vaulted with graceful stonework that looked more ornamental than functional.

The hall was filled with gold.

Each item in the room had its own pedestal or case. They all deserved special display. A wooden stand the size of a wardrobe but fronted with glass held a selection of crowns as delicate as birds' nests—woven of filigree, of gold and silver wire that held hundreds of gems aloft. A long case made entirely of crystal held rings in the shape of towers or horses or swords that curved around until their points touched their pommels. Each ring held a single perfect gem the size of a robin's egg. Along one wall hung tapestries made of cloth of platinum, cunningly worked with shining copper wire for contrast. The scenes the tapestries showed—including a view of the Vincularium from the top of the central shaft—were so finely detailed they might have been windows into a shimmering world.

A row of suits of armor lined the other wall, with additional suits mounted higher up to make a second array. One panoply was painted with black enamel, then worked with silver leaf to form a floral pattern so convoluted the eye could get lost in its twists and turns. Another suit was covered in gold-tipped spikes to give a fearsome aspect. Yet another looked to Malden as if it had been carved from stone.

Then there were the weapons. Axes and pikestaffs rose from the floor, gathered together by the hafts until they looked like deadly trees. The blades of some were inscribed with runes in a script so flowing, so elaborated with curlicues and sharply barbed serifs, that a single thorn rune could fill the entire available space. Others were engraved all over with characters so tiny Malden could not make out the individual runes.

There were cases of swords with blades so delicate and thin they looked like they would snap if they were lifted, or hilts so heavily encrusted with jewels that surely no hand could hold them. There were doubly recurved bows of laminated horn fitted with half a dozen strings—they looked like fairy harps to Malden.

The armor and weapons were so grand it took him a while to realize they all shared something in common, which was their small size. They were not made for humans, but for dwarves.

"It's illegal for a dwarf to use a weapon," Malden said, admiring a sheaf of perfect daggers that stood like pins in a velvet cushion. The pommel of one was a ruby as big as his fist.

"It is now," Slag explained. "Before we signed that damned treaty my people were hardy warriors. Lad, help me over to yon case of glassware. I'd stand on my own feet in this place."

Malden brought Slag to the case in question, which was full of fantastically elaborate bottles, decanters, and ewers.

"When we left the Vincularium, we had to leave all our weapons behind. That was part of the agreement we made with your king." Slag shook his head—a gesture that made him wince with pain. "We gave up a great deal."

Cythera held the lantern high to look at a collection of objects at the far end of the room. Malden went to her side and then wondered why she bothered. Unlike the gold and gems in the cases, these works didn't seem like treasures at all. Bolts of linen stood next to barrels of perfectly normal arrows. There were pieces of driftwood polished until they shone like glass, and plain bottles of clear liquids, and pieces of rotting parchment inscribed with simple runes. Yet these mundane pieces were mounted and displayed with as much care and ostentation as the finest jewels and the best gem-inlaid cloisonné. Most surprising were the stones. Simple, spherical stones—a lot of them—that shone in the light for the smoothness of their surfaces, but were made of common granite, basalt, or limestone. Malden accounted them little more valuable than pebbles washed smooth by a river.

"What's this dross?" he asked. "It's hardly treasure."

"To the dwarves who made those things, they were worth more than all the fucking gilt and samite in this room," Slag said, and nodded at Cythera. "Lass, you know your runes well enough, but you misread the name of this place. This ain't the Hall of Treasures. It's the Hall of Masterpieces. It's understandable, though—in my language, the words are almost identical."

"Masterpieces," Malden said. "Like a journeyman would make?" In the guilds that ran Ness's many workshops and yards, there were three basic ranks of worker: apprentice, journeyman, and master. To attain the rank of master a journeyman was required to create some piece of especially fine work—a perfectly balanced sword, a cloak dyed a new color, or the like—which proved he'd learned his trade.

"Exactly like that," Slag agreed, "except we take it more serious. When a dwarf figures out what craft he'll follow—stonework, goldsmithing, armoring, what have you—he spends five years' time making a perfect specimen of skill and design."

"Five years?" Malden said. "For one piece? The masters must be slave-drivers."

"While working on his masterpiece, a dwarf has no master. He gets no pay—he lives with his family, if they'll have him, and sleeps on stone, and eats crusts of bread."

"The law requires this?"

"Fucking pride requires it! A dwarf with a second-rate masterpiece will never be able to look another dwarf in the eye. The masterpiece makes the man, do you see? Everyone knows how it turns out, and everyone judges the dwarf based on what they've seen. Reputation means everything to us. Yon shiny balls of stone you sneer at, Malden, are the credentials of a generation of the finest miners and sappers that ever lived. They were cut down from blocks bigger than this room, cut and worked and smoothed out until they were as round as the sodding moon. There's a long tradition of dwarves competing to see who could carve the most perfect sphere."

Cythera picked up one of the pieces of polished driftwood. "That this would even last eight hundred years without rotting is a miracle," she said. She held it high so Malden could see it had been varnished so many times it seemed to be embedded in a thin layer of glass. "Five years of work, on this one piece . . ."

"Methinks that dwarf picked the wrong career," Malden said, shrugging. He was a thief, and he found the thought of so much hard work depressing. "All right, Slag, we're suitably awed. Now—which of these curios was it that made you cross half the world?"

The dwarf slumped against the case of glassware. "It should be over there," he said. "Five enormous barrels worth. It should be right fucking . . . there."

He pointed toward a corner of the room Malden had yet to explore.

An empty corner.

# CHAPTER FORTY-NINE

"No, damn you," Slag wheezed. "No! The book was clear. It was clear as fucking crystal! The barrels were stored here, in the Place of Long Shadows, in the Hall of Masterpieces . . . this is impossible. Impossible! The book said it, in black and white!"

"Books can be misprinted," Malden suggested, though the excuse sounded lame even to him. "Or perhaps someone moved your treasure after it was published."

"No. No!" Slag exclaimed. The force of his frustration was enough to send him into a coughing fit. "Trust me, this wouldn't have been removed. It was supposed to still be here when the elves were sealed inside. Blast!"

"I'm so sorry, Slag," Cythera said, and tried to rub the dwarf's back.

Slag would not be comforted. He pulled away from her and slumped forward across a display case. "It was going to . . . it would have . . . oh, sod it! My entire future was in those barrels. This was going to end all my miseries. It was going to put me back on fucking top. And it's gone. It's fucking . . . gone."

"But what was it?" Malden asked. He bent low and studied the floor where the barrels had supposedly been stored. A layer of dust—thinner than he might have expected—lay on the floor, but there were five large circles of bare stone where no dust had collected. "Were the barrels full of gold dust? Or maybe assorted gems of various sizes and cuts?"

"It was . . . a weapon," Slag explained. He sank down to sit on the floor. Dark rings surrounded his eyes and Malden could hear him wheezing from across the room. "I don't claim to know how it worked, only that—it was lethal beyond anything—anything that had been seen before. The dwarves who worked here invented it . . . just before they left." He shook his head and cringed in pain for a while.

"Don't strain yourself," Cythera said, squatting down next to the dwarf. She mopped his face with a kerchief.

Slag reached up to bat her hand away, but he was too weak to properly resist her. "We only have sketchy notes on what it was, what it . . . did. I won't bore you with the details, lad. I only know it could have killed a knight in full armor from so far away he'd never see you coming. We never told the humans about it, of course—imagine the fucking disaster that might have caused, if they got their hands on it. But when the treaty was signed, and we were forbidden from . . . from—" He started coughing then, long, nasty paroxysms that left his face red with congested blood.

"You didn't want us to have that kind of power. We'd already done enough harm," Malden conjectured. "So you didn't want to make us more deadly? I suppose I can see that. So you sealed up this magic weapon forever, and forgot it existed. Or almost."

"Not . . . not . . ."

"Malden, let him rest," Cythera insisted.

The thief nodded, and decided to ask no more questions—for the nonce.

"Not magic," Slag finally choked out. "Not . . . magic at all, or . . . I wouldn't . . ." He lowered his head to his chest.

"Just be quiet now," Cythera said.

Slag shook his head again, though this time it was voluntary. "I'm sorry," he said.

"What? You hardly need apologize for anything right now," Malden told him.

Slag scowled. "I led you both here. For fucking . . . nothing. I owe you an explanation. Though I'm . . . I . . . I'm loath to say it. There's some things you don't know about me, lad. Embarrassing things I never shared. I think . . . think . . ."

Slag's face went white again and he stared up at the door.

Carefully, painfully, he leaned forward.

"Slag, really, you need to lie down," Cythera suggested.

The dwarf fought her hands away and this time he had the strength to do it. "I heard something. Put out the light," he demanded in a hoarse whisper.

"But—" Cythera started, but Slag ignored her protest. He brought his own hand down hard on the flame of the lantern, snuffing it with a hiss and a curl of smoke. Malden blew out his own candle and they were left in utter darkness.

Not, however, in silence.

When his eyes were rendered useless by the lack of light, Malden's other senses grew stronger. Specifically his sense of hearing. He could make out, now, what had startled the dwarf so. A faint rapping sound. Something tapping on stone, not very far away, with bony fingers.

Perhaps—Malden's guts clenched at the thought—the revenants had followed them down from the top level. Perhaps even now a legion of undead elves was making its way toward the Hall of Masterpieces.

He tried not to breathe.

The rhythmic sound came closer. It was not like the sound a human makes while rapping his knuckles on a door. A human knocks two or three times, then stops to listen for a response. This was like a steady drumming, a cascade of taps that never stopped. There seemed no regular pattern to the sound—it came in fits and starts, *tip-tip-tap-RAP-tip-RAP-tick*—but it never faded away.

It came closer, inch by inch, until it was sounding on the open door.

*Tap-tip-tick-RAP-RAP-tap.*

And then it stopped.

If they can't hear us in here, Malden thought, perhaps they'll just go away. Perhaps they'll leave us alone and return to their graves, perhaps—

A light appeared outside the door. Long yellow beams moved up and down the wall, and around the edge of the door the light was bright enough to dazzle Malden's dark-adapted eyes.

Then a beam struck him square in the eye and he flinched backward—right into a sheaf of pikestaffs that fell clattering to the floor.

The door creaked open wide, and two figures stepped through, silhouetted by their own light. They were both rail-thin, but neither of them were tall enough to be revenants. One was barely four feet tall. The other only a quarter that height, the size of a cat.

As Malden's eyes recovered from being dazzled, he saw the light touch first Cythera, then Slag. The taller of the two newcomers laughed excitedly when Slag held up one arm to block the light. Then it set down its lantern, and for the first time Malden could see them properly.

The short one looked somewhat akin to a goblin. It had long floppy ears and a mouth full of crooked teeth. Its eyes were enormous and milky in color, with no pupils or irises. Its mangy hair was a shocking blue, and ran down its back in a wide pelt. Its hands and feet looked too large to be supported by its sticklike limbs, and it never quite stood still, instead bobbing up and down and slapping its feet. It tapped on the floor with long bony fingers, knocking randomly on the flagstones as if it couldn't help itself.

The taller of the two was a dwarf, dressed in leather coveralls. A female. Malden had never seen a dwarf woman before, and that alone would have been shock enough. She was as thin as Slag, though her hips and breasts were of generous proportion. Her long black hair had been tied up in a dozen braids that stuck straight out from her scalp. Her eyebrows met without interruption over the bridge of her nose, and her upper lip was dark with sparse hair. She had the smaller creature on a leather leash.

Her eyes were bright with malice.

She couldn't seem to stop laughing. She walked over to Slag crouched against a display case and leaned over to laugh in his face. "Looking for something in particular?" she asked.

## CHAPTER FIFTY

Croy went first down the secret tunnel, Ghostcutter drawn and held before him. The flame of the candle in his other hand streamed behind the wick and fluttered dangerously, but never quite went out.

Behind him Mörget had difficulty fitting through the narrow passage. He only had to stoop a little to avoid hitting his head, but he had to walk nearly sideways to get his broad shoulders through.

The passage took a winding course that went now down, now up by a sharp incline, so that Croy almost put Ghostcutter away so he could have his hands free to help him climb. He decided against it—who knew what waited for them just ahead?—and was forced to stumble forward by finding footholds in the rough stone.

Such were in plentiful supply. He had little time to spare for thoughts of who made this tunnel, or why, but he knew it was no dwarf. The rock was crudely cut, marked everywhere with the square white scratches of a chisel. The ceiling was uneven, and more than once he bashed his head on a place where the tunnel had not been properly excavated. In places it grew so narrow that he had to squeeze through sideways himself, and it was only with vigorous wriggling and much grunting that Mörget kept up with him.

Yet the barbarian never complained, nor suggested they turn back. He shared with Croy a certain outlook on enemies who ran away from you when you approached. It was highly unlikely they would just run and leave you alone—in all likelihood, the farm girl, or whatever it was that Mörget had startled, was going to seek help. Presumably armed and dangerous help. For a knight like Croy, that meant only one course of action was thinkable. You rushed in, as fast as you could, to find your enemies before they had a chance to regroup.

Croy was sweating and breathing hard by the time he reached the end of the passage. It terminated in a featureless brick wall, just like the one that had led to this secret way. He pushed at it, expecting it to open easily like the secret door they'd found back in the mushroom farm. When it failed to budge, his brow furrowed and he kicked at it and struck it with his shoulder and considered digging into the mortar between the bricks with his belt knife.

"Let me see," Mörget insisted, shoving his way past Croy. There was no room for them to stand side by side in the narrow tunnel so Croy squeezed backward, coming into far more contact with Mörget's flesh than he liked. Considering the fact that both of them were covered with manure, it was not a pleasant dance.

"It must open," Mörget insisted. "We saw no side passages, or any other way for her to escape."

"Unless there was another secret door, more cunningly hidden than the last," Croy suggested. "It's possible this door is false. A brick facade placed over a dead end in the tunnel."

"A false door?" Mörget asked.

"A false secret door," Croy agreed.

"A false secret door trap," Mörget growled. "Intended to leave us with no retreat possible, boxed in where we can't fight properly. Subtle! I like this not. I told you she was a sorceress. She's playing tricks on us."

Croy grunted in dissent. "I'm sure now she was no practitioner of magic at all," he said. "Just a simple mushroom farmer."

"She is a sorceress, and she must be destroyed," Mörget demanded. His rage seemed poorly contained.

Croy remembered something then. He recalled that when Mörget had told his story of coming from the eastern steppes to Ness, he claimed to have fought many sorcerers along his way. It was how he'd learned to fight like an Ancient Blade.

Now Croy wondered how many of those foes had been actual magicians—and how many just appeared so to the barbarian. How many innocents he might have slain in his berserker fury. The thought made Croy's blood run cold. Mörget seemed less than interested in rescuing Cythera and Slag as well—he was far more determined to find his demon, regardless of whether Croy's friends survived the quest.

For the first time Croy began to wonder just how honorable a companion Mörget might be. Croy had spent time guarding the mountain passes against barbarian invasions. He'd always been told that the easterners were vicious, savage people, barely human and incapable of moral behavior. When he first met Mörget and saw he bore an Ancient Blade, he'd come to believe that was all just prejudice, that it was possible for a barbarian to be an honorable warrior and a good man.

He tried to fight off such doubts. They were no help at that particular moment. "Come," he said. "Let's go back.

There must be another way up—some stairwell that will take us more directly to Cythera and Slag, and—"

Mörget was beyond talking, at that point.

The barbarian roared and charged at the wall with his shoulder, hard enough, it seemed to Croy, to smash his own bones if the bricks didn't yield.

Luckily, they did. The door shifted an inch or two, letting in a gust of foul-smelling air. Croy wrinkled his nose. At least this new reek didn't smell of excrement. Instead it stank of rotting vegetables and spoiled meat.

"Damn your tricks, sorceress!" Mörget cursed, and then struck the door again, hard enough to make the tunnel shake. The door shrieked as it opened another few inches—and then Croy winced as he heard something heavy and metallic fall away from the door. It clattered and rang as it fell to crash on a floor on the far side.

"Now at least they know we're coming," Croy said. He was not prone to sarcasm, normally. Maybe Malden had been rubbing off on him.

"That just makes for a fairer fight," Mörget replied. He pushed the door again and it opened easily. It must have been barred from the far side, that was all.

Mörget slipped through the opening and Croy followed close behind—just close enough that he could grab the barbarian's shoulders and pull him back before he fell to his death. Beyond the brick door was a narrow ledge looking out over a vast room. The floor of the room was a good fifty feet below them.

Mörget shouted in anger and struck the wall behind him with a closed fist. The blow made an echoing boom that rolled around the big room for long seconds.

We may not surprise them, Croy thought, but if luck is with us we'll scare them senseless.

Candlelight revealed few details of the room beyond, but enough at least to give Croy some idea of how to proceed. The ledge was only six inches wide, part of a stringcourse that ran along the wall. This at least was dwarven architecture—the stringcourse was made of carved dwarven runes, hundreds of them, with raised dots between every six or seven runes, probably to mark the end of one word and the start of another. Below the stringcourse someone had made a very crude ladder by chiseling holes into the wall for handholds.

Croy sheathed Ghostcutter and started down, lacking any better plan. He had never been a skilled climber, but he went down as quickly as he could, clinging desperately to the handholds.

They were too small for human hands, really, but he found he could grip them with a few fingers, and use other handholds for the tips of his boots. Carefully, and far slower than he would have liked, he climbed down the wall to the floor below. He was hampered in this by the need to hold his candle in one hand even as he climbed. He dropped the last five feet to the floor and unsheathed his sword the second he was standing on solid ground.

Behind him Mörget came down much faster, with Dawnbringer clamped tight between his teeth.

By the time the barbarian dropped light as a feather to the flagstones, Croy had made out more of the chamber. The room was perhaps a hundred feet long, and half that wide. Its walls were of fine marble veined with a deep green. No furniture, machinery, or other fixtures filled the space, but at one end a massive throne had been carved to abut the wall, a deep chair raised up on six steps of joined marble blocks. "An audience chamber. Or perhaps a place of judgment," Croy said.

"Once upon a time. Now it's a midden," Mörget replied.

They were both correct. At their feet lay the iron bar that had barred the secret door above them. It had dug a shallow gouge in the floor when it struck. It was, however, far from the only thing strewn across the floor. Rags, bits of broken wood, and countless pieces of cave beetle shell had been dumped here without heed. The floor was thick with rotting meat and cut-up pieces of mushrooms. Entire fish skeletons crunched underfoot.

None of it was fresh—but it was new. This was not garbage dumped by dwarves in ages past. Someone living had used this chamber to store their refuse.

"Gah!" Mörget shouted, and lifted up one boot to stare at its underside. The sole was clotted with fish guts. "What's next? Will we have to crawl through a charnel house before we find this demon? Or perhaps a latrine?"

"I don't think so," Croy said. He pointed with Ghostcutter at the far side of the chamber. A massive arched doorway stood there, open to darkness.

Oozing across the threshold was a thing perhaps fifteen feet in length, though its shape constantly changed so it was hard to tell. It had no fixed form, instead rolling forward like living water. Its skin looked slimy to the touch, and underneath could be seen shapes like organs and even faces, pressing upward against the skin in mute screams of torment.

"That's it, isn't it?" Croy asked.

"Oh, aye!" Mörget said, and let out a booming laugh that made the whole marble chamber buzz.

# CHAPTER FIFTY-ONE

The demon flowed across the floor, the edges of its shapeless form rippling as it glided over the refuse. A face pressed outward against its skin, the eyes protruding and staring in Croy's direction. A second face loomed toward Mörget. Both were stretched and distorted to a point of horror.

Croy set his candle on the floor, squeezing its lower end between two flagstones so it would stand upright. He couldn't fight this thing if he couldn't see it. Then he brought Ghostcutter down, the point near the floor. He put his left foot back to improve his stance.

He had no idea how to attack it. It did not have limbs to cleave or a proper head to target. He was not so foolish to think that the faces would be vulnerable. It had too many of them, for one thing. Mörget had spoken of a central organ that seemed important to the beast, but Croy couldn't see it through the skin. What could you do with such a shapeless abomination, save carve it up and then burn the pieces?

He doubted it would stand still while he did that.

It came on fast, faster than a man could run. Just before it would have lapped across Mörget's boots, it reared up in the air and struck at him with the edges of its envelope. Croy jumped in and brought Ghostcutter around in a wide arc intended to slice open the thing's back. The cold iron edge of his sword found little purchase—its skin gave too easily, so it was like trying to slice honey. He managed only to trace a shallow wound that oozed a clear fluid.

The monster did not roar in pain—if it had a voice at all, it had not used it yet. Croy knew he'd hurt it, though, because it stopped attacking Mörget and came at him instead. He expected it to turn around to face him, but instead it merely leaned over backward and splattered all over Croy's chest and face like a thing of pure liquid. Its back became its front, and Croy was overwhelmed instantly.

Sticky fluid splashed across his mouth and nose, sealing in his breath. He clamped his eyes shut and tried to bring Ghostcutter up, but the thing's infernal substance wrapped around his sword hand and squeezed, constricting the muscles in his wrist until he dropped the weapon. He fought and clawed against the stuff as it wrapped around his waist and pulled him off his feet, drawing him into its body.

The demon swallowed him whole.

He passed through its skin like diving into hot water and suddenly was inside the thing. Its blood burned his face and hands—anywhere it touched exposed skin—and slithered down the collar of his tunic and up his sleeves.

There was no air inside the thing. Its jellylike substance pushed at his lips, trying to get inside of him, to suffocate him. Wherever it touched his bare skin searing pain made his muscles twitch, while fear threatened to overwhelm him like a black wave. He was seconds from death—seconds at the very most—and his natural urge to panic, to scream, was almost uncontrollable.

Giving in to that urge would undo him, he knew. He would die the moment he gave up fighting. There had been a time when even reason would not have been enough to save him from his own fear. Only years of training allowed him to overcome that perfectly natural reaction. He forced himself into a kind of fragile calm. If he was to die like this, devoured by a demon, then that was acceptable. But only if he went down fighting.

He forced himself to open his eyes and saw a jeering face inches from his own. Its mouth opened in a mocking laugh and he saw right through its maw—there was nothing behind those cruel lips but dim light. Croy fought to bring one arm up and he punched wildly at the face. Every movement was constrained, slowed by the viscous medium of the thing's body. He barely had the strength to push his fist forward, to connect with that terrible face. Yet when his knuckles met its cheek, the face did not resist him but only folded around his hand like a wet leaf.

He felt the face's soft lips work at his fingers, and he yanked his hand back in disgust.

Croy's lungs heaved with the desperate need for breath. He fought down the spasm that threatened to force open his mouth and make him inhale the caustic substance of the demon, knowing that would be his death. Wildly he looked around him, even as his eyes burned with fierce pain, looking for something to grab, some organ he could rend and pull apart.

Then Dawnbringer plunged downward through the mass of the demon, missing Croy's chest by inches. The Ancient Blade burst with light as its point found its target—an enormous round mass that pulsed with wriggling dark worms. Dawnbringer pierced the organ through and it spilled open, the worms curling and shriveling as they were exposed to the demon's acidic blood.

Croy saw three more faces scream, and then a thick wet membrane came crashing down all around him, the thing's skin contracting as it died. He fought and pushed against the skin that wrapped around him like a blanket. His fingers dug through that gruesome envelope and tore it apart in long ribbons of clear flesh. Icy cold air struck his face, and he spat the creature's blood out of his mouth, then sucked in a sweet gust of breath that made him tremble with ecstasy.

Mörget pulled and scraped the skin away from Croy's body as he struggled to get up, to stagger out of the thing's clinging remains. He stumbled over to one marble wall and leaned hard against it, gasping and weak. Looking down at his hands, he saw they were as red as if he'd been scalded with boiling water.

The demon lay in a puddle of its own ichor, as flat and lifeless as a cast-aside tarpaulin. The faces buried in its skin stared upward at nothing, and its organs oozed dark fluids as they twitched and died, one by one.

Finally it lay still. Its corpse began to steam, and it shrank as it turned to fumes and vapor. Like any demon, like any unnatural creature, it could not exist in this world once its vital spirit had been dissipated. Only sorcerous energy could maintain its physical form, and now that was gone. In a few seconds it was nothing more than a stain on the marble flagstones.

"It is dead," Mörget said, and laughed wildly. "My demon is undone! Now I am a man—and even my father cannot gainsay it. Mother death, I thank you for this chance to kill, to send this thing into your arms. Croy! Brother! We have won!"

Croy nodded feebly and tried to slow the frantic beating of his heart.

"Yes," he finally wheezed. "Yes. Won. Now—we find Cythera."

"Of course!" Mörget chuckled. "Anything you like."

"Right now," Croy said, the words like knives in his throat, "I just need . . . to sit down."

# CHAPTER FIFTY-TWO

The blue-haired creature walked on its knuckles toward Malden and started tapping on his foot. He pulled his leg back and drew Acidtongue from its scabbard. "What in the Bloodgod's name is that thing?" he demanded.

"Just a . . . blueling, lad," Slag groaned. "Harmless. Your human miners call them knockers. They're blind but—"

He stopped to wince and try to cough. Nothing came up.

When Slag could breathe again, he went on. "They're bloody useful . . . underground . . . can see through rock with their . . . their rapping. Can find pockets of . . . gas . . . and . . ."

The female dwarf rolled her eyes dramatically. "And he can tell me if anyone's in a room before I open the door and get three feet of iron shoved up my arse," she said. She yanked viciously on the blueling's leash and it flipped over backward and groveled on the floor.

"All right, next question." Malden walked around the simpering imp and pointed the tip of Acidtongue at the female dwarf's throat. A drop of acid spilled from the blade and sizzled on the floor. She stared at it the way a jewelry appraiser might study a gem of a color she'd never seen before. "Who are you?" Malden demanded.

She smiled and bowed, careful not to impale herself on the sword.

"Balint's my name. I work for the dwarven ambassador at Redweir."

The city of Redweir—Skrae's third largest—was home to the Learned Brotherhood, the monastic order that preserved all of Skrae's knowledge. The city possessed the largest library on the continent, and also a thriving colony of dwarves, Malden knew. The dwarven embassy there controlled all trade between Skrae and the dwarven kingdom and was responsible for maintaining the treaty between dwarves and men. Balint could be a very powerful enemy to make, but Malden didn't much care at that moment.

"Where are the barrels that stood here?" he demanded. "We want our property back."

"Hmm, where could they be? Where, oh where? You can suck snot out of my mustache and have as good a chance of finding them. They weren't yours to begin with, and they sure as fuck aren't *his*."

She gave Slag a kick to the ribs. Slag cried out in pain and Malden brought his sword up to slash at her.

"Oh, now, that would be a fucking shame, wouldn't it? If you were to strike me down right now. Considering I'm completely unarmed, you bucket of puke."

Malden glanced down at her belt. She had a scabbard on either hip, but they didn't hold knives—the one on her left contained a screwdriver, while on her right she had a wrench.

"You know what human law says about pus-kerchiefs like you who kill dwarves, don't you?"

Malden did. The treaty that guaranteed Skrae its only source of steel made the punishment for harming a dwarf quite clear. If he murdered Balint, he wouldn't just be executed. He would be roasted alive and then fed to dogs. Of course, that would only happen if he was caught in the act.

"I don't see any witnesses around here," he said.

"I've got two of my kind outside this door, waiting for me to come back out. More up top, on the surface. You going to kill every last dwarf you can find? You going to tell them you just accidentally shoved that pig-sticker through my tits?"

"It might be worth a shot," Malden growled.

Balint just stared at him the way she might look at a stain on an expensive carpet. Not a trace of fear showed in her features, even with a magic sword drooling acid inches from her heart.

"Malden," Cythera said, "stand down."

Malden lowered his sword, but he didn't sheathe it. Cythera glared at him but he was damned if he would let this dwarf get away with poisoning Slag and stealing the most valuable treasure in the tomb, especially when he was in the process of robbing it.

"Please," Cythera said, addressing Balint. "You have us at a disadvantage. We thought we were alone here. We did not know that any dwarves had come to reclaim their property. When we ran afoul of the revenants on the top level, we assumed—"

"Reve-whats?"

Cythera frowned. "The reanimated elves. The spirits seeking justice for past crimes. How did you get down here without encountering them?"

"She didn't come . . . through the front . . . gate," Slag said.

Balint brayed at the idea. "*You* did? I knew you were a fool. But just how stupid are you?"

"I'm guessing—oh, bugger, this hurts—I'm guessing you came . . . through the escape shaft . . . in the residential level," Slag said.

Balint shrugged. "Why don't you guess in one hand, and shit in the other, and see which one fills up first?"

"But why now?" Malden demanded. "This is no coincidence, all of us here at precisely the same time."

"Hardly! We had to stick prods up our horses' arseholes just to get here before you lot. We spent the last week breaking through the seal on one of the emergency exits, and just got here a few hours ago. We almost didn't make it before you, but then, Urin here always was a tad off in his calculations." She gave Slag another kick.

"Hold—you know Slag?" Malden asked. "Except you called him—"

"Not now, Malden," Cythera cut in. "Please, milady Balint, tell me why you're here. Maybe we can help you with your needs."

The blueling tapped its way over to where Cythera stood. She allowed it to palpate her foot, though it looked to Malden like she was having a hard time not kicking it away.

Balint deigned to explain a few things. "About three months ago, some big futtock with a red chin like he was drooling blood came to Redweir. Asked a lot of uncomfortable questions about the Vincularium. Even knowing which questions to ask meant he knew too much already. Still, we figured he didn't have an arsehole's chance of getting inside this place, so we gave him one seriously nasty look and let it drop. Big mistake. Next thing we know, he's seen in that piss-pot Ness. Well, they take all kinds in that place, don't they? Isn't that right, you whey-faced catamite?"

She kicked Slag again.

Malden took a step forward and raised his blade. "If you strike him again, I'll shave you bald with this thing."

Balint snorted in derision. "He deserves a lot worse than that, the fucking debaser. Now, as I was saying, this big red-faced arsehole went to Ness, and there he found the one dwarf in Skrae who would even talk to him. Which meant he actually had a chance of finding a way in here. So we took it upon ourselves to make sure he didn't get what he was after."

"The barrels? But Mörget didn't come for them," Cythera said. "He came to kill a demon that he tracked here." She shook her head. "Please. It doesn't matter why we came. You have what you wanted. The barrels are out of our reach. I'm willing to accept that, and surrender them to you without further unpleasantness."

"Oh, aye? Well, I'm not!" Slag grumbled.

Cythera closed her eyes. "Balint. Our friend was struck by a poisoned dart. I hate to say this, but—I believe you placed that trap."

"Good one, too," Balint agreed. "One of my best."

"Now he's sickening, and he's going to die." Cythera lowered her head. "Since you've already won—perhaps you'd be gracious enough, in your victory, to give us the antidote to your poison."

Balint scratched at her mustache. "Antidote? Now why the fuck would I have any of that on me?"

# CHAPTER FIFTY-THREE

Cythera clutched her hands together, beseeching the dwarf one last time. "You have no antidote. I see. Very well. Then at least take us out of here. Please, I beg of you. Take us back to the surface. If you don't, he'll die."

"If you don't you'll be Slag's murderer," Malden added.

"Who? Little me?" Balint laughed. "I didn't shoot him with that dart."

"What difference does that make?" Malden said.

"All the difference in the world. At least as far as the law is concerned. A dwarf can't use a weapon, not anywhere in Skrae. So I didn't. I just built one. Oh, true. I left the thing where he was bound to stumble on it, clumsy fuck that he is. But he could have avoided it if he was a little more careful."

"You have a funny idea of guilt and culpability," Malden said. Though he knew she was correct. The law said that a human who killed a dwarf, even by accident, would forfeit his life. Dwarves, on the other hand, were held to a more lenient standard. They could not wield traditional weapons, and they were forbidden from attacking anyone directly. Yet if they caused a death indirectly—through, say, laying a poison dart trap—they were held free of guilt. That loophole in the treaty was why they'd become so good at building cunning and insidious traps—and why humans always watched their step around angry dwarves.

"Ignore him," Cythera insisted. She implored Malden with her eyes to hold his tongue. He just looked away. "He's just upset because his friend is dying," Cythera went on. "Listen to me, Balint. Slag still has a chance to survive if I can reach the surface. I can save him. But down here, he'll perish, surely."

Balint shrugged. "As far as the king of the dwarves is concerned, this motherless snot-drip died a long time ago. When we exile somebody, they stop being a dwarf, for all practical intents."

Balint kept throwing out references to Slag's past that Malden caught, but time was too short to follow up on them. Still, he filed them away for later. Slag had been exiled? He was a debaser? Whatever that was. His real name was . . . Urin? Malden had so many questions.

"You," he said, fuming with anger, "could stop being a dwarf right now." He began to lift the sword.

A hand grabbed his forearm and he spun around to find Cythera behind him, stopping him from killing the little monster. She slapped him across the face, very hard.

The rage inside him threatened to boil over. His vision went red and he growled, literally growled, in the desire to attack, to kill.

"Malden," Cythera said, "I understand."

His rage hit a brick wall. He was so surprised he couldn't move.

"I understand how you're feeling right now. Believe me, I do. But if you harm her, then you'll be throwing your life away. And you won't help Slag at all."

"But—she's so . . . she's—"

"She is within her rights, as far as the law is concerned. And you aren't. I know you break laws all the time. But only because you expect something out of it. This won't achieve anything."

"No, please, don't listen to her," Balint laughed. "Come on, boy. Try to hit me with that great big whanger of yours. I dare you!"

Malden stared at her. The fury was still inside of him, but instead of howling for blood now it was like a torrent of water penned up like a dam. He would not give Balint what she wanted. "I won't forget this," he said.

"No man forgets meeting me," Balint assured him.

"I assure you, that—" Malden began, but he stopped in mid-sentence. Outside the door of the Hall of Masterpieces, he could hear the sound of hammers striking metal. That, and a lot of cursing. Something was up. "What are they doing out there?" he demanded.

"My men? They're simply buying some time. I'm going to walk out that door in a minute. I'm not exactly wet in the trousers to have you follow me."

She yanked on her blueling's leash again and it climbed up her arm. Dancing along like a monkey, it wrapped itself around her shoulders and closed its eyes. In a moment it was asleep. "You know, Urin, I should drag your dog-hearted arse right out of here, right now, and let you die in the foundry out there. You've got no right to sully this place—this hall—with your debasing presence. But in a way, I suppose it's appropriate you'll die right here. Aye, it's got some fucking poetry to it, don't it? Surrounded by all the emblems of what you betrayed. In the place you nearly betrayed again."

She turned to go.

"Balint," Slag moaned. "Tell me . . . one thing."

She sighed dramatically, then turned to look at him.

"What will you—ugh—do. With the bloody barrels?"

Balint frowned. "I've got my orders. I'll set them ablaze. Watch them burn, every little bit."

"But . . . why? They're priceless!"

"They're worth about as much as a whore's hand-rag to me. They're *history*." She made this last word sound like a profanity far worse than anything she'd used so far. "It's taken a long time for our people to forget, Urin. To forget what we once were. The king doesn't want anyone reminded of what we can never be again. Now—you tell *me* one thing."

Slag looked up at her.

"What the fuck were *you* going to do with them?"

Slag managed to chuckle, a little, before his chest seized up and he lost himself in a wheezing cough that made tears squirt from his eyes.

"My plan was to sell them to our king. In exchange for . . . for . . . letting me . . ." Another half chuckle. " . . . letting me come home."

Balint nodded in understanding. Then she shrugged. "It'd take more than that to earn his forgiveness. As far as he's concerned, you stink worse than a goblin's codpiece." She strode toward the door. Just before she stepped out of the room, she turned to look back at the three of them one last time. "Farewell, cock-sniffers," she said, and then she was gone.

Malden stood there holding Acidtongue for a while, trying not to shout in frustration. Finally, careful not to drip any acid on himself, he sheathed the blade and went to Slag's side.

"Your countrywoman's got a nasty streak," he said.

"Not to mention an uncivil tongue," Cythera agreed.

"Yes," Slag whispered. A wistful smile crossed his face, despite the pain. "Wasn't she magnificent?" His eyes fluttered closed and his breathing grew shallow, if ragged. He had fallen asleep.

Cythera stood up and walked to the door. She placed a hand against it and held up one finger for silence. "I can't hear them out there. They must be gone."

"And good riddance," Malden said.

"No—hark, Malden. I'm relatively sure Balint was bluffing."

"About what would happen to me if I struck her down? Believe me, I considered that it might be worth it."

"Not about that. About not having an antidote. Did she strike you as a fool?"

"What? No—not that. Not a fool, at least."

Cythera nodded. He could see in her eyes that she was thinking hard. "She laid the trap. Coated that dart with poison. The first thing Mother taught me about working with venoms and toxins was that you should never even consider it unless you had an antidote at hand. What if she had accidentally pricked herself while loading the dart into the trap? She must have something that can help Slag."

"And you want me to steal it from her."

"Exactly."

Malden laughed. It would be a pleasure.

"Follow her closely. Even if you can't get it—or if I'm wrong, and she doesn't have the antidote—you'll at least learn where the escape shaft is. But be careful! We've already seen she's a mistress of traps. Whatever her people just installed beyond this door is sure to be deadly."

"Ah. So you want me to go alone."

Cythera blushed. "I need to stay here to look after Slag. I know this is dangerous. But it may be Slag's only chance."

Malden looked down at the sleeping dwarf. "How could I refuse? But give me a kiss for luck, before I go out there into certain peril."

She sighed and tried to peck his cheek. He swung his head around in time to steal a kiss, a real kiss, from her lips. She looked slightly shocked.

"I'll be back before you have a chance to miss me," he told her, and slipped out of the Hall of Masterpieces before she had time for a clever retort.

# CHAPTER FIFTY-FOUR

Malden stepped carefully outside the door, watching the floor carefully for trip wires or pressure plates before he put a foot down. He had Slag's makeshift lantern in one hand, the other free to react to whatever he found.

It did not take long to find the trap. Indeed, it had clearly been designed to be seen immediately. That fact made Malden's heart sink. Clever, easily avoided traps relied on subterfuge—the hidden dart, the covered pit. Traps that drew attention to themselves tended to be far more deadly and far, far more difficult to circumvent.

Balint's men had filled the entire foundry with this one.

Eyelets had been hammered into the walls, and between them were strung countless lengths of woolly red yarn. They crisscrossed each other from the floor to the ceiling, like the laces of an unbelievably complicated corset. They reminded Malden of a far more delicate version of the chains strung across the entrance to the Vincularium.

Of course, this was a dwarvish trap, which meant the threads would not be cursed. He would not be burned alive if he touched them. Yet they were taut as lute strings and he knew something ugly would happen should he disturb them in any way. Escape could not possibly be so simple as cutting or burning them either.

He sighed and looked for what they might be attached to. In the dim light he could only make out the square lines of a machine erected at the far end of the room. The threads all converged on a lever sticking up from its side. A shim had been jammed into the lever's pivot so it couldn't move, but it looked like the slightest motion would knock the shim loose. So if he tugged the threads, they would pull that lever. And then . . . ? He could not say what would happen then. But he was certain it would be lethal.

Looking up, he could see the threads reached all the way to the ceiling. So he couldn't just climb up there and somehow traverse the room above the threads. No, he was going to have to make his way through them.

It was not impossible. Though when viewed head on the threads seemed to cross every cubic inch of the foundry, in fact they were far enough apart that he could slip between them if he was very deft and very careful. Malden knew he was at least one of those things. Tentatively, convinced he might set the trap off merely by breathing on it, he ducked under one of the threads and stood up on the far side.

The hair on the top of his head brushed a thread and set it vibrating.

Malden ducked low and covered his eyes. When nothing exploded or caught on fire or rained boulders down on his head, he allowed himself to breathe once more.

The next thread ran across the room at ankle height. It was easy to step over it, but he had to lean back to avoid catching another thread with his throat. Twisting at the waist, he passed under that one, then held his left foot still in the air so as not to trod on the thread beyond.

With infinite care he slid his hand and shoulder between two threads, then braced himself against the floor as he lifted his legs carefully through the gap. Directly ahead, three threads crossed the room, close enough together that he could not pass between them. He moved sideways, walking like a crab, watching always what was ahead of and behind him, until he found the place where the three threads crossed each other. There was a gap underneath just big enough for him to roll through. He passed his sword and lantern over, then tucked and rolled forward, coming to an abrupt halt when something touched his face.

Every muscle in his body locked at once. His bones held his tremulous flesh back as he tried, desperately, not to twitch in his fear. He could feel something fuzzy stretched taut against his left cheek. His left eye saw nothing—but his eyelashes felt it.

Moving absolutely nothing but his arm, Malden reached over and picked up the lantern. He lifted it by inches toward his face, taking great pains not to let the candle flame touch a single thread.

When the light came within a foot or so of his face, Malden saw what he was touching. A thread, just like the others, stretched across the room. Except that where the others were bright red, this one was dyed black. It had been invisible in the dark room. Which was the point. Anyone foolhardy enough to try to climb through the red threads wouldn't be expecting a thread they couldn't see.

Malden would have laughed in admiration, if he dared move at all. Balint truly was a master—she had hidden a cunning and undetectable trap by concealing it inside a blatant one.

Moving very slowly, he craned his neck back to release the pressure he'd put on the black thread. Then he stood up, making sure to look above his head for any more black threads he might have missed.

There was one right above him.

Looking to the sides, he spotted more of them—and those were only the ones his light could illuminate.

Taking a deep breath, he started forward again, climbing through the threads while avoiding so much as touching any of them. Checking for black threads slowed his progress to a crawl—and with every minute that passed, Balint and her men were getting farther away.

He kept expecting Cythera to call to him, demanding to know what was taking so long. Worse, the slow pace was taking a toll on his muscles. Malden had trained his body to be a fine instrument. He had spent years climbing spires, jumping across rooftops, and most importantly, running very fast whenever the authorities came for him. Yet he had spent little time training himself to hold perfectly still in contorted positions. His legs were beginning to cramp from being held in unnatural attitudes, and his arms had started to shake.

It was not much farther, he could see. The threads stopped directly before the machine they controlled, and presumably after that he would be able to move normally again. Still, he just wasn't sure he would make it. He stopped to rest for a moment—only a moment, he promised himself—and to study the threads.

He was close enough now to see the deadly component of Balint's trap. The machine looked like an oversized wine press, of the kind that used a screw to push a wooden plate down on a pile of grapes. This one seemed to have far more gears and counterweights than any wine press he'd ever seen, however, and the plate was made of metal and lined on its crushing side with thick pyramidal teeth. Underneath the crushing plate lay a piece of corroded yellowish metal, presumably taken from one of the scrap piles along the walls.

Malden couldn't figure it out until he remembered what Slag had said about not touching anything. That yellowish metal piece of junk was made of pure arsenic.

If he put too much pressure on one of the threads, it would dislodge the shim and thereby the lever on the side of the press. The crushing plate would come down and pulverize the arsenic. Malden had enough imagination to envision what would happen then—the arsenic would be reduced to a fine powder that would billow through the foundry and hang in the air as dust. Extremely poisonous dust. He would breathe in enough of it to render him completely, irrevocably, and mercilessly dead.

He went back to searching for black threads.

His next move required him to bend double and lift one leg over a thread, then squeeze his torso through the gap between two more. He sucked in his stomach and swiveled through the air, then put his free hand down on the floor and twisted his legs up, through the air, and between the threads. Next came a place where he had to lie down all the way on the floor and roll sideways under a black thread, and then—

Malden heard a sizzling sound, and looked up to see that one of the threads was glowing a dull orange.

He stared at his lantern and realized the awful truth. He must have inadvertently gotten the candle flame too close to one of the threads. Now it was smoldering. In the span of a heartbeat or two it would burn clean through—and release.

"No!" he shouted, and reached for the burning thread so fast he completely missed seeing a black thread next to his free hand. It caught between two of his fingers and he tugged it hard as he tried to extricate himself.

The shim popped free and hit the floor with a dull sound. Instantly the lever on the side of the rock press swung forward, then flew back on a spring. The mechanical parts of the machine began to ratchet and whir. The crushing plate, with terrible slowness, began to descend toward the lump of arsenic.

Malden yanked Acidtongue out of its scabbard and ran forward screaming. Threads both red and black parted before him with a sound like bowstrings twanging. His feet pounded at the floor as he poured on more speed.

The crushing plate was only inches from the scrap

metal. It was moving faster now, as the gears and counter-weights added force to its descent.

Malden jumped forward, Acidtongue pushed out in front of him like an extension of his arms. His feet left the ground and he arced through the dark air, and after that there was nothing he could do but hold the sword out straight, as far as it would go—

—so that its point smacked against the piece of arsenic a bare instant before the crushing plate made contact. The chunk of metal flew out of the press and slid across the floor. Malden yanked the sword backward, tiny droplets of acid flecking his tunic. The crushing plate slammed down with stunning force on nothing at all.

Malden's body completed its arc through the air by smashing him, face first, into the side of the rock press. His skull rang inside his head like a bell as he reared back, unable to believe he was still alive. That the air around him was not deadly poison.

Then his heart started beating again, and he whooped in triumph.

# CHAPTER FIFTY-FIVE

Croy desperately needed to rest. Yet he would not, not until Cythera and the others were safe.

Mörget, on the other hand, had never seemed so vital. "I am a hero now!" he exclaimed, hefting Dawnbringer over his head. "I will be a great chieftain. You will see. Every-one will see!" he proclaimed.

"I'm sure your reign will be a glorious one," Croy agreed. He glanced up at the ledge, high overhead, through which he had entered the throne room. He did not relish the prospect of climbing up there again. The only other option meant proceeding through the arch ahead of him—through which the demon had entered. One way was as good as another, he supposed.

"Many nations will fall before me," Mörget told him. "Men will bow when I approach. Women will want to make love to me."

"That's often more trouble than you'd think," Croy warned him. He had some experience in that realm. "Especially when they're already married to other people. Hark at this arch—do you think it will take us back toward the central shaft?"

"They will clamor for my central shaft," Mörget laughed. "Yet I promise you this, brother. No matter how she begs, I will lay no finger on your bride."

Croy inhaled deeply. That was coming very close to impugning Cythera's honor. If Mörget took his jest any further, he would be required by his own honor to respond. He had no desire to have to duel Mörget just then, however. He wasn't sure he could lift Ghostcutter without exhausting his meager reserves of strength. "We should be quiet now," he told the barbarian. "The girl you saw will have had time to reach others by now. We could walk into an ambush in the next room."

"I will be as silent as death, my mother," Mörget assured him with a great bloodcurdling laugh. "I promise."

Croy shook his head but said nothing. He headed through the arch, the tiny light of his candle throwing long shadows into the room beyond. He could not see the walls of this new chamber at all, nor its ceiling. Just as on the top level, where they'd faced the revenants, the light made a small island in a sea of darkness.

Yet as he pressed forward, he thought his eyes must be playing tricks on him. It seemed almost as if the sun was coming up. He stared and closed one eye, then the other. He knew from past experience that when one spent too long underground sometimes one's eyes became differently adapted to the lack of illumination. Yet both of his eyes agreed, and he could doubt the evidence of his senses no longer.

A ray of red light stretched along the floor, flickering in and out of existence at first, then growing stronger. This was no beam shed by a lantern or a torch—even a bonfire would have given less steady light, and certainly the light of a normal fire would be a different color. Yet even as Croy watched, the light strengthened and grew more clear. Huge shapes loomed toward him out of the darkness—big, blocky silhouettes that he soon realized must be the walls of buildings. The red light grew even stronger, and it was just like watching the sun rise over the walls of Ness.

"Mörget," he whispered, "do you see this?"

"Aye," the barbarian answered.

Croy moved forward toward the light, uncertain of the dangers but needing desperately to know its source. This new light made long shadows of everything it touched. It made him think there must be some magic afoot, and he wondered if maybe Mörget hadn't been right after all, and the girl they'd chased was, in fact, some kind of magician. They had slain her pet demon—what mischief could she be making for them now?

Croy's skin prickled and he grew very, very aware of his surroundings.

In the new light, he could see they had entered a massive courtyard, an open space full of low buildings—houses, temples, granaries, who could say?—with, high overhead, a vaulted ceiling held up by stout pillars. Ahead, the red light came from between two buildings with massive marble walls. Behind him, he saw that the throne room was just one more of these large structures.

Up to this point the Vincularium had shown him only tunnels and enclosed spaces, but now it was like he had walked into a mammoth city, and he felt as if he had fallen through some magical portal and wound up outside of the Vincularium, perhaps hundreds of miles or more away. Only the vaulted ceiling assured him that he was still underground.

He passed between the two columned facades and crossed another hundred feet of flagstones before he came to the far end of the courtyard. It ended in a ledge over the central shaft, a broad viewing platform with a marble and bronze railing. He had been searching for the central shaft for hours now, it felt like, and he'd finally discovered it. Yet it was so wondrous in appearance he barely noticed where he was.

The shaft itself was lit up like full daylight. Croy could see all the way to the top level where he had entered the Vincularium, and up at that dizzying height stood the source of the reddish light. It was the crystalline orb that hung in the center of the shaft, suspended on its three massive chains. It burned now, with a roiling fire that almost hurt his eyes to look at, an incredible conflagration contained entirely within the transparent globe. He could see now that dozens of pipes crowned the orb, running away into the domed ceiling of the dwarven city.

Dawn had come to the Vincularium.

"Like an enormous oil lamp," he said, trying to puzzle it out. "But how—what— Ah, of course. It's magic."

No other explanation satisfied Croy's view of the world. It had to be magic that made the light burn. He marveled at it, having fit it neatly into his simple philosophy. If you saw something you couldn't explain, if it seemed to have no rational explanation, then it was undeniably magical in nature, and therefore it couldn't be explained, so you didn't need to worry about it. It was a common enough attitude in Skrae, at least among the human population. Dwarves, Croy knew, found this rationale endlessly frustrating, but then dwarves rarely needed much justification to be frustrated with humanity.

While he stood gaping at it, the light of the orb grew suddenly stronger and he had to look away with a gasp. If he tried to look at it a moment longer, he felt his eyes would be seared from his head. He blinked away blotchy afterimages of green and purple and looked down into the pool of water at the bottom of the shaft.

And then he got his next shock. A naked woman was swimming through the dark water, her limbs parting the surface with a languid motion. Her skin was as pale as ivory, and she struck him as being too slender to be human—though what he saw of her angular form did not make him think of emaciation and hunger, but of a sublime beauty. Starvation hadn't made her so thin. He'd seen human women who had gone too long without food, and it made them cadaverous and ugly. This woman looked like she was born to be willow-thin. Even her bones looked more slender than a human's. As she swam, her dark hair flowed behind her, buoyed by the water.

Croy stood enchanted, watching her stroke her way across the pool. He might have stood there and watched forever—had Mörget not grabbed his shoulder and hauled him bodily around.

"Brother—come quickly. Such wonders must wait."

"But—" Croy shook himself to break his reverie. The sight of the swimming woman had bewitched him. "What is it, Mörget? Why do you look like that?"

The barbarian had gone pale, even under the red ink that masked the bottom half of his face. His eyes stood out from their sockets as if he'd seen a ghost. "Just come with me," he said. "And have your sword ready."

He took Croy back to the center of the courtyard and shoved him behind one of the marble buildings. Together they peered around a twisted column of cyclopean blocks. "Behold," Mörget whispered, and pointed into the long shadows between the buildings.

At first Croy could see nothing. His eyes had adapted to the light of the Vincularium's artificial sun, and the shadows in contrast were too absolute. Then he spied a pair of figures emerging from the reddish light. They wore armor of bronze, and they were as rail-thin as the woman he'd seen swimming in the pool. Revenants, he thought. They must have tracked him and the barbarian all the way down from the top level. Well, he could still fight such, though—

His hand stopped before he could get his sword free of its scabbard. Moving between the two revenants was . . . something else. A creature of no fixed form, five feet in general diameter. Howling faces pressed outward from inside its skin.

"Another one?" Croy asked. "Another demon? The little brother of your beast—or perhaps its child?" Whatever it was, it chilled Croy's blood. If there was more than one— far worse, if this demon could somehow multiply—it was a far greater threat than he had ever imagined. He'd thought a demon so close to the border of Skrae could be a thing that undid the world if it wasn't stopped. Yet if there were more than the two, if the demon had been down here for centuries, reproducing, creating an army of itself—how could even the Ancient Blades ever resist it? How could they possibly win?

This could mean the end of the world.

Mörget, who should have shared Croy's apprehensions—the barbarian was an Ancient Blade as well, sworn as Croy was to checking the advance of demons—seemed more concerned with his own singular destiny. He seethed with anger, and Croy imagined he would start roaring at any moment. Yet when he spoke it was with the cool tones of a man estimating a job of work. "I know only this—my labor here is not yet done."

# PART IV

# The Shadows Lengthen

# INTERLUDE

Even as the red sun of the Vincularium flickered into a kind of dawn, outside, in the wider world, night was falling. On the road to the ancient city, Herward the eremite kept his watch, his eyes fixed on the dark hole in the once-inviolate seal.

He shuddered as the last purple light of day fled, and bolstered himself with a swig of black mead. His sole sustenance, it was a concoction of mead made from wild honey with fermented weeds and root vegetables, brewed and left to age until it resembled molten obsidian. The stuff had given his ancestors courage to charge into battle and to brave the tortures of the elves. It had sustained Herward for years without solid food, and opened his eyes to visions and hallucinations past number. No matter how hard his life in the ancient fortress had been, no matter what privations he faced, the black mead kept him going. It had kept him steadfast and strong.

It had no power whatsoever to give him the courage to step inside the Vincularium.

He could not say what he was so afraid of. Had he not spent much of his adult life yearning—hungering desperately—for the secrets of that place? And yet now those secrets seemed foul and horrid. He felt as if he put one foot inside that dark hole, it would be immediately chopped off. Or worse—a long-dead hand would grasp the foot and pull him inward, pull him inside out of the moonlight, and he would never reemerge.

His mind so full of dark fancies, his body trembling with fear, Herward nearly expired on the spot when someone crept up behind him and softly spoke his name.

His hand shot out and his clay bottle flew away to shatter on the stony road. So much for liquid courage. Slowly he turned to see what dread phantom had come for him, what horror he'd loosed from under the mountain.

Yet it was a smiling face that greeted him, a smiling face with twinkling eyes he could just make out under the shadow of a monkish cowl. The man who stood behind him wore no bronze armor, but instead the undyed wool habit of a priest.

"Oh, I—I'm sorry, you frightened me," Herward said, clawing at his wild hair, his scabrous skin. He must look a terror himself, he thought, though he felt like a lizard caught too far from its hiding place in the rocks. "I beg your pardon, brother. You know my name?"

"In Helstrow they told me I'd find you here," the newcomer said. He did not move forward to embrace Herward, nor even offer his hand, but he offered no violence either. There was a supernal calm about the man, an aura of perfected peace. He looked as if he'd been truly touched by the divine, and that calmed Herward a little. "There are many there who remember Herward the Holy."

"Herward the Mad, you mean," the eremite said with a laugh. "Oh, I bear them no malice. They made sport of me, it's true, but I know my ways are not those of others. That's why I came here, really. To live life in my own fashion."

"When we are touched by higher things, it is hard to stay worldly," the newcomer said. "May I sit with you? I'd talk awhile, if you'll have my company."

Herward nodded eagerly. By custom he was a loner, undesirous of human connection, but this night was different. He'd been plagued by doubts before as he sat and watched the hole in the side of the mountain. He'd started to think he heard things moving around just inside, and was grateful for someone else to share his vigil. "Of course, of course! You are a fellow holy man, I see. Yes, I can sense it about you, you know the calm of communion with another world. Please, please join me, friend, brother, ah . . . ?"

"Call me Prestwicke," the newcomer said. He found a boulder by the side of the road and sat down upon it. His habit was dusty, as if he'd come a long way. "It's good to sit, and rest awhile."

Herward sat down in the road and folded his skinny legs in a pose of meditation. "Have you come far?" he asked, because he knew not what else to say.

"From Ness, and lately," Prestwicke assented. "The miles are long, but the work is the important thing. I do not shirk my duty, nor do I complain. But . . . it is good to sit, and rest." He looked toward the hole in the mountain but did not remark on it. For a long quiet time the two of them simply sat and shared each other's company without words. Herward was just grateful not to be alone.

When the newcomer did speak again, his voice was soft and pleasing to the ear. "You were visited recently, weren't you? By armed men, no less. That must have been hard for you. That sort are so full of bodily desires and greedy aspirations. Their very presence must have tried your devotion."

How Prestwicke could know that was a mystery, but Herward kept doubt from creasing his face with a frown. Perhaps Prestwicke had been given that information in a vision. "As you say, I do not shirk my duty. The Lady asked me to help them."

"Now this, Herward, is why I wanted to meet you," Prestwicke told him. "How long has it been since I met another who really understood what holy work means? Too long I've been surrounded only by common folk, or worse—priests."

Herward cringed at the man's tone. "Now, the priests of the Lady are good men, and learned, and wise," he said, almost rising to his feet to defend them. "They are touched by Her hand just as much as—"

Prestwicke interrupted him. "They lead the people in

prayers that go unanswered. They sing . . . hymns." He lifted one hand in dismissal.

"The Lady places us each in our station, and gives us our work. Her priests She chooses because they can teach, and heal, and bring to the people a—"

"They do nothing of value. They take money from the people to burn incense and read from books. Bah! Do you know, Herward," Prestwicke went on, "there was a time—long passed, of course—when priests were *feared* by the common herd? When they inspired awe wherever they went?"

"The Lady's chosen ministers bring only comfort and—"

"The days I speak of were before the Lady came to our world," Prestwicke said with a little shake of his head. "It was the first work of Her clergy to track down and destroy the old priesthood. Because they knew, Herward. They knew what real priests were capable of. They could make the rain fall. They could change the course of battles. They could perform wonders, Herward. Wonders."

Herward felt as if icy water had been poured over his shoulders and back. He began to think this visitor was not what he seemed. He might not even be human. There were old tales of demons that took human form, of tempters and cajolers. "You're speaking of sorcery," he whispered.

"I most certainly am not," Prestwicke said, and though he did not raise his voice, it seemed to echo like a thunderclap. "Sorcerers are vile creatures, despoilers of ancient ritual. They steal scraps of incantations and chants from the old priesthood, and use them for their own venal purposes. I'm talking of the old priests of Sadu. The holy brotherhood that placated and worshipped the Bloodgod, in the name of all humankind."

"Lady preserve me," Herward said. "Why have you come to me? I'll resist you, I swear. If you try to take my soul—"

"Their ways are lost now. Their books destroyed. But secrets have a strange way of being remembered. I'm going to find the old ways, Herward. I'm going to bring them back. I can't let you stop me." Prestwicke rose to his feet. "Back then, in the old days, the priests of Sadu would perform sacrifices. Human sacrifices. The people would choose who amongst them must die. It mattered little to the priests who was chosen—any life would do as far as Sadu was concerned. Any life would give them the power, the strength to do His work in the world."

The knife did not suddenly appear in Prestwicke's hand. It had been there for a while, but Herward had not noticed it before. Now he saw nothing else.

There are many kinds of fear. There is fear of the unknown, and fear of immediate violence. There is a kind of supernatural dread, too, when one realizes that a painful, bloody death may only be the prelude to something much worse.

"I don't know if the Lady is even real," Prestwicke said. It was ugly blasphemy just to say that out loud, but Herward did not challenge it. "I know She doesn't protect Her priests. I've seen them bleed. You, on the other hand, are different, Herward. You seem to have genuinely been touched by something bigger than yourself, just as I have. Of course, it's possible you're just insane."

Herward raised one hand to make a holy sign across his chest. Prestwicke moved faster than a striking snake and knocked his arm away. The knife did not touch Herward's skin, but he heard it slash through the air, an inch away from his throat.

"It might be interesting to see just how much power you have. It might be entertaining to test my god against your goddess, and find out which one can actually protect their chosen. But then again, there's a chance I might lose. *You* might kill *me.*"

Prestwicke chuckled. Herward found himself unable to resist, and he made sounds that might have been giggles or might have been tiny screams.

"But the people didn't choose you for my sacrifice,"

Prestwicke went on. "They chose another. I have to go inside the Vincularium now, Herward. It's better—more proper—if I don't kill anyone else until I finish this task. So I'll ask you politely. Are you going to try to stop me?"

Herward opened his mouth to speak, but no words came out.

The knife was only a hairbreadth away from his eyeball. Herward was a man of celestial visions, of grand thoughts encompassing the whole of the cosmos, but in that moment, in that slowed-down time, he could see nothing—nothing at all—but the shiny, sharp point of that little knife.

"No," he said.

Because sometimes fear is stronger than faith.

# CHAPTER FIFTY-SIX

Malden lifted the lantern high and scanned the rest of the foundry for traps. He saw none, though he knew Balint's skill now, and could never be sure she hadn't hidden something so devious he would only discover it by stepping on it.

Time was precious now, however, so he moved quickly—if quietly—toward the lift. Much as he'd expected, the brass cage was not where he had left it. Balint must have gone that way.

Or, possibly, she had moved the lift to throw him off her track.

Such thinking had no end, though. If he doubted her

every move, and thus dithered until he was paralyzed and unable to act, she would already have beaten him. He had to catch her before she escaped the Vincularium—and without letting her know that he was on her trail.

He risked shining a little light up and down the lift shaft. Far below, he could just make out a glint of brass— that must be the cage down there. He blew out his candle immediately, lest she see its light. In the darkness he grabbed hold of the lift's main chain and slid down the shaft. The chain was well greased, and he fell faster than he'd meant to, but he managed to clutch it tight enough that when his feet struck the top of the cage they made only a little sound. Even so, he froze in place and listened carefully before he climbed down the side of the cage and dropped to the floor.

Now he was faced with a quandary. He could see nothing, hear nothing. Yet he dared not make any light until he was sure Balint wouldn't see it. Fortunately, the chamber he was in proved almost identical to the one above, a round room of narrow diameter with a single exit. He moved along the wall, one hand on the smooth bricks, using caution every time he took a step. This meant moving at a slower pace than he liked, but it would make him all but invisible to any dwarf watching for pursuit.

Outside the lift chamber, he found himself on an open floor. He headed forward quietly, knowing he would soon have to make a light or risk stumbling and breaking his neck. He was unsure how to proceed, but he knew he had no choice but to keep moving. Slag's life depended on what happened next.

In the utter darkness his ears grew keenly sensitive. It was not long before he heard a distant, patternless drumming. Surely it was the sound of the knocker's fingers tapping on some wall or floor. He expected to see a light ahead at any moment, for Balint could see no better in the dark than he could. She would need a lamp to guide her to the exit shaft.

Yet when he did spy a light, it was not the color he expected, nor did it flicker like a candle flame or a torch. A red beam of radiance split the floor ahead of him. As he watched, it grew more intense and spread across the flagstones.

Malden saw that he stood on the central avenue of a warren of low structures, most likely the houses of dwarves long dead. In shape they were uniform to a surprising degree. He was used to cities where wealth and ostentation were celebrated, where having the biggest house made you the better man. Here all the houses were alike, drab huts no more than six feet high with flat roofs. In places, tiers of such houses had been piled atop each other to form misshapen towers, with ladders leading up to each doorway. Standing outside each tower was a high pole, topped with a globe a foot across. What function these standards once performed was an utter mystery to him, so he ignored them and instead studied the squat shapes of the houses.

They looked to Malden more like the chambers of a cut-open ant colony than the domiciles of a residential district. These were not homes in the human sense, places of warmth and security where families would gather around communal fires. It seemed to him more a place, simply, where workers went to sleep when their labors were done. The closest analog in his experience was a monastic dormitory.

Malden could make little sense of it. He knew dwarves wasted little thought on luxury or appearances, even though they prized gold and wealth above everything except good craftsmanship. But what did they want with money at all, if this was how they lived? The dwarven houses confused him deeply, as did most things concerning dwarves. One thing was clear, though. This must be the residential level—where Slag said the escape tunnel was located. Balint must be on her way out of the Vincularium, intending to leave as quickly as she might. Malden hardly blamed her. He could only wish his own egress would come so soon.

The red light continued to strengthen, showing more and more of the dwarven dormitory. He had no way to account for the light, and at the moment had no taste for mysteries. He'd assumed, on first seeing it, that Balint had some source of light more advanced than humble fire, some dwarven machine whose workings would be like unto magic as far as he was concerned. Yet this light resembled most the breaking dawn of a newly risen sun.

He crept forward, trying to stay always out of those red beams. They made the shadows deeper and he was thankful for that. His senses were tuned toward finding the dwarves, and it wasn't long before he saw them ahead of him, turned to silhouettes by the crimson rays. There were but three dwarves, and of course the knocker. They cast long stripes of shadow behind them, like ribbons of darkness.

The Place of Long Shadows, Malden thought. The ancient dwarven name for the Vincularium suddenly made a great deal of sense.

If the idea of a sun rising underground was a marvel to the thief, it seemed no less awe-inspiring to Balint and her crew. The dwarves stood as if transfixed by the light. Balint and one of the others stared up through a broad opening before them, a gallery, Malden surmised, that looked out on the central shaft.

The third dwarf, however, kept staring at the shadows. In the new light, Malden could see that his eyes were enormous and he was trembling. "I tell you true, Balint—I saw somebody back there. Just for a second, and then it vanished again. Ducked back into the fucking shadows or something. Weren't one of your humans neither."

"Shut your hole or I'll stick something in it," Balint said, and struck the trembling dwarf.

"It was wearing the most beautiful bronze armor, too," he responded, flinching away from her blow.

"Don't go jumping at fancies," Balint told him.

Malden felt a chill fear creep down his back as he listened. Bronze armor—that could only mean one thing. The frightened dwarf must have seen a revenant. Had the undead elves really come this far down the shaft? If one had, and it discovered the dwarves, why hadn't it attacked at once? The revenants had no reason to love Balint and her crew—in fact, they had every reason to hate dwarves more than they hated humans. It was the dwarves, after all, who betrayed the elves into coming down here. Now that they were undead spirits of justice, the elfin revenants must long bitterly for dwarven blood. Yet it sounded like this dwarf had seen one and it had hid from him.

Malden could make no sense of it. He told himself it didn't matter, at least not in the immediate moment.

He snuck up behind the four of them, sticking close to the shadows they cast. He was certain that the knocker would hear him at any moment, but if he was fast enough—

Then new light, the same reddish hue but not as intense, burst into life behind him, and the shadows around him evaporated like morning mist. Malden glanced back to see the light came from the poles that stood outside the dormitory towers. The globe atop each pole proved to be a lamp of strange design. Most of them remained unlit, and he saw that some of the globes were cracked or even shattered. Yet they cast enough light to mimic bright day on the surface.

He sought around him for shadows to conceal him, but before he could move he heard the dwarves cry out. He was discovered.

# CHAPTER FIFTY-SEVEN

"There!" one of the dwarves shouted.

Balint spun around, her eyes wide in surprise. "You survived that trap? How?"

"Did you leave a trap for me?" Malden asked, his face a mask of nonchalance. He blew out the candle of his lantern, since there was plenty of light to see by now. "I didn't notice."

Balint turned to her confederates. "Make sure he doesn't get past the next one," she told them.

Malden started to rush forward, intending to grab Balint and force her to give him the antidote. It was the best plan he could come up with, having no time to think anything through.

It nearly got him killed.

The law said Balint could not use any weapon, even in her own defense. Over the centuries the dwarves had found more than one creative loophole in the treaty. Before Malden even got up to speed she took a glass flask from off her belt and smashed it against the floor between them. Pungent liquid splashed across the flagstones. She must have drilled her men in what to do next, as one of them tossed a lit taper into the midst of the puddle thus formed.

Malden reared back as a wall of flames leapt up at him. He overbalanced and fell on his posterior, his hands stretched out behind him to catch his fall. Scuttling like a crab, he raced backward, away from the spreading fire.

In a moment the fuel was all consumed and the fire died, but it left a thick bank of greasy smoke hanging in the air. By the time Malden batted away the fumes the dwarves and the knocker were nowhere to be seen.

Cursing silently, he jumped to his feet and raced for

the few remaining shadows in the dormitory level. He had no doubt the dwarves had done the same. They could be anywhere around him, hiding perhaps in one of the drab houses of their ancestors—or they could be even now running down a side passage, away from him. There were far too many such avenues to choose from. The dormitory was a maze of narrow lanes with nothing to recommend one or another.

He tried to think what Balint would do next. Retreating was certainly what he would have done—he was an expert on running away from trouble. Though he had always felt most comfortable running along rooftops, high above his pursuers, up where he could observe them without being seen himself—

He clamped his eyes shut and listened.

Yes.

He could just make out the faint tapping of the knocker. The creature was blind, Slag had said. Its only method of sensing its environment was to listen to the echoes of its own drumming.

After a split second the tapping stopped—perhaps Balint had silenced her creature to better hide her escape—but Malden knew where to head next. He raced up a ladder, heading to the top of one of the towers. When he reached its highest level, he grabbed the edge of its flat roof and pulled himself up to catch a glimpse over the edge.

Immediately he dropped back, as a mouth full of peg-like teeth and two white, blind eyes came screaming toward him. The knocker wasn't constrained by the law. It came scampering over the edge of the roof, its long fingers reaching to grab and rend Malden's face.

He swung aside, balancing all his weight on one foot on the top of the ladder. The knocker went hurtling past him, gibbering horrible curses Malden couldn't understand. It fell nearly all the way to the flagstones below before catching a rung of the ladder and bouncing there like a ball on a string.

Its momentum shook the ladder and Malden nearly fell

himself. His arms out wide, wheeling for balance, he felt his foot begin to slip on the rung. It was all he could do to get his other leg jammed between two rungs so he didn't slip and fall to his death.

When his heart stopped hammering in his chest he took a deep breath and started up again. This time when he got his eyes above the edge he saw what he'd been looking for—Balint's back, running away from him at speed.

He hauled himself over the edge of the roof and ran across its flat expanse. There was no rain in the underground city, and no snow, so the dwarves had built their houses without sloped rooftops. Malden found the going much easier than what his legs were trained for: the shingled roofs of Ness. His legs were much longer than Balint's as well. It wasn't long before he reached the far side of the roof and saw her crossing a rope to the next roof over. He looked down and saw she'd thrown a grapple to make herself a bridge. As small as she was, it was easy for her to swing across, hand over hand.

"You won't get away that easy," he called.

Balint glared at him over her shoulder and spat out a curse in a language he didn't know. Exactly as he'd hoped, his taunting had slowed her down. He reached the near end of the rope before she was even halfway across.

This end of the rope was tied to a narrow chimney pipe. It would be child's play to cut the knot and let her fall. It was a good forty feet down. He doubted even a dwarf as tough as Balint could survive a plummet like that.

Of course, the antidote she carried was probably held in some fragile bottle. If she fell it might shatter. He left the knot alone. Instead he danced forward along the rope, one foot in front of the other. As easy as breathing, he thought, making sure not to look down. I can do this, I can—

Balint got to the far side and started cutting through the rope while he was still running on air between two buildings.

Malden felt the rope twang and shudder beneath him,

knew that he only had a split second before he fell himself. At this height he wouldn't just break his neck when he hit the ground. He would splatter.

He had no choice but to jump. He timed his leap just as the rope went slack beneath him. His hands shot forward and grabbed the ledge of the far roof, and he pulled himself over, rolling away in case Balint had any more traps waiting for him. When no metal jaws clamped shut on his face and no bursts of fire singed his eyebrows, he leapt to his feet and found her cowering away from him, her eyes hard as she waited for him to attack. "You have something I want," he told her.

She looked him up and down. "Do I? But what's in it for me? I doubt you could satisfy a bedbug."

It took him a moment to work out what she was saying. Then he growled in anger and stepped toward her—

—and right into a rope snare lying before him on the rooftop.

Malden threw his hands out to his sides, expecting the rope to close around his ankle and haul him up into the air while Balint made a clean getaway.

Instead he just stared down at a length of rope that didn't move at all. He didn't understand. It was an obvious trap. He'd fallen for it like a novice at this game. Yet for some reason it hadn't triggered.

Balint's eyes burned with fury. Ignoring him, she ran to the side of the rooftop and stared down at the street. "Murin! I told you to secure that fucking line!"

There was no response from below.

"Murin! You answer me right now!" She ran to the other side of the roof. "Slurri! Get your thumb out of your arse and come up here!"

"They don't seem to hear you," Malden said, stepping toward her. "Perhaps they grew tired of listening to your curses. Or maybe something else found them. Something in bronze armor. Something that isn't bound by any laws or treaties."

Balint turned and glared at him. Then she looked behind her. She had very little room to back up, and no more grappling hooks to throw. Her trap had failed—and now she was snared herself. She had nowhere to go. Malden took another step toward her.

"They're probably already dead," he said, thinking revenants must have come down to this level. Thinking that even if they were still alive, he had to keep her thinking she was out of options. "Come, Balint. The antidote. And then we can go our separate ways. Maybe you'll even make it out of here alive."

She took a half step backward and nearly fell off the roof. He saw her teetering, her arms flying outward, and he rushed forward to grab her and pull her back.

"Fucking get off of me," she said, batting at his hands as soon as she was steady on the roof again.

"Damn you, Balint, I just saved your life! Be reasonable!"

"No human gets the better of me! I'll suck your eyes out and fuck your skull!" she shrieked.

Then she drew the wrench from its scabbard at her hip, and smacked him across the jaw with it.

# CHAPTER FIFTY-EIGHT

Malden's head spun. Lights burst in the backs of his eyes and drool fountained out of his split lip. He reeled as he staggered to keep his feet, one hand reaching for Acidtongue.

"Oath-breaker," he swore, as he rubbed at his hurt jaw. "The law—"

Balint's eyes were wild. She stared down at the wrench in her hand as if she were holding a feral animal that was likely to bite her. Her mouth opened to form words but for a moment she was so stunned by what she'd done (perhaps more stunned than Malden was by the pain of it) that she could not speak.

Considering the mouth on her, that was a marvel in itself.

Then she seemed to recover a bit of her composure. "I . . . don't see any witnesses," she said, and changed her grip on the wrench.

Malden drew Acidtongue a few inches from its sheath.

"Is this really what you want?" he asked.

She swallowed noisily. "Fuck you."

Malden stepped backward. His head still rang, and he wouldn't have been surprised if his jaw was broken. It hurt badly enough. Still. He could focus enough to draw Acidtongue free of its scabbard and hold it out to his side, the way he'd seen Croy hold Ghostcutter many times.

Balint looked terrified when she saw the sword. She was trembling visibly. She clearly wasn't afraid enough to give in, however. Malden watched in grudging admiration as she drew her screwdriver with her free hand. It would make a serviceable dagger, more than capable of putting out his eyes.

Assuming he bent over so she could reach, and that he was obliging enough to hold still while she did it.

Malden took a step toward her. His magical sword dripped acid onto the rooftop. It would cut through her like a loaf of bread the first time it touched her. He had a longer reach. He was faster than she was. He outweighed her—a fact he'd seen end more fights than any other factor.

She started shaking. The wrench rattled in her hand.

"Just give me the antidote," Malden said. He frowned, then added, "The barrels, too. Then you can run away."

"I . . . can't do that," Balint told him. Her whole body was shaking now.

"Of course you can."

"No! The barrels must be destroyed!"

"By the Lady's eighty-nine nipples! What's in those barrels that makes dwarves go crazy?" he asked. "What could possibly be so important?"

"You don't know anything. You know nothing of our history, and don't even pretend otherwise. I have my orders, straight from the lips of my king. No human—nor any dwarf—can ever have the barrels. I'll give my life for that command."

"A pox on your orders!" He lifted the sword higher, preparing to bring it down in a killing stroke.

"Why don't you go shit blood?" she asked. Her mouth closed tightly as if she were trying to keep her teeth from chattering. "Go ahead and kill me, you—you . . . girl-slayer. My men will still get away with the barrels, and Urin will still die."

Malden lifted the sword and pointed it at Balint's face. She yelped in terror.

And then his heart broke inside his chest. *What in the name of the Bloodgod's trousers am I doing?*

Malden had grown up hating swords. More accurately, hating anyone who wore one on his belt. Swords were the answer to any question, it seemed, for those who had them always got their way over those who didn't. In his experience most swordsmen took advantage of that fact and abused their power. How many times as a child had he seen a client refuse to pay one of his mother's colleagues, and get away with it because he had a length of iron on his belt? How many times had he seen tradesmen and merchants and the abject poor of Ness shoved to the side of a street, thrown in the gutter, because they were in the way of a man with a sword?

It wasn't until he'd met Croy that he even considered that there might be armed people in the world who didn't want to steal from, lie to, and cheat everyone else, and then claim that was their right because they were born to the proper parents.

And now here he was. About to slaughter a dwarf—a dwarf, in Sadu's name!—to get what he wanted. With a sword.

He had fallen in with low companions, he thought. Croy possessed a terrible influence on him. Made him forget everything he'd once believed. Croy had given him Acidtongue as if it was some great prize, some mark of esteem. In the process the knight had turned him into one of those arseholes he'd grown up hating. The ones who used to make his blood boil. He'd always considered himself an enemy of power, of the abusive system of knights and lords and kings that held Skrae in an iron grip.

When he accepted Acidtongue from the knight, he'd joined that crew.

He moved the sword back to his side. He wanted to throw it away. He didn't sheathe it, though. He still needed that antidote, at the very least.

"Keep your benighted barrels, then. Give me the antidote and I'll leave you in peace."

Balint stopped shaking immediately. A look of incomprehension crossed her face—but then, suddenly, her eyes went sly. "I have your number now. You've got grease for guts," she said. A nasty smile split her face. "You can't do it. You can't kill me, even with that length of iron in your hand. What is it? Are you just a coward? Or are you going to tell me you've got too much honor to slaughter an innocent?"

"I'd hardly put that label on you," Malden told her. "But I won't cut you down. Not like this. Give me the antidote."

"I told you, there isn't any."

Malden sighed. "And I know you're lying. Cythera— you met her back at the Hall of Masterpieces—told me so. She's the daughter of a witch, and she's worked with poisons herself. She told me no poisoner is so foolish not to keep the cure for her own venom somewhere on her. So you must have it. Hand it over. Now."

She watched his face for a while, perhaps trying to judge just how far she could push him before he attacked her in blind rage. Then she reached down inside her shirt and took out a tiny glass vial with a cork stopper. A few drops of brown liquid rolled around inside the glass.

"Put that iron prick-replacement away and I'll consider it," she told him.

He scowled at Balint, but then he shoved Acidtongue back into its glass-lined scabbard, as she'd asked. He kept his left hand near his belt, where his bodkin was ready to be drawn at a moment's notice. If he was going to have to kill her, he wanted to do it with a poor man's weapon.

"How do I administer it?" he asked, nodding at the vial.

"One drop is all he needs. Any more and the antidote will make him shit out his bowels, his brains, and everything in between," Balint said.

She might be lying, but he reckoned Cythera would know the truth.

"He won't be much good for anything for a day or two. Of course, a debaser like that isn't fit to lick clean my privy any day."

"Just give it to me," Malden said.

"Certainly. Here you go!" she cried, and flung the vial past his outstretched hands and over the rooftop.

# CHAPTER FIFTY-NINE

Malden howled in anger and horror. He forgot all about Balint as he twisted on one foot and jumped into the air, trying desperately to catch the vial before it smashed on the flagstones far below. He gave no thought whatsoever as to where he, himself, would land.

The glass vial arced through the air, spinning end over end. His fingers barely touched it as he hit the top of his own parabola, and he nearly flicked it away by being over-zealous. He shot out his other hand and just managed to grab it and hold it tight in his fist. He had it! He had the antidote!

Too bad it looked like he was going to die for it.

He had expected to land face-first on the rooftop but hadn't realized how far he'd jumped to catch the vial. So focused was he on catching it that he had overshot the edge of the roof completely. Now there was nothing beneath him but empty space.

Time seemed to stretch out and an awful sort of peace suddenly came over him, as his brain chose to retreat into pure reason rather than scream in horror. He seemed to have all the time in the world to think as he fell. He looked down and saw the rooftops of a lower building come shooting up toward him, and wondered if he'd just thrown away his own life to save Slag's.

How unlike me, he considered as he dropped through the dim red light. Normally I put myself first and above all others. For perhaps the first time in my life, I've acted nobly and selflessly.

He looked down again.

*What a terrible mistake that turned out to be.*

When Malden had taught himself to climb on the rooftops of Ness, one of the first things he had to learn was how to fall properly, but now there was no time to put that knowledge into practice. He tried to roll as he struck a rooftop two levels down, but still he took most of the impact in his shoulder. He felt the bones in his arm flex and start to crack, but before anything could shatter he was falling again, bouncing off the one roof to land on the next one down. This time he landed with a crunch that stole all his momentum and left him at rest.

That's odd, he thought. I don't appear to be dead. This doesn't even hurt all that much. He rolled over and tried to sit up.

What he accomplished instead was that he started to scream in agony.

He grunted through the pain, forcing himself to rise to his knees. His left arm felt like a piece of crazed pottery, like it would shatter into a million pieces if he moved it even a fraction of an inch. He had wrenched his shoulder badly, and the ribs down that side of his chest throbbed with agony.

He had to know, though. He forced his hand to open, and saw the vial lying on his palm.

Intact. The cork had worked its way partially out of its collar, but he pressed it back down with his good thumb.

Then he dropped onto his back and just stared up at the red-lit ceiling for a while, trying to not pass out from the pain.

For a long time that was all he could do.

There was no sign of Balint. She wasn't peering down at him from a rooftop high above. She wasn't approaching to hit him with her wrench again. Most likely she'd done the wise thing and just run away. He supposed he should be grateful for small favors.

He knew he had to get up. He had to get to his feet and get back down to the street level. He had to take the lift back to the foundry and get the antidote to Slag before it was too late. If he failed, the dwarf would die.

He tried to roll over, and screamed in pain again. He had no control over it—his hurt arm took control of his lungs and made him scream. Sweat poured down his face and his breathing came in hitches and starts. The red light pulsed behind his eyes, keeping time with his pulse.

He felt sick. He knew if he vomited now it would just make him weaker, so he choked down his stomach contents and struggled to get up on his knees. His legs worked just fine. They didn't hurt. He climbed to his feet—hard to do without using his hands, but he managed. He exhaled deeply, once, twice, three times. Then he walked across the rooftop to its edge, where he looked down and saw a ladder below him. He could climb down a ladder with one good arm, if he had to.

He had to.

He was halfway down the dormitory tower when a new scream ripped through the red-lit air.

Malden froze in place and stared at the wall in front of him for a long time before he realized that the scream had not come out of his own mouth.

Who had made that sound, then? He couldn't know. It didn't matter. He climbed down another rung.

"Slurri!" he heard Balint call, from somewhere else in the cavernous dormitory level. "Murin! Where are you?"

No answer came.

Malden took another step down.

The light changed subtly and a long shadow passed across the wall in front of Malden's face. He ignored it and took another step down the ladder.

"Human!" Balint called. "Human! Answer me!"

Malden ignored her and kept climbing.

"What did you do to Slurri? Where's Murin?" Balint shouted.

"I've done nothing," Malden said. He didn't have the strength to make his voice very loud.

"What? Speak up, arsehole. I can't hear you."

Malden turned his head to look up at her. She stood on

a rooftop across from him, one level up. Her face was lit from below by the red streetlamps, giving her a ghastly aspect.

"Look at me," he said, with as much force as he could muster. "I'm right here. I did nothing! If your friends are gone, it must have been the revenants that got them!"

"Dead elves? Ha! Your lies stink worse than your moldy bollocks. You must have laid a trap for him. I swear, if they're dead, I'll go to Helstrow myself and demand justice of your human king. I'll make sure they cut you open and draw out your intestines on a windlass!"

Malden shook his head and climbed down another rung. Every time his foot landed it jarred his whole body and his left arm flared into agony again. "I don't—lay traps. I defeat them. You're the one who—sets traps."

Balint said nothing more. She disappeared behind the edge of her rooftop and was gone. Malden was glad for it.

As he was about to place his foot on the flagstones at street level he heard another scream. This time he was sure he wasn't the one who made it. Perhaps it had been Balint, meeting her first revenant. That had to be it—the dwarves must have fallen afoul of the Vincularium's guardians. They were dead, then, all of them. Even Balint's wrench would be no match for their clutching, bony hands.

It didn't matter.

Nothing mattered but getting the antidote to Slag.

# CHAPTER SIXTY

Outside the throne room, Mörget and Croy hid behind thick marble columns and did their best not to make a sound.

The patrol that sought them—the demon's smaller twin and the two armored revenants—was getting close. Close enough that Croy could hear their footfalls echoing. From his place in the shadows he got occasional glimpses of them as they moved around the room, poking their swords into various shadows and hiding places. So far they had failed to find anything, but they seemed resolved to check the entire chamber. As they drew closer, he wondered what he should do if he was discovered.

Every one of his sinews and tendons were tensed for him to jump out from behind the pillar and attack. He longed for the fight. He had taken vows to slay demons wherever they were found. Yet he had taken other vows as well. Vows of love.

He must find Cythera. He must get her out of this terrible place. And that meant that no matter what else, he had to keep himself alive.

He still felt weak from his last encounter with the formless demon, when he had nearly been devoured. His face and hands still stung from the touch of the creature's blood. He was in no shape for a desperate fight now. And even if he prevailed against this patrol, how many more of them would there be? How many revenants, hiding in the deepest recesses of the Vincularium, waiting for the proper moment to spring forward and take their revenge—and how many demons?

Just on the other side of his pillar, the new, smaller demon stopped moving forward. Its substance bunched up in the middle and it grew taller. Faces appeared under its skin, stretching outward as if they sensed something.

A few feet away, protected only by shadows, Croy held his breath and waited. Then he glanced over at Mörget.

The barbarian had Dawnbringer half out of its sheath.

Croy shook his head violently. Mörget frowned and lifted his sword another few inches clear of its scabbard. No, Croy thought, desperately trying to communicate with the barbarian. No, not now. He wasn't in any shape for a desperate fight. One demon had nearly butchered him. Backed up by undead elves, another might succeed. If he was slain now, what hope would Cythera have? She was trapped down here, surrounded by nightmarish creatures and unknown dangers. And she had only Malden to protect her.

Croy stared directly into Mörget's eyes and pleaded with him silently. He reached out and grabbed Mörget's sword arm. He felt the barbarian's arm tense, and for a moment thought the bigger man would attack him rather than the elves. But somehow Croy's desperation won through. The barbarian relaxed his arm. Croy held up a hand for patience. Mörget looked deeply disappointed but nodded and put his sword away.

Croy let out a breath in relief. He was careful to make no noise.

Still, it was enough to give them away. One of the revenants froze in place, then turned slowly to face the shadows where Mörget and Croy hid, its eyes scanning the darkness. The other moved back to cover it while the demon stayed where it was, its faces craning toward the shadows.

It was over. The revenants had found them, and Croy knew he could not win. He reached for Ghostcutter's hilt anyway—

—but did not draw it. The revenant took a step into the darkness. Croy felt like it could reach out and grab them, like it would lunge at any moment. Yet it waved its sword around ahead of itself as if it were blind in the dark.

How was that possible? The revenants they'd seen on the top level had no trouble seeing in the dark. None of them even had eyes. Why was this one so tentative? It almost seemed afraid of finding them.

In the shadows, Croy could barely make out its features. Yet he sensed there was something different about this one. It wore the same bronze armor as the revenants he'd fought, and it carried the same bronze sword. Yet it didn't move like they did. It was at once more graceful and less resolute. As its sword came closer, pointing almost directly at him, he squinted hard and studied its face, and got quite a shock.

Its skin was intact—he couldn't see the bones breaking through rotted flesh. Its nose was unscarred by time, its lips not even cracked. And its eyes glinted with the few stray beams of red light that made it back into the hiding place.

In fact, it didn't seem to be dead at all. It seemed . . . alive.

It looked almost exactly like Croy's idea of what a living elf would look like.

Of course, at that moment its looks mattered far less than the fact that it was about to stab him through the vitals. He pressed himself back against a wall and prayed to the Lady that he would not be discovered.

"Aengmar!" someone called from out in the main room. "Over here!"

The revenant—or whatever it was—in front of Croy turned and looked over its shoulder. "I thought I heard something over here," it shouted back, its voice enormous in the shadowy hiding place. It had an accent Croy didn't recognize, thick enough that he had trouble understanding even the simple words. Yet he knew one thing for sure. The revenants didn't talk. They couldn't speak.

"Never mind that! Quickly!" the other cried.

The revenant—the elf—Aengmar—turned away from the hiding place and dashed off to catch up with its partner. Leaning out of hiding—exposing himself a little to the light—Croy saw the demon and the two armored figures run into the throne room, out of sight.

Croy gestured for Mörget to emerge from their hiding place. Still keeping silent, the two of them moved away from the arch, their only light the reddish glow that spilled in through the gallery ahead of them. Croy moved cautiously around a building with high marble walls and headed to his left, looking for any way out of the level. He found a side passage leading along another gallery. It looked deserted. When he was reasonably sure they were alone, he leaned close toward Mörget's ear and whispered, "Did you see that thing? It was no revenant."

"Aye, I agree. But so what?" Mörget asked.

"So what? I think we both know what those were. They were alive. That woman we saw swimming in the central shaft—the girl you saw back at the mushroom farm. It adds up, now, to only one thing. Those weren't revenants. They were—Lady preserve us all—they were living elves!"

The barbarian shrugged. "Probably easier to kill than the dead kind."

Croy shook his head in frustration. Didn't this mean anything to Mörget? The fact that there were living elves in the Vincularium was extraordinary! It meant—it meant—

"It means nothing to us," Mörget pointed out. "We are here to kill demons. Any other inhabitants of this place are merely in the way. Now I understand you wished to avoid detection back there. At first I thought you were a coward."

Croy's brain was so wracked with understanding what living elves could mean that he didn't register that at first. Only slowly did the heat of anger light up the chambers of his heart. "I beg your pardon?" he asked, very carefully. If Mörget said that again, it would be a slight that had to be answered.

"I thought it briefly, but then realized the truth. You simply wish to lay an ambush for them, yes? It makes sense. You do not let the enemy come for you. You lay in wait for them! I am learning so much from you, western knight."

"You thought I wanted to . . . no," Croy said. "No, no—we can't fight those things now. We must find the others. If there are more of these elves here, then—"

"You think a thief, a dwarf, and a witch's useless daughter will be any help against them?" Mörget demanded.

Croy studied the barbarian's face. "Not at all," he said. "But that's exactly the point. We must get them to safety."

"And postpone my glory even longer," Mörget said. "I like it not."

"I like nothing about this," Croy said. "But I know my duty. Innocent lives are at stake."

Mörget snarled in disgust. "Innocence is not a quality admired by my people," he said. "It's just another name for weakness."

"I've taken a vow to aid those who can't help themselves. If you want my help with your demons," Croy said, "you'll have to do this my way."

The barbarian glared at him, clearly estimating how much he valued Croy's help after all. Croy very much hoped he would come around and see reason. He had no desire to split up, not as weak and tired as he felt. He did not want to have to leave Mörget here and go looking for Cythera on his own.

But if that was what it came to, so be it.

Luckily the barbarian was still capable of seeing reason. "All right," Mörget said. "All right! We'll do it your way."

# CHAPTER SIXTY-ONE

Malden hurried forward through the red-shadowed streets of the dormitory floor, retracing his steps toward the lift. Every footstep made his arm bounce and throb, but it wasn't as bad as when he'd been on the ladder. Every rung had been a new chapter in a book of agony. Now he just ached abominably.

It didn't matter. He had to keep moving. He heard the sound of the knocker desperately tapping its way across the floor, moving fast, its rhythm even more broken than usual. It had nothing to do with him.

The lift cage waited for him in its chamber. The lift shaft was mostly in darkness—the red light from the main shaft didn't reach that far, and the streetlamps had stopped at the edge of the dormitory. Yet there was enough light for Malden to crouch into the cage and close its door and start to pull on the loop of chain inside.

As the cage began to climb up the shaft, toward the foundry level above, he heard one last shriek of surprise from Balint. "Don't you touch me," he heard her screaming, "Or I'll cut off your prick and use it as a paperweight!"

Something had her. The revenants, or, who knew, Mörget's demon, or—

It didn't matter.

It had nothing to do with him. He kept pulling, and pulling, and pulling on the chain before him. The mechanism was so simple anyone could use it, not just a dwarf with a brilliant insight into engines and devices. You pulled on one side of the chain to make the lift go down. If you pulled on the other side the lift went up.

Inch by inch the cage rose through the shaft. Soon Malden was thrust into inky darkness again. He still had

Slag's makeshift lantern, and the flint to light it with, but he kept pulling on the chain, pulling and pulling and pulling until his good arm felt numb. Better, he thought, to balance the searing pain in his bad one.

Even in the dark he could sense when the cage had reached the foundry level. He stopped pulling and let the chain go, so that it rattled in the dark. He pushed the door of the cage open and stepped out. He fumbled with his pack, intending to strike a light. Just getting the knapsack off his back was a trial. He clamped it between his knees and reached inside with his good hand until he found the flint. He drew it out of the pack.

Then, in the dark just behind him, he heard a clink of metal.

The lift chain started to rattle and move and he knew someone was pulling the cage down through the shaft.

The revenants must have finished off the Redweir dwarves. Now they were coming for him.

Panic gripped Malden's brains as he listened to the lift chain rattle. He wanted to sit down and just gibber in fear. He wanted to run away.

He forced himself to stay calm. To stop himself from following his natural instinct—which was to find the darkest place he could and hide there until all the bad things and nightmarish enemies went away.

In a place like the Vincularium, that meant hiding forever.

Malden cast about him in the foundry and quickly discovered what he sought—a long rod of iron, thin but strong enough so it wouldn't snap. He set his lantern down and hefted the rod like a javelin. He watched the lift chain ascend for a moment, then shoved the rod forward as fast as he could, trying to thread it through one of the links. The first time he missed, and the rod was deflected to the side, jangling in his hand. The second time he drove the rod home perfectly, tangling it in the lift chain.

The chain continued to rise through the shaft. As it rose

it took the rod with it until the rod hit the ceiling with a sharp crack of noise. It held against the ceiling, obstructing the hole there and keeping the chain from climbing any farther.

Instantly the lift chain froze in place. Malden peered down the shaft and saw the cage stuck down there, well below the foundry level.

The chain jumped and the rod nearly came free. It jumped again, and again, as whoever—whatever—was in the lift cage tried to unjam the mechanism. It was to no avail. The rod wedged the lift in place.

He had bought himself a little time.

It was the most precious commodity he could imagine. One thing mattered, still, and only one thing. He had to get the antidote to Slag. He lit his tin lantern and then hurried through the foundry level, careful not to trip on the red strings that hung loose now from the walls. Ahead of him lay the door of the Hall of Masterpieces. He could hide in there with Cythera and Slag, he thought. They could barricade the massive stone door and—and—

—and wait for Croy to come rescue them. Croy, who was probably dead, and who anyway wouldn't be able to fight his way through a legion of revenants, even with Mörget's help.

It wasn't a wonderful plan, but there were no options. Malden hurried up to the door and was only a little surprised to find it closed. Cythera was no fool. She lacked any weapon better than a belt knife, and if anyone but he came by, her best defense lay in keeping that door closed. Malden thumped on it with his good fist, then found a piece of iron and started prying it open once more. He expected Cythera to come and help him from the other side once she realized he had returned, but he had to fight with the door unaided, just as he had the last time. A little annoyed, he heaved and shoved at the bar. It took far too long—his pursuers could arrive at any moment!—and it made his damaged arm ache fiercely—but he kept at it, grunting and cursing and pulling until the door opened just wide enough to let him slip inside.

Beyond the door, the hall lay in perfect darkness.

Malden frowned. That seemed odd. Cythera had a good store of candles—there was no reason for her to conserve them, and surely she would not want to sit in the dark in this place if she didn't have to.

He called her name, softly at first—then louder. There was no response. Malden slipped into the hall and held his lantern high.

Gold, gems, glass, and polished stone all threw back bright and cheery reflections at him. Of Cythera, or Slag, there was no sign.

They must have left, he thought. Cythera must have decided to move Slag somewhere else—somewhere safer. Maybe she'd heard something of the screaming down on the residential level. Though that seemed unlikely—there was far too much stone between here and there. But perhaps Cythera had another reason to flee. Maybe the revenants had come here first.

It was just possible that Slag had thought of some way for the two of them to escape the Vincularium, and they seized the opportunity. But surely they would have left some message for him, some words traced in the dust, or, or . . . something.

He could find no clue at all to their disappearance.

There was no sign of a struggle. No blood on the floor. Nothing knocked over or moved out of place. Malden frowned. He very much wished he knew what was going on. Or what to do next.

He slipped back out of the hall, intent on finding his friends. Yet when he looked across the foundry level toward the lift shaft, a new terror crossed his soul.

He could see light there. It wasn't the flicker of candlelight but the great guttering flare of torchlight, and there was a lot of it. He could hear footsteps, and thought there might be as many as a score of revenants coming for him, from elsewhere on the foundry level. He imagined they must have followed him up from the dormitory level, using a flight of stairs he had not seen. They didn't need the lift after all, and jamming it had only slowed them down.

Wherever they came from, though, didn't matter at all—what did was that they were coming closer. Coming right for him.

Malden had a magic sword on his belt, and one good arm to swing it with. He had never trained as a swordsman, though, and lacked any manner of killer instinct. He knew he would be no match for even one persistent revenant, much less twenty of them. He had trained as a thief—and so he did what a thief would do in that circumstance.

He hid.

## CHAPTER SIXTY-TWO

The foundry offered a hundred good places to conceal Malden. He considered hiding inside the great furnace. Perhaps up in the smelting ladle—but no, he would be trapped up there. If the revenants spotted him, he would have nowhere else to go. The same difficulty eliminated the Hall of Masterpieces as a refuge: again, there would be no way to escape once he was inside. If his pursuers found him there, he would be cornered.

In the end he chose a hiding place out in the open—a place, perhaps, that would be overlooked in the abundance of more secluded spots. Moving aside some of the pieces of scrap, he buried himself as best he could inside the small mountain of copper heaped up against one wall. He chose the copper because its color was obvious—he had no desire to accidentally bury himself in arsenic, or something else poisonous that he didn't recognize. Once he was concealed, he put out his light, then pulled more pieces of copper on top of himself. He left just a bit of his face exposed, enough that he could breathe, and see.

Then he settled in and tried to make himself as quiet as possible.

He did not have to wait long. Torchlight filled the foundry, and he heard footfalls coming toward him. Many footfalls.

He didn't dare raise his head to see the revenants coming for him. He would have to wait until they came closer.

He was not prepared at all to hear Cythera's voice.

"He's not here, you see?" she insisted. She sounded very tired, and even more frightened than she had been before. It sounded like she was over by the lift room. "I told you. He's a thief. A scoundrel! At the first sign of trouble, I'm sure he fled this place entirely. He's probably running for Helstrow, as fast as his legs can carry him."

Malden almost climbed out of his hiding place then, intending to tell her she was wrong. That he would never desert her. That he had the antidote.

But then another voice spoke.

It was a sneering voice, high-pitched but distinctly male. It dripped with sarcasm and had an accent Malden couldn't place, so thick he could barely make out the words. He'd never heard that accent before, he was sure of it.

"I'm certain you wouldn't lie to me. Humans are known far and wide for their scruples, after all. But I think we'll have a look anyway."

He heard many people moving around, and then the jingling of the lift chain. "What's this? Look! A piece of iron has jammed itself in the chain, all of its own accord. Fascinating. Pull that free." The iron rod was removed from the lift chain and fell to the floor with a noise like a church bell ringing out an alarm. Malden's body tensed as his ears thrummed with the noise. They'd found his clever ruse, it seemed. Silently he cursed his luck. There would be no doubt that he had been in the foundry, then, and recently.

"You three—search this area completely. Find him and bring him to me. Don't be gentle about it either."

Malden tried not to even wince.

He was deeply confused now. The revenants they'd seen on the top level did not speak. Even if they could, he doubted they would sound so jaded or so bored. Who was taunting Cythera? Had some other group of explorers entered the Vincularium? Between Mörget's demon-hunting party, Balint's dwarves, and the revenants, it seemed the deserted tomb of the elves was experiencing a population explosion. But who were these new people, and what had they come for? The mystery was solved quickly enough. His pursuers came into the dark part of the foundry, carrying torches to light their way, and he saw they weren't revenants at all.

They wore the same bronze armor he'd seen before, battle scarred and falling apart, held together with patches and bits of string. They were as gaunt as the revenants, and as pale. And yet—they were beautiful. They were graceful. And they were decidedly *alive*.

The three soldiers who hunted him had long angular faces, their features sharp and elegant. Their eyes were cruel but sparkling, their lips thin but red. Their hair fell around their shoulders but could not conceal their delicate pointed ears. Their skin had little color to it, true. Like dwarves, they were so pale that they might have been albinos if not for their dark hair. Yet if a dwarf's skin was like marble, cold white veined with blue, the soldiers' complexions had the warmth and subtlety of fine alabaster.

They were elves. Living elves, in this place—living, surviving, after eight hundred years in the long shadows underground.

Malden nearly gasped in astonishment.

The elves searched the foundry as if it was beneath them. They poked their bronze swords into various piles of scrap. They picked at the lengths of red string that crisscrossed the floor, the remains of Balint's trap. They seemed wise enough to avoid disturbing the pile of arsenic. When they reached the door to the Hall of Masterpieces, one of them sighed in distaste.

"I suppose we'll have to open it," he said. He looked to the others and rolled his eyes. One of them snorted out a laugh. The three of them found a bar and started to pry open the door.

Malden knew how much resistance it would give them. They could not be as strong as humans, not with those stick-thin arms, so they would have to struggle with the door. He waited until they were wholly occupied with this task, their weapons stowed securely on their belts and away from their hands.

Then he jumped out of the pile of copper scrap and ran as fast as he could toward the lift shaft.

# CHAPTER SIXTY-THREE

A cry went up immediately, and someone shouted, "He has a sword!" but Malden paid no attention to the clamor. He reached inside his tunic with his good hand and skidded to a stop as he came before the great furnace.

More elves waited there. More heavily armed elves, and while some of them slouched against the walls, he knew he would never make it past them all and reach the lift unmolested. But that had never been his plan.

Cythera was there as well, all but carrying Slag. The dwarf looked as if he had only minutes to live. Just one guard stood near the two of them, and he looked more confused than vigilant. Malden shifted the antidote to his bad hand—he could barely close his fist around it—and yanked Acidtongue from its scabbard. As he leapt toward the guard, he shouted, "Only one drop!" and threw the vial of antidote toward Cythera's outstretched hand.

The guard was taken completely by surprise. Had Malden any training with his sword, he could have taken the elf unawares and cut him in half. Instead he merely managed to swing at the guard's head, and miss completely.

Behind him, he heard a great clattering of bronze armor as the other elves—he didn't bother to count how many—came rushing to attack him. The guard he'd threatened lifted his own weapon high in both hands, ready to defend himself.

"What a fool," one of the elves said. "Take him."

It had never been Malden's plan to fight his way out, however. "Hold," he called, and shoved Acidtongue back into its glass-lined scabbard. "I surrender." He lifted both hands in the air, fingers spread wide to show he meant it.

Out of the corner of his eye he saw Cythera dab a drop of the antidote on her finger and stick it down Slag's throat.

The dwarf gagged and spat, but she held her hand where it was.

"What is she doing?" One of the elves came forward. He wore a circlet of fine silver on his brow, and his armor was in far better condition than the others'. He had a short cape across his shoulders made of very fine cloth, and as he walked he leaned on a slim-bladed sword as if it were a cane. Malden decided he must be the commander of this elfin company. He grabbed Cythera's hand out of the dwarf's mouth and held it up to the light.

She stared at him with fierce defiance, but the look in her eyes burned out quickly. When she'd lost her rage, she stared down at her feet.

"Milord," one of the soldiers near Malden said. "What should we do with him?"

The lord's face flared with anger. "Get his sword away from him, obviously! And then strip him naked and check him for other weapons. And then—and I really shouldn't have to tell you this sort of thing *again*—beat him until he can't get up."

Malden's eyes went wide. He considered drawing Acidtongue and fighting desperately for his life, but he knew that was futile. Reasoning with the elf might prove the better course. He kept his hands above his head as an elf soldier unbuckled his sword belt and took away his bodkin. "I offer you no resistance. I've hurt none of you!"

The elfin commander favored him with a thin smile. "And I have express orders to take you alive, if possible." His eyes twinkled. "But you know, I've never actually seen a human before. I'm curious what color your blood is. Finding out might alleviate a little tedium."

An elf grabbed Malden's cloak and tore it from his neck. Malden's bad arm was wrenched badly in the process and he cried out in pain.

"No!" Cythera shouted. She tried to run toward Malden, but the elf commander still held her hand. He must have been stronger than he looked, because she couldn't break his grip. "No, you can't, I—I love him!" she screamed.

"Why, that just adds a certain—" the commander began, but then stopped abruptly and stared at Slag.

The dwarf convulsed around his middle and made a horrible gagging sound. Then he leaned forward and vomited all over the foundry floor. Great gouts of black liquid rolled across the flagstones, edging toward the bronze boots of the elfin soldiers.

Every single one of them danced backward, gasping in

disgust. Not one of them stood their ground—not even the commander, who yelped like a girl.

Suddenly Malden, Cythera, and especially Slag were standing alone, with no one guarding them or in a position to stop them from running away. Malden would have made a break for it, except that he was watching Slag. The dwarf slumped forward, falling down into the pool of his own sick. Then he vomited again. The elves cringed backward again, while Cythera bent down to grab Slag's shoulders and pull him back before he drowned in his own vomit.

"In the name of the ancestors—what a stink!" the elfin commander wailed. He pulled his cape up around his nose and mouth and wiped at the tears that dripped from his eyes. "I'll have no more of this." He turned and started walking toward the lift.

One of the soldiers managed to regain enough composure to ask, "But milord, what should we do with the prisoners?"

This is the moment he orders us all killed, Malden thought. This is the end.

But it seemed the lord had lost his desire to see the color of human blood. "Follow your orders! I don't really care!" he shouted back over his shoulder.

Stepping gingerly over the mess on the floor, the soldiers moved in and grabbed at Malden's arms. He offered them no resistance at all. Others grabbed Cythera, who didn't even look at them—she was clearly too concerned for the health of the dwarf. There was a great deal of discussion and argument over what should be done with Slag. None of the elves wanted to touch him, and they argued bitterly over which of them should have to do it. In the end, the three of them were searched and all their possessions taken way. Then they were marched toward a section of the wall that looked different from the rest. It was made of crude brick, and when an elf pushed on it, it opened like a door. Beyond lay a narrow tunnel bored inexpertly through the rock.

# CHAPTER SIXTY-FOUR

Croy signaled for Mörget to come forward. It looked like the way was clear. They had been traveling for miles through empty halls and dusty corridors, intentionally staying away from any place that looked like it might have been recently occupied. It wasn't difficult—the enormous volume of the Vincularium seemed mostly to be deserted, unused for centuries. However many elves might still live, there certainly weren't enough of them to fill the place up. So far they'd seen no more elves or demons or revenants or anything else.

Croy imagined that a paltry few survivors must be clinging to life in some tiny corner of the vast place, as afraid of the haunted corridors as he had been. He thought of how they had blundered through the place, all through its long night, and not seen any elves at all until the dwarven sun had come to life. Perhaps if they'd been quicker, if they hadn't been separated by the revenants, they could have gotten into the place, killed one of the demons, and gotten out before the elves even knew they were there. How he longed it had been so. Mörget would have been satisfied, his manhood thoroughly proven. He and Cythera could have left without incident. This whole adventure could have been over in a few hours. Something they could laugh about whenever they recalled it in their later life, something to tell their grandchildren about.

Instead, now, he had slogged for hours through a place that offered death at every turning.

He estimated they had come halfway around the central shaft, and passed through miles of dark rock, when they came into the dormitory level.

He gestured for Mörget to follow him while he crept

forward, seeking danger wherever it might hide. The two of them crept up a spiral ramp into the reddish light of this new level. A wide plaza opened onto another gallery before them. Croy stood well back from the opening on the central shaft—there was no telling who or what might be watching, and he tried to stay out of the light as much as possible.

Silently, he moved away from the gallery, deeper into the level. In his hand Ghostcutter moved back and forth, covering every shadow.

This place was supposed to be deserted—yet clearly it was not. The revenants on the top level, the demons on the lower floors, were not the only enemies he must be wary of. Elves might be the worst threat yet. They would be capable of subterfuge, of laying traps and ambushes. As he studied this new district he was constantly in fear of discovery.

He found himself in a place of narrow towers and squat structures that must have been residences for dwarves long since gone. It looked a great deal like the living quarters he'd seen in more modern dwarven cities—unadorned, perfectly functional, but far from what a human would have considered so. It differed only in that here there were so many more rooms than he was used to, so many that they had to be piled atop each other in great towers. He leaned in through the door of one of the low rooms and saw only scraps of rotting wood—what had been furniture, perhaps, centuries ago. Now it was nothing but rubbish. He stepped back outside and continued his search. Moving carefully through the red-lit lanes, he saw that outside each tower stood a spherical lamp on a pole. A fountain stood in the midst of the towers, its spouts crusted with white mineral deposits now, but the water still flowed. It smelled faintly of sulfur, but it was clear and free of scum. He stopped to take up a handful and scrub some of the grime off his face.

Ahead of him, Mörget clucked his tongue. A small sound, but in that empty place it made too many echoes.

Croy hurried forward to chide his friend for disturbing the stillness.

Yet when he saw what Mörget had found, he let out a quiet sigh himself.

Lying on the flagstones was the body of a dwarf. The corpse's face and hands had been slashed violently, and its blood pooled beneath it and ran away through the cracks between the flagstones. In the reddish light of the streetlamps, the blood looked almost black. An expression of utter terror had frozen on the poor dwarf's face.

It was not Slag. "A dwarf, here? He didn't come with us, and we know the builders of this place abandoned it long, long ago," Croy whispered, shaking his head. "What does this mean? What is he doing here?"

"It means the Vincularium is getting crowded," Mörget said, frowning. "Perhaps we were followed. Perhaps this dwarf came in on our heels, hoping to steal something of value while we fought the demon."

Croy shook his head. "Dwarves don't steal. Nor do they have any interest in their own history. Or at least, I thought they didn't. There are abandoned dwarven cities and mines all over the continent, and I've never heard of dwarves returning to any of them before. Honestly, I was quite surprised when Slag said he wanted to come here. In my experience, dwarves are content to leave their old places to molder and collapse. Yet here we see evidence to the contrary—this dwarf must have come here for some good reason. But why? It's a mystery. I'll admit I'm confounded."

"Does it really matter?" Mörget said.

"In times of danger, the unknown is one's greatest enemy. At the very least I'd like to know how he died. If we knew who killed this dwarf, we might be better prepared when they come for us, next." Croy knelt down to close the corpse's eyelids. The flesh did not resist him. "He died recently," he whispered. "He's not even stiff yet. And these wounds weren't made by your demon, I can tell that much. These are sword cuts."

Mörget nodded but wasn't looking at the body. He was staring down a side street. Croy looked and saw the end of a rope lying on the flagstones. It ran toward one of the towers, and then up its side.

"That looks like some kind of trap," Croy suggested. "Dwarves make them all the time. Perhaps this poor fellow was hoping to catch his killer in it."

Mörget approached the rope cautiously—then reached up and pulled it down, even as Croy waved his hands in warning. The rope fell with a thud from the top of the tower in an untidy coil. The other end was tied off in a loop to make a snare. "This trap was not set properly. There's no counterweight," he said.

Croy raised an eyebrow.

"In the East we make similar snares, for hunting," Mörget explained. "You suggested the dwarf must have been setting this trap when he was killed. Which meant he wanted to ensnare someone up there." The barbarian pointed at the top of the tower. "Maybe the killer came from on high." Before Croy could stop him, Mörget scurried up the ladder.

Croy followed close behind, not wanting to get separated. When they reached the rooftop, he found it deserted and empty. Mörget gave the barest of glances around, then went to the edge of the roof to look down.

Croy took a slightly closer look—and found something that excited him. "Here," he said, running a finger across a small grouping of pits in the stone at his feet. "Look! These marks were made by vitriol." Mörget looked at him without comprehension. "Acid! I've seen similar spoor before, many times. Malden must have been here, holding Acidtongue. The blade drips its essence constantly, etching the floor wherever it's drawn. Malden was here!"

# CHAPTER SIXTY-FIVE

"Malden stood here, yes. He must have been under attack as well, for he was holding a naked blade," Mörget said. "Perhaps that explains this." He went back to the side of the roof and pointed down. Another dwarf lay on a rooftop far below, half its body cloaked by shadow. Its face was even more bloody than the other's. Croy couldn't even tell if it had been male or female. "The dwarves must have beset our little thief. He defended himself ably."

Croy shook his head. "No—Malden didn't slay these dwarves. He couldn't have. Our laws are very strict on that sort of thing."

"And he is known for abiding your laws," Mörget said. "Our thief?"

Croy supposed the barbarian had a point. Malden was a criminal. But he wasn't a killer. Croy had known him long enough to understand that Malden had his own moral code. It might be quite liberal, and include all kinds of things that he himself wouldn't countenance, but Malden wouldn't kill unless his life depended on it. And no dwarf would ever attack a human, not unless they had no choice. So how could such a fight have even started? "I just don't know," Croy admitted. "This does mean one thing, though."

"Oh?" Mörget asked.

"Malden was here. Not so long ago. And that means Cythera must be close by. We're on the right track."

"Good," Mörget said. "The sooner we find her, the sooner we can get back to our real purpose here." He headed to the edge of the roof and started climbing down the tower. Croy followed close behind, invigorated by what they'd found.

They began to head deeper into the residential level, toward a place where the walls narrowed to a point, when Croy called a halt.

Mörget grimaced in annoyance at yet another delay, but he waited expectantly while Croy craned his ears back the way they'd come.

"I know I heard something back there. A grunt of pain—or fear," Croy insisted.

"Then we are best served going the other way. We cannot waste time investigating every little noise."

"I suppose you're right," Croy said, and started walking forward again—only to freeze in his tracks a moment later.

"No!" someone screamed. He didn't recognize the voice but it had a dwarven accent. "No, you stinking sack of pus! You can't have him! Get back!"

"Someone's in trouble," Croy said.

"Good! One less enemy for us!" Mörget growled. But Croy had already turned on his heel and was headed back into the dormitory. His boots beat like drumsticks on the flagstones as he pulled Ghostcutter free of its scabbard. He came around a sharp corner toward the fountain, then drew up short as he viewed a scene of horror.

The demon—one of the demons—had come to claim the body of the dead dwarf. Its amorphous mass had flowed over the lower half of the corpse and it was absorbing the rest while Croy watched.

Yet not without resistance. Another dwarf—a female—beat at the faces under the demon's skin with a wrench. She had a bad cut across her face and another gash in her leg, but she battled more fiercely than a wounded badger. Still, she couldn't possibly win. Already the demon reached a thick tendril of its substance toward her, clearly intending to have two meals for the effort of securing one.

She looked up when Croy approached and stared at him with blazing eyes. "Stop fiddling with your dubious manhood and help me!"

Croy leapt in immediately, slashing away with Ghost-cutter at the demon's thick skin. Its glassy blood poured out in gouts but it only redoubled its efforts at seizing the female dwarf, shooting forth a second rope of pale flesh to snare her ankle. She fell backward, her arms wheeling in the air, and dropped her wrench. Inch by inch the demon started reeling her in.

"I've never seen them do that before," Mörget said, rushing in to slice through the tendril with one quick stroke of Dawnbringer. The blade flashed with light as the dwarf tumbled free.

"What's that?" Croy asked as he cut again through the thing's hide. He couldn't seem to find the central mass, its only truly vulnerable spot.

"Grow arms," Mörget said. A new tentacle slapped out toward the dwarf, but the barbarian grabbed her by the belt and tossed her to safety. As the tentacle attempted to grab Mörget around the waist, he brought his sword down in a close arc. The limb came off neatly and spun in the air for a moment before splattering wetly on the flagstones. As Croy watched, the monster surged forward to reclaim this piece of itself. It absorbed it as hungrily as it was swallowing the dead dwarf.

"We know little of these things," Croy agreed. "Yet I fear learning more would be a dangerous enterprise."

"Perhaps," Mörget said, slicing off a wide strip of the demon, "yet it might profit us well, should we encounter very many more of them."

"Excuse me!" the female dwarf shouted, drowning out the warriors. "If you two giant teat-suckers don't mind winding up your colloquium—I want to kill this thing."

"What do we appear to be doing?" Mörget asked, civilly enough.

"Wasting my fucking time." The female dwarf ran off, toward the fountain. "Draw it this way! I have a plan!"

# CHAPTER SIXTY-SIX

The female dwarf hurried ahead, while Mörget and Croy took turns slashing at the demon and then dancing back before it could strike them with its fleshy appendages. Croy was growing tired again, and he hoped she was as good as her word—he could not keep this up much longer, nor could he see the spherical mass inside the demon that he must strike to kill it once and for all. If her plan did not succeed, he would have to suggest that they run for it, something he liked not at all.

Yet the female dwarf showed no sign of flagging confidence. Her wounded leg slowed her down but soon she had taken up a position near the fountain and started waving her arms, trying to draw the demon's attention.

Mörget laughed wickedly and stabbed deep into the demon's body, then jumped away. Croy pushed forward, slashing shallow cuts in its back with Ghostcutter. The demon was as easy to herd as a sheep, once you knew the secret. It would always move forward to attack whomever had struck it last. Between the two of them they got it to move exactly where the female dwarf pointed, toward a particular flagstone that looked exactly like the others.

"This was meant for that poxy prick with the magic sword," she explained, "but it might work on yon pimple-leaving as well."

"Might?" Croy asked.

She shrugged. They all held their breath as the demon flowed over the indicated flagstone.

Nothing happened.

"Blasted buggering bastard! Murin never could set a trap right. You," she shouted, pointing at Mörget, "cut that rope over there."

Croy turned and saw the rope, hidden along one side of a tower block, but only for a moment. One of Mörget's throwing axes cut through it neatly. The lower end fell instantly to the ground, while the upper part disappeared, flashing up toward an eyelet mounted on the side of the tower. Meanwhile something dark and huge came hurtling down from the ceiling.

It proved to be a sheaf of paving stones tied together in a stack, suspended from high above by the rope Mörget had just cut. They came down straight and true, right on top of the demon's body. With a sickening wet crunch they struck and sent vast wet ripples through the monster's body. Its blood squirted out through the perforations Croy had made in its skin, hot clear fluid splashing on nearby walls, landing with a grotesque sloshing noise in the fountain. The faces under its skin pushed hard against the fleshy envelope, their mouths open wide in silent howls of torment. The whole creature writhed in pain and rage, slapping wildly at the floor with its tendrils, stretching them out toward the knight, the barbarian, and the dwarf.

It was pinned, trapped, grievously wounded. The blow must have missed the central mass, however, for the demon did not perish instantly. Instead it raged and struggled and threw out wild tendrils, as if trying to crawl out from under the weight by moving in every direction at once. No matter how hard it flailed, however, it could not seem to get free.

"That should hold it," the female dwarf said, panting for breath. She took a long stride back from the demon, never lifting her eyes from its squirming mass.

"It certainly makes our job easier," Croy said.

Mörget sneered. "A coward's way. A creature like this deserves to be beaten in close combat, not trapped like a food animal and slaughtered at our leisure."

Croy found it difficult to agree. Killing demons was a sacred duty—he'd taken vows to that effect. Yet nothing in the oaths he swore ever said he had to do it the hard way. He hefted Ghostcutter and stepped warily toward the convulsing monster, intending to cut pieces off of it until he found the central mass and could finally kill it.

A tendril whipped out toward his leg and he danced back. He started to bring his sword down to sever the tendril, but instead of rising to meet his blow, the appendage reached out farther—past his foot—straining and pulling on the flagstones until its substance was stretched like taffy. Then, with a sudden snap, it broke off from the main mass. The broken-off tendril flattened out and quivered while Croy watched, nauseated and fascinated at once. It formed a puddle on the floor, no wider than his two hands could cover. A single small face peered up out of its skin. And then it started to slither away, a tiny replica of the demon from which it had split.

"Don't let it get away!" the female dwarf insisted.

Croy did his best to stab the thing, driving downward into its flesh with Ghostcutter's point again and again until he worried he would blunt the sword on the flagstones. This miniature demon moved far faster and with far more agility than its larger parent had, however, and in moments the thing had escaped him, racing for the gallery. It did not slow as it reached the edge, but instead flung itself into empty space and the water below.

"Oh, for fie," Croy said, one of the worst profanities he ever used. He leaned out over the edge and looked down but could see nothing but a faint splash, far below.

"Croy!" Mörget called. "Beware!"

Croy turned around, not knowing what to expect. He changed his grasp on Ghostcutter's hilt and ran back toward the trapped demon, only to see that it had spawned more limbs, which stretched and strained outward like the first.

With a series of sickening popping sounds, the arms snapped off and quivered to life on their own. One by one they started rippling across the floor, straight toward where Croy stood waiting for them.

"Any suggestions?" Croy asked, but Mörget could only

shrug. The barbarian drew Dawnbringer and came running toward the smaller demons, howling in battle fury, but there were far too many targets and they clearly had no intention of engaging him.

Croy whirled and struck as fast as he could, slicing at each of the miniature demons as it came past him. Most merely veered away from his blade. He caught some of them, but managed to do little more than spill their glassy blood, which barely slowed them. Mörget smashed one with his boot, but as soon as he lifted his foot the demon reshaped itself and came dashing for the edge of the shaft again. Croy had time only to leap out of the way as an especially large one came oozing toward him at speed. One slid over his foot and he felt its corrosive touch burn into the leather of his boot. He yanked his foot backward and then spun around to watch the horde go flying off the edge of the gallery, to splash into the dark water far below.

"They're gone," he called, and Mörget nodded. "The main body, though—what of it?" Croy asked.

The two warriors traded a look of horror, then hurried back to see what remained of the demon they'd trapped.

Not much, unfortunately. It had ejected most of its mass, leaving behind nothing more than its skin, which it shed like a snake. The limp envelope of the demon was already fuming and decaying in the cool air.

"No!" Mörget howled. "No! This is too much!"

# CHAPTER SIXTY-SEVEN

Malden and Cythera each took one of Slag's arms, but the dwarf had to move his own legs. He stumbled forward, clearly moving only by instinct. His eyes rolled in his head and eventually caught on Malden's face. "Lad," he moaned. "Lad. Is that you?"

Malden hoisted the dwarf's head up so he could see better. "It's me," he said. They were marching still through the rough tunnel, with elfin warriors ahead of and behind them. "Are you feeling any better?"

"I think I was sick," Slag said.

"Many times," Malden told him.

"Oh. That explains it, then."

"What's that?"

"Why my beard smells like somebody's arsehole."

The dwarf's head drifted forward abruptly and he stopped walking. His dead weight was too much to bear and he slid toward the floor, out of Cythera's hands, even as she tried to grapple him and keep him upright. Malden tried to prop him up again, but Slag had gone completely limp. He wouldn't take another step. Malden looked over at Cythera and shook his head.

"You," she said, addressing the elf in front of her. "Our friend can't go any farther. He's sick and he needs to rest!"

The elf turned to look her up and down, as if sizing up a horse he was buying. "Carry him. Or, if you prefer, I can run him through and we can leave him here to die."

Cythera glared at the elf. "Your orders are to bring us in alive."

The elf shrugged. "Orders! We receive so many of them, honestly. And sometimes they contradict each other. By the time we reach home the Hieromagus will have forgotten why he gave that order. Pick him up, keep moving, and don't bother me again."

The elf turned away, and Malden knew it would be no use arguing further. He'd met far too many watchmen, guards, and soldiers in his life—and been on the receiving end of their ire more often than not—to mistake the look on the elf's face. The elf had been given a job to do, a job he didn't care for and wanted to get over with as quickly as possible. Slag was merely an element of that task, an impediment at best. Any minor irritation, anything that made the elf do more work, would be enough to spur him to violence. Malden turned to Cythera and whispered, "They may not be human, but it's nice to see some things are universal."

"Please, Malden—I can't hold him on my own," Cythera said as she wrestled with keeping Slag from lying down on the floor and going to sleep.

Malden sighed and bent to help. He got his hands underneath Slag's armpits—they were slick with sweat—and lifted most of the dwarf's weight while Cythera took the ankles. She had to walk backward, facing Malden.

"Watch your head," he told her. "The ceiling gets lower ahead of us."

She ducked her head just before it struck an overhang.

"I've been trying to think of a way out of this," she told him, keeping her voice low. "I've come up with nothing useful. I could turn invisible and make a run for it. I could go and look for . . . help. But I fear they would hurt you two in reprisal."

Malden knew she was probably right. "They have orders to bring us in alive, but clearly they don't care what state we're in when we get there. We just have to be breathing. I fear we have no option but to see where they're taking us."

Cythera nodded. She pursed her lips and looked down at Slag. "Will he be all right? You must have caught up with Balint. Did she tell you what poison she used, or what the antidote was?"

Malden shook his head. "She was hardly forthcoming. She hit me with a wrench."

"No!"

Malden grinned, though it made his jaw hurt. "In her place I would have done the same. She told me only that the antidote will keep him alive, though he will be sick for a time."

"You saved him," she said. She favored him with half a smile. Then she blushed and looked away.

"I'm glad for one thing, at least," he told her. "I got to see you smile one more time. I would have preferred different circumstances, of course. But when I got back to the hall and found the two of you gone—well, I didn't know what to think."

She frowned. "They came with no warning. They pushed open the door and suddenly they were all around us. I couldn't fight them all, and Slag was barely conscious at the time. So I surrendered."

Malden nodded in understanding. "I don't think any of us were expecting living elves down here."

"There was no time to leave you a message, or any kind of warning. They asked me where the others were and I said the two of us were lost and alone. Then Slag woke up a little and asked if you had returned yet." She closed her eyes in frustration.

"Mind your head again," he told her.

"I think they've been watching us since we arrived. They know about Mör— I mean, they know there are more of us. I don't think they've caught the others yet. I said a lot of things to try to convince them you had fled the Vincularium, but—"

"I heard some of them. You called me a scoundrel."

"I was trying to throw them off your track, Malden." Her face changed. "What of Balint and her crew? Did they make good their escape? I suppose it's unlikely they would help us, but—"

"They're most likely dead," Malden told her. He didn't

know it for a fact. But he had heard their screams, and hoped, for their sake, it was true. Those screams had not sounded like the cries of people who were surprised by being taken captive. They were shouts of agony. "Though I don't know why they were killed, and we were spared."

Cythera looked down at Slag's feet. "They have orders to kill dwarves on sight," she whispered. "I think they blame the dwarves for their imprisonment more than they blame us."

Malden frowned. "It was the dwarves who betrayed them, and sealed them in here. But then—why is Slag—"

She glanced over her shoulder, as if to see if any elf was listening. Then she whispered to Malden, "I told them he was a human."

"Slag? A human?"

"A very short human. He wears human clothes, after all. And none of the elves have ever seen a human *or* a dwarf before. They asked a lot of questions, but I managed to convince them."

"And saved his life. I wish Balint and her friends had been so quick of mind. No, they won't be coming to help us, not now."

"So our only hope is . . ."

He knew she didn't want to say Croy's name out loud. She didn't want to give the elves any information they didn't already have. "Assuming he's still alive. And that he can stay free, with every elf in the Vincularium looking for him."

"You two," the elf behind Malden said, and jabbed him in the back with the point of a spear. Not hard enough to pierce his skin. "What's that you're saying? Your accents are so thick I can't understand you. Are you scheming something? Humans are supposed to be tricky sorts. What are you planning?"

"We were discussing which of you is the prettiest," Malden said.

The elf jabbed Malden again with his spear, harder this time.

"Actually," Cythera said, "we were just wondering about *your* accent."

"Accent? I haven't got one," the elf replied. "I talk like an elf." He did not seem to possess much in the way of imagination.

"Of course, of course," Cythera said, her voice warm with soothing tones. "Forgive me. I actually meant to inquire how it is that you speak our language, the tongue of Skrae?"

The elf looked deeply confused. Judging by the way his brow beetled and his eyes narrowed, it was a common expression for him to wear. "I don't speak Skraeling. I speak the tongue of the ancestors."

"Ah, well," Malden said, "that explains everything." He made a face at Cythera, crossing his eyes and sticking his tongue out of one side of his mouth. She almost giggled in response. She had to raise one hand to her mouth to stifle it.

In the process she dropped one of Slag's ankles. The dwarf stirred in Malden's arms. One of his eyes opened a crack. "Lad? Am I dead?" he asked.

"I got your antidote, old man," Malden told him.

"Ah," Slag said, his chin drifting up and down with the rhythm of Malden's footsteps. "And then . . . the elves . . ."

"They've taken us captive. But they have orders not to kill us. We don't know why that is."

"Well," the dwarf slurred, a sleepy smile playing around his mouth, "that's easy. They haven't killed us yet because . . . because . . ."

"Because?" Cythera asked.

". . . because they'll want to torture us first. That's an ancient elfin custom."

# CHAPTER SIXTY-EIGHT

"I'm Balint, by the way," the female dwarf announced when the two warriors had accepted that their demon had gotten away.

"Well met, milady," Croy said, bowing low. "I am Sir Croy, a knight of Skrae, and this—" He turned to indicate Mörget, but the barbarian was halfway across the room, pouncing on something. Croy thought he must have found one of the demon's animate pieces, but when Mörget stood up with a nasty grin, he held something small and wriggling and humanoid in his clenched hand.

"Got you!" the barbarian announced. "Croy, look what I found!"

"That would be mine," Balint said, sounding annoyed.

Croy shook his head. "It's all right," he told Mörget.

"Some kind of cave imp! It was spying on us!"

Croy smiled as politely as he could. "It's just a knocker," he explained. "The dwarves use them to scout their tunnels."

The barbarian stared at the blue-haired thing he clutched. It was tapping frenziedly at his forearm with its long fingers.

"You can put it down now," Croy said.

Mörget scowled, but he dropped the thing. It came running over to Balint and hid behind her legs. Croy bent low to pat it on the head, but it snapped at his fingers with its nasty teeth.

"Does it have a name?" he asked.

Balint stared at him. "It's not a pussycat," she said. "It's a tool. I don't name my hammers either."

"I see." Croy glanced at the barbarian, who had crouched down and was staring at the knocker with the shrewd eye of a hunter. "Ah, this would be Mörget," he told the dwarf.

"We've met before," Mörget said. He turned his head and spat copiously on the ground.

"You . . . have?" Croy asked.

"Briefly," Balint concurred. "Though our meeting was approximately as enjoyable as having the skin flayed off my buttocks."

"Oh," Croy said.

"At Redweir," Mörget explained, "I sought information on this place, and on my demon. The dwarves there were less than helpful. She is the lieutenant of the dwarven envoy there."

"Ah," Croy said, "so you must be of noble blood. Well, milady, I—"

"Fuck nobility," Balint said, scratching one armpit. "My father was a bricklayer, and my mother a cook. I got my job by being more useful than the dwarf who had it before me."

"I see. And what do you do for the envoy? See to his appointments, watch his accounts, that sort of thing?"

Balint laughed. "Mostly I go in for surprising his enemies with nasty traps." She shrugged. "It's what I'm good at."

"And . . . is that what you came here to do?" Croy asked. "Forgive me, but I've never heard any dwarf mention a desire to enter the Vincularium before. Those of my experience always seemed willing to leave the past alone. Yet you came here, facing terrible dangers, and—here's the rub—at exactly the same time as we did. I suspect that might not be a coincidence."

Balint glared over at Mörget, who refused steadfastly to look back. The female dwarf squinted one eye, but when she failed to cause Mörget to so much as turn his back on her, she sighed. "In my line of work secrets are a valuable commodity, but I don't suppose that matters now. All right. When yon friend of yours came to Redweir, we could tell he wasn't the sort to be turned away by a friendly warning. He was going to come to the Vincularium, open it up and stir up the past, whether we liked it or not. There are some old secrets buried here we didn't want disturbed, and a lot of history we didn't like thinking on. The history of this place ain't something to be proud of."

"I suppose not," Croy admitted.

Balint scowled. "I was sent here, tell the truth, to keep an eye on your barbarian. Make sure he didn't find some things we didn't want found. The dwarven king had no idea this place was as full of squatters as a goblin's larder is full of roaches. We didn't know anything about the squishy bastards, for one thing."

The knocker climbed up her arm and perched on her shoulder. Balint headed back to the body of her fellow dwarf. Croy saw that much of the corpse had been devoured by the demon despite her efforts. She wasted no time on tears, however, nor did she offer any prayers for the dead dwarf's soul. Instead she merely picked up his remains and hauled them into one of the nearest houses. "We need to make haste. One of those wet farts will come soon enough—the little ones that got away will come back, or send one of his brothers. There are more of them out there than I have traps to deal with."

"You've seen more of the demons?" Croy asked. "We thought there might only be three. One of which we already slew."

Balint gave him a nasty look. "Really, now? And how did you manage that?"

Croy looked away. "We . . . allowed it to swallow me, and then Mörget stabbed its . . . heart."

"Sounds like a wonderful plan," she told him. "Here, help me, will you? Or did you just want to watch me break a sweat? Maybe that's what gets you stiff, sweaty dwarf girls."

Croy frowned, deeply discomfited by Balint's words. Yet he knew that she meant no real offense. Dwarves made an art of vulgar oaths and blasphemous curses. Instead of poetry they wrote bawdy farces, and instead of high-minded rhetoric and grand speeches they tended to tell jokes about—well, about bodily functions.

So he did not chide her for unladylike speech, but helped her move the other body—the one with the ruined face—inside the house as well. Then she started to wall off the doorway with paving stones that she pried up from the floor, gluing them in place with paste from a pot affixed to her belt.

"You wish to give them a proper tomb," Croy said, admiring her quick and thorough work.

"I just don't want them getting eaten and then shat out by the likes of that thing," she told him. "Murin and Slurri were layabouts and scum, honestly, and not worth the salt they put in their soup. Just two fools I picked up in Red-weir who needed a quick bit of coin. Still, I'd hate to see them end up as luncheon for those snot monsters. Murin knew some jokes even I thought were nasty, and they were both at least adequate at fucking."

Croy tried not to let her see him blush. Instead he turned to look at Mörget, who was busy sharpening his weapons over by the fountain. Apparently the barbarian had no desire to renew his acquaintance with Balint.

Croy watched as she put the last stone in place, sealing the doorway. Then she stepped back and dusted off her hands. On her shoulder the knocker mimicked her gesture.

When she spoke again, her voice was very different—almost reverent. "Anyroad, there aren't enough of us dwarves left not to show each other a little respect. Barely ten thousand of us now, in the whole wide world. There were five times that many living in just this city, back in its heyday."

"We humans try to protect you as best we can," Croy said. He needed to ask her a very delicate question, and he was looking for a way to lead into it.

"That's the law," she replied. "And like most human

laws, if you put what it's worth on a scale and balanced it against a fly's turd, you'd still find it wanting."

She walked away from the impromptu tomb and started gathering up lengths of rope from her various traps. These went into a pack she wore on her back.

"I'm sorry you feel that way," Croy said. "But I swear on my honor I won't let you be harmed again. I'm afraid we can't leave just yet, not until we find our friends. But I'll make sure you get out of here as soon as possible."

"You think of leaving now?" Mörget said, looking up from his axe. "While the demons still live?"

"The thing we came here for seems undoable now." Croy sighed. "We came to slay one demon and we find an army of them. I think a judicious retreat is our best option. We'll go to Helstrow, summon the rest of the Ancient Blades. Maybe raise an army. Then we'll come back here and purge this place of them all." He turned back to Balint. "You must have seen one of our friends here. The, ah—the man with the sword. I need to know. Was it him who killed your crew?" Malden was his friend, and he had no desire to be obligated to chase him down like a common murderer. Yet the law—and his duty—was clear.

"That sheep dropping? Hardly," Balint snorted. "He hadn't the guts to carve a roasted chicken. I dealt with him handily."

"Oh, thank the Lady," Croy said, though he'd meant not to speak. It was such a relief to learn that Malden was no dwarf-killer.

"No, it was them that came later. They appeared out of nowhere. Right out of the wall—dozens of them, skinny as a whore's breakfast and paler than mother's milk. I thought they were ghosts, to start with. They cut down Murin and Slurri without so much as a by-your-leave. Then they came for me. I took my licks, then did what a human girl does on her wedding night: lie down, pretend it isn't happening, and wait for it to stop. They must have thought I was dead, too. I bled enough."

"You mean the elves," Croy said. "Were they living elves, or the undead kind?"

"Living," Balint told him.

"Did these elves kill our friend?" Croy asked.

"No. He was too busy running back to the others. That moping slattern of his, and the debaser, Slag."

"You know where they are?" Croy asked, his eyes growing wide.

"What's left of them, more like," she told him.

# CHAPTER SIXTY-NINE

Croy barely noticed the brass lift. It was magical in nature, of course—some kind of invisible spirit of the air carried the cage on its back, he imagined, its labors spurred on by the simple ritual of pulling on a chain—and therefore of little interest to him. He was far more intent on finding Cythera. Balint had given him some veiled hints that he might not like what he found, but he had to see for himself.

In the foundry level, he lifted his candle high and stared at a sticky black stain that spread across the floor. It couldn't be blood. He was certain of that much. It wasn't Cythera's blood.

It couldn't be.

He registered the threads hung from the walls and the various pry bars scattered outside the door of some vault of treasures. He saw the piles of scrap metal and the incomprehensible machinery of dwarven manufacture. The odds and ends strewn from torn-open knapsacks. These things meant nothing. The black stain, well, it meant nothing as well. It couldn't be blood.

He knew, with a perfect certainty, that it was not Cythera's blood.

"Show me what we came here for, Balint," he said, growing impatient. Clearly Cythera wasn't here. He needed to find her as soon as possible, before she ran afoul of the elves. That was what was important.

The knocker ran around the room in circles, tapping at the floor, the walls, the trash strewn across the flagstones. Balint turned to face Croy. "Smells like someone's guts exploded, doesn't it?" she asked, wrinkling her nose. "Look, my blueling found something. What's this?"

The knocker had found a knife tossed haphazardly into one corner of the room. Croy took it from the diminutive creature and recognized it instantly. It was Malden's little bodkin. Little more than a belt knife, but the thief treasured it.

"I see no sign of Acidtongue," Mörget announced. The barbarian sifted through some other detritus. It looked like Malden's pack had been rifled and its contents discarded when they failed to prove valuable. "The elves must have taken the blade."

"They must have gone through your friends' belongings, taking what they counted valuable, discarding the trash. Now, what's this?" Balint said as the knocker handed her more objects. "Ah, this is a little hammer. This must have belonged to your Slag." She held it out toward Croy. He glanced at it. Shrugged.

"Something else, maybe," Balint said. She sent the knocker forth again and it returned with a small piece of worked horn. Croy thought he might recognize it, but he didn't look very closely.

"Ah," Balint said. "Now, what have we here? A lady's comb."

Croy grabbed it from her.

For a while he didn't look at it. He couldn't.

"It must have belonged to the thief's bit of tail."

Croy's hand ached and he realized he was crushing the comb. Its tines dug into his palm until one of them snapped off. He forced his fingers to relax. "You won't speak of Cythera like that again," he told Balint. "She is my betrothed."

The dwarf looked confused. "Really? I could have sworn she was spreading her legs for the craven."

"You . . . were wrong," Croy said, his teeth grinding together. She had made a mistake, that was all.

Just like she was mistaken in thinking Cythera was dead.

"Your woman, eh?" Balint asked. There was a gleam in her eye Croy did not care for at all. "I'm sorry, then. This must be very hard for you, knowing the elves got to her. Took her here."

"There are no bodies in this room," he said. "No blood either. That stain . . . is not blood," he insisted.

"You saw what the porridge monster did to my Murin," Balint told him. "They eat our dead, and leave no bodies behind."

"Perhaps," Croy said, squeezing his eyes shut at the thought. "But—".

When he opened his eyes again, Balint was staring at him expectantly. Across the room Mörget watched him with the dead, emotionless eyes of a hunter.

"Yes?" Balint said.

"What? What, blast you?"

Balint rubbed at her furry upper lip. "You said 'but' as if you had some point to make. But then you said nothing more."

"There was nothing more to say. Cythera is not here. We should go. We should go and find her, wherever she is."

"I know you don't want to hear this," Balint told him, sounding almost compassionate. "It might be easier to deny that it happened."

"There's no need to deny anything. I'll admit it looks like Cythera was here at some point," Croy said, trying to stay calm. He needed to think this through. He needed to think, period. It was hard when a little voice in the back of his head wouldn't stop screaming in terror. "Cythera, and Slag, and—and Malden. And clearly they were surprised by—by something. Something that searched their packs. Beyond that—"

"It was elves. You know it was," Balint said.

Mörget nodded. "Revenants wouldn't have searched their things. Nor would the demons."

"And you know the elves, at least by reputation," Balint went on. "You know what all the stories say they used to do to their human captives."

"Be silent!" Croy thundered. Then he calmed himself. Forced his passions to cool themselves. "Please."

"I don't think there's two ways to read this," Balint said. "I'm sorry, but you must see it, too. The elves slew your woman. Your beloved."

Croy wished she would let him think. "You can't know that. You can't know for sure that she's dead—"

"Tell me, human. If the elf who butchered her was standing right here, right now, would you hail him and say, 'Well met'? Or would you stick your sword so far down his throat it would come out brown on the other end?"

"That sounds reasonable," Mörget pointed out.

"Cythera isn't dead," Croy insisted. He could feel the blood burning under his skin. "She lives, still. I would know somehow, I would feel it in my bones if she had perished. The love we share is so strong that I am bound to Cythera by holy chains. It was my sacred duty to protect her. If I had failed her so thoroughly, the Lady would strike me down with lightning out of heaven."

"Maybe She's just waiting till you're outside," Balint interrupted. "Hard to throw a levinbolt through a hundred feet of solid rock."

"My soul would have shriveled inside me," Croy stated. "My heart would have broken. I would feel—"

"The world doesn't work that way," Mörget growled.

"I would feel—something."

But he did feel something, didn't he? He felt doubt. For the first time since they'd been separated, he truly doubted that Cythera was still alive.

"I feel—I feel—"

"These are elves we're talking about," Balint said. "They probably had her sixteen different ways before they let her die."

He knew he was being goaded. He knew she was manipulating him. It didn't stop him from feeling the guilt. Guilt, for letting Cythera come to this haunted place at all. Guilt for not protecting her better. Guilt for leaving her side, even for an instant.

"I—feel—"

"Do you think she was the kind to scream when they tortured her, or would she not give them that satisfaction?" Balint asked.

"I—"

But Croy couldn't finish the thought. His vision went red. His sword jumped from its sheath and he slashed at the air in front of him, not caring what he struck, only needing, desperately, to cut and thrust and stab anything that was in front of him. *For Cythera*, he howled in his head. *For Cythera. For Cythera.*

"That's the spirit," Balint said, with a nasty laugh.

He could barely hear her over the roaring of the blood in his ears.

"What do you want from me?" he demanded. "Why do you torture me like this?"

"I want revenge," Balint told him. "Against the arse-holes who killed Murin and Slurri. I might need your help to get it. So I'm asking. Do we team up and get our revenge? I aim to pull their giblets out their arses and strangle them with their own guts. What say you?"

"I say yessss," Croy hissed.

"And you, Mörget?" Balint asked. "You have no reason to love me. But will you help?"

"This design of yours, to slaughter elves. Does that extend to their pets as well? Their demons?"

"Of course," Balint told the barbarian.

"Then my axe is yours," Mörget told her.

# CHAPTER SEVENTY

The elves took them down a crude flight of stairs carved out of the rock of the winding tunnel and down to another brick door. By that time Slag was able to walk a little on his own. Malden's feet were sore with the constant marching, and his arms ached from carrying the dwarf, but those pains couldn't compete with the searing agony in the muscles of his back.

He was afraid. Terrified, in fact. His back hurt because his body was in a constant state of tension. It had steeled itself for the blow it thought was coming, the moment when the elves turned on him and started to torture him.

His rational mind could not compete with the part of his brain that knew he was going to die, and that it would happen in the most horrible way imaginable. The part of his brain that only wanted to run away, to hide, to curl up and perish on its own rather than face that torment.

He tried to keep cheerful, to laugh and smile and raise the spirits of his companions. To help alleviate the fear he knew they felt as well. Yet he knew once they passed through this last door, only gruesome fate and inevitable death awaited him.

One of the soldiers rapped on the door with the pommel of his bronze sword, and it swung wide on its hinges.

Light, warmth, and music spilled into the tunnel. Malden smelled meat roasting over an aromatic fire. The elfin guards stepped aside and gestured for the prisoners to step forward, into the hall beyond.

"Let everyone have a good look at you," one of them told Cythera. "This should be quite diverting."

Malden watched her walk through the door, with Slag leaning on her arm. She craned her head upward to see her new surroundings, and her mouth fell open in awe. Malden followed close behind and could scarcely credit what he discovered.

The darkness of the Vincularium gave way to dazzling light. Standing lamps lit this room, just as they had the dormitory, but here their reddish light was mellowed by the yellow glow of a thousand candles that chased every shadow out of the hall. He could not imagine what the room might once have been used for, as no sign remained of the cold, cyclopean stone halls of the kind favored by dwarves. The elves had made this room their own, paneling the walls with elaborate wooden carvings or hanging them with rich, warm brocades that spilled out across the floor to become luxurious carpets.

Musicians in motley and crimson danced through the room, no two playing the same instrument. They seemed to be competing with one another yet their melodies wove together seamlessly, filling the air with bright piping and vigorous drumbeats. Jugglers lofted blazing torches high in the air, catching them behind their backs as they bowed to passing ladies in diaphanous gowns that trailed unheeded across the floor. Elves in heavy plate armor bashed away at each other with wooden swords, laughing as their armor rang, again and again. A groaning board ran the full length of one wall, laden with meats and wheels of cheese and enormous flagons of brown liquid.

Malden realized his jaw was hanging open, and he forced it to close. He caught Cythera's eye and imagined his own face looked much like hers—wide with uncontrolled surprise.

Despite what the elfin soldier had told them, the gathered elves did not seem at all shocked to see humans enter their home, nor curious to get a good look at the newcomers. They seemed too enveloped in their own revelry, too devoted to their own amusement, to even notice a change in the hall, or the arrival of three beings whom they had reason to hate. Malden was glad enough for that. He saw no instruments of torture in that place, no real weapons, even, other than those carried by the guards that brought them hence. If the three of them were to be tortured to death, it seemed they must wait until the party was finished.

Above them a wide balcony let out onto the hall, its far side hidden by thick red curtains. One of these curtains twitched aside and an elf strode out onto the balcony to stare down at the prisoners. Malden could see at once that this one was different. He had an aura of command about him, and Malden thought the elf must be their king or maybe some kind of high priest. He wore a black garment that started as a cowl around his head, revealing only his face, then fell without seam or fastening to the floor, as if he were covered in a sheet with a hole cut out for him to see through. Small bells were sewn everywhere onto this mantle, and they rang with a shrill sound as he moved. He was tall and his face was sharply featured, but his eyes were strange. From a distance it was difficult for Malden to tell, but he thought one of the elf's pupils was much larger than the other.

"Silence," he said, in a voice that conveyed no emotion at all.

Instantly the clamor in the hall ceased. The musicians stopped playing in mid-chord. The jugglers caught their torches and held them. The warriors drew apart and came to attention. The ladies stopped exactly where they were, and lowered their hands to their sides. Around Malden, Cythera, and Slag, the guards all stood up very straight and held their arms down at their sides.

"What," the black-robed elf asked, "are these?"

As if noticing the newcomers for the first time, the gathered elves all turned to stare at the two humans and the dwarf. They grabbed at one another's arms and pointed. Some pressed hands to their mouths, or their nostrils flared in surprise. None of them made the slightest sound.

The soldier who had threatened to kill Slag if he couldn't walk hurried forward. The clattering of his armor sounded very loud in the still room. He dropped to one knee and raised his hands in supplication.

The black-robed elf stared down at him for a moment as if he had no idea who the guard was. Then his face cleared as if he'd suddenly remembered something. "You . . . may speak."

"Your excellent presence be preserved, your beneficence praised in every quarter, Hieromagus. These are the human trespassers you sent us to retrieve."

"I sent . . . you? Trespassers?"

Malden started to quake. He remembered the elf—the one who'd been so horrified by Slag's vomit—say that a Hieromagus had ordered them to be brought in alive. The only reason they hadn't been killed already was because of this elf's command. If this Hieromagus couldn't remember why he'd wanted them alive, they might very well die in the next moment.

"Hold," the Hieromagus said. "It is time for my sacrament."

The curtains behind him moved again and an elf hurried out. She wore a shift made of patches and rags. In her hand she held something small and dark. The Hieromagus opened his mouth wide and she placed the thing on his tongue. Before he closed his mouth again, Malden saw that it was the cap of a black mushroom. The Hieromagus swallowed it like a pill.

"I sent you," he said. "I sent you to retrieve the tres-passers. That happened in the past. Yes. I have it now. I see again their future. Very . . . very important, that they are . . . alive. It will be very important. Though . . . though . . ."

He fell silent then. Seconds passed but he said no more.

One of the soldiers, standing just to Malden's left, moved his hand very carefully up to his face. He scratched his nose discreetly, then very quickly lowered his hand again, as if afraid someone would see him moving.

The Hieromagus suddenly slumped forward, leaning hard on the railing of the balcony. His eyes opened so wide Malden thought they might fall out of his head. His mouth twisted in a grimace of utter horror and his whole body convulsed.

Then, a moment later, he stood back up as if nothing had happened. In a quiet voice, the voice of a boy asking for a candy, he said, "Is it time for my sacrament? Why is there no music? When there's no music I hear . . . I hear everything . . ."

The musicians launched back into their riotous song. The jugglers tossed their torches in the air. The warriors began to fight once more in jest. The ladies giggled and whispered among themselves. None of them looked at the newcomers anymore.

The Hieromagus walked through the curtain, not even bothering to lift it away from his body. With a sigh, the leader of the soldiers rose to his feet and gestured at his warriors. "Take them inside and lock them away. Maybe he'll remember what he wanted them for, or maybe he'll order their deaths. Who knows? I can't say I find this game entertaining, either way."

"That fellow's in charge of our fates?" Malden asked. "I cannot describe the depth of relief that I feel."

The guard behind Malden jabbed him in the back with a spear. The three of them were marched forward, only to stop again after a moment as the leader grabbed hold of

Malden's sleeve. "Don't be fooled," he said. "The Hiero-magus sees everything—the past, the future as well. His sacrament allows him to confer both with his ancestors and his descendants. If he seems scattered about the present, it is only because he sees so much."

Malden knew enough to stay silent, yet he had so little left to lose. "He didn't seem scattered," he answered. "He seemed insane."

He fully expected the soldier to strike him with a mailed fist and break his already bruised jaw. Yet the soldier only laughed. "Right now his madness is the only thing keeping you alive, human."

# PART V

# The First Duty of Prisoners

# INTERLUDE

A elbring climbed the stairs to the top level of the Vincularium, dreading what he would find. Like most elves, he hated the cemetery of the dwarves. The elves lived in a relatively small section of the lower levels and shunned the rest of the underground city, and for good reason. There were too many memories up high. When one got too close to the world outside the mountains, the ancestors refused to be quiet in one's head. They remembered that world, even if Aelbring didn't. They wanted so badly to escape the darkness and the dust. Maybe the Hieromagus could bear their whispering voices, but for a low-ranking soldier like himself, they threatened to overwhelm his senses. It just wasn't fair.

And today of all days to draw this duty! There were humans down below—humans! After all this time. He wanted to see them. Wanted to know if they were as ugly as the ancestors said, or as hairy. Maybe the old legends were wrong. They said there was a female human among them. Aelbring had a secret yearning, a half-formed hope that maybe she would be different from the others. Maybe she would have an exotic beauty unfound among his own people. He burned with curiosity. Maybe he could arrange to have himself assigned to guarding her. Maybe he could show her some small kindness, some bit of unexpected compassion that would cause her to look on him with whatever humans had that resembled affection . . .

He had his orders, though. Something had stirred up the revenants on the top level. Well, of course it had—the humans who broke in through the seal, yes? But no, he had been told this was some new intrusion. The eternal guardians had calmed down since the humans arrived, but now some new excitement was brewing among them. The revenants did not speak, nor did they have any way of sending a message down to the lower levels. The queen, however, was in tune with them in some arcane fashion, and she said she'd felt their rage burning stronger than ever. Which meant something had set them off. And someone had to go up and find out what had so upset them.

And of course that someone had to be him.

At least it wasn't nighttime up there. The red sun burned as it did every twelve hours, and this high its light went everywhere, illuminated every dark corner. Its beams were almost too much for Aelbring's eyes to bear, accustomed as they were to the gloom of the lower levels. The geometric tombs of the dwarves draped long shadows along the far walls.

At first he could see nothing out of place, no horrid surprises waiting for him in that haunted region. No revenants waited to greet him, but of course they wouldn't make it that simple, would they? He checked the bronze sword he wore at his side and went to look for them, intent on getting this over with as soon as possible.

Up ahead, just to the side of a tomb shaped like a marble column, he saw something scattered on the ground. Some refuse left behind by the invading humans, most likely. Animals that they were, they could hardly be expected to pick up after themselves. He jogged over to see what it was, but before he'd taken half a dozen strides he tripped and nearly fell on his face.

"Human bastards," he said, catching himself with his hands. He got one knee under him and rose gracefully to his feet, then turned to see what he'd stumbled on. For a moment terror gripped him when he saw it was a length of bone, ending in a skeletal hand.

Then the hand twitched, the bony fingers contracting on rotten sinews, and he laughed out loud. "Did one of you fall down and hurt himself?" he called out, thinking to draw the revenants. It would not be the first time they had grown excited over nothing. One of them would walk too close to the edge of the central shaft and fall into the water below, and the whole lot of them would panic, thinking they were under attack.

The revenants were strong, and nearly indestructible, and they burned with a desire for vengeance. But they weren't very bright.

Aelbring kicked the bony arm away and headed again for the columnar tomb. The smile on his face faltered— but only a little—when he saw that what he'd taken for human garbage was in fact all that remained of a revenant. Its skull had been smashed in and its rib cage broken into a hundred pieces. One of its legs still kicked feebly at the cobblestones. The other had been ground nearly to powder.

"You haven't been fighting amongst yourselves, have you?" he called out. They'd never done such a thing before.

"I'm afraid not," someone said. Someone standing very close.

Aelbring gasped in surprise and whipped out his sword. He'd had no sense of anyone nearby, had heard no footfalls, seen no movement. And that voice—it had a human accent. Another of them? Maybe the first three had just been the advance guard of an invading army. The elves had been living in terror of such a thing for centuries. "Show yourself!" he demanded.

"Certainly." The human moved into view, and Aelbring was glad to see it was no knight in iron armor. Instead this one wore a colorless robe, with a hood to hide his features. This the human pushed back, and Aelbring was surprised to see not the savage ape-face he expected, but the refined features of a scholar.

"You're a human," he said.

"And you're very perceptive. I see you speak my language, too. Wonderful! That will make things so much easier."

Aelbring licked his lips in confusion. It had not surprised him when the human addressed him in the elfin tongue. It had never occurred to him before that there could *be* more than one language.

"Hark, I'm really very sorry about what I did to your guardian there." The human gestured at the broken bones on the floor. "I did what I could to communicate with it, but it wouldn't stop attacking me."

"They have reason to want your blood," Aelbring told the human. He lifted his sword. "As do I." He readied himself to charge, to run this human through. He would need to strike hard and fast. The ancestors were quite clear on the fact that humans felt no pain, and that they could survive injuries that would slaughter three elves with one stroke.

"Wouldn't you rather take me captive?" the human asked, his voice quite calm. He sounded as if he were asking if Aelbring would like his wine served hot or cold.

For a moment the elf could only stare at the human, unsure what was happening. Luckily for Aelbring, there were certain forms one followed, certain protocols one learned as a soldier, for dealing with just such situations. None of them were particularly complicated.

If you caught an enemy defenseless, for instance, you threatened him into submission. It was just how these things were done.

"You fear me? You should," Aelbring shouted. "I will strike you down if you show me the slightest sign of resistance."

"I will be as meek as a little lamb," the human said. And then he smiled. It was a gentle, kindly smile, the kind of smile one would give to a child.

So then why did it make his blood run cold?

"You should take me to your superior officer," the human said. "Right away. I have much to discuss with him."

"I'm sure he'll—he'll want to—" Aelbring didn't like this at all. "He'll have questions for you, I can guarantee it."

"And I hope I have answers he'll like," the human replied.

Aelbring tried to remember the protocol for this situation. Ah, right. "This way," he barked. "Walk ahead of me, where I can see you, and don't try anything!"

"But of course," the human said, chuckling to himself.

# CHAPTER SEVENTY-ONE

Once the Hieromagus had withdrawn, the revelers in the great elf hall seemed to lose all interest in the humans and the dwarf. They barely moved out of the way as the soldiers pushed the prisoners through the hall. "They don't seem as surprised to see us as we were to meet them. You'd think they were expecting us," Malden said to Cythera.

An elfin lady, exquisite in gemstones and a mauve dress, failed to get out of the way at all. The soldiers begged her to move but she just laughed at some jest made by her companion, a warrior wearing a silver circlet.

"Rather it seems that they already know us, and have for so long that they've discounted our value as curiosities," Cythera said, while they waited for the soldiers to make a new path around the lady. "I think they're feigning, though. Do you feel like someone is watching you?"

Malden had a thief's instincts for such things, but he'd been ignoring it until she spoke. Now he let the hair on the back of his arms rise up and felt the muscles of his back shiver. "Interesting." He tried an experiment. Turning his head, he tried to catch the eye of the first elf he saw—a juggler. But the performer was, at that moment, turning away to make some saucy comment to a mailed warrior. "Ah," Malden said. He turned his head again and looked right at an elf who was tuning a lute. The musician's head fell forward as he studied his strings. "Yes, yes, I see it now. They are watching us, all of them, and most closely. Yet they're doing their level best to seem as if they don't even know we're here. Very interesting."

"Fucking fascinating," Slag muttered. "In a few minutes, I wager the torture's about to start. You think maybe there are more pressing mysteries to solve?"

There was no time for further conversation. Malden was shoved forward by the elf behind him and the three of them were hurried out of the hall and down a side corridor. The walls of this passage were as rough as the winding tunnel that brought them to the elf hall, but its ceiling was at least high enough that they didn't need to keep ducking.

Alcoves and doors opened on the passage at irregular intervals. In most of them, elves stood waiting to watch them pass. These elves, at least, shared nothing of the bizarre affected quality of their cousins in the hall—they gawked openly, and whispered with agitation among themselves. They also lacked the finery of the hall, instead being dressed in the tattered patchwork of the Hieromagus's assistant. They must be servants, Malden thought, or peasants, or whatever passed for slaves in elf society. Yet they were as beautiful as the others, radiantly, transcendently beautiful, their skin creamy and perfect, their limbs of perfect proportion on their lanky frames. He tried smiling at one, a tall elf woman with beads in her hair. She looked terrified and ducked back into her alcove as if running from a demon.

"They're all as mad as their Hieromagus," Malden said with a sigh. "I can understand being tortured to death for breaking and entering, that's just how society works. But if it turns out we're going to be killed for wearing the wrong color tunics, or for some offense we made against the invisible giant tortoise they worship, then—"

"I think you were wrong about him," Cythera said. "The Hieromagus."

Malden turned to look at her. "Oh?"

"He isn't mad. At least . . . I don't think so." She shook her head. "The sacrament he took, did you see it? That was a cap of death's helm mushroom. A very rare fungus, and very, very dangerous. It's used sometimes in witchcraft, though my mother claims it's a crutch for those who lack the proper gift of second sight. A few shavings, when steeped properly in a tea, will grant visions of other times. Vivid, terrifying visions—powerful glimpses of other lives. The visions are not phantoms either, but true memories of those who lived before. It's a seductive drug. Take too much of it and your—well, call it your soul— can become lost and not be able to find its way back to its own body. If he eats entire caps at once, on anything like a regular basis, I don't know how he could ever know what time he was in. Did you see his eyes?"

"The pupils were different sizes."

"Yes," Cythera said. "I think his individual eyes were looking into different times. If I'm right, that explains the merrymakers as well."

"An unusual lot," Malden said.

"All there for his benefit. Playing out a scene, a great torrent of sensual delights, to entice him to stay close to his own body."

"Let's hope they don't falter, then," Malden said. "At least, not before he remembers what he wanted us for."

Slag snorted. "More like, not until he fucking forgets again. The longer it takes him, the longer we don't have to find out what our fate is to be."

That sent a new twinge of fear and pain up Malden's spine.

The side corridor ended in another hall, this one much smaller. It opened via a narrow window onto the central shaft. Spiral staircases pierced its floor, leading down to a lower level.

"I'll ready the gaolers," one of the elf soldiers said, and descended with a torch.

For a moment, then, they were allowed to just stop and stand there. It was a blessed relief. Malden considered sitting down on the dusty floor to give his legs a rest but didn't want to risk the displeasure of his captives.

Slag started walking toward the window. One of the elves drew his sword, but Slag didn't stop. When he reached the opening, he placed his hands on the sill and Malden thought he might intend to climb over and jump out. Instead the dwarf just looked upward, his body shaking with sobs.

Malden realized that this was the first time Slag had seen the manufactured sun of the Vincularium. He went over to look up at it with the dwarf. "It came to life a while back, like dawn breaking."

"It's fucking beautiful," Slag said.

"Your ancestors made it?" Malden asked.

"It's certain as shitting the elves did not. Look at those pipes coming out of the top. They must carry flammable gas to the lamp . . . there are pockets of such vapors everywhere underground. They're a hazard when you're digging a mine—but the builders of this place must have found a way to harness the stuff. I'll be buggered."

The thief smiled. "Strange. I was always under the impression that dwarves hated the true sun and shunned its light. Isn't it odd they should make their own, here under the ground?"

"'Tis a puzzler," Slag agreed. "True sunlight burns my skin and dazzles my eyes. Yet this is a different color, and somehow that makes a difference. It's almost soothing to look upon. Hah. Thur-Karas. Place of Long Shadows. I understand now." He glanced up at Malden. "Lad, leave me be a moment, will you? I want to see this by myself a bit. I have a feeling I won't get another chance."

Malden squeezed the dwarf's shoulder, then went back to stand next to Cythera. The elves eyed him warily but offered no threat. When Cythera slipped her hand into Malden's, two of the guards nudged each other and traded leering winks.

Malden ignored them, and focused his attention on the soft hand in his. Cythera's fingers trembled along with her pulse. He tried to meet her gaze, but she just looked straight ahead, lost in her own thoughts.

It was not much longer before the elf returned from below to announce that the gaol was ready to receive them.

## CHAPTER SEVENTY-TWO

The elves led them down the spiral staircase to a dark room below. The walls were unadorned and the floor was covered in a thick layer of wet silt. They must be very near the bottom of the shaft, Malden thought—and this room must periodically flood with water. In the middle of the room was a cage made of wooden bars, large enough to hold a dozen prisoners.

His bladder started to give way when he saw where he'd be held. He forced himself not to soil his hose, but it wasn't easy.

The gaolers came forward to receive the prisoners. There was no formal ceremony involved, which made sense since the gaolers were revenants. One was missing both eyes and part of his cheek. The other had no face at all. The living elf soldiers treated the revenants with a certain disdain that seemed odd to Malden—these were, after all, the undead remains of their own ancestors, and he'd been told the elves worshipped their forebears. Yet the soldiers spoke to the revenants the way a man would speak to his dog. It confused him, but he had other concerns to occupy him.

The gate of the gaol was opened and Cythera was forced inside. She grabbed at the bars and stared out at Malden, as if asking him silently to do something, to do something right now. To make some grand gesture of bravery and save them all.

He could do nothing. Without waiting to be pushed, he entered the cage. Slag followed, his head drooping against his chest.

The gate of the cage was closed and locked behind them. Then the living elves filed out of the room, while the two revenants took up positions on either side of the stairwell. Once they were in place, the gaolers remained utterly motionless. Each had a bronze sword held before him, its point touching the stone floor. They looked like grisly statues more than animate things.

There was no light in the room save what filtered down through the stairwell. Just a few stray beams to divide the shadows. There was no furniture in the stockade other than a pair of buckets. Malden could guess what those were for.

He went to the far side of the stockade and sat down in the silt. His breeches were instantly ruined but he couldn't bear the thought of standing any longer. All strength seemed to have fled him as his fear transformed into despair.

Eventually Cythera came and joined him. She put her head on his shoulder but did not speak. Slag stood awhile longer, but Malden could see the dwarf swaying on his feet. Eventually weariness overcame Slag—he was still recovering from being poisoned, after all, and the violent purgative of the antidote—and he sat as well.

And then . . . nothing happened.

A great deal of nothing. A long span of nothing, not even talk. Time passed, though it felt like it did not.

They might have been hours in that place before anything occurred. Days might have passed down there—Malden had no way to measure the time, other than by how hungry he grew. The air around him seemed to hang as motionless as their revenant guards, and each breath he took was like some crime against the terrible timelessness of that place where nothing ever changed.

Eventually a loaf of mealy bread was brought down to them and tossed through the bars. Malden caught it before it landed in the muck, then broke it carefully in three pieces and shared it out.

When it was consumed, they went back to doing nothing.

In time Cythera began to snore. They had all gone a very long while without sleep. Malden made a pillow of his cloak and laid her head gently upon it, so her face would not be in the silt. Then he headed over toward where Slag sat by the gate. He could no longer stand the silence or the waiting. He intended to get a conversation going, regardless of what the dwarf might want.

The dwarf was picking at one of the bars with his fingernails. He stripped a long fibrous sliver of wood from the bar.

"Trying to escape, Slag?" Malden asked.

The dwarf didn't answer. He studied his sliver intently.

"Slag," Malden said again.

The dwarf pulled the sliver into tiny strips. "It's not wood," he said, though clearly he wasn't addressing Malden. "I wondered where they could get wood from, down here. The answer is they fucking don't. It must be some kind of mushroom, perhaps those big tough growths we saw on the walls of the central shaft."

"Slag," Malden said, annoyed at being ignored. Still the dwarf didn't look up. "Urin," he tried.

That got a reaction. The dwarf stared at him with fierce eyes. "I don't use that damned name anymore."

"I can see why, since in the language of humans it sounds a great deal like—"

"It's a proper dwarven name! Uri was the inventor of glass-blowing. My father was his direct descendant. For a hundred generations the men in my family have been named Urin, you human fuck."

"But now you're Slag. A name my people gave you. You've turned your back on your ancestors."

Slag scowled. "You heard Balint. I'm an exile. She doesn't even consider me a dwarf at all."

"You were exiled for being a debaser."

"Aye," Slag admitted. "A debaser of the coinage. I won't deny it."

"What does that mean?"

"I worked in a mint, before I came to Ness. Back when I lived in a proper town, down in a tin mine. I had a life back then, and work to do. I know you humans are all shiftless bastards, but for a dwarf, having a profession means everything. I was proud of what I did. I oversaw the production of gold coins. It was good work, but in the end it didn't pay enough. I had debts, and when a dwarf owes money, he pays it back one way or another. There's no mercy for the lazy in our land."

"What kind of debts?"

Slag stared at Malden with angry eyes. "Gambling debts, if you must know. That's something that never used to happen. We didn't go in for games of chance, back in the old days—we stuck to sure things. One more damned vice we learned from you humans. Not that I trusted my luck. I thought I had a system, and I could bet on the fall of the dice and make some coin if I was careful. It turned out I was dead wrong."

"I had no idea," Malden said.

"What you don't know about us, lad, is—" He sighed. Malden could tell the dwarf had been working up a powerful obscenity but lacked the strength to finish it. "I needed money in a hurry. It occurred to me one day that if I added small impurities to the gold I worked with, I could make more coins out of less gold. I thought I was so brilliant. That no one had ever thought of that before."

"Most thieves feel like that, on their first job," Malden sympathized. "Most learn otherwise to their dismay."

"I was no thief! At least, I didn't think of myself that way. I thought I was improving efficiency. That's all."

"So what happened?"

Slag sighed deeply. "Nothing, at first. My coins were accepted by the fucking exchequer, same as always. It wasn't till later that I was found out. Dwarven coins are never counterfeited, so it's rare anyone would want to test one. But human merchants aren't quite as trusting. A big buggering miner came to our city, looking to sell some iron he'd dug up. When he was paid, he bit into one of my coins, the way humans do."

"That's how we know it's real gold, and not polished brass. Real gold is soft enough to take an impression."

"Aye, I know it too fucking well, lad. This miner broke his tooth."

Malden chuckled.

"You can't imagine the uproar! Dwarves are honest folk, everybody knows that. It's something they count on. If there's ever even the slightest whiff of corruption in our dealings with humans it could be a fucking catastrophe. There was an investigation, and all the evidence led straight back to me. I was tumbled, all right."

"And so they exiled you. There are worse punishments?"

"We don't do capital punishment, not my people. There aren't enough of us left for that," Slag said. "And we consider exile bad enough. It's different for us than for humans, ain't it? It's fucking worse. An exiled human just goes to the Northern Kingdoms and starts a new life. There is no other dwarven land. You have to go live among humans, finding what work you may. Never to see your family again. Never to marry, never to have a family of your own." He sighed deeply. "It's worse'n hanging, frankly. I'm like the opposite of one of yon undead bastards. They're dead but refuse to accept it. I'm still alive, but I feel half the time like I'm already dead."

"I had no idea that living in Ness was so hard on you. There are plenty of dwarves living there, and they don't seem to mind it as much."

Slag shrugged. "It was worse for me than for others. They know that once they make some money they can go home again. When they turned me out I had no choice but to head south. Even in Ness, though, no other dwarf would hire me. They couldn't trust me, you see? Never again. That's how I ended up with Cutbill." Slag looked Malden up and down. "Cutbill takes any old baggage that comes along."

"Did he know this story?"

"Much of it. That's why when you told him you were going to the bloody Vincularium, he thought I'd be interested. He knew I was always looking for a way back home. Figured there'd be something here I could trade for forgiveness. Our people are the same as yours in one way— if you're rich enough, nobody asks how you came by the money."

"Oh, aye," Malden said. "A rich man can buy his way out of a noose."

"Or out of exile, mayhap. But you heard what Balint said about that. You were there. I've got an arsehole's chance of ever going home. And now—well, if I'm still alive this time tomorrow, I'll probably be wishing I weren't. This whole venture was one colossal cock-up. I've got nothing left."

"Which means nothing to lose," Malden said. "So you're trying to break this bar." He ran a finger along the surface where Slag had peeled off his sliver. "So we can escape."

"No, lad. I was thinking if I could get a piece of it sharp enough, I could cut my own throat and get this over with faster."

# CHAPTER SEVENTY-THREE

Eventually the light at the top of the stairs went out, leaving them in total darkness. Slag snored noisily by the gate, but after a while even that sound stopped registering on Malden's ears and all was still. Cythera wrapped her arms around him, and he held her close. She had stopped shaking. The pain in his back was still there, though. It felt like his body expected at any moment to be stabbed through the vitals.

It was not a good feeling. It left him restless and irritable. The third time he shifted his weight, Cythera sat up and whispered in his ear, "Every time you move you wake me. Try to get comfortable, Malden. Or it will be a very long night."

"I'm sorry," he said. She settled back into his arms but her shoulder blade jabbed him in the side and he moved again.

He felt her weight leave him, and he panicked. Like a babe separated for the first time from its mother. "No," he said, his voice plaintive and hurt. The emotion in his words surprised him, but he couldn't help it. "No, please. Don't go away."

"I'm right here. I couldn't go very far if I wanted," she told him. "What's wrong? Beyond our obvious predicament."

"I can't take this," he told her. "Being confined. It's— It's worse than torture. My whole life I've been fighting to be free. To do as I choose, go where I want—and it seems like I've been running from one cage to another!"

She kissed him gently on the temple. Her hands caressed his face.

He was breathing heavily but not with lust. The comfort

she gave him was something he desperately needed, something he could not live without. "At least you're here with me," he told her.

"Always," she said.

"I almost believe you when you say that. You've forgiven me for my fancies. And my liberties," he said, thinking of how angry she'd been with him in the Hall of Masterpieces. "You love me. You said as much when you thought the elves were going to kill me."

"I remember. I was foolish enough to think that would save you. I thought it might move them and they would take pity. It seems stupid now, but at the time it was all I could think of."

He bit his lip. He was certain there had been more to it. That she was making an excuse now. If he gave her any leeway, she would slip from his grasp again. He wanted to keep silent but he couldn't. "If we get out of this alive—"

"Suggest no other possibility," she told him.

"When we escape," he told her, "you have to tell Croy about us."

She sighed deeply and put her arms around his waist. "And why do I have to do that?" she asked, sounding as if she knew she would regret the answer.

"Because we're in love! Because you don't love him. He still thinks you're going to marry him when we get home."

She was quiet for a time. A time far too long for Malden's liking.

"If Croy were here right now, before me, I would marry him on the spot," she said. "Malden—I said what I said. And I can't lie to you now, I do care for you. But I would have said anything at that moment, anything that might have swayed them. Anything that might have saved you. What I feel for you, Malden—it isn't right. It isn't the way my life is supposed to work out. I'm sorry."

He started to protest but suddenly realized he could see her face. Light was streaming down from the top of the stairs.

An elfin soldier came clattering down, carrying a torch. The two revenant gaolers lifted their swords, but the soldier said something soothing and they lowered their weapons again.

When he peered into the stockade and saw Malden and Cythera holding each other, a wicked smile twisted his thin lips. "If you were about to mate, please don't let me stop you. I'll just wait here and observe."

"Piss off," Slag moaned, sitting up. The dwarf wiped sleep from his eyes and rose to his feet.

The elf kicked the bars. Slag jumped backward and the elf laughed.

"You," the soldier said, pointing at Malden. "When we captured you, weren't you wearing a sword?"

Malden blinked at the elf but said nothing.

"What is your name?"

"You might as well tell him," Cythera said. "What difference does it make?"

"Malden," the thief said.

"What? Speak up. Is it Croy?"

Cythera's arms gripped him tighter.

"No," Malden said, raising his voice. "I'm Malden."

The soldier frowned. "How vexing. I'm supposed to fetch a Sir Croy. I was told he would be among the captives, and you were the only one with a sword, so—"

"Well, you've fucking found me," Slag announced.

For a moment no one at all spoke.

"You're Sir Croy? You're a knight?" the elf asked.

"That's right."

The elf laughed heartily. "You're not tall enough!"

"How dare you, sir," Slag said, in a passable impersonation of Croy. "I may be short in stature but—"

"You were wearing no armor when we caught you. Nor did you have a sword. Knights are supposed to have swords." The soldier frowned. "Aren't they?"

"The boy was just holding my sword for me at the time. If I'd had it to hand, the lot of you would be so many spitted roasts right now. Well, you've got me. You fought dirty, but I suppose that's what one expects from you dog-hearted elves. Take me away, you bastard. Do your worst."

The elf's brows knitted together. But then he shrugged and unlocked the cage. "Things must have changed outside in the last eight centuries." He pulled Slag out of the cage and then locked it again.

"Might as well get it over with," Slag said as he was marched up the stairs.

Malden turned to Cythera with a look of horror. "They're going to torture him to death," he said.

"But why?" Cythera looked deeply confused. "Why would he pretend to be Croy? He can't hope to benefit from such a ruse. Was he trying to protect you?"

"I don't think so," Malden told her, remembering what the dwarf had said earlier, while she was sleeping. "I think he just got tired of waiting."

# CHAPTER SEVENTY-FOUR

Croy's blood pounded in his temples. His fingers twitched and tapped at Ghostcutter's pommel. He needed to fight. He needed to kill something.

Balint had pushed him to this violent edge. She had bade him look over it, into the depths of his anger and his need for vengeance, and showed him there was no bottom to that gulf. There had been a time in Croy's life when he thought mercy was a virtue, and that restraint had its place in battle.

That was before Cythera was taken from him. Before he saw what bloodlust truly meant. He had possessed a future before he came to the Vincularium. He had seen a wife, and children, a family of his own. Heirs to pass his name to, and perhaps even a son who could lift his sword when he was gray and old and unable to carry the Ancient Blade himself. He had dreams then.

Now he had a desire to kill, and not much else.

Supposedly Balint had a plan. She had some scheme that would let him kill every last elf, and end their race forever. He barely listened to what she had to say. He would happily have run back down to the throne room and started hacking and slashing, but she had stepped him back from the abyss just enough to suggest there was a quicker if less direct route to sating his hunger for elfin blood.

He was still considering whether to take her option and go for the surety of destruction, the total eradication of the elves—or follow his own instincts, which was only certain to be more gratifying.

"If you kill them one by one, are you sure you can get them all?" she asked. "Are you quite sure you will finish what you start?"

"Ghostcutter has never failed me yet," Croy pointed out.

"And if one of them does get away—worse, a pair of them, a male and a female. If they outlive you, and restart their generation. Rebuild their numbers. What then? If the elves survive your attack, will you be satisfied? Letting them have what they took away from you?"

He frowned, liking none of this. "You want me to delay my revenge."

"I want you to be smart about it, you pillock! There are too many of them for a direct assault, surely even you can see that. We'd be slaughtered."

"If I die seeking vengeance, I die a noble death," Croy told her.

"No, no, no! We have to get all of them, or it doesn't count. And that means we have to be a little sneaky. When you make love to a woman . . ." she said, looking Croy up and down. The knocker on her shoulder waved its fingers in his direction, too. She frowned before continuing. "Not you, of course—I imagine you don't have much experience in that regard." She turned to face Mörget. "When you make love to a woman, do you just rip her dress off and bend her over whatever happens to be handy?"

The barbarian laughed gleefully. His eyes grew wistful and he hugged himself.

"I can see," Balint said, "that I've picked the wrong metaphor. No matter. When a real dwarf wants to woo, he flatters his sweetheart, and gives her little gifts, and kisses her gently, first. He doesn't make a rush for the goodies until she's already begging for it."

"So your plan is to give the elves gifts, and tell them how beautiful they are before we slaughter them like pigs?" Croy asked. "That sounds like folly."

Balint sighed deeply. "Perhaps you two should just follow me, and do what I say. It'll make this much easier if you don't ask a lot of questions."

"Fine," Croy said. "Just tell me when the time comes for vengeance."

The dwarf led them up a long ramp toward the level above. They emerged into a darkened infirmary, with rows of short beds lining the walls and in the middle a great slab marked with ancient bloodstains. Hundreds of iron tools—most gone to rust—hung by chains above the slab, knives and saws and pincers. Compared to the surgical equipment Croy knew, it all looked quite hygienic and advanced.

Beyond the infirmary ward the hall opened up into a broad cobbled space that was empty save for a pile of wheeled carts, heaped up and left to fall apart and rot. Wide-mouthed passages led away from the main chamber in every direction, heading straight out into darkness, some tending upward, some down.

"Mine shafts," Balint explained, "probably long since played out."

The knocker jumped down from her shoulder and ran along the floor, tapping its fingers arrhythmically on the cobbles. It scurried away into the darkness, then hurried back and tapped out a complicated pattern on Balint's leg.

"Our way leads through there." She pointed toward a stone arch at the far side of the big room. Beyond lay a staircase that curved away from view. "Up that way are the kitchens, and past them the leather works. Our destination's there. But we have to be careful now. My blueling tells me there are revenants up those stairs, standing guard."

Croy nodded grimly. Then he glanced over at Mörget.

The barbarian met his eye and smiled broadly. He nodded and hefted his weapon.

"Wait here," Croy told Balint.

"No! We must be circumspect as a whore with her hand in a man's pocket, unsure if she's found his purse or his pr—"

Croy interrupted her foul figure of speech by dashing up the stairs. Mörget came after, bringing a single candle to light their way. At the top of the stairs they found three revenants waiting for them, lipless mouths wide open in noiseless screams, hands and weapons already groping toward the two humans.

Mörget took one apart with his axe before it could even reach for his throat. Croy brought Ghostcutter up and decapitated one, then sliced the hands off another with his backswing. The revenants kept coming, so he kept carving—hitting hard at their bony knees, slicing one in half and taking the arm off another. Mörget took the other arm, then reached down and pulled the remaining bits to pieces with his bare hands.

The two of them headed back down the stairs. Balint waited for them there. The knocker's blind face was wide with astonishment.

"The way is clear," Croy told her. "Find me some living elves next time."

# CHAPTER SEVENTY-FIVE

After Slag was taken away, the night passed without further incident.

Malden slept, finally—after a fashion. He mostly drifted on dark currents of his own thoughts. Sometimes those thoughts grew bizarre in character, sometimes incomprehensible, and he would realize that he had been dreaming. Yet there was no sharp disconnection between wakefulness and slumber.

Certainly he got little rest.

Cythera woke when they were brought food so they could break their fast. More mealy bread, this time accompanied by small beer with a distinct mushroomy flavor. It occurred to him to wonder how the bread was made without wheat flour. Probably ground bits of mushroom.

He wondered what had happened to Slag.

He was almost certain he didn't want to know.

Cythera said little that morning, and moved less. She mostly sat watching the gaolers, the revenants who were themselves motionless. Malden wondered if she were doing something witchy. Trying to take control of their rotting brains with the hypnotic power of her gaze, perhaps. Or cause them to erupt into flame with an ancient incantation in some language lost in the mists of time.

Perhaps—maybe just perhaps possibly—she was coming up with some way of freeing them from the gaol. Maybe she had some brilliant idea. Maybe she could spring them from the stockade. Together they could make it up those stairs, slip past the guards that were sure to wait at the top. Find some way through the maze of elfin tunnels, then past the demons and the revenants. Perhaps together the two of them could make it back to the surface. To real daylight, to freedom.

He started sweating just thinking about it. He wanted out. He wanted out so badly he started convincing himself she was going to say something, that at any moment she would speak and tell him what she'd realized, what she had discovered, that would save them both.

He watched her face more carefully than he'd ever watched a guard patrolling outside a warehouse, with more rapt attention than he'd ever wasted on a fat purse he planned to snatch or a lock he planned to pick. He watched every twitch of her mouth, watched her eyes move from one revenant to another. When she was about to speak, he was ready, he could see her tongue start to form the words, and he nodded in excitement, in anticipation.

"That one's taller," she said finally.

Malden shook himself out of his reverie. "I beg your pardon?"

"The one on the left is taller. They look like they're exactly the same height. But there—look. The floor isn't quite level, so the one on the left is actually a hair taller than the one on the right."

Malden's entire body sagged with disappointment, every one of his muscles giving up a little more hope. "I think you have something there," he said, and decided not to rely on her for any daring escape plans.

He'd gotten himself so worked up that when an elfin soldier came down the stairs, he jumped up and grabbed at the bars with white knuckles. It was probably just their next meal being delivered, he told himself. This soldier didn't look nearly as bored as the others had, though. One of his pupils was larger than the other, as if he'd stolen a taste of the Hieromagus's sacrament.

"Are you . . . Malton?" he asked.

"No."

"Oh." The soldier looked confused and stared through the bars for a moment as if he couldn't remember why he'd come. Then he turned and started to head back up the stairs.

"Wait," Malden said. "We need blankets. It got very cold last night. And we can't live on just mushrooms. We need better food."

The soldier turned around slowly. "You," he said.

Malden waited for something more. Eventually he grew tired of waiting. "Yes?" he asked.

"Are you Sir Croy's squire?"

"No," Malden said again.

"Oh." The soldier went away, back up the stairs without another word.

He came back an hour later. This time he asked no questions, but threw open the gate of the cage and grabbed Malden. Cythera screamed and begged him not to take Malden away, but the soldier ignored her.

"It's all right," Malden told her. "You'll be all right. Croy is coming. Croy will save you," he told her. Croy is dead, he thought. If he was coming, he'd be here by now. "Cythera. When I die—your name will be on my lips."

She was still screaming when he was pushed up the stairs. As he was marched down the hallway, he could hear her.

The soldier dragged Malden down a side passage, then pushed him through a door. The room beyond could not have shown a greater contrast to the stockade, a riot of color and sound and fragrant smoke of incense, and the transition was so jarring that Malden fell to the rich carpet and barely caught himself on his hands.

Slowly he looked up to see where he was. The room's walls were lined with tapestries in every color imaginable, its furniture of varied styles and bizarre forms. A group of elfin musicians up in a choir loft played very loud. In the center of the room, the Hieromagus lay on a bright yellow divan, his shapeless robe spilling out across the floor.

"Your exalted presence radiates the light of the soul, Hieromagus," the soldier said. "This is Malton, as you requested."

"My name isn't Malton!" the thief shouted.

The Hieromagus slowly sat up. As distracting as the room's contents might be, his gaze was fixed on something wholly elsewhere. "He's telling the truth. You brought the wrong one."

The soldier dropped to his knees. "My honor, my allegiance, my life, my love, all for you. This was the only male remaining in the stockade."

"He must serve, then," the Hieromagus said. "Come closer, child."

"I'm no child either," Malden protested.

"To the Elders, all other races are children," the Hieromagus said. He was smiling with real warmth. "Come a little closer. I need to make sure you will not run away. Sir Croy gave me his word, which is good enough from a noble man. From a commoner, I'm afraid I need better assurances."

Malden guessed what was about to happen a moment before it was too late to run away. The Hieromagus shot one impossibly thin hand out from under his robe and grasped Malden's ankle.

An invisible serpent wrapped around Malden's leg and sank its fangs deep in the meat of his calf. The muscle there stretched painfully and refused to relax, no matter how hard Malden tried to command it.

He attempted to draw back, to get away from the evil touch of the Hieromagus. It didn't work. His leg was frozen in a stranglehold of pain. He could barely walk on it, and he knew he would never be able to run until that muscle was released. Which, of course, was the point.

He had been hobbled.

# CHAPTER SEVENTY-SIX

"Good," the Hieromagus said, sinking back on his couch once more. "It is done. Take him to . . . the . . . why do I keep seeing—my own reflection? But not one reflection. Hundreds of them, everywhere . . . in mirrors of crystal . . . is it time for my sacrament?"

"Your grace be remembered until the earth boils away at the end of time," the soldier said, "if it please you my orders were to take him to the queen."

"Ah. Yes, they were. I see it," the Hieromagus agreed. "I remember. I remember . . . so much." Then he looked away, into the middle distance, and Malden felt like he had left the room.

"Let us go," the soldier said, and shoved Malden forward.

Malden swung his hobbled leg out in front of him, to catch his fall. It was an automatic act, with no thought behind it.

When his boot touched the floor, he howled in agony and fell to the flagstones flopping and screaming.

The elf soldier waited for him to finish and to rise again.

When he did, pulling himself upward on an ornate carved armoire, sweat poured down the back of his neck and he felt his lips shiver.

"Now, Malton," the soldier said, "let us go."

"I told you," Malden spat, "that's not—my name."

With infinite care, expecting blinding pain at any moment, he put his foot down again. A tingling feeling, as if he were being jabbed with thousands of tiny needles, started to run up his leg. He held his calf perfectly still and hopped forward on the other foot, staring the whole time at the soldier.

The elf returned his stare, looking bored. How many times had he performed this duty? Yet certainly he'd never been in charge of a human prisoner before. Malden wondered how common crime was in elfin society—and how often this elf had performed this particular service.

"Do you like this job?" he asked, taking another careful hop forward. Doing so made his ankle move and sent pain lancing up as far as his knee.

"Sorry?" the elf said, when Malden had stopped grimacing. "You mean being a soldier?"

"Yes," Malden said. "Do you take satisfaction in your work?"

"What an odd question. I was born into harness. My father was a soldier. So, too, will my sons be."

"You have no hope of being a commander someday? Then you could torture other soldiers, instead of poor bastards like me."

"I don't understand you at all. Not altogether surprising, I suppose. Now, walk. I have other duties to perform before I can take my supper, and I'm already getting hungry."

Malden found, by process of trial and error, that if he did not bend or flex his ankle in any way, he could walk. It was a slow, limping gait, but it did not cause him undue pain. He headed in the direction the soldier indicated, stumping along until he came to another room. This place had bare stone walls and was simply furnished with a table and a large basin. An elf dressed in patchwork stood at one side of the table holding a pitcher.

"Your clothes are filthy. Take them off," the soldier insisted.

Malden did as he was told. He did not wish to be taken back to the Hieromagus to have his other leg withered. When he stood naked in the chill room, the elfin servant poured water over his head until he sputtered and cried out.

Then he was dried with towels—the elfin servant did a brisk but thorough job of it—and wrapped in a white robe. The fabric was not silk, but something like it. It felt like a very thick cobweb. He was given slippers of the same material and then told to move on again.

Strange torture, this, he thought.

Unless he wasn't the one being tortured. Perhaps they had taken him away—so they could have Cythera alone, and defenseless.

He did not like that thought at all.

They headed next down a tunnel of the sort he'd seen before, crudely carved with an uneven ceiling. It was next to impossible to cross the equally uneven floor with one leg hobbled, but he made a point of not complaining, and the soldier didn't shout at him to hurry. The tunnel wound back on itself, always rising higher, until it became a flight of stairs hewed through the rock. Malden mounted these steps one at a time, having to lift his cursed leg very carefully onto each riser.

At the top was a door. Elf guards stood on either side. One of them rapped sharply on the door with his knuckles, then threw it open and gestured for Malden to go in. None of the soldiers followed him across the threshold. The door was shut quietly behind him.

The room beyond the door was all of carved wood (or carved woodlike fungus, he supposed), graceful in its paneling and in the lacy rafters that held up its ceiling. The furniture had been polished until it gleamed, and was so carefully matched it seemed each piece was not placed upon the floor, but had grown, naturally, from it. The far wall of the room was a curtain of flowing water that gently plashed into a runnel carved into the floor.

A table near him held sweetmeats that looked suspiciously like honeyed mushrooms, but dyed all the colors of fresh fruit. Crystal flagons full of what Malden sincerely hoped was red wine stood on a sideboard at the far side of the door. He began to salivate just looking at the spread of hot loaves and wheels of cheese on a third table just before him.

"Her nibs thought you might be hungry. I imagine she

was fucking right—I know I was when they brought me here. She didn't know what humans like to eat, so she just had them bring everything."

Malden's eyes went wide. Despite the pain, he ran to a divan over by the wall-length waterfall and dropped to his knees as he grabbed Slag's hands.

The dwarf smiled wickedly at him. Slag had been dressed in a silken robe much like Malden's, though the dwarf's was embroidered with an interweaving pattern of gold thread.

"But how?" Malden asked. "When they took you, I thought it was to torture you to death!"

"So did I, lad." Slag picked at a golden thread in his robe. "Then they brought me before the Hieromagus. He made me swear I wouldn't run away. I swore on all kinds of gods that Sir Croy wouldn't run away, and the weirdest fucking thing happened—he bought my line. Said he knew, that he had seen the future, and that Sir Croy didn't run." Slag shook his head. "Crazy bugger. Then he sent me here. I had no idea why. I'm still not so clear on it. I think I'm supposed to be a pet for—" He struggled to sit up on the divan and then peered over its back. "She's coming. Lad—whatever you hear me say, just play along, or we're fucked. Do you get my meaning?"

"I think so," Malden whispered back.

Slag's face changed then. The grin disappeared from his lips and his countenance grew harsh. "Boy!" he shouted. "Stop simpering and see to my shoes." Slag waved impatiently at a pair of ornate slippers tucked under the divan.

Malden was deeply confused, but he knew a scam when he saw one. He picked up the shoes and polished them with the sleeve of his robe.

Behind the divan, the waterfall parted, just like cloth curtains being drawn back. And then the queen of the elves walked into the room.

# CHAPTER SEVENTY-SEVEN

Every elf Malden had seen was beautiful—their grace-ful, exotic features, perfect clean skin, and shining hair mocked his own human looks. But if they stood beside their queen, even the elfin lords and ladies resembled a herd of warthogs.

She had the delicacy of aspect of the shadows moon-lit leaves make on the surface of a tranquil pool. She had copper-colored hair that fell across her shoulders in perfect ringlets, hair held back only by the spun-silver filigree of her crown. She had eyes the color of the last day of winter, lips the soft red of the interior surface of a rose petal.

She wore a long yellow gown with tight sleeves that trailed on the floor. The garment was a rag on a woman like this. Malden could see it must have been quite elegant once—perhaps eight hundred years ago. Unlike the robes he and Slag wore, it was made of true silk. The cuff of one sleeve looked as if it had been nibbled at by mice, and round blotches of mold, in black and white, decorated its hem.

Behind her the waterfall closed again, hiding whatever lay beyond.

"You must be Sir Croy's squire," she said. Her voice was clear and musical. "Your name is Malton?"

"Yes," the thief told her.

Slag slapped him across one ear. Not hard enough to hurt, but it must have looked like a nasty blow, so he ducked his head and raised his hands as if to ward off an-other strike.

"Yes, your highness," Malden said, and bowed his head.

"Rise, please, and be welcome to my apartments. I fear Sir Croy has been quite at odds and ends without your services. If you ease a trifle of his cares, I shall be very glad for your company, and will find you a proper reward."

"I'll try to do that. Ease his cares. Sir Croy's cares," Malden said.

"I've grown very fond of your master," she said, and came over to the divan. She reached down and tousled Slag's hair, then walked over toward the sideboard to pour herself a goblet of wine.

When her back was turned, Malden shot a questioning glance at Slag.

The dwarf could only shrug in return.

The queen turned back to face them. Slag frowned and stared up at the ceiling.

"Your highness—" Malden began.

"You must call me Aethil," she told him. "As we are all friends in this room."

"Thank you, Aethil," Malden said. "I wonder if I might trouble you for that reward in advance, perhaps—"

"Friends!" Slag moaned. "Friends, she says. For fie!"

Aethil's face fell and she rushed over to the divan to kneel next to him. "Don't say that, Sir Croy!"

"She calls us friends. Yet when I ask her for a simple favor, she refuses me. It's like she doesn't care for me at all. Isn't it, squire?"

Malden held his tongue.

"I said, lass, and I thought I made this fucking clear, that I require both my servants if I'm to be imprisoned in this cramped cell." Slag pulled away as she tried to stroke his face. "My squire, *and* my shieldmaiden."

Malden saw instantly what he was driving at. "Yes, of course, you can't possibly be expected to be at peace without Cythera here to—to—bear your shield," he said.

The dwarf scowled at him. "Quiet, boy," Slag said, and made to slap him again. Perhaps he saw the steel in Malden's eye because he did not complete the blow.

"But, Sir Croy," Aethil protested, "it was so hard getting them to release just Malton to my custody. And you don't even have a shield here. And you certainly don't need one to protect yourself from . . . me."

"She has other duties," Malden said. "The shield-maiden. Vital duties. Really, she must be brought here, to live with us."

"She must be brought here at once," Slag insisted.

Aethil pouted. "I'll do my best."

"Milady," Malden said, and before Slag could slap him, corrected himself, "your highness. Aethil. You are the queen here. Could you not simply command it and have it done? Cythera could be brought here on the moment."

"It's not that easy," Aethil sighed. "I am the queen, yes, and in theory I'm quite powerful. At least, I am among the working classes. The warriors and the nobility tend to see me as a figurehead, though, and give the Hieromagus and his council of lords all authority."

"Oh, for fie! They've foisted me off on a creature of convenience. A fucking puppet," Slag said. "How I deplore this."

Aethil's eyes went wide and she rushed to the door. "Don't fret, Sir Croy! You know I can't stand it when you fret!"

"Without my shieldmaiden I feel as if I can't so much as get up off this couch. You do understand, Aethil? Don't you?" Slag said. "How hard it can be to get through the day without a little help."

Malden thought the dwarf was pushing it too far, and that at any moment the elf queen would roll her eyes and tell Slag to find a way, somehow, to make do with only one servant. But she didn't. "There are political necessities," she said, in that tone people use when they've already been convinced, when they are going to give you what you ask for but they want you to feel sorry for what it's going to cost them. "The lords won't like it, having so many humans around me, but . . ."

"But?" Slag asked.

"I hate to deny you anything," Aethil said. And then she pouted.

Malden had to remind himself that this was the queen of an ancient race of evil warriors who tortured men for sport and had nearly driven his ancestors off the continent.

"Will you make me beg?" Slag asked, his tone hard.

"Let me see what I can do." She pulled the door open and hurried out.

The instant she was gone, Malden turned and glared at the dwarf.

"What did you do?" he demanded.

"Nothing, lad! It was all her fucking notion. She's as mad as that poncing wizard-priest thing in the black bedsheet. She knows absolutely nothing about humans, except what she read in some epoch-old storybook. Piece of bloody fiction, all about valiant knights slaying dragons and winning the hearts of lovely bits of tail like her. When she heard there was a knight in her arse-smelling dungeon, she just knew she had to have it for a pet. So she summoned Sir Croy."

"And she got you instead."

"I'll admit, I expected a certain level of disillusionment," Slag said, almost grinning. He seemed to find the situation as bizarre as Malden did. "I thought she would just send me back, as deficient to specification. I mean, clearly I'm not a storybook knight with a rearing charger and a six foot bloody lance. But the look in her eyes, lad." Slag shook his head. "You'd think I was some piece of delectable man-meat wrapped up in too-tight hose and a ripped tunic. I feared for my virtue, I did!"

"Your . . . virtue."

Slag lifted his hands in confusion. "Son, you have never known real fear till you've seen a woman half again as tall as you are rushing forward to embrace you and smother you in kisses."

"It sounds just terrible," Malden agreed.

"I didn't know she was going to fall in love with me. It just happened!"

"She fell . . . in love . . . with a dwarf," Malden said.

"Shh! A very short human, remember! And a fucking knight of fucking blasted, misbegotten Skrae. You bloody well better remember!"

Before Malden could reply, the door opened again, and Aethil stepped through, beaming.

# CHAPTER SEVENTY-EIGHT

B alint had led them to a great communal kitchen on the sixth level, a room full of long low stone tables and endless rows of sealed pantry closets. These proved to be full of nothing but dust when they were opened. They were too small to hide an armored man, so Mörget and Croy ducked behind stoves big enough to be the furnaces of great smithies and waited in the dark.

They had heard an elfin war party coming long before they saw them. The elves made no attempt to be quiet. Their bronze armor jangled and rang as they moved, marching in double time. Croy had no doubt they had orders to butcher any human they came across. Already, it seemed, the elves knew that he and Mörget were haunting the Vincularium, killing every living thing they found.

This was the biggest company of elves they'd discovered so far. At first the elves had sent only pairs of soldiers after them, then pairs of soldiers accompanied by small demons. When that proved not enough to bring down the human invaders, the patrols had been doubled in size, and doubled again.

Now they were moving en masse. They were definitely

getting the message. Croy smiled hungrily in his hiding place. Good, he thought. Let them know their doom was coming. It made revenge all the sweeter.

In the dark they only saw the elves as they crossed the kitchen, and then only by a few stray beams of red light from a lamp hung in the vaulted ceiling overhead. It was enough for Croy to see that the elves were wary and prepared. Their bronze armor had been browned by time, but the swords in their hands were keen and bright as gold. With them they had a demon perhaps ten feet across, which rippled along the floor as flat as an animate carpet. The staring faces under its skin lifted now and again to peer into a shadow or the cobwebbed interior of an oven.

Croy knew well the military posture, the perfect formations of these elves. He had fought in his share of battles. He knew what well-trained troops looked like. He'd watched common soldiers drilled by serjeants, grizzled men who forced their charges through endless repetitions of the same basic, time-honored tactics until they could march in lockstep and turn with an infantry square in their sleep.

So he knew how they would approach, and how they would react when they first made contact with their enemy. And he knew the precise moment—the moment of maximal surprise—to step out of hiding, and bring Ghostcutter down on the exposed neck of an elfin soldier. Blood spurted in the dark, wetting Croy's face. He did not blink.

Well over to his right, on the far side of the formation, Mörget leapt up with a roar. His axe swept left, Dawnbringer cut right, the blade flaring with light. Two elves were decapitated before they'd even had time to know something was wrong.

Like good soldiers, the elves did not waste time shouting among themselves in surprise or demanding orders from their captain. They broke ranks flawlessly, spreading out so they could swing their weapons without striking each other. Those too far from Croy or Mörget to attack immediately moved quickly, trying to get behind one of the humans or at least flank them.

Ghostcutter rang on a bronze shield, denting its boss. Croy danced backward, drawing his opponent, trying to force the elves to clump up again. He parried a bronze sword that came in from his right, then whirled around for a riposte, sinking his point deep in the throat of an elf.

Another sword came in low, trying to get under his guard. Croy jumped over the blade, pulling his feet up high. Before the attacker could recover and catch him on the backswing, he grabbed the elf's arm with his free hand and pulled, hard. The elf screamed as he clattered to the floor, striking the flagstones face-first. Before he could even roll over, Croy stomped on his back with one boot.

Then he tossed Ghostcutter in the air, caught it in a reverse grip, and stabbed downward into his fallen enemy's spine with a thunderous blow.

An honorless attack. The kind of attack a noble knight should not countenance. Croy had never struck such a cheap blow in his life before.

Of course, he'd never fought to avenge his lady love before either.

His face was a mask of iron hatred as he pulled his sword free and faced another attacker. An elf came running toward him, sword held low and point-on. The soldier gripped his blade around the ricasso to add stability to the lunge, which would run Croy through if he couldn't knock it away.

Before the running elf could take another step, though, Mörget's axe slammed through the armor protecting his side. It bit deep and true, cleaving through bone and muscle and into the vitals beneath. The bronze sword jumped out of the dying elf's hands. The weapon spun in the air, flashing, before it fell to clash and clatter on the flagstones.

Mörget boomed with laughter, and lifted the elf into the air, still stuck on his axe. As the rest of the company swept forward, the barbarian flicked the axe toward them and their companion's body flew through the air to smash against their shields.

"Now?" Croy asked. Fury was a cold blue flame in his heart. He was ready to take on the rest, and the demon, single-handed.

But that wasn't the plan.

"Now," Mörget agreed.

The two of them brandished their weapons in the direction of the remaining elves. They gave their best war cries—Mörget's was far more intimidating than Croy's, but he strained his throat with it.

"More flesh for Mother Death!"

"For the Lady, and for Cythera!"

Then they both turned hard on their heels and ran for the darkness at the back of the kitchen.

The elves came screaming after them, the demon racing along the floor in the midst of them. Croy's knees flashed in the air as he dashed toward a wide open space in the floor ahead, then wheeled to one side at the last moment. Mörget executed a similar maneuver.

The elves came on, their course as straight as an arrow's flight.

Enraged, perhaps terrified, desperate to catch the humans, they paid no heed to the horse blanket spread across the floor in the middle of the kitchen.

The blanket that had been pulled taut over a vast open fire pit.

Elves and demon alike fell with a terrible rattling din into the pit, arms flying, swords jumping out of hands. Those who landed atop the demon screamed and tried to scurry off its back as it thrashed in blind panic, the faces under its skin stretching outward open-mouthed and wide-eyed. Wherever it touched their bare skin, its corrosive touch scorched and seared, and the elves screamed.

Balint stepped out of the shadows and chuckled. The knocker on her shoulder grabbed at her pack straps to keep from being thrown off. "Boil-brained hedgepigs. You fell for literally the oldest trick in the book. Just be glad I couldn't get the gas pipes to light, or you'd be a demon omelet by now!" she crowed.

"What now?" Croy asked.

"Now we slaughter them before they can get out of there," Mörget suggested, as easy as if he'd said they should clean their swords and polish their armor.

"Leave them there, to fight it out with that crawling pockmark of theirs," Balint told the warriors. "We just needed to clear the way to the leather works. And so we have. Come along, you two."

Croy stared down into the fire pit awhile longer. The elves were too busy trying to get away from their pet beast to pay him any attention. He considered spitting on them.

But no. There were some things a gentleman didn't do, even to the murderers of his betrothed.

Instead he glared down at them and shouted, "You're going to die. Every last one of you will die! It's less than what you deserve for what you did to Cythera!"

# CHAPTER SEVENTY-NINE

"Stop, please," Cythera begged. "I feel I might burst!" She put her hand over her goblet before Aethil could pour her any more wine.

"More fish?" the queen of the elves asked, picking up a flat-bladed silver knife.

"No, no, thank you, your highness, but I really couldn't

swallow another bite." Cythera laughed happily and dabbed at her mouth with a beetle-silk napkin.

It matched the dress they'd put her in, an elegant gown of the same cut and style as the ones Malden and Slag wore. Aethil had told them that the silk was made from threads secreted by cave beetles. The thought had discomfited Malden considerably, even after Slag told him where real silk came from.

The fish bothered him as well. Its flesh and skin were both snowy white and it had no eyes—the dome of its forehead was just smooth skin from the dorsal fin all the way to its toothy mouth. It looked unnatural to him, especially after being roasted and swimming in thin mushroom gravy. But it didn't bother him enough that he didn't eat it. He was still hungry after days of wandering in the dark and being locked up in a filthy gaol.

Every food the elves had brought for their queen's special supper was questionable in one way or another. The wine was good but smelled of damp earth. The bread—far better than the mealy loaves they'd been given in the stockade—was the wrong color. The filets of cave beetle even tasted different underground, not nearly as gamey as the one he'd had up on the surface, in the forest, before they'd come to this benighted place.

But at least Cythera was there to share it.

Her release from the gaol had been the occasion for this feast. When she arrived, Slag—or rather, Sir Croy—actually smiled and wept a little. That had made Aethil so happy she ordered a grand celebration for the four of them. The feast was served by elves in patchwork shifts carrying platters of tarnished silver, while a musician playing a lute made of cave beetle shell serenaded them softly from one corner.

It almost felt like they weren't prisoners anymore.

Yet when the musician had been sent away, and Aethil excused herself from the table to make water, Cythera drew up her gown to show Malden one of her legs. A tattooed vine ran up her calf, spreading spiky leaves and studded with tiny, vividly purple flowers. "He couldn't cripple me," she said in a very low voice. "But I know what he was trying to do. You, as well?"

Malden nodded and hauled his own hobbled leg up onto a bench. "If I move my foot at all the pain is unbearable."

Cythera reached for his ankle before he could pull it away. "Be still," she told him. "This won't hurt." She pressed her hands around his calf and gasped a little. "It's a strong enchantment," she said, and sank back into her chair.

The muscles in Malden's leg relaxed instantly, and a wave of pure relief flushed through him. When he recovered, he grabbed Cythera's hands to look at them. On the palm of each a violet flower bloomed, and as he watched they started to send out creepers.

"It's all right," she told him. "Just try to remember to limp, or they'll know something's up."

"You worry too much," Slag said. He was drunk on mushroom wine and smiling quite a bit. "She's in the palm of my hand, I tell you. She'll do any fucking thing I say. If I tell her to let you two go—"

"I don't advise trying that," Cythera said. "This is an improvement in our situation," she whispered, "but not a reversal of fortunes."

"You mean they're still going to kill us," Malden said.

"Yes. But not immediately. Which means we have some time to work out how we're going to escape. First we need to—"

But she had to stop then, because Aethil was coming back.

"Oh, this is so nice," Aethil said, looking at her charges. "It can get so lonely in these rooms. But now—now we're like a happy family. Like a human family! The mother," she said, pressing a hand to her bosom. "The pretty children," she went on, gesturing gracefully at Malden and Cythera, "and of course," coming over to put her arms around Slag's shoulders and put her lips next to his ear, "the daddy."

She cooed and leaned her head on Slag's chest, her ringlets of coppery hair tangling in his greasy dark beard.

Cythera shot him a querulous look, but the dwarf could only raise his eyebrows to indicate his own confusion.

Getting up from her place at the table, Cythera walked over to where Aethil was trying to climb into Slag's lap. Slender as she was, it was still too small for her to fit properly. "Your highness," Cythera said, "you have such lovely eyes. May I look at them more closely?"

Aethil laughed musically, pleased by the flattery. She let Cythera peer deep into her pupils and even pull one eyelid to the side. Then Cythera took one of the queen's hands in her own and studied the lines on her palm.

"Thank you," Cythera said, and went back to sit by Malden.

"This was a perfect feast, was it not? I'm so glad you three came along. You're going to make me so happy, until you have to go away."

Malden frowned. "Perhaps we could stay here forever," he said. "If your highness wills it."

Aethil frowned and looked away from him. "I've told you, there are limits to my power. The Hieromagus has plans for you three, and I can't gainsay him. You have . . . other enemies as well. The lords are not happy about having humans in our midst."

"Maybe you just don't know how much authority you truly wield," Malden beseeched. "Maybe if you talked with him, tried to find a way to—"

Aethil started squirming on top of Slag as soon as Malden began speaking again. His words were clearly causing her great distress. Slag sat up suddenly, nearly dumping the queen onto the floor, and said, "Squire, be still. Your words are an annoyance to our fu—to our hostess."

Malden closed his mouth.

"Let's speak no more of such things," Cythera said

quickly. "Instead, let's think of what pleasures this day may bring. Your highness, your kingdom is lovely, but we've seen so little of it. Do you think it might be possible for us to walk about a bit, and view the triumphs of elfin society?"

"Now that suggestion," Aethil said, "is pleasing to my ears. Yes! I shall give you all the grand tour of my domain. I'll show you everything! Oh, you'll be amazed and delighted by our mushroom farms, I'm sure. They're so cleverly made. And you must see some of our better tunnels. Oh! Wonderful!"

She jumped up and ran to the door. "Wait here while I arrange for our escort," she told them. Before she left she turned around and looked at them. "What fun!"

"Good thinking," Malden said when she was gone. "We can look for an escape route while she's showing us where they turn beetle brains into soup."

"Indeed." Cythera got up and went over to Slag, as if she'd barely heard Malden. She peered deeply into his eyes, then grabbed one of his hands. "Hmm. You're not affected. You don't find her attractive at all, do you?"

"Who? Aethil? She's a nice enough brat, but no, my tastes run shorter and more generous in the arse."

"Just as I thought." Cythera let go of his hand. "She's completely in love with you, though."

"So I noticed. Well, can you blame her? I am a fucking perfect specimen of manhood. As far as dwarves go, anyway. Or very short humans."

"Don't flatter yourself. She's been enchanted."

"What?" Slag demanded.

Cythera scowled. "Someone gave her a love potion. Probably just before you met her for the first time—whoever walked in through that door would have looked to her like her ideal husband, the person she couldn't live without. I don't know what kind of potion they used, but it was strong enough to make her fall in love with a cave beetle if it knocked on her door."

"I'll choose not to be insulted by that comparison," Slag said.

"Such philters are dangerous to brew, much less to consume. Too strong a dose and she would have—well, she would have attacked you, rather than doted on you. She would have exerted herself," Cythera said, blushing a little, "until you both were exhausted unto death."

"Lass, come now. I wouldn't have let her do that," Slag pointed out.

"You wouldn't have had a choice." Cythera rubbed at one eye with the heel of her palm. She looked quite tired, perhaps from the work of absorbing Malden's curse. "She would have had her guards strip you and hold you down. She would have had you crippled for real, just to keep you where she wanted you. On your back and helpless."

"I suppose I'm glad they got the dosage right. But why, lass? Why do this bloody stupid thing? Just to play a trick on her? On me? And if it's magic—you don't suppose it's going to just stop working at some point, do you? Fucking magic."

"Such potions can be made to work for a single night, for a year and a day, or for a lifetime," Cythera said. "It's been long enough that I think we can rule out the mildest form. I doubt this one's going to wear off anytime soon."

"That's a relief, I suppose," Malden said. "At least we know we'll have one friend here we can count on."

"Indeed." Cythera stroked her chin. "It makes me wonder, though. A deep game is being played here. Why would anyone want her to fall in love with—with Sir Croy? Clearly that was the intention. They believed they had Croy in their gaol, so they sent him to her just after she took the potion. It must have been some elf or other who did it. But why in the world would they want that?"

"By the sound of it, there's some kind of power struggle between her and the Hieromagus," Malden suggested. "If it got out that she was sleeping with a dwarf—"

"Very short human!" Slag reminded him.

"—it would make her look bad," Malden finished.

"Perhaps. Though it sounds like the Hieromagus has little to fear from Aethil. I'd think it more likely they would give the Hieromagus the potion, to make him look silly so that Aethil gained power." Cythera shrugged. "It must be something of the sort, though. Politics. Elfin politics. I don't claim to understand. But we can make it work for us, I'm sure of it."

# CHAPTER EIGHTY

"Eight hundred years ago," Aethil told them, as they trooped through one of the winding, unfinished passages through the rock, "my ancestors came here seeking a better life. The war with the humans was dragging on and we had tired of always fighting. We're a gentle, peaceful people by nature."

Except for all the torturing and evil magic, Malden thought. Though he had to admit that it was difficult to look at Aethil and imagine her torturing anyone. Croy had made the elves sound like sadistic bastards. The Hieromagus fit that description pretty well, but perhaps—like humans—elves weren't all of a sort. Maybe only some of them were cruel and decadent villains. Malden had always found there was more than one way to look at any given story. Certainly Aethil's version of the events leading to the elves being driven into the Vincularium and buried there to rot differed considerably from the historical accounts he'd heard.

"We sealed ourselves in, because we didn't wish to be followed. In the early days we expected always to be invaded. The humans really had treated us very badly." She stopped and put a hand to your mouth. "Not that I blame you for that, Sir Croy!"

"It's all right, lass," Slag told her. "All water under the fu—under the bridge, right?"

"You're so generous and forgiving," Aethil said. She slid her hand under his gown and touched his chest with her fingers. "Such a good heart."

"These tunnels," Cythera said. "The dwarves didn't build them. I assume the Elders dug them?"

Aethil blinked and looked at the human woman. "What? Oh. Yes—as I said, we expected at any time to be attacked. We fortified this place as best we could, and our ancestors built secret tunnels so that we could surprise any invaders. The entire Vincularium is riddled with them now. We can go anywhere we like, to any hall or chamber, without being seen."

Slag slapped the wall with one hand. "Not the best plan, honestly. You've weakened the mountain, like worms digging their way through a moldy apple. I'm surprised the whole place hasn't fallen on your heads by now."

Aethil shrugged prettily. "Sometimes there are cave-ins. But they're very rare, and I try not to think about the ones who get hurt."

Malden remembered to pretend to limp as she led them out of the tunnel and into a long hallway where mist wreathed the floor and the stink of manure was thick in the air. "In the early days there was no food down here," Aethil told them. She wrinkled her nose but didn't lift her gown from where it trailed on the wet floor. "We never had to cultivate crops before—always we lived on the produce and game of the forests up on the surface. Our ancestors had to teach us what kind of plants would grow down here, so far away from the sun, and how it could be done."

She showed them endless racks of wrapped cylinders, and had an elf in a patchwork smock unpeel one to show the mushrooms growing inside. Other workers were busy cleaning up a mess in one part of the farm corridor. Malden saw manure splashed across one wall, and some of the racks had been knocked over. "What happened there?" he asked.

"Vandalism," Aethil said, her voice thick with sadness. "It's—not my favorite thing about our life here. But sometimes we get very bored, with so little to do. The soldiers and especially the nobles sometimes break things or make messes just to alleviate the tedium. And then, of course, my little friends have to clean up after them."

One of the workers came over and knelt before Aethil. "It is our joy to work in your service, highness," he said.

Aethil let him kiss her hand. He seemed near tears when he rose to his feet again and went back to work.

"They do work so very hard, and get so very little for their labors," Aethil said. "I try to make their lives easier when I can. But with so many nobles and soldiers to support, there's always more work to be done than we have workers for."

"How many nobles are there?" Malden asked, frowning.

"About half of us come from ancient stock," Aethil explained. "And of course, any elf whose ancestor was a lord or lady is exempted from all labor. Is this not the way in human lands as well?"

"Our highborns are shiftless parasites, yes," Malden said. "But only one in a thousand, say, can make that claim. Are you saying, though, that an entire half of your people are doomed to endless servitude? Is there no way for them to improve their station?"

Aethil seemed confused by the question. "How would they do that?"

"By proving themselves in battle, perhaps." That was the traditional way for commoners to become knights in Skrae, and once a man was a knight there was no limit to how far he could rise.

"We have nothing to do battle with down here," Aethil replied. "Except our memories."

Malden ignored the wistful look on her face. "But there are other ways, surely. In the city where I was born—it is called Ness—men are free to improve their lot through labor, and they can leave their wealth to their children, to try to give them a better life than they knew."

Aethil gave him a smile that clearly was meant to be pitying. To Malden it just looked condescending. "Wealth. You're speaking of money. I understand the concept from my books—and that it seems to be the main source of unhappiness among humans."

"Fair enough," Malden granted, "but it also allows us to better ourselves."

"Such distinctions are unknown among the Elders. We are each born to our rank, as appointed by our ancestors."

Malden thought of the elf soldier he'd spoken with, who said his father had been a soldier and his son would be one, too. He'd assumed the soldier merely hoped for his sons to take up the family trade, but it sounded as if they had no choice.

In Skrae they had the Lady—the Goddess Croy worshipped—who was supposed to place everyone in their appropriate station. It was a pleasing theology if you happened to be born to high estate. There was good reason why the poor of Ness tended to worship Sadu the Blood-god instead, who judged both the high and the low. "This system leaves no room for ambition, for talent, for merit," he pointed out. "The poor are all doomed to work like slaves, while the rich—"

"Quiet, boy!" Slag said.

Malden looked up in surprise. He saw for the first time that Aethil looked distinctly uncomfortable with this turn of conversation. He bit back angry words for fear of offending her. No good could come of that.

Slag quickly apologized for him. "You'll have to forgive him. He's from a poor family, and one not known for its wisdom. He doesn't understand how hard it can be to be the one in power, the one who has to make all the decisions."

The one with all the servants, Malden thought, but he kept his peace.

"Ah. Well, your race is very young, still. In time I'm sure you'll all find a way to accept the natural order of things, as we have. Come this way—I want to show you our flocks."

She took them down to the end of the tunnel, to a wide room that got very little of the red sun of the Vincularium. A herder lit torches for them so they could see better. They were on the lowest dry level of the Vincularium, and its gallery was half submerged in the pool of water at the bottom of the central shaft. Hundreds of giant cave beetles had congregated there, grazing on the green scum that coated the walls and floor.

"Can you imagine," Aethil asked, "that before we came here, Elders actually considered insects to be inedible? They even thought they would sicken and die if they accidentally swallowed a gnat or a spider!" She laughed. "We would have starved centuries ago if that was actually the case. Our ancestors must have been very stern with us back then, to be able to convince us that we could actually eat beetle steak."

Or her forebears were just that hungry, Malden thought. How desperate had that first generation gotten, he wondered—had they considered cannibalism? Had they come down here themselves and gnawed at the green stuff on the walls? He shuddered at the thought. Yet he knew that people would eat anything if there was no choice. He'd seen it plenty of times in Ness, where the poorest of the poor lived off the kitchen scraps of the wealthy, all the small bones and bits of stringy hide that proper folk considered worthless garbage.

"You've mentioned your ancestors a few times now,"

Cythera observed, "as if they were creatures separate from yourselves. Do you mean the revenants we've seen? Were they the ones who taught you what was good to eat?"

"The revenants?" Aethil asked. She laughed uproariously. "You mean the undying bodies we use as guards? Oh, no! Those are only the empty vessels of the ancestors. I speak of the *souls* of those who went before."

"Their memory, then, written down in books, or passed down orally from one teller to the next," Cythera pondered.

"Hardly. I'll show you what I mean, at the end of our excursion. It really is a wonder to finish with. First, though, come this way. I want to show you our nursery, where our little elf babies are raised and trained to their stations. They're so cute!"

# CHAPTER EIGHTY-ONE

Ghostcutter sliced through the bones of a defleshed arm and cut deep into the side of a revenant who was reaching for Mörget's throat. The barbarian's mace, held in his weaker left hand, caved in the abomination's skull. Still it kept grasping for Mörget's neck, so Croy yanked his sword free of its armor and wheeled around to cut its remaining arm to pieces.

Cold hands dragged at Croy's cloak from behind. He growled and flung himself backward, but couldn't break the grip. Mörget brought Dawnbringer high, gripping its hilt in both hands now, and cut a revenant in half, slicing through its wasted body right down the middle. The Ancient Blade lit up with brilliant fire as it cleaved through collarbone, ribs, and pelvis.

The light was bright enough to blind Croy, if only for a moment. Among the undead warriors it had a far more devastating effect.

The revenants convulsed in holy terror and staggered back. The hands holding Croy released him. He kicked backward with one boot and felt a near-skeletal warrior's midsection crumple into dust. As the revenants threw up their thin arms to block the light of Mörget's blade, Croy took his chance and swung Ghostcutter through a wide arc that severed finger bones and elbows and ended with the blade embedded in a silently screaming skull.

One revenant, scuttling back to get away from the light, put a bootless foot down on what appeared to be a loose flagstone. The stone retracted on a hidden spring and Croy heard a clicking sound.

"Get down," he shouted at Mörget. The two of them ducked at the same moment a load of stones tied into a ball came whistling over their heads. The massive stone orb swept through every revenant in its path, shattering their bodies and scattering their fragile bones all about the room.

Croy leapt up to face a headless corpse that swung a morningstar at Mörget's back. Ghostcutter whistled through the air and the weapon clunked to the floor, still clutched in a disembodied hand. Croy ducked again as the ball of stone came back on its return swing and utterly disintegrated the headless foe, sending an arc of bone fragments high into the air.

Mörget rolled to the side, out of the path of Balint's swinging trap. He sprang to his feet, sword and mace held high. Croy leaned back out of the way of the stone ball and pointed Ghostcutter toward the end of the hall, where the revenants had first appeared.

None showed there now. In the vast hall of the leather works, not a single revenant was left standing.

Croy heaved for breath, his body still twitching with bloodlust. He looked over at Mörget and saw a bodiless arm crawling up the barbarian's leg.

Mörget followed his gaze down, then laughed wickedly and tore the arm free of his boot. As if he were plucking petals from a daisy, he tore off the finger bones one by one and tossed them over his shoulder. The arm kept twisting, trying to break free of the barbarian's grip, but it was harmless now and he dropped it without ceremony.

"Done?" Mörget asked.

"Done, with this bunch at least," Balint agreed, stepping out of the shadows. Her knocker jumped down to the flagstones with a gentle thud and went running forward, rapping on the flagstones over and over with its knuckles.

Croy wiped sweat from his upper lip and looked around. They'd been so busy fighting the revenants he hadn't had a chance to study his surroundings. The leather works weren't much to see, it turned out. The hall was filled with stone benches, and boxes of rusty tools filled high shelves against the walls. Hooks hung down from the ceiling in a hundred places, but any hides that might have been cleaned or cut or tanned here had long since rotted away.

"There's an escape shaft that way," Balint said, pointing into the darkness. "It's how my crew and I came in, back when I still thought this place was emptier than a spinster's womb. We planned on taking the barrels out that way, so I had Murin drag them up here. If Slurri and I had come with him . . . but instead I had to go find Urin and gloat over his failure." She shook her head. "I could be halfway to Redweir by now, and a good bath, and a session with the best mustache plucker in town."

Croy only half heard her. "The barrels will be up there?" he asked. He still had no idea why Balint wanted the things now, but she swore they would be instrumental in slaughtering the elves. Therefore, he intended to get to them as soon as possible.

"Aye."

He nodded and strode toward the arch at the far end of the room. Ballint and the barbarian followed.

"How can five barrels destroy an entire city?" Mörget asked. He was not consumed by vengeance, and therefore was still thinking. In an offhand way, Croy was glad one of them was still asking questions.

"I told you, you daft pillock. The barrels contain the most powerful weapon the dwarves ever built. It's terrifying, what they're capable of. If everybody had what's in those barrels, they would never make war again because they'd be too horrified to use them."

"Even if they were full of magical swords," Mörget said, "we still only have six arms between us to swing them."

"Not every weapon in this world needs a strong arm to wield it," Ballint replied.

"If you say so. But it also occurs to me it's been eight hundred years since those barrels were stored away. Won't the weapons inside have rusted or rotted or—"

"No, no, no, the barrels are sealed tighter than a toad's arsehole, for one thing, and any way, the substance inside has a high measure of hydrophobicity—"

"High what?" Mörget asked.

"It's—It repels water, and that means it should last near on forever if it isn't—"

"But how? How does it do that?"

Croy roared and turned to face the other two. "It's magic, of course. That's what she's saying. It's magic, so it doesn't wear off. Now let's get on with it!"

He passed through the arch, not waiting for a reply. The room beyond was filled with enormous tanning vats, great stone cylinders far taller than Croy's head. Sitting between two such vessels stood the barrels in question. They were good-sized hogsheads, made of a greenish stoneware. They gleamed dully in the candlelight.

"That's them," Ballint said, crowing in excitement. "Now we just have to move them up to the top level."

"Where all the revenants gather? But why?" Mörget asked.

"Let's just do it," Croy said, and bent to pick up one of the barrels. "I tire of waiting. I tire of questions. I want vengeance on the evil ones, and I want it now."

# CHAPTER EIGHTY-TWO

The elfin children were as beautiful as their parents, and they laughed even more. Aethil led the three of them through the nursery, pausing frequently to coo over the babies where they slept in narrow cribs made out of beetle shells. "They're so adorable. I envy the mothers so. Sometimes I come down here and just watch them sleep, when I'm feeling sorrowful."

"You have no heir as of yet, Aethil?" Cythera asked.

"What? No, of course not, I—ah . . . But you can't know. We queens of the elves are different from others. When the time comes to produce an heir, I will find my proper mate and for the first time I will know real joy." She glanced at Slag as if sizing him up as a candidate for that position. The dwarf was chewing on his fingernails. He seemed to have no interest at all in elf babies. "I will conceive immediately, and bear a single child, a daughter, who will become queen as soon as she is born."

"You don't get to finish your reign?" Malden asked.

"I . . . cannot. You see, I will die in childbirth. Just as my mother did."

Cythera made a sound of utter pity, a kind of deep, heartfelt moan. Aethil favored them with a bright smile that had little warmth in it.

"Enough—we need not speak of that. Let me show you the rest of the nursery." She led them out into a larger cavern full of noise, where children were playing elaborate games. Malden recognized most of the games at once, as he'd played them—or something very like them—as a child himself: seek-the-hidden-one, catch-the-ogre, even knights-and-elves, where pairs of boys sparred with flimsy swords of scrap wood. He wondered if they called it by the same name.

"Until they are seven years old," Aethil said, raising her voice over the noise, "they are schooled here. We make sure they're educated in their history, in the vital arts, and given a smattering of arcane knowledge. Not enough to let them do any serious mischief, of course."

Malden saw one little boy being chased by dragons of smoke, long ribbony illusions cast by a girl who laughed to see him run. Such a spell, he knew, would take a human sorcerer decades to master, and the sorcerer would pay a terrible price for the knowledge. Here it was a commonplace.

"What source of power does your magic draw on?" Cythera asked, in awe of even this small magic. "Surely they don't summon demons to teach them these spells, and no child that young could ever master even the basics of witchcraft."

Aethil laughed at the idea. "Our ancestors provide all the magical power we could ever require. Demons! Such foolishness! No one would ever be so foolish as to *summon* one of those."

Malden and Slag shared a knowing look. Someone had to have summoned the demon that Mörget came to slay. It was impossible for demons to come into the world unbidden—that was the pact the Bloodgod had made with humanity, that he would keep his terrible creatures walled away in the pit of souls. A sorcerer had to release them, and hopefully control them. So who had summoned the amorphous demon if not an elf? Malden suspected it must be the Hieromagus. The wizard-priest would certainly have enough power to do it, and his forgetfulness might explain why the demon seemed to be loose to prey upon men and animals at its leisure.

Aethil wouldn't know about that, it seemed, and there was no point questioning her on the point, but Malden filed it away as another mystery of the elves.

The elf queen led them farther into a library, where older children were taking a lesson. While the very young had been dressed all alike in simple smocks, those of six and seven years were variegated in their garb. Half of them wore patchwork shifts, old and tattered and ill-fitting. The other half wore sumptuous robes and gowns. These must be the children of the noble class, Malden surmised— though he was confused as to why the poorer children were receiving the same education. "In human lands, only the very rich teach their children to read," he said.

"But then how are the laboring classes expected to learn anything?" Aethil asked, quite scandalized.

"Mostly, they aren't," Malden told her. "They either learn a trade, through apprenticing to a master, or they work as unskilled labor all their lives." And that was only in the Free City, he thought. Outside of Ness, nine of every ten humans spent their lives on a farm, and never learned more than how to hold a sickle properly or how to plant seed. In the whole kingdom of Skrae perhaps only one man in twenty knew how to read and form letters.

"Why—that's—barbarous," Aethil said. She made the word sound obscene. "You keep your people ignorant? They can't even read? I thought you humans were nothing like the old stories, but this—"

Cythera stepped in hurriedly to change the subject. "All this talk of education has made me remember something I wanted to ask you."

"All right," Aethil said. She had a new look on her face, a kind of guarded doubt that Malden didn't like at all.

Cythera spoke quickly, though, and soon Aethil was

nodding along. "When we first encountered your soldiers," she said, "I was surprised to find that they spoke Skraeling—the language of my people. The accent is different, and the pronunciation of some words radically so, but we seem to be able to understand each other just fine."

Malden had wondered about that himself. In the course of subsequent events—their capture, their imprisonment, the threat of immediate death, and being forced to act as if he were Slag's servant—he supposed he'd put it out of mind. Yet it was wondrously strange. Not even all humans spoke the same tongue. He'd met sailors from Skilfing and the Rifnlatt and the other Northern Kingdoms, and was unable to understand a word of their speech—much less the courtly and decadent language of the Old Empire, with its myriad tenses and declensions. The dwarves had their own language as well, and even used a different alphabet. Yet the elfin and Skraeling tongues sounded almost identical.

"Your soldier told me that I was speaking elfin," Cythera said with a little laugh. "I was hoping you might shed some light on this puzzle."

The doubt on Aethil's face had turned to pity by the time Cythera finished. "You poor creatures. You don't know your own history, do you?"

"I beg your pardon?" Cythera asked.

"But of course, your lives are short, and you have no ancestors to teach you." Aethil placed a delicate hand on Cythera's arm. "You speak our language and we speak yours because they *are* the same language."

"But—how?" Malden asked.

Aethil tilted her head to one side. "What do you know of your past? Do they teach you even that your people came from the Old Empire, exiled by decree? That you landed on the shores of this continent with nothing but what you could carry away? It sounds as if they don't teach you at all about the age of brotherhood our people shared."

"No, they never mentioned that," Malden agreed. "Because there was no such age." He looked at Cythera. "Was there? We fought the elves, and we won. That's what I learned."

Aethil laughed. "Oh, perhaps. But not until later. When you landed here, it's true there were a few skirmishes, as we didn't know what you wanted. Soon, though, we realized you couldn't even feed yourselves. You didn't know what plants were edible and which were poisonous. You had never seen snow, and you weren't ready for the first winter. You would have died out if we didn't take pity on you."

Cythera shook her head. "You're saying that our forebears relied on the elves for survival? That we weren't matched in constant warfare for the land?"

"Hardly. The continent is enormous! There was plenty of room for both our nations. We took you under our wing. Taught you how to survive here, and more. We taught you our language and even how to work magic. For centuries we lived amongst each other—even intermarrying, though, sadly, our unions never bore fruit." This with a longing glance at Slag. "Oh, you humans. We loved you, as Elders should love their juniors."

"But something happened," Malden said. "Something changed. There was a war. There was a war that lasted what, twenty years?" He looked to Cythera and she nodded.

"Oh, yes," Aethil agreed. "And it only ended when we came here."

"But—why? If we were so happy together?"

Aethil blinked her eyes. "You don't even know about the Prophetess? How one of our own—an Elder, one of our Hieromagi—betrayed her own people? How she taught your people religion and turned them against us? She demanded that the humans worship her, and they did. Then she went too far, and demanded we worship her as well, that we renounce the ancestors and take her as our only goddess. When we refused, she set you at our destruction."

"We— She— Who— But what . . . ?" Malden was so

confused he couldn't speak. He'd never heard any of this.

"You rose up against us, and we were caught unawares," Aethil went on. "It was all done with great stealth and cunning. In one night you slaughtered nine of every ten Elders in their beds. Those few who survived held out for twenty years, but in the end we retreated here."

"That's not the story we tell at all," Cythera said.

It damned well wasn't. Malden felt the blood rush out of his face at the thought. If all this was true . . . He'd never been particularly proud of his country, or his people. They were far too base and hypocritical to allow that. But he'd never thought their history was one of mass murder and deceit.

It seemed his people had good reason to want the elves locked away and forgotten. Suddenly he understood why nobody had broken open the Vincularium in so many centuries—because they didn't want to learn the secrets it held.

# CHAPTER EIGHTY-THREE

Perhaps discomfited by the story she'd told them, Aethil took her leave of them for a while. She went and sat with a group of children struggling over a history lesson, and coached them through the hard words and the complicated tenses of elfin writing. Malden saw how much love and reverence even these children showed their queen, and he thought he finally understood her place in elfin society. She gave the workers something to believe in, an emblem of their traditions and heritage. The Hieromagus must find her very useful, he thought, for keeping the workers in line. So then why, he pondered, had he gone to the trouble of making her fall in love with Slag, which could only discredit her with these people?

Speaking of the dwarf, Malden looked around and saw him climbing on a high bookshelf. A ladder had been mounted on the wall for this purpose. Slag drew one slim volume off a top shelf, then scrambled down to floor level and started paging through it. Apparently he didn't find what he was looking for, because he started to climb back up again.

Cythera grabbed the hem of his robe and pulled him back down. "We need to make a plan," she said. "This tour is almost over. We'll never have a chance like this again."

"You mean to make a run for it now," Malden said, nodding. "We'll need a diversion. Slag, you could grab one of the children and threaten to—"

"Absolutely not!" Cythera cried out.

Aethil looked up from the lesson to study the three of them with questioning eyes. Cythera made a great show of smiling and bowing before Slag, as a proper shieldmaiden should.

When they were unobserved again, she went on. "I won't allow that, Malden. These children are innocents. Don't you believe in anything?"

"Not if it keeps me imprisoned in this pretty cage," he told her.

"Lad, lass, calm yourselves. We can't make a break for it now anyway. Where would we go?"

"The escape shaft. The one Balint opened up for us," Malden insisted.

The dwarf shook his head. "Forget it, lad. That's clear on the other fucking side of the Vincularium. Assuming we even made it back to the central shaft, I could lead you there, aye, but you saw those worm tunnels the elves have made. They'd be there waiting for us. No, we need a better plan than just legging it. I still think if we work on yon queen of peons, we can convince her to make a case for us, and get us released. She'll do anything I—"

He stopped speaking because Aethil had finished her lesson and was coming toward them. "I'm so sorry for that," she said. "You've been so patient, waiting for me. But now, let us return to our tour. I have something very important to show you."

"Of course, your highness," Cythera said.

"Sir Croy?" Aethil said. "Now what are you doing up there?"

The dwarf had returned to the bookshelves. He was leaning far out across the top shelf, stretching his arm to reach a book that was just too far away.

"What? I just—"

His fingers snagged the book he wanted and sent it flopping down to the floor. Its spine broke instantly and half its pages turned to silvery flakes.

"Shit-sucking cock bollocks!" the dwarf shouted.

Suddenly every elfin child in the library was staring at him. Slag's face went bright red and he hurriedly climbed back down.

Aethil had picked up the book he'd knocked out of its place. Carefully, she tucked the loose pages—those that hadn't turned to dust as she touched them—back inside the loose covers. "What did you want this one for?" she asked.

"It's a book the dwarves thought didn't exist anymore!" Slag exclaimed. He reached for it, but Aethil held it out of his grasp. "I can't believe I found it!"

"A dwarven book? Yes, I can recognize a few of these runes, though not many." Aethil frowned. "But, Sir Croy, what would a human want with such a thing?"

Slag's eyes went wide and his mouth opened but no words came out.

What would a human want with a dwarven book?

Malden, never at a loss for a quick cover story, raced to the rescue. "Sir Croy is a man of great learning. He's studied the lore of all the races of Skrae," he said. "Even those treacherous cutthroats, the dwarves."

"Fucking bastards, them," Slag agreed. "Never trust a dwarf, I always say."

"I didn't even know we had any of these," Aethil said, looking down at the book. "I suppose it must have been left behind when the dwarves abandoned this place. It is of interest to you?"

Slag nodded carefully. "Of—some—small academic interest only, but—"

"Then you shall have it, as my gift," Aethil said. She knelt down and handed it to Slag. "Perhaps you'll think of something you can give me, in return." The look on her face left no doubt in Malden's mind what she hoped her present would be. "But read it later. We really should go see the hall of the ancients now."

"What's there?" Malden asked.

Aethil smiled. "Our ancestors. As promised. I want you to meet them."

# CHAPTER EIGHTY-FOUR

Aethil led them down a long series of curving tunnels that ended in an irregular cavern—no dwarven hall, this, but a natural cave. Torches standing in cressets here and there lit the place near as bright as day. Stalactites hung down from the high ceiling, reminding Malden of the spires of Ness, but inverted and hung from a stony sky. He touched one as they passed and felt its wet, stony surface.

"How do they not fall?" he asked, imagining how little he would like to be underneath one when it did.

"No one knows that," Aethil told him, "nor why they grew like this in the first place. I've heard a theory, though I give it little credence, that these are the roots of some enormous tree high above us. Though how a tree's roots should come to be made of stone I cannot say."

Once the floor must have been equally covered in stalagmites, but many of these had been cut down to make a walkway—the floor of the cave would have been impassible otherwise. A trail of them like stepping-stones ran from one end of the cave to the other. They looked a great deal like tree stumps, which got Malden thinking. "Trees. They say the elves loved their trees, when they lived above the ground."

Aethil's face grew wistful for a moment. "I've read about trees. They do sound lovely. I'd like to see one . . . but of course, that can never be."

"They're . . . even lovelier than you can imagine," Cythera said. She looked at Malden with wide eyes, and gave him a barely perceptible nod. "The way they are—so—green. And tall." She shook her head and looked to the thief. "Words fail me, I—"

"They shimmer," he said, catching on. "In the summertime, when they are cloaked in verdant leaves, every gust of breeze that comes by makes them shiver. The leaves rustle together until it sounds as if they whisper secrets amongst themselves. The shade they make is dappled, and cool, and a blessing on a hot day. Ah, but they save their best beauty for the days of autumn, when the air grows crisp, and they turn all the colors of fire. A thousand trees in serried ranks, orange and yellow and red, shimmering like a sea aflame, the trunks bending in the wind, the leaves falling like a rain of gold . . . 'Tis a glory to see."

Aethil's face went completely blank as she listened to him. She didn't move a muscle as his description went on.

He thought he had touched something in her, something deep in her ancestral memory.

Then she recovered herself and looked down at her hands with sad eyes. "Forgive me. I was lost there for a moment." She laughed prettily. "You fill my head with fancies! Almost you make me think I'd like to go up to the surface, just to see all the things I've read about."

"The seal that locked your people away has been breached. The way is open, for one who is not afraid of revenants," Cythera pointed out. "You could just go up there to the entrance hall and peek out. There are trees not a hundred yards from where we came in."

Aethil shook her head, her copper curls dancing in the torchlight. "I'll thank you to stop tempting me now. We have much to see today, and tomorrow—tomorrow things will be different. Come."

Malden opened his mouth to speak again, to describe the feel of wind on one's face, the warmth of the sun, the serene majesty of clouds—but Cythera pinched his arm, hard, and he realized that this was not the time to push.

The four of them passed through the cave and came to a stone arch at its end. There, a pair of revenants stood guard. They stirred when the humans approached, but Aethil spoke soothing words and they stood down.

Beyond the arch was a wide mezzanine that looked down into a vast hall of dwarven work, with marble floor and walls and countless columns holding up a vaulted ceiling. The walls below them were pockmarked, however, with hundreds of narrow tunnel mouths. Strangely, the tunnels could not be reached from the floor—anyone seeking to use them would have to scale the smooth marble blocks, which even for Malden would be a challenge. The vast chamber was empty, the distant floor looking scoured clean.

"I've shown you how our lives begin," Aethil said, her voice quite serious and even reverent. "Now you'll learn how they end. Or rather, how they are transformed, for in a very real way, we elves are immortal. When our bodies reach a certain age, when they slow down and are beset by aches and pains, we come to stand here and join with the ancestors. It is a profound event in our lives, and one we take with utter solemnity. What I am about to do is mild sacrilege, honestly, but it's important you see this."

A large brass bell with a handle hung from a hook near the door. Aethil took it down, then holding it carefully, rang it once, loud and clearly. Then she put it back on the hook.

"Nothing is lost," she said. "Our memories, our souls, join with those of all our ancestors here. Our bodies become empty husks but they walk still, and are given simple tasks to perform. Like guarding the arch back there."

"You're talking about the revenants," Cythera said.

"Yes. That is how our bodies become immortal. But for our souls, a far better future awaits."

Malden heard a faint rushing sound, like water flowing through pipes. He stared down into the marble hall, wondering what horror he was about to witness.

He did not have to wait long.

Whitish fluid sluiced down out of one of the tunnel mouths, then another. Soon, from every conduit the viscous stuff poured in a torrent. It splashed and sloshed as it hit the marble floor, then gathered in a pool that rose to fill the open space. As Malden watched, repulsed, it grew thicker and climbed toward them, bits of its substance shooting forth like tendrils to reach ever higher.

In that white pool, faces loomed toward them, pressing against the skin that formed over the fluid. Angular, beautiful faces—the faces of elves. There were thousands of them, and they lifted toward Aethil, smiling, laughing silently. Beckoning.

Aethil took a step back from the edge of the mezzanine. Her face flushed and she turned her eyes away. "Even now, I feel the desire to enter the mass," she said. "Though my time has not come. It is so hard to resist. How I long to see my mother's face for the first time, and to see again friends I've loved who have gone on . . . Sir Croy, please, take my hands. Hold me to this place, so that I am not tempted to leap into my destiny too soon!"

"Bloody fuck," Slag said, forgetting that he was trying not to swear. He grabbed the elfin queen to hold her back. "This is your—"

"The ancestral mass," she confirmed. "The life force of every Elder who ever lived, every one of us who perished—their memories, their dreams, their thoughts, made tangible. It preserves our history. It sustains us—it dug the tunnels you've seen, and it taught us how to grow mushrooms and harvest the meat and milk of the cave beetles. In the early days it went so far as to gather food for us, and tend to us when we were sick."

Malden could only sneer in horror at the thought of that stuff touching him, that gooey, dreadful substance. It looked soft in the way dead things are soft, pale in the way corpses are pale. The curdled souls of millions of dead elves, all of them swirled together in a shapeless accretion. It lived, after a fashion, but only in a fashion that made him want to kill it. Though how anyone—even Mörget—would go about destroying something so large and so lacking in qualities, Malden could not imagine.

"Without it, we would have perished centuries ago," Aethil said. She sounded like a woman looking in awe into a majestic canyon, or a mother watching her baby take its first steps. She loved the damned thing, he thought. She truly loved it, because it wasn't just some pile of memories. It was her family—her legacy and her loved ones, all at once.

Malden tried to see it through her eyes. He tried to understand what the elves must think of this thing, this slimy savior. He couldn't do it.

He just wanted it to die.

The psychic effect of the mass didn't just effect Aethil. Cythera reeled, too, and pressed her hands to either side of her head. She seemed desperate to get away, edging slowly back toward the archway—if the mass attracted Aethil, it repelled Cythera equally. Malden supposed it must know of the magic in her skin, or perhaps it had this effect on any daughter of a witch. He grabbed her arm to help steady her and she met his eyes. "You recognize it, from his—from the barbarian's—from the description," she gasped.

"Aye," Malden whispered.

It was Mörget's demon, all right. Though a thousand times bigger than the barbarian had thought.

Pieces of the mass—mere drops of its substance—splashed up onto the mezzanine. Some were ten feet across. They drew themselves up into amorphous blobs, the faces under their skin crowding toward Aethil, beseeching with her. Clearly the mass could split off small parts of itself to perform various tasks. One of those pieces must have been the thing Mörget fought on the eastern slope of the Whitewall Mountains.

"We must go," Aethil insisted. "Please, lead me away. I cannot seem to take a step on my own."

The three of them helped propel her back through the archway and into the cave of stalactites beyond. Once out of the hall of ancients she seemed to recover quickly. She looked to them all with grateful eyes.

"You needed to see that," she said softly. "You needed to see how beautiful the ancestral mass is."

"For fuck's sake why?" Slag demanded.

Aethil looked away. "It has been decided. Tomorrow you—all of you—will be joining it. It's a privilege beyond compare. The first humans to enter the mass! You should welcome this, with happy countenance. Though I'll admit, I'll miss you all when you're gone."

# CHAPTER EIGHTY-FIVE

"Heave!" Balint called. Croy and Mörget hauled on the ropes they held, their backs straining. Croy's arms felt as numb as wood, but still he pulled. "Heave!"

The barrels shifted a foot farther up the ramp.

They were a quarter of the way up, with a good hundred feet of incline to go.

Each of the barrels was too heavy for the knight or the barbarian to carry themselves, and the five of them together made an immense weight. They could be turned on their sides and rolled across flat stretches of floor, but getting them up to higher levels was beyond human strength.

"Heave!"

Luckily Balint had a pulley in her pack, and enough rope to make a block and tackle. Croy understood little of how that actually helped—something to do with multiplying the force involved, the dwarf had said. He hadn't really been listening. What he did know was that the barrels were moving, inching their way up a long ramp to the top level of the Vincularium.

"Heave!"

Of course, once the humans and the dwarf did get up there, the revenants would certainly come to kill them. Croy and Mörget would have all the grim work they could handle, fighting off the undead elves long enough to get the barrels into place.

He didn't worry about that. He kept all his attention on his rope. It helped if he thought there was an elf in a noose on the other end.

"Heave!"

"Useless dwarf, be still!" Mörget shouted. "You aren't helping."

Up on top of the barrels, Balint looked down at the barbarian with a hurt expression. "If you don't pull at the same time, we run the risk of breaking the rope. At which point the barrels will slide all the way back down—and hopefully, roll right over your bloody big foot in the process," she said. "Now, together, heave!"

Croy pressed his boots hard against the surface of the ramp and pulled for all he was worth.

"I don't understand why we're doing this at all," Mörget said. "Yes, yes, it's a powerful weapon. More powerful than anything I've seen before, you say. But my sword and my axe are good weapons, too. Good enough, if you ask me."

"Heave! And what of your demons, friend? What of those creeping birdshits you came to slay? You've seen how hard it is to kill them with your pig-sticker and your wood-chopper. Wouldn't you prefer to kill them all in one stroke? Heave!"

Mörget grunted explosively, but he heaved.

"Tell me again, then, why this will work," he insisted.

Balint sighed dramatically. "Heave!" Her knocker tapped away at the top of one barrel as if trying to guess what was inside. "The entire Vincularium is held up by three massive columns. Heave! It's an elegant design, a real joy to look at, but it's about as vulnerable as a maidenhead when the fleet comes in. Heave! It's like a three-legged stool. Not much use if you—*heave!*—remove one leg. Shatter one of those columns, just one, and—"

"And the whole thing crashes down," Mörget said.

"Heave!"

Croy's back burned with the effort, but he heaved.

"The weapons in the barrel will let us cut through such a column?" the barbarian asked. "Won't one of us need to be here to use the weapons, though? And that one will be killed, too."

"Heave! That's the best part. We can set the barrels so they activate only after we leave. By the time they take light, we'll be in the escape shaft and headed home. We'll have to run like a pregnant—*heave!*—a pregnant lass for the privy, but we'll escape with our hides intact, and the whole damned mountain will come down, crushing every living thing in this hole. Heave!"

"The whole mountain, you say," Mörget repeated. Then he let out a booming laugh.

"Heave!" he called, in chorus with Balint.

Croy pulled hard on the rope. Would he go with them, he wondered, when the time came? What remained for him outside this dark pit? Perhaps he would stay, and watch, and listen to the elves scream as their bodies were crushed to pulp.

Yes. He thought he might enjoy that.

"Heave!"

# CHAPTER EIGHTY-SIX

On their way back to Aethil's chambers they were stopped by an elfin soldier who gasped for breath. He took the queen aside and gave her some desperate message that clouded her face with worry. When she came back to them, she looked confused and hurt. "Something terrible has happened," she told them. "A group of our soldiers has returned from patrol, with only half their numbers—and that half terribly wounded." She shook her head. "The messenger did not know what befell them. It must have been a cave-in in one of the tunnels. I'm sorry, my friends, but I must go help tend to the injured. I'll see you again, Sir Croy, before you—before—well, I'll see you tonight. Perhaps . . . perhaps you'll give me some token of your esteem, to strengthen me for the ordeal I am about to face."

"To be sure, lass, if you want my kerchief to wear, or—"

Aethil bowed low and grabbed the dwarf by the beard. Without further warning she pressed her mouth to his, kissing him long and deeply. Her arms wrapped around his neck and she sank against him, pushing Slag back until his back collided with the cave wall. "There," she said when she broke the embrace. "That will sustain me. Until later . . . my love."

She departed then, with many a backward glance over her shoulder. When she was gone, Slag rubbed at his face and combed out his beard with his fingers.

"Like being sucked dry by a moray eel," he said.

The messenger remained behind to take them back to the royal apartments. At least, Malden thought, they wouldn't have to wait for their doom in the elfin gaol. When the messenger brought them to Aethil's door, he saluted the guards stationed there and said, "The queen's pets are your responsibility now. Make sure they don't leave this room."

The soldiers leered and shoved the humans and the dwarf through the door. It was bolted behind them, and though Malden knocked again and again on the door, demanding food and drink, there was no answer.

Out of options, the three of them made themselves as comfortable as they might. Slag sat down to pick at the rotten pages of his book, laying out pieces of time-browned paper carefully on a table, as if assembling some puzzle. Cythera dropped heavily into a cushioned chair and put her hands over her eyes, as though the lamplight in the room was too strong for her.

"Tomorrow, she said." Malden paced back and forth across the floorboards, feeling like a fox caught in a trap. "Tomorrow we'll be fed to that demon."

"No," Cythera said. She looked distracted.

"I misheard her? We're not going to be dropped into that mass, to dissolve into goo ourselves?"

Cythera sighed. "No, I meant it's not a demon. More like a god."

"I will make sure to be suitably reverent, then, when it chews on my flesh tomorrow, and sucks my soul to wash down my giblets."

Cythera got up and went to a side table to pour herself some mushroom wine. "I should have realized, when I heard Mörget's description of the creature he saw in the mountains. It's not a pit-spawned abomination. Sorcery didn't draw it up from the Bloodgod's domain. In substance it much resembled ectoplasm, the immanentized stuff of psychic energy. I imagine a powerful enough witch could generate a gallon of the fluid during a trance session, but—"

Malden had been staring at her in incomprehension for a while before she noticed.

"If you like, you may think of it as a more-solid kind of ghost," she said. "It is made, truly, of the memories and thoughts of Aethil's ancestors. All those elves who have gone before. It's strange, though. There was never any mention of such a mass in the legends of the elves I've read. There were old stories of their ancestors living in the trees, of how we angered them by chopping down their sacred groves, but that . . . that made it sound more like ghosts, more like immaterial beings. This is different—something has changed. Something has changed in the very nature of their life force. It must have been emanated only after they came here. Perhaps, in their desperation—when they realized they were sealed in and could not escape—their fear and their anger reified the etheric currents of the—"

Malden stared at her again.

"Oh, fie! Malden, why must you look at me like that?"

"Because I care very little what that thing *is*. I care very much about how to avoid being eaten by it. We need a plan. We need to think of how we're going to escape, and we need to think of it now."

Cythera inhaled deeply. "Yes. Of course. Slag?"

"Hmm?" The dwarf didn't look up from his scraps of paper. "Ah!" he said, and moved one to lie next to another. "Yes . . . there . . ."

"Slag," Malden said. "Sir Croy. Urin!"

"Busy," the dwarf told him. With trembling hands, Slag picked another scrap of paper from a pile by his elbow and turned it sideways, then laid it down atop the others. "Hah!" he shouted, and jumped off his chair.

"Are you all right, Slag?" Malden asked.

"I have it! So simple! Lad, lass, this is a wonder! Three ingredients only, all readily available. Why this was lost so long—why no one stumbled on it since—I will never know. Huzzah! Fucking huzzah!"

Malden looked at Cythera. She shrugged.

"I have it! I have it precisely—when I saw this book, I knew there would be secrets inside. It's the *Manual of Applied Combinations*. One of the greatest works of all dwarven literature, a compendium of formulae for creating various substances of use to dwarvenkind. It's been lost for centuries. No copy is known to exist in any dwarven library, but here, here in this musty old deathtrap, this fucking hole—I have it!"

"What have you?" Malden asked.

"The nature of the powder. The recipe for its admixture. I don't need those barrels. Balint can bloody have them! I can make as much of it as I like, for farthings on the hogshead. Fucking brilliant—I'm going to be rich, lad. Exile be damned, I'll be richer than the dwarven king. I'll buy the fucking crown off the top of his head, and we'll see who's a real dwarf then!" Slag pounded on the table merrily. Malden had never seen him so happy. "Rich!"

Malden sighed in exasperation and pushed a hand through his hair. "Both of you! You're lost in mysteries and might-bes! Cythera, everything we learned today, everything we saw, will mean nothing tomorrow. Slag—this discovery of yours—"

"Means we have to escape," Slag said, nearly jumping up and down with excitement. "Money's no use to a dwarf who's been et by a demon. Lad, lass, stop your moping. We must come up with an escape plan—and we must have it now. I have to get out of here and start formulating the compound, if I'm ever going to make any money from this." His lips curled into an irrepressible smile and he burbled with laughter. "Rich!"

# CHAPTER EIGHTY-SEVEN

When Aethil returned, Slag lay slumped on the divan again, one forearm pressed against his eyes. "Oh, woe is me," he moaned, and rocked his head back and forth.

Malden hoped he wasn't overdoing it.

The elf queen, however, for once didn't seem to notice her paramour's emotional state. She went to her sideboard and poured a goblet full of dark wine, then lifted it with a shaking hand. She looked even paler than she'd been before.

"Sir Croy," she said, softly, "you didn't . . ." She couldn't seem to finish the thought. After a moment she swallowed her wine and shook her head. "No. Of course not. I refuse to believe it. You're an honorable human. Not at all like the ones in the stories."

Cythera stood up from her chair in the corner. "Your highness," she said. "You don't look well."

Aethil gave her a bitter smile—then sighed and favored them all with a more sincere countenance. "Just a trifle tired. The soldiers were wounded most horribly, and many of them didn't survive. I . . . I don't normally see so much . . . blood."

"A cave-in must be a terrible thing down here," Cythera sympathized.

"It was no accident. The wounds I saw were made with swords. Iron swords . . . they tell me there are other humans in our home now. Two fierce warriors, brutes who offer no quarter or mercy. Supposedly they're even being helped by a dwarf, of all things. They lay ambushes for our soldiers and cut them down without warning."

Cythera gasped, though Malden was certain it wasn't out of horror. These two warriors the queen described could be none other than Croy and Mörget. The dwarf with them must be Balint or one of her crew.

"I know," Aethil said, draining more of her wine, "that you three had nothing to do with this. You couldn't have— it's—it's impossible. You were with me, or in the gaol, this whole time. So I will not say more, for fear of offending you. Yet when these two men are caught—and their traitorous dwarf—well, justice must be done."

"Of course," Malden said. He sidled over to the queen and went to one knee before her. "Perhaps you'll let us see them when they are brought in, so we can revile them with you."

Aethil shook her head. "I would grant that wish if I could, but I'm afraid right now I have little ability to arrange things." She looked at Malden, and for a moment he thought she was looking at a thinking, rational being. Always before she'd regarded him like an especially talented pet. "The lords have been in close council with the Hieromagus. They have a plan, they claim. Some method to capture the fugitive humans without losing any more of our people. They wouldn't tell me the details—already they've stopped trusting me. They've also been saying things about me. Hurtful things."

Malden was so shocked by her confiding in him that for a moment he could only respond in kind. "They threatened you?"

The queen shook her head. "I've told you. I have very little real power. For simple things, for things that don't matter, sometimes my words are heeded. But this is different. Those soldiers . . . they died to protect me. From humans. And the lords are saying I've already shown you three humans far too much compassion. They fear you, squire. They are afraid, and they are men, and when men are afraid, they think only of violence. I'm not sure but I think they may try to harm you, and Cythera, and Sir Croy."

Malden wasn't sure what the elfin lords could do to him worse than throwing him into their ancestral mass. But then he remembered they had a reputation as torturers. "If there's anything we can do, anything to help—"

Apparently Slag hadn't forgotten that they were trying to use Aethil to aid their escape. He went on with the scheme, as planned—exactly according to the script they'd worked out. "Oh!" the dwarf moaned, more loudly this time. "Woe is me!"

Aethil dropped her goblet on the floor, spilling wine across the hem of her gown. She rushed to the divan and knelt beside it, grabbing up Slag's hands in her own. "Sir Croy! Are you sick? What has befallen you while I was gone? Oh, I hurried back here as quickly as I could. You must believe me!"

"Oh, to die, to perish here, in this dark place," Slag moaned.

"You won't die at all!" Aethil's voice was near hysterics. "My love, you're going to live forever. And I can come visit you as often as you like, once you're part of the ancestral mass."

"To live . . . forever," Slag said. He shook his head wildly. "In the dark!"

Aethil looked up at Malden and Cythera, her eyes pleading.

Malden almost regretted what they would say next. He was not pleased with the harm they'd already done to Aethil. But he knew this was their only chance.

"Sadness has gripped him like a fever," Cythera explained.

"He longs for one thing only," Malden added, perhaps not with the same theatrical plaintiveness he'd originally planned on putting into the words.

"What is it? My darling, tell me, and I'll give it to you with all my heart. Is it another kiss? Is it a caress? I'll gladly give to you my virtue, if it will—"

"I must feel the sun's light on my face, one last time," Slag whispered. "Or my soul will shrivel and fucking perish."

Malden's hands were balled into tight fists at his sides. This was the moment that could be their undoing—or mean their escape. If Aethil agreed to let them go up to one of the exits from the Vincularium, they could slip past any escort and be free. If she refused, there would be no more chances, no more possibilities—

"Of course you can see it," Aethil said.

The dwarf's body stiffened on the divan. "Really? I don't mean the red bauble you've got chained up down here either. I mean the sun that warms the surface world. The—The—"

"The golden orb of day, the fiery chariot of heaven," Malden supplied.

"Aye, that one," Slag concurred.

"Well, yes, of course I knew which one you meant," Aethil told him. "Nothing could be simpler. Are you too gripped by sadness to walk? I can summon servants to carry you there, if you like."

Slag sat up and then slid off the divan to his feet. "I can manage."

"Then come this way," Aethil told him. She looked back at Malden and Cythera, and for a moment Malden was terrified she would tell them to wait there, that she and Slag would go look on the sun alone. "Your servants must come with us. Though they lack your sensitive nature, I'm sure they'll want to see this as well."

"I wholeheartedly agree," Slag said, and started toward the door.

"Oh, no, not that way," Aethil said. "I've been given instructions not to let you leave my chambers. Luckily we don't need to, for this." She walked toward the back of the room, to where the curtain of water fell constantly. She lifted a hand and the waters parted, revealing a dark room beyond. Lifting a candlestick from one of her tables, Aethil stepped through and into a sumptuous bedchamber. "I had planned on showing you this room anyway," she told Slag. "Though not in such company."

The queen led them through the bedchamber to a broad archway. Myriad glinting beams of light emerged from beyond the arch. One by one they filed through, into a cave of unsurpassed beauty.

At first Malden thought the walls were decked with snow, and that icicles of impossible size and profusion had grown from the ceiling. It was no colder in this hidden cave, however, than in the rest of the Vincularium, and he quickly determined that the "snow" was in fact a dense encrustation of rock crystals. They covered every surface, sending up faceted spearheads both minuscule and gigantic, sticking out in every possible direction. One spar fifteen feet long crossed the cave on a diagonal slant, and as Aethil's light touched it, beams of pure color shot out to dazzle Malden's eyes.

"This is my personal grotto," Aethil explained. "For centuries, only royalty have been allowed back here. Please, don't touch that!"

Malden looked up just moments after he'd touched a rock so covered with crystal spines that it resembled a sea anemone. Even the softest contact was too much, as it turned out—the crystals snapped off one by one and fell to the floor to shatter.

"Oh, they're so delicate," Aethil said.

"I am sorry," Malden told her.

She shook her head prettily. "Never mind. Come this way."

Deeper in the cave, its natural shape curved around an entire pipe organ's worth of standing crystal columns, each thicker and taller than the last. In the next section a perfectly still pool of water covered most of the floor, with islands of crystal rising from the yellowish water here and there. Still farther on, a narrow path led upward, fringed on either side by perfect growths, like a garden of diamonds.

Slag must have seen him slipping crystal shards into a pocket of his robe. The dwarf shook his head and leaned back to whisper, "They're worthless, lad. Too fragile to use as gemstones, and common as crap."

Malden frowned. He'd thought perhaps to make his own fortune here. He still hadn't forgiven himself for failing to rob the Hall of Masterpieces when he had the chance. Yet all expression left his face when he followed Aethil up the path—and sunlight fell across his hands.

Real sunlight.

The light of day—the light of the surface world.

Its color, its warmth, its clarity, all proclaimed its provenance. He hurried after the queen, and nearly trampled on a patch of crystals grown into the shape of flowers.

"Here, stand just here," Aethil said. She showed Malden the exact patch of cleared ground she meant. "Now. Look—there."

Malden looked up, following her pointing finger.

And saw a patch of blue sky.

It was beyond being beautiful. It was the coolth of summer shade, the first taste of ale after a day of thirst. It was perhaps six inches on a side. The cave stretched onward and upward, he could not say how far—perhaps hundreds of feet. It opened on what must be the side of the mountain, a natural exit from the Vincularium. Too bad, then, that it was so encrusted with crystals that not even Balint's knocker could have fit through that gap.

Of course, if one were to break the crystals out of the way, say with a hammer, uncaring of their beauty in the desperation of one's need to get out—

"Let Sir Croy look now. He feels the need the most," Aethil said.

Reluctantly, Malden stepped away from the viewing place and let Slag take his spot.

"I used to come here when I was a young girl, and dream of what strange lands might lay out there," Aethil confided. "I think even then I knew that my lover waited for me out there in the other world, waited for the day when he would come find me. Is it not beautiful?"

The tears that came to Slag's eyes, Malden thought, might be tears of desire. Or they might be tears of irritation—a dwarf's eyes were far too sensitive for the sun's pure light. He could not know.

"Aye, lass," Slag said. "Pretty as a fucking picture."

## CHAPTER EIGHTY-EIGHT

Mörget slammed Dawnbringer against the side of a dwarven tomb. The blade flared brilliantly, shedding daylight stronger even than the light of the false red sun behind him. The revenants threw up their arms to protect their eyeless faces and staggered backward, away from the barbarian.

A few of them had the strength of will to try to surge in low, under the sword's glare. Croy smashed in their heads with Ghostcutter and sliced off their hands before they could grab Mörget and quench his light. The revenants shook and their feet scrabbled on the cobblestones as they tried to escape. Yet they could not, for just behind them another wave of undead elves was rushing in, rushing to attack, to destroy, to avenge themselves.

Croy could sympathize, in a way. It didn't stop him from slicing them to pieces.

One of them came straight at Croy, a bronze flail whirling around its head. Mörget smashed through its rib cage with his axe, the bones splitting apart like dried wood, the bronze armor squealing as the steel axe tore through it like paper.

On Croy's other side a revenant rushed at him with nothing but its bare hands. Croy got his shoulder down and leaned forward into the revenant's charge. He caught his shoulder in the arch made by its rib cage and sternum and then stood up straight, lifting the dead thing up into the air. Its fingers grabbed for Croy's hair, but Mörget smashed the revenant away with his sword. Light blossomed over Croy's head and the revenants drew back, arms flailing in horror.

"Quickly, dwarf," Croy shouted. "We can't keep this up much longer!"

Mörget made his sword ring on the cobblestones again. Did the revenants fear the light because it reminded them of their failures in the world above? Did it remind them of battles lost, and hasty retreats? Or was it simply that they were unholy monstrosities, and the pure light of the Lady's sun was enough to pain them?

It didn't matter. The revenants attacked and were repulsed. The light drove them back, and the steel and iron blades hacked them apart.

The two warriors had been holding them off for nearly half an hour this way.

"Just a little longer," Balint shouted back.

The revenants seemed far less aggressive when the red sun shone on them—or perhaps Croy had simply learned better how to fight them. Their attacks were nowhere near as fast or furious as the first time he'd faced them, back when he first came into the Vincularium.

Perhaps he was the one who'd changed. Perhaps the need for vengeance drove him now just as it propelled them. Back then he'd come here to slay a demon. Now he just wanted death, endless death. One could take strength from a drive like that, he knew. Patriotism, piety, vows sworn, and the hands of ladies fair, those things gave a man the spirit to fight. But hatred trumped them all.

"I just have to make a—what's the word—a fuse," Balint shouted back. She'd wrangled the five barrels around until they encircled the massive, arching support pillar. Now she took a hammer from her belt and knocked a hole in one of the barrels.

Mörget struck the stones, and his light bought them a moment's breathing room. Croy looked back and saw black dust spill from the hole Balint had made.

"No!" he cried. "You were wrong—it's rotted away to dust over the centuries!"

"Don't take me for a dizzy virgin. That's what it's supposed to look like," Balint told him. "For fuck, it's pretty. Now—if I'm right, I can fill this pipe with the powder, and it'll burn steady as a candlewick. Just one touch of fire will be enough to bring this place down. And then no dwarf will ever be tempted to come back here."

Mörget's sword rang. A revenant came in from the side and Croy cut it in half. "What? I thought you did this for revenge, like myself."

Balint shook her head. "I didn't care about Murin and Slurri that much. It's not elves I hate, but this place. Its history—it holds my people back. How can they face a dismal future knowing what glory they once possessed?" She glanced up from her work to stare at him. "But why do you care what my reason is for doing this? You'll still have your revenge, and the pillock will still slay his demons."

Croy scowled. He didn't like this. His own thirst for revenge had not receded, but he understood now that he'd been tricked into such fury. Still—she was right.

It didn't matter.

Mörget raised his sword to strike it off the stones again. As if anticipating the light it would shed, the revenants stumbled backward. The barbarian paused.

"What are you doing? We need that light," Croy said, grabbing Mörget's arm.

The barbarian shrugged him off. He held Dawnbringer high, the blade still dark.

The revenants were retreating.

One by one they pulled away from the main group and ran for the shadows. They did not look back. They made no last attempt to kill the warriors. They simply turned and ran.

Then Croy heard a low chanting. In the distance he could just make out a human figure. It sat cross-legged on the cobblestones, hands pressed together as if in prayer.

"What do you make of this?" Croy asked Mörget.

The barbarian shrugged.

When the last revenant had gone, the figure rose to its feet and walked slowly toward them. In the red light of the subterranean sun Croy could just see that it was a man—a human—wearing the undyed woolen habit of a priest.

"Be not alarmed," the newcomer said. "I am a holy man, and I drove the fiends away with the blessing of my god. That is all. You are Sir Croy, are you not?" The man had come close enough that Croy could see his round, smiling face. His eyes were small and dark but they glinted in the red light. "My new friend Herward told me you had come inside the Vincularium."

"Herward?" Croy frowned. "The old hermit sent you in here? Why, to aid us?"

"I came for my own reasons. You must be Mörget, the man of the East," the priest said. "You're bigger than I expected." He reached into one sleeve of his habit and twisted something Croy couldn't see. "I was under the impression your dwarf was male as well. My new friends weren't entirely clear. That may change things slightly."

The knight shoved Ghostcutter into its scabbard. "If you've come to do the Lady's work," he sneered, "you've come too late. What's your name?"

The priest laughed pleasantly. "I didn't say I was a priest of your Lady." He brought his hands down to his sides. "My name is Prestwicke."

His left hand shot upward and something flickered across Croy's vision. Balint screamed, and her knocker leapt down to the cobbles and ran off into the shadows. Croy stared in horror as he saw a dart sticking out of Balint's neck. Her scream ended in a gurgling hiss and then she slumped against one of the barrels, her eyes fluttering closed.

Croy gasped in surprise and reached for Ghostcutter's hilt. Before he could even reach it, the priest threw another dart that struck Mörget right in the chest, just left of center.

"The elves had a very poor description of you. Never mind. The dosage may be too low for your weight, but applied directly to the heart, it should be effective," Prestwicke said as Mörget came storming toward him. Dawnbringer came up to slice the priest in half, but before the blow could connect, Mörget stumbled and pitched face-first onto the cobbles.

"Not now," Croy growled, and yanked Ghostcutter free of its sheath.

The priest flicked his wrist. Croy couldn't see the dart coming—he only felt a sudden pinprick in his shoulder. He howled and lifted his weapon high, but before he took a step toward the priest, his blood slowed in his body and his head spun.

And then everything went black.

# CHAPTER EIGHTY-NINE

For a long while Croy heard nothing but a voice roaring close to his ear. He could not seem to open his eyes, or move his hands, but he could hear just fine. Unfortunately all he could hear was Mörget.

"—pull your tongues from your mouths, flay the skin off your backs, the clans will tear you out branch and root, your stomachs burst open, your eyes spitted, your—"

Croy felt like he was trapped at the bottom of a well, with only the curses echoing down to him from above. He tried to swim upward, to reach for the light, but his body felt like it was made of lead. Straining and groaning, he stretched his consciousness as far as it would go and it snapped back, rubbery and ineffectual.

He was moving, always moving. He very much wanted to lie still. He felt sick and afraid. He felt like he was going to throw up, but still he couldn't see where he was. *Open one eye*, he told himself. *Just open one eye and take a quick look. Find out where you are, at least.*

His body refused to acknowledge his desires. He was barely aware of it at all, aware only of the motion and the noise.

"—guts steaming on the hot ground, eat your liver, tear it apart with my own teeth, smash your brains with a rock—"

If Mörget would just be quiet—but no. No, it was helping. The bellowing imprecations were anchoring his consciousness. Without them he would be lost, adrift. So instead of ignoring the foul words, Croy focused on them. Struggled to hear them better.

"—grind your bones, stretch your skins on frames, the

death of one cut, blood on the rocks, blood to paint our tents, blood, blood, blood—"

*Open one eye.*

*Open it.*

Croy's left eyelid parted, only a crack. Light streamed in and for a moment he was swimming again, swimming and spinning and lost, but then the light dimmed, became almost bearable. He turned his eye left and right.

He was in a room with walls of every possible color. Music was playing somewhere, no, not music, just the sound of bells, rattling bells.

If he pushed his eye all the way over to the left, he could just see the side of Mörget's face. Thick cords bound the barbarian's head, one holding his chin, others crossing his forehead, holding him in place. Croy grunted and tried to move his arms, and felt similar cords holding him down as well. He was bound. Immobilized.

An elfin face surrounded by black cloth appeared before him. The bells were attached to the elf's black cloak, and they stirred and jingled every time he moved. The elf was speaking. Croy had to force himself to ignore Mörget so he could hear what the elf said. He was soon sorry for it.

"—in a different era, we had a special torment for humans who despoiled our lands. We would stake them out in the forest, in a clearing where a little sunlight came, and underneath their bodies we would plant the seeds of fast-growing trees. Over a period of months, the trees would grow, spreading branches upward toward the light—through the bodies of the interlopers. The agony was supposed to be beyond measure, as the woody growths pressed against their skin, then penetrated their flesh. Special care was taken to make sure no branch pierced a vital organ, because then the human would die too quickly. No, we wanted them to understand why this was done. We wanted them to know what despoiling felt like. Intimately. Of course, now we have no trees. I imagine we can think of something else, given time."

The black-clad elf fell silent. He nodded politely as someone else spoke. Who, Croy could not have said—he couldn't see the other party. He tried desperately to open his right eye, to twitch his fingers, anything, but it seemed his strength was used up.

"Of course," the elf said, replying to something Croy hadn't heard. "You have done us proper service, and you will be rewarded. You will have the one you seek, to kill as you desire. His name was . . . Malton?"

"Malden, milord." Croy heard the other's voice this time. It was the voice of the priest, the man in the undyed habit who had drugged him. Who had captured him and turned him over to the elves.

"Malden. I must . . . . remember that." The elf's eyes turned inward then, and he sank back onto a waiting couch. "I must take my leave of you now," he said. The elf lay on his couch and stared up at the ceiling.

Croy searched the room with his one open eye but could find no one else in it. Nothing moved, nothing made a sound, except Mörget, still raving:

"—slit along the forehead, just at the hairline, then slip the knife under the skin and cut a flap, peel back, we will take your hair and make plumes for our helmets, we will slaughter your children and make slaves of your women, we will—"

It was too much. All too much. What little energy Croy had marshaled had been used up, just for that one moment of lucidity. His eye fluttered closed again. He could not have kept it open for any price. Soon even the sound of Mörget's cursing receded, and he sank into a heavy velvet sleep, fighting all the way down.

In the last part of his mind to stay awake, his own voice rang out, echoing off the walls of his skull. *Malden. You're still alive. Malden, you're alive.*

Though not, apparently, for much longer.

# CHAPTER NINETY

Cythera stretched upward on the balls of her feet to bring her face into the little patch of sunlight. She closed her eyes and sighed in deep pleasure. "I'd begun to think I'd never smell fresh air again," she said.

Aethil smiled sadly and turned away.

It was Malden's only chance.

He grabbed the elf queen by the shoulder and pulled one arm across her throat. She screamed and every crystal in the grotto shivered. Pulling the queen off her feet, he held her close to his body to keep her from breaking free.

He'd been considering this move for some time. He'd put it aside for a while—when Aethil confided in him, when he felt sorry for her, it seemed like the last thing he should ever do. He still felt terrible about it, guilty almost to the point of letting her go. But not quite.

There was no other way. Their best plan had been to get Aethil to let them see the sun. Their only plan. But this route wouldn't work—he couldn't fit through the crystal tunnel, couldn't escape that way. And now he was out of time.

"I'm sorry," he said. "If there was any other way, I'd take it. But I will kill you if it means we get out of here alive."

"What are you doing?" Aethil demanded. "Sir Croy! Defend me!"

Cythera wheeled around and stared at Malden. "No—not like this," she said, shaking her head. "Please, Malden."

"You asked me once if I believed in anything," Malden told her. "Well, I do. I believe in freedom. I won't let myself be dissolved in that slime pit. I will not be imprisoned with a thousand dead elves for all eternity. I won't be this one's pet any more either."

Aethil started to scream again. Malden put pressure on her windpipe until she stopped. He felt like a cad. He felt like a villain. It didn't matter. This was their only chance. He would save Cythera and Slag, and he would buy his own freedom at any price.

"But what of Croy and Mörget?" Cythera said. "We know they're alive, now—would you leave them here to be tortured to death?"

"What choice have we?" Malden demanded. "Slag, grab that candlestick," he said. "We can use it to break away the crystals. I don't know where we'll find ourselves once we climb up there, but it's better than being stuck down here."

The dwarf didn't move. He looked like he'd seen a ghost.

The body in Malden's arms went limp. White smoke wreathed Aethil's head, streaming out of her mouth and nose and eyes. As Malden watched in horror it coalesced and formed a demonic visage, all horns and gnashing teeth. The white face came looming toward him, jaws stretched wide to snatch him, and he panicked.

He fell backward, crashing against a wall of sharp crystals that exploded into choking, glittering dust. His arms flew back and Aethil was free. She did not waste another moment on beseeching Slag's aid, but dashed toward the exit of the grotto, back toward her apartments.

The demonic face broke up into swirling vapor that dissipated almost instantly.

"Blast!" Malden shouted. "She'll have every elf in the Vincularium down on us in a moment. I'll go after her. Cythera, Slag, start breaking the crystals. Don't wait for me, just get out of here!"

Malden ran toward the grotto's exit and into Aethil's bedchamber. Ahead of him the waterfall curtain had become a pounding torrent, a cascade of water that roared violently and foamed on the floor. He put one arm over his face and dashed through—

—and felt watery hands grab at him, holding him in

place as the rushing water bashed and beat at his face. Water filled his mouth and nose and he had to fight his natural instincts to keep from breathing it in. A trap, a magical trap.

But Malden was very good with traps.

The hands that clutched at him weren't solid enough to be beaten away with his flailing fists. He couldn't move his torso or his head, for they were held fast by the very same water—it was solid enough when it wanted to be. Everywhere the water touched him he was stuck fast. One of his legs, however, had passed through the curtain before the trap activated—and now it was mostly dry. It extended out into the main chamber beyond. He could see nothing out there—the water filled his eyes—but he could still move the leg. His foot struck the floor and found the leg of a table. Hooking his foot around this anchor, he dragged himself out of the waterfall, pulling for all he was worth against the watery hands that tried to hold him fast.

When his face broke the surface of the water, he sucked in air and made one desperate, convulsive push that sent him sprawling onto the carpets beyond, soaking wet and bruised. Black spots swam before his eyes.

Ahead of him the door to the royal apartments stood open. Just a few feet away. He pushed himself up, forced himself to stand. He ran out through the door and into the stone passage beyond. An elf maid in a patchwork dress stood there, staring at him in horror. Malden pushed past her and kept running—

—straight into a massive intersection of tunnels, where a dozen elf soldiers in bronze armor stood waiting for him. Aethil stood among them, her face a mask of imperious rage.

Malden stopped where he was and raised his hands in surrender.

He expected Aethil to speak, to say how disappointed she was in him, or to chide him for abusing her hospitality. Instead she simply turned her face away. Then someone else pushed through the rank of soldiers to face Malden. Not an elf—a human, dressed like a priest, with tiny dark eyes that displayed a malicious intelligence.

"Prestwicke?" Malden asked. "But . . . how?"

"Not easily. I followed you all the way from Ness. I've never had to travel so far on a contract," Prestwicke told him.

"But the elves—"

"My new friends? I did a small service for them. In exchange they've agreed to give me a gift. Your life."

# CHAPTER NINETY-ONE

The elves dragged Malden back to the gaol. It was exactly the same as before, except this time he was alone.

In the dark, sitting in the wet silt of the floor, he could only lay his head in his hands and try not to weep. Sometimes he failed.

It was over—all his dreams, all his plans. He had failed. He was going to die down here under the ground, of that he was certain. The elves would never slip up, would never stop watching him. Even now they had a half dozen revenants guarding him. If he could get through the bars, he had no doubt they would strangle the life out of him with their bony claws.

Perhaps that was better than waiting to see what Prestwicke would do to him. The murderous little bastard was going to cut him up with those little knives. Already he could feel his skin tingle as if they were slicing away at him, carving him up piece by piece. It was too much to bear.

"I demand to see Aethil! I demand an audience with the Hieromagus!" he screamed, running to the bars and grabbing them with both hands. It was pointless, but he couldn't help himself. "Does a condemned man have no rights in this place? Where is the rule of law? You call yourselves civilized! I demand to see your queen!"

"Very well," someone said.

Malden jumped back in surprise as a light appeared at the top of the stairs and he heard footfalls coming down toward him. Had his time come already? No. No, it couldn't be. Surely he had a while longer before they turned him over to Prestwicke.

Surely.

Aethil appeared at the bottom of the stairs, an oil lamp in her hand. She waved one slender hand at the revenants and they moved to one side to let her pass.

"You called for me," she said. "Now I am here."

Anger deranged her fine features, and made her as ugly as any weathered old fishwife of Ness. Her tiny nose scrunched up as if she was disgusted by the stink of the gaol, and the light streaming upward from her lamp made her features alien and ghastly.

"I—I only wanted to apologize," Malden said, standing well clear of the bars. Had she come to torture him, before he was to die? "My actions were foolhardy, and . . . and ill-considered. I never meant you any harm."

"You *touched* me," she said. As if it were an unpardonable violation. "Now you won't go to the ancestors with your friends. You won't live forever. You'll simply die."

"You think that bothers me?" Malden asked, regaining some of his composure. "You think I wanted to be absorbed into your ancestral slime? Fie on that." He turned away from her. If she was going to torture him, clearly nothing he said would change her mind. Not now.

"It's a great honor—"

"It's just another way to kill us, you stupid cow," Malden shot back. "Your council of lords doesn't give a damn about adding our memories to your stock. They just want us dead, but they know you wouldn't let them just hang us!"

"Cow," Aethil said. "Cow," she said again, as if she'd never heard the word before. "That's a kind of domestic animal, isn't it? Like a cave beetle. So. You're not only a violent beast. You're also rude."

Malden sighed and sat back down.

"One more vice my people do not share with yours," Aethil said. "I came down here to give you one last boon, and instead you insult me. I'm of half a mind not to let you see Cythera at all."

"Cythera?" Malden asked. "She's here?"

"I am, Malden," Cythera said from the top of the stairs. "Aethil, may I come down? I beg you to forgive my friend. I know if Sir Croy were here he would say the same. Malden's merely frightened—you must understand that."

"Of course," Aethil said. "Please, join us."

Cythera came down the stairs then. She looked very pale. When she saw the revenants she flinched, but then she rushed over to the bars and grabbed Malden's hands through them. "Such a stupid man," she said.

"I only—"

"Such a stupid, brave man," she said. She was weeping.

"I'll leave the two of you alone," Aethil said. "You don't have much time, but I'll see what I can do about delaying the execution a few minutes."

She turned to go. Malden called her name through the bars, and she looked back.

"Aethil—thank you, for this."

The queen looked no less haughty, no less angry. But she nodded. "I know what love is, now that I've met Sir Croy. Even a human deserves to say goodbye."

She left them then, but Malden had already forgotten she was ever there. He could only stare into Cythera's face, for what was surely the last time. He tried to memorize every curve, every wrinkle, the down on her cheek. If he was going to the pit of souls this day he would at least have that face to take with him.

"There's not much time," Cythera said. He barely heard her. "Slag is working on Aethil as best he can, trying to persuade her to forgive you, and help us in some way. I don't know how much luck he's having. Croy is here somewhere, and Mörget as well—that was the deal this Prestwicke made with the elves, apparently. Croy and Mörget were killing every elf they could find, and the elves couldn't stop them, and then Prestwicke showed up and just captured them. I have no idea how he could do that. He certainly doesn't look like much of a warrior."

"Cythera," Malden said, almost a whisper.

"The important thing is they're here, somewhere close by. I'll try to reach them somehow, at least get a message to them. Our chances don't look good, but we'll do everything we can to—"

"I'm so sorry," he said.

"Malden, there's no time for that," she pleaded.

"I've been nothing but a hindrance for you since we left Ness. I've gotten you in terrible trouble. Please. There's no way out for me now. But you and Croy—you'll find a way to get free. To get out of here. And when you're back in the world above, I want the two of you to—"

"Malden, be still!" Cythera hissed.

"You deserve happiness," Malden said.

"I beg of you, stop it! I can't marry Croy now!"

The thief blinked in confusion. "But—"

"I met Croy when I was still a child, a girl of eighteen. I thought he was some kind of demigod come to walk the world, and I believed what I felt for him was love. Later on I dreamed of all the things he could give me. Things you never could, Malden, and I thought that mattered. When I was convinced he was dead I saw my entire future die with him, and I thought I had to honor that memory. I thought I

owed him. But now . . . Malden, when the elves first captured you I said it, and it was true. It's you I love."

"But now—"

She leaned forward and kissed him. Deeply, passionately. "I can't have any kind of life with Croy. Every day
of it I would think of you, and what I'd lost. Instead I'll
go to my mother and have her teach me to be a witch. It
will burn, Malden, what I've lost will always burn, but it
won't be a lie. It's you who should forgive me. Forgive me
for wasting our time together. Forgive me for how I've
failed you."

"There's nothing to forgive," Malden said. His heart
was so full he thought he might perish on the spot, and
cheat Prestwicke out of his due. "Just—kiss me again. Just
once more, before they come for me. Please."

# CHAPTER NINETY-TWO

They dragged Malden through their twisting stone tunnels and brought him to a wide hall, a place where massive columns fronted buildings that were full of nothing but
cobwebs. A gallery let out onto the central shaft, and the
red light of the dwarven sun cast the place in sunset hues.

Malden was tied to a marble column thicker than his
waist, and left there, all alone. Not for long, though.

One by one elves in patchwork smocks or the finest beetle-silk livery came to the hall's many entrances. At first
they arrived only to peek inside at the man who had assaulted their queen, but soon they grew bolder. Elfin maids

perched on high cornices while dandies leered out from behind archways. Soon groups of them lined up around the far walls of the grand hall, and Malden realized that his execution was to be a grand spectacle. An event not to be missed in an underground world where diversion was a rarity.

Soon enough the hall was half filled with elves of every station. The humblest mushroom farmer and the grandest nobleman of elfinkind had come. The soldiers in their bronze breastplates, the jugglers and musicians and duelists, the Hieromagus and, yes, Aethil, all were in attendance. And then the others were brought in. Cythera and Slag were hauled out onto the flagstones for the elves to jeer at. They each wore a silver chain around their neck. There seemed to be no more doubt that they were kept as pets for the queen. Malden tried to catch Cythera's eye but she was too far away. Besides, she was watching the archway through which she'd entered the chamber. It seemed there were more guests yet to arrive.

A great booing and hissing commenced as three more trespassers were wheeled out. Malden gasped in surprise to see Mörget and Croy—still alive, though worse for wear. The warriors were bound to a cart, their arms bent up behind their backs and tied to a post. They looked drugged—their faces slack, drool sliding down their chins. At their feet lay Balint, her eyes wide open and staring up at nothing.

"Together," the Hieromagus said, and the murmuring crowd fell instantly silent. "Together . . . at last . . . all of them."

The throng held its collective breath as they waited to hear what their wizard-priest had to say. Yet the Hieromagus seemed even more distracted than usual. His eyes were as vacant as Balint's, and his hands occasionally flew up around his face, as if to drive away bothersome insects. He was ushered to a good viewing spot, then left alone by his attendants.

Last to arrive, Prestwicke entered the hall and strode across the flagstones, bowing deep as the crowd cheered him on.

"This is not how I wanted things to end, dear Malden," he confessed, coming close enough that he could speak to the thief in a conversational tone, though the marble walls around him reflected his voice so that Malden was sure the elves could hear him, too. "I wanted to do things *properly*. There are forms to follow, rituals to carry out. I wanted to make this *clean*. But you forced my hand."

"So sorry for the inconvenience," Malden said, intending the words to come out clear and defiant. Instead they sounded like a panicked mumble.

Prestwicke drew an oilskin bundle from inside his woolen habit and unrolled it carefully. Inside, his knives gleamed as bright as polished silver.

"What are you?" Malden asked, in his desperation. "You're no assassin. I've known bravos before, jaded men who would cut a throat for the price of a cup of wine. Stupid, brutish fellows with no imagination. You're different from them."

Prestwicke smiled broadly. "Flattery," he said, "will not save your skin, Malden. But I'll answer your question. I am exactly what I look like."

"A priest?"

Prestwicke bowed again. "Exactly. I serve Sadu, the Bloodgod. I do not assassinate my victims. I sacrifice them, in His exalted name."

Malden frowned. In Ness there were still plenty of people who worshipped Sadu, of course. The Lady was the official religion of Skrae, but her tenets meant little to the poor, and they had kept the old religion alive through centuries of persecution. It was hardly an organized faith, however. "There are no priests of Sadu," Malden said.

"Not now. Yet once there were, and there will be again. I will be the first," Prestwicke said. "I will renew the church. I will bring back the old ways."

"I'm no scholar of theology," Malden admitted, "but I know Sadu's priests never took gold for their ceremonies."

"You're assuming I will be paid in coin. Malden, I will gain so much more than that from your death! My employer claims to have certain books that were long thought lost. Books I would give anything to see. The secrets I will learn—the prayers, the ceremonies, the sacred lessons, will bring great honor to Sadu. But I say too much." He took a knife from his pouch. "I shouldn't waste time with chatter, when there's work to be done."

He brought his knife up to Malden's forehead. Malden tried to jerk his head backward but Prestwicke grabbed his chin and held him in a viselike grip. He had forgotten how surprisingly strong the killer was.

The knife touched Malden's skin. He tried his hardest to keep his eyes open, to stare his hatred into Prestwicke's face while he was slaughtered, but the pain was too much. He squeezed his eyes shut and gasped as blood rolled down through his eyebrows.

Prestwicke moved his knife to Malden's cheek.

Before he could press it home, though, a terrifying shriek split the air. The gathered elves murmured and cried out in surprise, and even Prestwicke stopped what he was doing to look.

The Hieromagus had jumped up from his chair and was clawing at nothing as if he were beset by wild animals.

# CHAPTER NINETY-THREE

"Not like—not this way—the thief doesn't—doesn't die like this! History—so much history—all here—*so long*. So long! The chains cannot be broken . . ."

Malden shook his head to clear the blood that threatened to roll into his eyes. He craned his head farther to the side to see better what was happening. The Hieromagus slumped forward, his body wracked by spasms. He was caught by a pair of elfin soldiers who looked terrified.

"The Hieromagus!" a lord shouted. Malden recognized him—he was the same one who had wanted to watch him bleed, and who was only kept from that pleasure by Slag's sudden attack of vomiting. It seemed he'd finally gotten his wish, but he was too distracted to enjoy it. "The Hieromagus is undone—lost in time! Quickly, bring jugglers, and dancers, and . . . anyone, sing a song, call him back!"

Musicians gathered on the flagstones before the delirious priest-wizard and started into a jaunty tune, but the Hieromagus did not look up.

"Bring perfumes and spices. Put pepper on his tongue," the lord pleaded.

"Hold still," Prestwicke told Malden. "That does not concern us."

But then Aethil stood up and rushed forward. "Wait!" she called.

The gathered elves fell silent. Even the musicians ceased their playing. It seemed that in the absence of the Hieromagus, Aethil could still command a certain respect.

"Stop the execution," she commanded.

"But—your highness," the lord pleaded. "Now? We must see to the Hieromagus, and—"

"You heard my order," Aethil said. "Will you defy me?"

The lord looked confused. He reached for the Hieromagus, perhaps intending to simply ignore his queen.

"I asked you a question!" Aethil shouted.

It was another lord who answered, however. One Malden didn't know. "The human assaulted your person."

"And he shall die for it," Aethil agreed.

Malden's heart sank.

The elf queen wasn't finished, however. "But let his death serve some purpose. Let him fight the other human. That should be diversion enough to arouse the Hieromagus."

"A fight to the death?" the lord asked. "But we've never stooped to bloodsport for his amusement before."

"Exactly. It will be a novelty, sure to bring him around."

Malden frowned in confusion. He had no idea where this sudden inspiration had come from. It didn't seem Aethil's style at all. Then he looked over at Slag, and the dwarf winked back.

Malden started to laugh.

He still expected to die. He still had no hope of ever leaving this place. But at least he wasn't going to be butchered like a hog. It was funny what you could be grateful for, when fate played its tricks.

"No!" Prestwicke screamed, a strangely high-pitched noise. "No," he repeated, in a more measured voice. "This is not what I was promised. I made a deal for this man's life. I intend to see that deal honored."

"If you feel slighted, human," Aethil said, "you may seek redress from the Hieromagus. Once he comes back to himself, of course."

Prestwicke seemed near to tears. "I was promised—"

"I made you no compact," Aethil said. "Unbind the prisoner! Bring out the iron swords!"

A gasp rose from the audience.

An elf in a tattered smock came running toward Malden and Prestwicke. The Bloodgod's priest raised his knife high and the elf flinched back, but then Prestwicke turned

away and wiped the blood from the knife with his sleeve.
The elf untied Malden's bonds and then ran off again as
fast as he could.

Malden staggered forward and rubbed furiously at his
wrists. His hands ached with being tied for so long.

Next, an elfin soldier hurried into the hall, carrying
a burden wrapped in rough cloth. As if he was afraid to
touch its contents himself, he opened the bundle with a
flourish and dumped three swords onto the flagstones.

Ghostcutter, Dawnbringer, and Acidtongue.

# CHAPTER NINETY-FOUR

Croy's arms felt like they were being torn from their
sockets. He gasped in pain and his eyes shot open. He
was still only semiconscious, but the pain was good—it
helped drag him back from the black void he'd been swimming through.

What he saw shocked him even further into wakefulness.

Before him, lying on the ground like the spoils of war,
lay three Ancient Blades—Ghostcutter among them. He
tried reaching for the sword, only to find his arms were
securely fastened behind him. They had been chained together and pulled upward, forcing him to bend low.

It was a kind of torture known well in Skrae—the strap,
accounted by some the most painful excruciation of all. As
ingenious as it was devious. The chain was not quite long
enough to let him stand comfortably, but just long enough
that if he tried to drop to his knees it would pull his arms

back and wrench them from their sockets. His own body weight would pull him to pieces if he didn't stand perfectly still, and fatigue would eventually claim him no matter what he did.

The elves . . . he remembered now. But it wasn't an elf who'd taken him when he was captured. It was . . . some human in a priest's robe, wasn't it? That made very little sense, and he wondered if he had hallucinated it.

Weariness passed through him in a wave. He longed to just surrender to it, to drift off into sleep. Yet as his eyes fluttered closed his arms were pulled up behind him. The drug in Croy's system kept him from feeling the pain fully, but every time he tried to move, white light threatened to explode behind his eyeballs.

He stopped struggling—and saw more to confuse and confound him.

Malden was there. Malden—Malden was still alive, he remembered now—Malden was alive, but . . . but the elves were going to . . .

Malden dashed toward him, and Croy wondered if he was being rescued. That would be . . . nice. But no. No, it was too much to hope for. Instead of releasing him from his chains, Malden rushed instead to the swords and snatched Acidtongue from the ground. Croy tried to call to the thief, but before he opened his lips he saw Malden run away again, as if he hadn't even seen him hanging there. It was all Croy could do to follow Malden with his eyes. The thief was running again, headed over toward a group of elves, elves and—and some others, among them—

Cythera.

Cythera was alive. She was—alive.

There was a silver chain around her neck but she looked unharmed. He had been living with the fact of her brutal death for so long he could scarce believe it. She was alive! His heart sang, his body thrummed with waves of joy, and—

Cythera grasped Malden's face and then leaned in to kiss the thief with passion and desperation.

Was this some drug-induced nightmare? Croy wondered. Had his sanity itself deserted him? He could make no sense at all of what he saw. He could only stare with wide eyes at this vision before him, and hope that it was, in fact, delusion.

Then his arms were hauled upward again and a brilliant wash of pain swarmed over all of his senses. His eyes squeezed shut and he felt his face contort in a grimace of excruciation.

"Knight! Wake up, Sir Knight!"

It was Mörget's voice calling him. Mörget his brother, Mörget his fellow Ancient Blade. Croy fought through the pain and opened his eyes to look for the barbarian. He found Mörget and saw at once that they were chained together. The chain had been looped over a post, high above their heads. Mörget hauled downward on the chain, which had the effect of pulling his own arms ever farther, painfully, upward.

"Help me, knight," Mörget demanded. "Are you too addled to even hear me? Help me—pull with all your strength, and we're free. Our swords are right there—we can fight to freedom."

Croy watched the barbarian's face as the words formed. Mörget's red-stained mouth snapped and bit at the sounds. His eyes rolled in fury. It was like the man's face and his voice were separated, as if the words emerged from him long seconds before his lips started to form them. More hallucinations. More delusions brought on by the drug, of course. How much of this was real?

"Knight! Pull, for all you are worth!" Mörget howled.

Croy pulled downward on the chain, and at the same time Mörget pulled down on his length of it. Croy nearly lost consciousness as the links bit deep into his wrists, chewing on the tender flesh there.

"Again!" Mörget screamed.

Croy pulled downward. The skin on his wrists stretched and tore.

"Again! Once more!"

There was a creaking sound and then a snap, and a piece of wood fell and struck Croy on the ear. It made his head ring. He barely heard the chain rattle and fall and smack the wooden cart. Mörget's booming laugh was the sound of distant thunder.

Croy slumped forward, free of the chain. Free of the only thing that had been holding him upright. He crashed to the stone floor, his face not inches from Ghostcutter's sheath.

He was . . . he was free. Free.

He thought he might be sick.

# CHAPTER NINETY-FIVE

Malden moved slowly, watching always the little knife in Prestwicke's hand. He circled the priest, heading to his right to keep the knife in view.

Prestwicke didn't move. He didn't turn to follow Malden. He didn't even seem to be watching him very closely.

Prestwicke didn't so much as flinch as Malden roared and came at him. He stood perfectly still—until the last possible moment, when he stepped away from the descending blade. Acidtongue came crashing down on the flagstones, its foaming vitriol burning a deep trench into the stone. Only when Malden was committed to the swing did Prestwicke move. The priest stepped inside of Malden's reach until their shoulders touched.

Then he pulled his knife across Malden's back, digging deep through robe and skin and the muscles beneath.

Malden screamed and staggered forward, past Prestwicke. The weight of Acidtongue dragged him downward until he was doubled over in pain.

For a long while he could do nothing but try to breathe through the agony. Prestwicke could have finished him off easily while he was down, but instead the priest merely stood to one side, waiting for him to get up.

Malden caught his breath. He pushed himself upward, using the sword like a cane. Eventually he regained his feet.

From behind him, he heard a sound as soft as a lover's whisper. The noise of soft shoes slapping on flagstones. Malden whirled to see Prestwicke dashing at him. The bright knife in his hand came for Malden's kidney, and Malden just managed to roll away from the attack.

He had let himself get distracted. It nearly cost him his life.

Or, no, not his life. At least not yet. He understood now why Prestwicke had kept to his little knife. Why he was taking so long to finish this. Prestwicke wanted him to bleed. He wanted his blood to flow.

Little cuts, but deep ones. Blood loss would kill him—eventually. Malden had seen men bleed to death before, and he knew how it would progress. He would weaken, and then falter, and then struggle for breath. His skin would pale and his lips turn blue. Eventually he would lose consciousness, and drift off to a sleep from which he would never awake. That was exactly how they said the priests of Sadu had once slaughtered their sacrifices, by bleeding them dry.

It was a painful way to die.

Desperate, driven by fear, Malden wheeled up to his feet, Acidtongue flashing out in a broad arc before him. Prestwicke was nowhere close enough to be cut.

Damn. Malden could feel blood sheeting down his back. The cut there had not severed any of his muscles, but it bit deep enough that he could feel blood rolling down his legs. He did not have much more time.

The priest raised his knife high and started to chant. Malden cast a quick glance toward the onlookers. Cythera looked terrified. Aethil the elf queen was staring with eyes that showed no emotion at all. What was her game? Why had she consented to this grotesque spectacle? Malden knew Slag had beseeched Aethil on his behalf—but surely this wasn't the dwarf's idea.

He needed to concentrate. He needed to focus. None of it mattered—not Mörget's escape, not what Cythera was doing. Nothing but where Prestwicke happened to be, and where his knife was.

The next attack came while he was still turning in place, looking for the priest.

The blow came down fast. Malden managed to parry it with Acidtongue, thinking the blade's acid would burn right through the knife. But Prestwicke must have thought the same thing, for he withdrew his attack before it had even really begun. Then, while Malden was bracing for the impact, Prestwicke slipped the knife under his guard and stabbed him in the stomach.

Malden shrieked in pain and jumped back, away from the knife.

Blood from his newest wound splattered on the flagstones. He had yet to even touch his opponent.

# CHAPTER NINETY-SIX

Croy's breath came in ragged pants. His eyes snapped open and he saw Malden again. Malden, with Acidtongue naked in his hand. The thief was advancing on a man dressed like a priest. Priest—priest—Prestwicke. Croy knew the priest's name. For some reason Prestwicke was holding a very shiny knife.

Mörget tore at the chain around Croy's wrists. It came off with scraps of his skin still woven through the links. Croy gasped in pain, but he was still watching Malden. The thief was—was—what in the Lady's name was the thief doing?

As Croy watched in horror, Malden took a step toward Prestwicke. He held Acidtongue high over his head, as if he were going to chop wood with it. Then he started to circle toward the priest's right.

Toward his strong side. What was Malden thinking? No trained swordsman would ever make a mistake like that.

"Knight! Collect yourself! Take this." Mörget shoved something into Croy's hand. It was Ghostcutter's scabbard. Croy looked down at the sword, thinking that at least one thing still made sense. He still had the blade that he thought of as his soul.

The familiar weight of the blade and its scabbard helped bring him to his senses. How many times had he held this sword? How many times had he drawn it, and turned to fight an enemy?

He turned now, and saw a dozen elves holding drawn swords come screaming toward him.

Ah.

That, he understood.

Yet as he drew Ghostcutter from its sheath, he felt like

he was struggling through a mire. He moved so slowly, and the elves were so fast.

"This way! Only cover my move, and I will love you forever," Mörget shouted at him. Croy lifted the sword. It felt far heavier than it used to. "This way!" Mörget said again, and grabbed his arm and spun him around.

Ahead, he saw a wide gallery lit red by the dwarven sun. Mörget was running toward the light. Croy followed, unable to make his legs move very fast. Soon the elves were upon him, hacking and slashing at the steel-plated brigantine he wore.

Croy brought Ghostcutter up in a defensive posture. Bronze swords rang off the silver edge of his blade. A blow came in from his left that Croy barely had time to parry. Another darted in low and he shifted his leg back an inch, so the weapon merely grazed his flesh.

He turned his head and saw Mörget run for the gallery, and then leap over its railing. What was the barbarian doing?

A bronze sword struck the side of Croy's head. Only the flat of the blade connected, but it was enough to knock Croy sideways and throw him off balance. He went down on one knee, and then a dozen more blows dropped him to the flagstones. A boot came down toward his jaw. Croy grabbed it and twisted with all his strength, and its elfin owner fell backward, into the surprised faces of three of his comrades.

Croy's blood surged in him. Heat burst in his chest as his heart, made sluggish by the drug, labored to keep up with his screaming muscles. The fog started to lift as Croy stretched and danced, holding off his enemies. The exercise was burning off the drug and he was starting to move faster, to think more clearly.

Then the flat of a bronze blade struck him across the ear, and he dropped like a bag of stones.

Around him the elves debated his fate. "Are we supposed to kill him, or take him alive?" one asked.

"Kill him quick! No one will blame us," another said. "How many of us did he slay?"

"But we had standing orders not to—"

"He's a beast, a wild beast!"

Croy struggled to get one hand under him, to push himself up off the flagstones. The elves drew back in terror as if they couldn't believe he was still standing. Free of them for a moment, Croy raced over to the edge of the gallery. He looked for Mörget again, and saw the barbarian on the far side of the central shaft. How had Mörget gotten all the way over there so quickly? It seemed impossible—yet the barbarian seemed a man possessed as he leapt from gallery to gallery, his hands barely connecting with the wall of the shaft before they reached for another handhold. He climbed up the sheer wall as quick as a spider, hauling himself upward by the woody growths of fungus that studded the wall.

But—why?

Croy's brains had cleared enough that he had it in an instant. Mörget was headed to the top level, to the support column where they had left the barrels. Where Balint had placed them, in just such a way that they would break through the column and bring down the entire mountain on their heads.

Mörget was going to finish what had been interrupted. He was going to put fire to the—what had Balint called it?—the fuse. It was his last chance to kill the demons, to end his personal quest.

And it meant the death of every living being in the Vincularium.

"No," Croy said, because his brain had finally started working again. "No—he's going to—to bring this place down! But Cythera is still alive!"

Then a boot connected with his jaw, and elves piled on top of him until he was unable to move at all.

# CHAPTER NINETY-SEVEN

Prestwicke came at him again, and Malden barely managed to dance away from the flashing knife. He tried bringing Acidtongue around for a slashing cut, but the knife gleamed in the air between them and Malden had to jump back again. Prestwicke drove him toward the gallery, as if he intended to push him over the edge and into the waters below.

Malden had no illusion that he would get off that lightly.

He tried a thrust with Acidtongue, not aimed at Prestwicke's chest or face, but at his knife hand. The priest darted away more quickly than Malden would have deemed possible. Had Sadu given the little man supernatural powers? The knife came swinging toward him again, and Malden had to jump out of the way.

He was up against the railing of the gallery when thunder cracked over his head.

Despite his peril, Malden glanced upward, and saw a cloud of brown dust flash across the top level of the Vincularium. It obscured the red sun and for a moment darkness descended, making Malden blind.

Then a single stray ray of light illuminated Prestwicke's knife, not inches from Malden's throat. He dodged sideways and it missed.

More thunder came from above. Thunder, and a sound of rocks tumbling down the shaft. They fell in the water with tremendous splashes, water surging so high Malden felt its spray on his back. The roar of the water nearly concealed the sound of massive chains creaking and snapping high above.

And then, for the first time since it was put in place, the red sun of the dwarves moved in its artificial heaven.

Malden knew that he needed to drag his eyes away, that he had to watch Prestwicke and keep the assassin at bay—but he found it impossible to not look at the spectacle above. He had never seen destruction on such a massive scale before, and he was dumbstruck, awed by what he beheld.

One of the three chains holding up the red sun had been severed by the explosion. The other two could not hold it in place. It tore loose from its pipes in a great gout of fire that rushed down the central shaft, tongues of flame licking down around Malden and then dissipating so fast he wasn't even scorched. He looked up and saw the pipes sheared off where they had once entered the crystal sphere. Flames jetted from the loose ends of those pipes, casting a furious dancing light.

Then he saw the sphere itself, dull and empty, fall to smash upon the side of the central shaft. It collided with the wall at high speed, and shattered into a million shards of crystal.

Directly overhead.

"In Sadu's name," Prestwicke said, "I shed this blood, for—"

Malden jumped. He had no choice but to leap right toward the priest's knife—there was no time for anything else. He twisted in midair and the blade passed his jugular by a hairbreadth. He hit the flagstones hard, his own blood flecking the air all around him as he rolled and jumped to his feet. He didn't stop running.

"Malden," Prestwicke called, "you cannot escape me."

The priest didn't move to follow. He stood still by the railing of the gallery, as if he could simply wait there and Malden would have to return to him.

When a thousand spears of broken crystal fell on him, his eyes went wide. When they pierced his flesh and thudded into the flagstones like frozen lightning bolts, he opened his mouth as if to speak. But then a shard of crystal sliced off the front of his head, obliterating his face, and he moved no more.

Elves were screaming. Cythera called Malden's name. He heard Croy groaning under a pile of struggling elves, and Slag shouting for him to get away from the gallery, that it wasn't over.

"No," Malden said. No, not yet—not like this—not before he could demand to know who'd sent Prestwicke after him. "No. No!"

Prestwicke was dead. There could be no doubt about that. He was impaled in place, still standing on his feet, his arms and his chest transfixed by long shards of crystal. Malden rushed forward and grabbed the priest's woolen robe. It was wet with blood.

"Who sent you after me?" Malden demanded, frenzied by being cheated this way. "Who was your employer?"

Prestwicke could not answer, of course. But as Malden pulled at the priest's garment he heard a rattling little sound, like a tiny snare drum. He tore open Prestwicke's habit and saw a piece of parchment folded neatly against the dead man's breast. He plucked it free.

Then he ran like every demon in the pit was after him, for he could hear the entire Vincularium shaking itself to pieces above him.

## CHAPTER NINETY-EIGHT

When Malden was halfway to Cythera and Slag, the entire hall felt like it had fallen away under his feet. He tottered and fell, slamming onto the flagstones, his hands over his head as if that would do any good, and prayed for the world to stop moving. Eventually the shaking stopped—but when he looked down and saw his own blood on the flags, the drops were rolling to the left as if the floor had been tilted a few degrees out of true.

The elves didn't stop screaming. The soldiers were running about as if looking for something to attack. The nobles in their finery were shouting for their servants, while the servants in their patchwork clothes were huddled together, crouching on the floor and staring up at the ceiling with wild eyes.

For good reason. A fine drift of powdered stone was raining down from the vaults high overhead.

Malden got back up and kept running. As he passed the cart where Mörget and Croy had been bound, he heard high-pitched laughter and stopped to see Balint lying in the cart, staring up at him. Her whole body was trembling with mirth. "He did it," she said. "He blew the fucking thing up. It's all over now! We're all going to die!"

Malden ignored the crazed dwarf and ran to Cythera's side. She and Slag were clutching each other. They looked confused and very frightened. He grabbed Cythera's shoulders and tried to force her to look at him. "I think," he said, when she finally met his gaze, "that we should get out of here."

Cythera nodded and pushed her hair out of her eyes. "Good plan," she said. "But how will we—"

"We'll figure it out. Come on," Malden said, and grabbed at her arm.

"Help me get the elves moving," Cythera said.

He could only stare at her. Even as parts of the hall above began falling down to the floor with thunderous crashes, he couldn't think of the words he needed to respond.

"We can't leave them here to die," she said, as if it was obvious.

"Really? I believe we can," Malden tried.

"Malden—please. You're not that callous. I know you," Cythera said.

It was Slag who made the best point, however. "Lad," he said, "do you remember what you told me, once? That the elves were evil and deserved to be entombed? You still think that?"

"They've done nothing but imprison us and try to kill us since we got here," Malden pointed out. "I'd call that evil."

"All of them? You'd call 'em all evil, then? Even Aethil? After all she fucking did for us?"

"Well . . . no," Malden said. "She treated us well enough. But—"

A chain of explosions far off in the Vincularium made it impossible to speak for a moment. When it was over, Cythera grasped Malden by the arms. "Remember what Aethil said. There was a time when elves and men were brothers—we share the same language, Malden. Don't you understand? Help me save them."

Malden thought back to when he had grabbed Aethil, intending to hold her prisoner so they could escape. Was that really so different from what the elves had done to him? Cythera had a point. He needed time to think this through, to make a rational decision.

Unfortunately at that moment giant stones started falling from the ceiling, and all rational thought became superfluous.

He nodded and raced over to where Aethil stood, staring upward at her collapsing kingdom. Before he could reach her, she saw him and came storming toward him, her eyes sparkling with anger. "What have you done?" she demanded of him.

"I survived your little sport, that's all," the thief told her.

The elf queen raised one hand and made claws of her fingers. She started to speak in low, ugly syllables, and Malden realized she was about to cast a curse on him.

"Wait," Cythera said, from behind him. "Your highness, please—listen to me."

Aethil let the curse dissipate and stared at Cythera.

"Please, Aethil, I know you have no reason to love us anymore. But we must make common cause. If we don't leave here now, we will all be killed."

"Leave? Yes, I suppose we must withdraw to the tunnels our ancestors made. It seems the dwarven halls are no longer safe."

Cythera shook her head. "No, your majesty. I mean we must leave the Vincularium altogether."

Aethil's brow furrowed. She didn't seem to understand. "But we can't do that. This is where we live."

"It will be your tomb," Malden told the queen, "if you like."

"I must consult with the Hieromagus," Aethil said. "Surely this cataclysm was enough to bring him back to the present." She stood up on her tiptoes and looked around the hall. "Where is he?"

Malden searched the crowd of milling elves for the priest-wizard but could find him nowhere. "Aethil," he said, "he's gone."

"Impossible. He wouldn't desert us at a time like this."

Malden might have argued with her further, but just then the floor of the hall split open. Cracks ran crazily between the flagstones, and an elf fell into the gap between two stones. His screams filled the air for a moment, then ended abruptly.

Cythera exhaled in frustration and grabbed the elf queen's forearm. She twisted it, hard. When Aethil turned to face her with a look of rage, Cythera said, "You can save your people. Right now. Or you can wait for his approval. Are you a queen, or not? Do you lead the elves?"

"I—" Aethil stopped in mid-thought. "There was a time when my forebears, the ancient queens of the elves, had that power, but—"

Slag stepped forward and took her hand gently. "My love," he said, and swallowed thickly. "It's time to restore your authority. Before we all get fucking crushed to death."

Aethil's face slackened for a moment, and Malden was

sure she would lose her composure and start screaming. Well enough, he thought. At least he could count on Cythera and Slag to act rationally. And he had done his best to convince the elf queen. If the elves perished now, it was their own fault.

Yet something strange happened then. Aethil straightened up and seemed to grow an inch or more in height. Her eyes snapped into sharp focus and she reached up to straighten her gown.

Then she walked out into the middle of the chaos and started shouting for everyone to listen to her.

And they did.

"Friends. Subjects. Fellow nobles—the Hieromagus is nowhere to be found. So we must proceed without his counsel. You must come with me."

The elves all turned to watch their queen with a kind of reverence and respect Malden had never seen in human faces. The poor folk stood up straight and rushed toward Aethil. The nobles stopped shouting at one another and gathered their families together.

"We will be leaving this place that has always been our home. Any other place has been forbidden us, for a very long time. Now," Aethil said, as the hall shook all around her, "we have been given a sign. The ancestors have given their blessing. Together we will return to the world above, and there we will rebuild our former glory."

There was more to the speech, but Malden bent to confer with Cythera and Slag. "The best way out is probably the escape shaft on the other side," he said.

"Forget it, lad," Slag told him. "There's no way we'll make it over there before this place collapses." He sighed deeply. "Such a waste."

"Surely we can't reach the main entrance on the top level either," Cythera said. "No. We must exit by Aethil's secret grotto."

"But that's blocked by the growths of crystal," Malden pointed out.

"With enough hands, we might clear a way," Cythera pointed out. "The crystal is delicate. We can smash through."

"Doubtful," Slag told them.

"Perhaps," Cythera went on. "But I'd rather die in the attempt than die here because we wouldn't try it."

"That, lass," Slag admitted, "is an *excellent* fucking point."

"Good, we're agreed," Cythera said. "Now let's find Croy and go!"

# CHAPTER NINETY-NINE

"Croy! No!" someone shouted.

Someone who sounded like . . . Cythera.

After escaping from the cart, Croy was beset by warriors on every side. It had been all he could do to fend them off. And then half the ceiling had fallen, and was suddenly free of his attackers. Either they'd been crushed by falling debris or had run off in terror. He'd been deeply confused for a moment—and then rocks fell on him, and a small mountain of dust, and he lost consciousness again.

Now hands were reaching for him, dragging the rocks away from his sore and bruised body. He tried to fight the hands away at first, thinking the elves had come back for him, but eventually he realized he was being rescued.

By then he had overcome most of the influence of Prestwicke's drugged dart and could think again. He at least knew where he was. He saw Cythera and embraced her passionately, though she seemed strangely impatient to escape his arms.

"I thought you were dead," he told her. There were tears in his eyes.

"I always believed you were still alive," she told him. "Croy, please, there's no time—we need to talk, but only once we're out of here. Mörget did something—he started some kind of avalanche or . . . I don't know what, exactly. But Slag insists the entire Vincularium is about to come down on top of us."

"He used the dwarven weapon," Croy said. Cythera didn't seem to understand. "I'll explain later. Slag is right—I know that much. We need to leave, now." He looked around and saw the entire nation of elves screaming in terror and running for the exits. "But how will we fight our way through all these soldiers?" he asked. He reached down to touch the hilt of Ghostcutter. Even panicked and in wild disarray, there were far too many of them for comfort.

"We don't," Malden told him. "Right now we're all on the same side."

Croy frowned. "But . . . they're elves. They're evil. They consort with demons."

Cythera sighed deeply. "Croy—the ceiling is about to fall in."

"Let me try," Malden said. He grasped the knight's shoulders and looked right into his eyes. "Those weren't demons. Those things you fought were ghosts. Ghosts of the elves, of their ancestors."

"Oh?" Croy said. He didn't understand what that meant, but he didn't doubt Malden was telling the truth. "But the things I did . . . I thought they had killed Cythera. And you and Slag. It's why I did what I did. Normally I would never have—"

"I understand," Malden said, "but right now you need to grasp this. Everything you thought was wrong. The elves are decent folk, and they're going to die."

He stopped talking then as a series of explosions like very close thunder tore across the roof of the hall. Beyond the gallery, the central shaft was a cascade of falling rock and dust, so Croy could no longer see the far side. He turned and looked back at the thief, raising one eyebrow in question.

Malden sighed and closed his eyes. Croy wished he understood what was going on. "We have a couple hundred good, innocent people here who are about to die," the thief said, "and if they do, it'll be a tragedy of historical proportions, and—"

"Innocents? In peril?" Croy asked, his heart singing. That was all he needed to know. "Let's go! We must save them!"

He charged forward, in the direction the elves were already headed. Then he stopped at the cart and gathered Balint into his arms. She didn't look like she could walk.

"*She* betrayed you," Malden pointed out. "And she tried to kill Slag. Not to mention me. Several times."

"She's a dwarf," Croy said, wondering why Malden didn't understand. The law required one to protect dwarves. That was enough for the knight.

The great surge of elfinkind headed up a long ramp and into a region of tunnels that were far too irregular and rough-walled to have been made by dwarves. Croy expected the crowd to back up and stall in the narrow tunnels, but someone seemed to be leading the elves from the front and doing a very good job of it. They passed through a wider space where a dozen revenants stood guard before a door. Croy started to draw Ghostcutter, but it wasn't necessary.

As he watched, the revenants fell to pieces. Bones fell apart, flesh sloughed off their frames. Their bronze armor clattered to the floor.

"The ancestors!" some elf screamed. "The ancestral mass must have been crushed! The magic that animates the revenants is loosed. What hope have we now? What will become of us?"

"The real question," Slag shouted back, "is how tall

you'll be in a second, when this whole place falls in." The dwarf hurried forward and grabbed the hand of an especially pretty elf maid. Croy wondered what that was about.

No time for questions, though. He handed Balint's limp form over to a pair of slender elfin warriors and then hurried to catch up with Slag. He passed through the door with the others and into a very pleasant room, one wall of which had already collapsed. A curtain of water cut across another side of the room, and he thought perhaps some underground river was about to flood in on them.

Then Slag's elfin friend lifted one delicate hand. She spoke a word and the water stopped falling instantly. They all hurried through a bedchamber beyond, and then through an arch filled with light.

Beyond, there was a cave full of diamonds. Croy's eyes went wide as he saw enormous growths of crystal protruding from every surface, sticking out in all possible directions. Broken crystals littered the floor like the gem hoard of some ancient dragon. When his feet kicked through the drift of stones, they skittered and chimed away from him.

He was so busy looking at the glittering detritus at his feet that he walked right into Malden, who had stopped in the middle of the cave.

"What's the problem?" Malden asked.

"The Hieromagus," the thief told him.

Croy looked up and saw an elf standing in the middle of the cavern before them. He recognized this one—it was the same one he'd heard describing ancient elfin torture techniques. The one in the black robe covered with tiny brass bells. Apparently he was called the Hieromagus.

"Hold," he said.

Slag's pretty elf maid bowed to the dark-robed elf and said, "Exalted presence whose shadow is like the cool blessing of night, please, get out of our way!"

"History . . . is . . . here," the Hieromagus announced. "So many lifetimes . . . have I waited. In darkness."

Behind them something massive crashed to the floor.

The whole cave shook so violently that crystal shards were launched into the air. More than one of the elves fell down and cut themselves on the gemstone growths.

"We must pass," Malden said. "Cythera, if we have to hurt him—"

"This time I understand, Malden," she said.

"I'll take care of him," Croy announced, and drew Ghost-cutter. He strode forward, toward the black-cloaked elf.

The Hieromagus lifted one hand from beneath his garment and squeezed it into a fist. Croy's arms pressed tight against his sides and his legs locked at the knees. He couldn't move—he fought desperately with his own body but could not move one inch. He just managed to move his eyes far enough to see Malden beside him, also immobilized in mid-stride, the thief's arms twisted painfully before him.

Only Cythera was still able to move, but she was not unaffected. Painted flowers bloomed on her left temple and her right wrist. Creepers slithered around her throat, as if to strangle her. Vines ran up her arms and into her sleeves.

She screamed in frustration and tried to run past the elf.

He brought up his other hand and pointed directly at her. His mouth started to form words in a language both ancient and evil. Sores erupted on his lips as if the words themselves could corrode his skin.

"You can't hurt me. I'm immune to your magic," Cythera protested.

Then her back arched and light shot from her eyes.

The Hieromagus coughed blood into the air, but he kept chanting. Croy could almost see the evil magic in the air between them, a distortion of reality itself.

He could not turn his head to look, but behind him he heard a noise like bedsheets being torn, only much, much louder. The sound didn't stop, but rolled on and on. He understood that the Vincularium was tearing itself to pieces. If this went on much longer they would all be killed, stopped from escaping by a sorcerous duel.

The painted flowers on Cythera's face bloomed, and wilted, and bloomed again. Vines and tendrils and fronds curled and lashed across her features. No patch of skin visible on her body was uncovered. Her mouth opened and smoke began to trickle out.

"We must stop him!" Croy shouted.

Beside him Malden nodded, almost imperceptibly. The fingers of his hand twitched as he reached for the hilt of Acidtongue.

It was hopeless, but the thief kept trying. Croy struggled and fought with his own legs to make them move forward. He could do no less.

Cythera screamed. Her body shook convulsively as the Hieromagus's endless stream of curses poured into her.

Yet the elf was suffering as well. His lips pulled back from colorless gums. His skin lost what little color it had and started to crack and bleed.

Cythera managed to take one step toward him. Then another. She shot out one arm and grabbed his hand.

When their skin touched, the Hieromagus bellowed in anguish and thick blood leaped from his mouth. His bones glowed with infernal light until they could be seen plainly through his skin.

And then he slumped to the floor, his face burning with green flames.

There could be no doubt that he was dead.

Instantly the immobilizing spell was lifted. Croy ran forward, intending to wrap his arms around Cythera and hold her forever.

"No!" she shouted. Croy grunted in horror when he saw that even the whites of her eyes were covered in tiny painted flowers, and that her hair had taken on the appearance of writhing vines. Every inch of her skin was covered in writhing tattoos that seemed to fight each other. She was suffused with dark magic, carrying more of it than he'd ever seen on her before. "Stay back—all of you. And close your eyes!"

Then she turned away, facing farther up the cavern passage. She lifted her arms, palms stretched forward, and whimpered in pain.

Croy just managed to turn his face from Cythera as she released all the magic energy her body had stored. Every iota of the Hieromagus's power flowed out through her hands, toward the crystals that choked the passage.

Flickering lightning leapt from crystal to crystal and a sound like a hurricane wind tore through the narrow space. Croy pressed his hands over his eyes to save himself from being blinded. He felt something hot and wet roll over his boots, and when he dared look, saw molten crystal sloughing back down the slope of the cave.

He looked up and saw Cythera, then, her skin completely clear once more. It seemed she was about to faint, so he grabbed her up in his arms.

Ahead of him the cavern was now completely stripped of its former crystal growth. It was a natural, winding cave tunnel, leading gently up toward light and warmth. The walls were perfectly smooth and the way was clear.

Croy carried Cythera forward, into sunlight.

# CHAPTER ONE HUNDRED

The danger wasn't over. Behind them the grotto began to collapse, even as the last elves pulled their way up through the tunnel and into the open air. Malden and Slag helped injured elves out of the cave mouth, while Croy and

Aethil directed the others to head down the mountainside as fast as they could run.

The elves looked startled as they emerged, unable to understand where they were or what it meant. Malden figured that their confusion might just save them. If they stopped to think about what had just happened, they might despair and stop moving.

And that would be fatal. The whole mountain shook, again and again. High overhead snow and rocks were cascading down. The peak of the mountain looked far different to Malden than when he first saw it. Cloudblade, Croy had called it—now it looked more like a dozen blades, tilting against one another. As he watched, terrified, one of the blades collapsed and shattered as it struck the slope beneath.

"That's the last of them, son," Slag shouted over the deafening rumble of a mountain taking itself to pieces. "Everyone's clear! Now, scarper for dear fucking life!"

Malden didn't have to be told twice. He ran down the slope, jumping over rocks and rolling every time the shaking earth threw him off his feet. He whooped in panic but kept moving, running, always downward, always away from the rocks that came bouncing and shooting past him. A stone the size of his fist shot past his ear fast as an arrow from a bow. Grit filled his mouth and nose so he could barely breathe.

He didn't stop running until he was suddenly going uphill again, and then only because he was at the end of his physical endurance. He kept climbing, as fast as his muscles would let him, even as the top of Cloudblade disappeared in a vast roil of dust and vapor, even as the earth bounced and heaved underneath him. He kept climbing long after his fingertips bled, long after the pain in his side, in his lungs, in his cuts and bruises and countless scrapes, had devoured every rational thought in his head.

And then—finally—he climbed up over one last rock

and before him stood an open fortress gate, beyond which hundreds of angular elfin faces looked out at him. Elves, and Croy and Cythera, and Slag—and Herward.

He had made it to the fort that Herward the hermit called his home.

Malden hurried inside. The gate was slammed shut behind him. He threw himself full length on the ground. The world was still moving, though not as violently as before. And then he did nothing for a long while but breathe, and stare up at the smoke and dust in the air, and finally—finally—long after the rumbling and the shrieking of broken rock and the howling winds of dust had ground away, he looked up once more, and saw blue sky over his head.

Nothing but blue sky above him, as far as he could see.

When he could hear again, he heard the lamentation of the elves. They had lost everything—their home, their ancestors, their Hieromagus. Everything but their lives. He heard someone sobbing then and he turned his head to the side. Across the courtyard of the fortress he saw Cythera weeping by herself.

He went over and squatted next to her. He did not speak.

"He knew," Cythera said quietly. "The Hieromagus had seen the future. He saw *this*, all of this. In his last moments, his mind spoke directly to my mind. For an instant I saw into his heart. He knew that what he'd seen could not be changed. That this was the only way for his people to survive."

"What are you saying?" Malden asked her.

"He wasn't our enemy. He was never our enemy. Everything he did was to lead us to this moment. He was deeply confused, Malden, lost in time—so lost he couldn't just tell us what he was doing. So it looked like he was our enemy, but . . . no."

"Then why did he resist us so fiercely?"

"But that's just it—he didn't. He helped us every way he could," she explained. "It was he who gave Aethil the love potion—so that when the time came, when Slag called on her to be a true queen, she would listen. His idea to release us from the gaol, and let us see so much of his domain—so we would understand, and know his people were not evil. That once we lived together, and could again." She shook her head. "Even at the end, even in the passage back there. He wasn't trying to hurt me when he poured those curses into me. Malden! He knew it was the only way to open the passage. He knew only I could do it. He spoke to me, in silence, with his last thought before he died."

"What did he say?" Malden asked.

"'Save my people. Show them a forest, and let them live there.' He knew, the whole time, how this would end. And he sacrificed everything to make sure we lived."

Croy came over and held Cythera close and kissed the top of her head. "He was a true leader, willing to die for what he believed in. Not evil at all. Just like Mörget, who died to destroy the demon he'd pledged himself against. They were both heroes."

"If you like," Cythera said.

Malden watched them clutch each other tightly and tried not to let jealousy overcome him. He walked away, to a corner of the courtyard where he could be mostly alone. Then he took the piece of parchment out of his tunic. The one he'd found on Prestwicke's body.

He started to unfold it, but before he could Aethil stood up in the center of the courtyard and called out, "Sir Croy? Where is Sir Croy?"

Before Croy could answer her, Slag jumped up and waved his arms in the air. "Over here, darling," he called back.

Aethil ran to the dwarf and lifted him off the ground in a passionate embrace. "Sir Croy, you are a noble knight indeed. You have saved my people from utter destruction. The time ahead will be fraught with difficulties. We will need to learn once more how to live above the ground. But we will live. We will live, thanks to you. My love, I cannot repay you, ever, for all you have done. Ask of me any reward you would have, any favor, any liberty you desire—"

The real Croy cleared his throat.

Malden saw Slag's face flush red. "Aethil, my, uh, my dear, sweet, forgiving Aethil," the dwarf said. "Let's go somewhere private."

"Oh, yes!" Aethil exclaimed.

"To . . . talk. There's something I need to tell you."

Malden smiled, but could not bring himself to laugh.

He had other thoughts on his mind. Carefully, he unfolded the parchment, and studied the words written on it. There weren't many. There was a short description of his own physical appearance, and a list of the taverns in Ness he was known to frequent, and that was all. Information that might be useful to an assassin looking to track his target. There was no formal warrant for the thief's death, no flowery language about why it was justified. No explanation at all as to why he had to die.

Nor was there any signature. Yet at the bottom of the page there was a small mark, a crude drawing. It showed a heart, transfixed by a key.

# EPILOGUE

The water surged furiously, smashing its way back and forth through the submerged shaft. Pebbles and small stones went streaming past like shots from a thousand slings, smashing into his body and cutting his skin to ribbons. The last trapped breath in his lungs, long since gone stale, sought desperately to get out. It pushed at his battered rib cage and filled his mouth, yet opening his lips now would mean certain death by drowning.

It was impossible to swim up the shaft. It shook wildly every second, and he could feel the immense pressure of water building behind him as parts of it collapsed. His cloak wrapped around him like the coils of a constricting serpent. He tore it away and kicked to propel himself up the passage, the water pushing him from behind like the cork in a bottle of shaken beer.

He bounced off the walls of the shaft many times, hard enough that he could barely feel his arms as he was launched out of the mouth of the shaft, back into the clean sunlight of the surface world. The shaft was set into the face of a sheer cliff, and the water that came spurting out fell away into open air. It was all he could do to grab at the edges of the shaft's mouth to avoid being hurled into the chasm below. With fingers like iron claws, he dug into the rock and held on for dear life. He could only watch as the body of a dead elf was ejected from the shaft and went spinning down into empty space below. When he heard the crunch of the elf's eventual impact, he winced and looked down to see the corpse in a heap on the rocks far below.

Eventually the water subsided, filling the shaft but no longer lapping over its edge. He climbed down the cliff face, finding easy handholds in the broken rock.

He knew this cliff.

When he had thrown himself into the central shaft of the Vincularium, a bare moment after he'd touched flame to the black powder in the ancient dwarven barrels, he had not expected to live. He'd been thrown this way and that by the explosions and the shifting ground, tossed about with the water until he couldn't even think straight. He had fully expected to die. Yet somehow his body had been sucked into one of the emergency escape shafts—the same one, in fact, that he had watched the demon slither through years earlier. The pressure of the water behind him had been enough to shoot him free just before the mountain collapsed inward on itself.

And now—now he was still alive.

The landscape before him he knew. It was the land of his birth, the eastern steppes of the clans. He turned and looked back, and looked for the familiar shape of the mountain Cloudblade, that stood as a sentinel between this land and the more civilized kingdom of Skrae, to the west.

The mountain was gone.

Utterly gone.

In its place was a wide valley of broken rock, filled with smoke and roiling dust. When the Vincularium collapsed, it had taken Cloudblade with it. Now there was a gap in the Whitewall. What had been an impassible barrier of rock and snow that no man could climb was now . . . open. The mountain had fallen and become a pass. A serviceable, if rugged, new pass through the mountains. A pass so wide that an army could march through it.

Looking out on what he'd wrought, Mörget tilted his head back and laughed, and laughed, and laughed.

If you enjoyed DEN OF THIEVES and
A THIEF IN THE NIGHT,
don't miss the next adventure in
The Ancient Blades Trilogy,

# HONOR AMONG THIEVES

# PROLOGUE

The Free City of Ness was known around the world as a hotbed of thievery, and one man alone was responsible for that reputation. Cutbill, master of that city's guild of thieves, controlled almost every aspect of clandestine commerce within its walls—from extortion to pickpocketing, from blackmail to shoplifting he oversaw a great empire of crime. His fingers were in far more pies than anyone even realized, and his ambitions far greater than simple acquisition of wealth—and far broader-reaching than the affairs of just one city. His interests lay in every corner of the globe and his spies were everywhere.

As a result he received a fair volume of mail every day.

In his office under the streets of Ness he went through this pile of correspondence with the aid of only one assistant. Lockjaw, an elderly thief with a legendary reputation was always there when Cutbill opened his letters. There were two reasons why Lockjaw held this privileged responsibility—for one, Lockjaw was famous for his discretion. He'd received his sobriquet for the fact he never revealed a secret. The other reason was that he'd never learned to read.

It was Lockjaw's duty to receive the correspondence, usually from messengers who stuck around only long enough to get paid, and to comment on each message as Cutbill told him its contents. If Lockjaw wondered why such a clever man wanted his untutored opinion, he never asked.

"Interesting," Cutbill said, holding a piece of parchment up to the light. "This is from the dwarven kingdom. It seems they've invented a new machine up there. Some kind of winepress that churns out books instead of vintage."

The old thief scowled. "That right? Do they come out soaking wet?"

"I imagine that would be a defect in the process," Cutbill agreed. "Still. If it works, it could produce books at a fraction of the cost a copyist charges now."

"Bad news, then," Lockjaw said.

"Oh?"

"Books is expensive," the thief explained. "There's good money in stealing 'em. If they go cheap all of a sudden we'd be out of a profitable racket."

Cutbill nodded and put the letter aside, taking up another. "It'll probably come to nothing, this book press." He slit open the letter in his hand with a knife and scanned its contents. "News from our friend in the north. It looks like Maelfing will be at war with Skilfing by next summer. Over fishing rights, of course."

"That lot in the northern kingdoms is always fighting about something," Lockjaw pointed out. "You'd figure they'd have sorted everything out by now."

"The king of Skrae certainly hopes they never do," Cutbill told him. "As long as they keep at each other's throats, our northern border will remain secure. Pass me that packet, will you?"

The letter in question was written on a scroll of vellum wrapped in thin leather. Cutbill broke its seal and spread it out across his desk, peering at it from only a few inches away. "This is from our man in the high pass of the Whitewall Mountains."

"What could possibly happen in a desolated place like that?" Lockjaw asked.

"Nothing, nothing at all," Cutbill said. He looked up at the thief. "I pay my man there to make sure it stays that way. He read some more, and opened his mouth to make another comment—and then closed it again, his teeth clicking together. "Oh," he said.

Lockjaw held his peace and waited to hear what Cutbill had found.

The master of the guild of thieves, however, was unforthcoming. He rolled the scroll back up and shoved the whole thing in a charcoal brazier used to keep the office warm. Soon the scroll had caught flame and in a moment it was nothing but ashes.

Lockjaw raised an eyebrow, but said nothing.

Whatever was on that scroll clearly wasn't meant to be shared, even with Cutbill's most trusted associate. Which meant it had to be pretty important, Lockjaw figured. More so than who was stealing from whom or where the bodies were buried.

Cutbill went over to his ledger—the master account of all his dealings, and one of the most secret books on the continent. It contained every detail of all the crime that took place in Ness, as well as many things no one had ever heard of outside of this room. He opened it to a page near the back, then laid his knife across one of the pages, perhaps to keep it from fluttering out of place. Lockjaw noticed that this page was different from the others. Those were filled with columns of neat figures, endless rows of numbers. This page only held a single block of text, like a short message.

"Old man," Cutbill said, then, "could you do me a favor and pour me a cup of wine? My throat feels suddenly raw."

Cutbill had never asked for such a thing before. The man had enough enemies in the world that he made a point of always pouring his own wine—or having someone taste it before him. Lockjaw wondered what had changed, but he shrugged and did as he was told. He was getting paid for his time. He went to a table over by the door and poured a generous cup, then turned around again to hand it to his boss.

Except Cutbill wasn't there anymore.

That in itself wasn't so surprising. There were dozens of secret passages in Cutbill's lair, and only the guildmaster

knew them all or where they led. Nor was it surprising that
Cutbill would leave the room so abruptly. Cautious to a
nicety, he always kept his movements secret.

No, what was surprising was that he didn't come back.

He had effectively vanished from the face of the world.

Day after day Lockjaw—and the rest of Ness's thieves—
waited for his return. No sign of him was found, nor any
message received. Cutbill's operation began to falter in his
absence—thieves stopped paying their dues to the guild,
citizens under Cutbill's protection were suddenly vulnerable to theft, what coin did come in piled up uncounted and
was spent on frivolous expenditures. Half of these excesses
were committed in the belief that Cutbill, who had always
run a tight ship, would be so offended he would have to
come back just to put things in order.

But Cutbill left no trace, wherever he'd traveled.

It was quite a while before anyone thought to check the
ledger, and the message Cutbill had so carefully marked.

# CHAPTER ONE

On the far side of the Whitewall Mountains, in the grass-
lands of the barbarians, in the mead tent of the Great
Chieftain, fires raged and drink was passed from hand to
hand, yet not a word was spoken. The gathered housemen
of the Great Chieftain were too busy to gossip and sing as
was their wont, too busy watching two men compete at an
ancient ritual. Massive they were, as big as bears, and their
muscles stood out from their arms and legs like the wood

of dryland trees. They stood either side of a pit of blazing coals, each clutching hard to one end of a panther's hide. On one side, Torki, the champion of the Great Chieftain, victor of a thousand such contests. On the other side stood Mörget, whose lips were pulled back in a manic grin, the lower half of his face painted red in the traditional colors of a berserker, though he was a full chieftain now, leader of many clans.

Heaving, straining, gasping for breath in the fumes of the coals, the two struggled, each trying to pull the other into the coals. Every man and woman in the longhouse, every berserker and reaver of the Great Chieftain, every wife and thrall of the gathered warriors, watched in hushed expectation, each of them alone with their private thoughts, their desperate hopes.

There was only one who dared to speak freely, for such was always his right. Hurlind, the Great Chieftain's scold, was full of wine and laughter. "You're slipping, Mörg's Get! Pull as you might, he's dragging you. Why not let go, and save yourself from the fire? This is not a game for striplings!"

"Silence," Mörget hissed, from between clenched teeth.

Yet his grin was faltering, for it was true. Torki's grasp on the panther hide was like the grip of great tree roots on the earth. His arms were locked at the elbows and with the full power of his body, trained and toughened by the hard life of the steppes, he was pulling as inexorably as the ocean tide. Mörget slid toward the coals a fraction of an inch at a time, no matter how he dug his toes into the grit on the floor.

At the mead bench closest to the fire a reaver of the Great Chieftain placed a sack of gold on the table and nudged his neighbor, a chieftain of great honor. He pointed at Torki and the chieftain nodded, then put his own money next to the reaver's—though as he did so he glanced slyly at the Great Chieftain in his place of honor at the far end of the table. Perhaps he worried that his overlord might take it askance—after all, Mörget was the Great Chieftain's son.

The Great Chieftain did not see the wager, however. His eyes never moved from the contest. Mörg, the man who had made a nation of these people, the man who had seen every land in the world and plundered every coast, father of multitudes, slayer of dragons, Mörg the Great was ancient by the reckoning of the east. Forty-five winters had ground at his bones. Only a little silver ran through the gold of his wild beard, however, and no sign of dotage showed in his glinting eyes. He reached without looking for a haunch of roasted meat. Tearing a generous piece free, he held it down toward the mangy dog at his feet. The dog always ate first. It roused itself from sleep just long enough to swallow the gobbet. When it was done, Mörg fed himself, grease slicking down his chin and the front of his fur robes.

A great deal relied on which combatant let go of the hide first. The destiny of the entire eastern people, the lives of countless warriors were at stake—and a debt of honor nearly two centuries old. No onlooker could have said which of the warriors, his son or his champion, Mörg favored.

Torki never made a sound. He did not appear to move at all—he might have been a marble statue. He had the marks of a reaver, black crosses tattooed on the shaved skin behind his ears. One for every season of pillaging he'd undertaken in the hills to the north. Enough crosses that they ran down the back of his neck. Not a drop of sweat had showed yet on his brow.

Mörget shifted his stance a hair breadth and was nearly pulled into the fire. His teeth gnashed at the air as he fought to regain his posture.

Nearby his sister, herself a chieftess of many clans, stood ready with a flagon of wine mulled with sweet gale. Mörgain, as was widely known, hated her brother—had done since infancy. No matter how hard she fought to prove herself, no matter what glory she won in battle, Mörget had always overshadowed her accomplishments.

Letting him win this contest now would be bitter as ashes in her mouth. Nor did she need to play the passive spectator here. She could end it in a moment by splashing wine across the boards at Mörget's feet. He would be unable to hold his ground on the slippery boards, and Torki would win for a certainty.

"Sister," Mörget howled, "set down that wine. Do you not thirst for western blood, instead?"

Mörg raised one eyebrow, perhaps very much interested in learning the answer to that question.

The chieftess laughed bitterly, and spat between Mörget's feet. But then she hurled her flagon at the wall, where it burst harmlessly, well clear of the contest. "I've tasted blood. I'd rather have the westerners alive, as my thralls."

"And you shall, as many of them as you desire," Mörget told her, his words bitten off before they left his mouth.

"And steel? Will you give me dwarven steel, better than the iron my warriors wear now?"

"All that they can carry! Now, aid me!"

"I shall," Mörgain said. "I'll pray for your success!"

That was enough to break the general silence, though only long enough for the gathered warriors to laugh uproariously and slap each other on the back. The shadow of a smile even crossed Torki's lips. In the east the clans had a saying: *pray with your back turned, so that at least your enemies won't see your weakness.* The clans worshipped only Death, and beseeching Her aid was rarely a good idea.

"Did you hear that, Torki?" Hurlind the scold asked. "The Mother of us all pulls against you now. Better redouble your grip!"

The champion's lips split open to show his teeth. It was the first sign of emotion he'd given since the contest began.

And yet it was like some witch's spell had been broken. Perhaps Death—or some darker fate—did smile on Mörget then. For suddenly his arms flexed as if he'd found some strength he'd forgotten he had. He leaned back, putting his weight into the pull.

Torki's smile melted all at once. His left foot shifted an inch on the boards. It was not necessarily a fatal slip. Given a moment's grace he could have recovered, locking his knees and reinforcing his strength.

Yet Mörget did not give him that moment. Everyone knew that Mörget, for all his size and strength, was faster than a wildcat. He seized the opportunity and hauled Torki toward him until the balance was broken and the champion toppled, sprawling face-first on the coals. Torki screamed as the fire bit into his skin.